The shining ~~...~~ jewel in the mightiest
empire the world has ever known!

THE KINGPRIEST

Absolute ruler of Istar, he speaks with the voice of the gods.
All bow beneath his power and glory.

And yet a shadow has crossed the sun . . .

and an evil has awoken in the heart of Istar.

In the first book of a powerful trilogy, Chris Pierson brings
to life the world of long-ago Krynn. Before the Cataclysm.
When the Kingpriest of Istar was

CHOSEN OF THE GODS

Also by Chris Pierson

Spirit of the Wind
BRIDGES OF TIME SERIES

Dezra's Quest
BRIDGES OF TIME SERIES

Kingpriest Trilogy
CHOSEN OF THE GODS

DIVINE HAMMER

SACRED FIRE
(December 2003)

CHOSEN OF THE GODS

KINGPRIEST
TRILOGY

VOLUME ONE

CHRIS PIERSON

CHOSEN OF THE GODS

©2001 Wizards of the Coast, Inc.

Distributed in the United States by Holtzbrinck Publishing. Distributed in Canada by Fenn Ltd.

Distributed to the hobby, toy, and comic trade in the United States and Canada by regional distributors.

Distributed worldwide by Wizards of the Coast, Inc. and regional distributors.

Cover art by Marc Fishman
Cartography by Denis Kauth
First Printing: November 2001
Library of Congress Catalog Card Number: 00-191036

9 8 7 6 5 4 3 2

UK ISBN: 0-7869-2676-7
US ISBN: 0-7869-1902-7
620-88694-001-EN

U.S., CANADA,
ASIA, PACIFIC, & LATIN AMERICA
Wizards of the Coast, Inc.
P.O. Box 707
Renton, WA 98057-0707
+ 1-800-324-6496

EUROPEAN HEADQUARTERS
Wizards of the Coast, Belgium
T Hofveld 6d
1702 Groot-Bijgaarden
Belgium
+ 322 467 3360

Visit our web site at **www.wizards.com**

For the Turbinites, past and present, who innocently asked, "How's the book going?"— and for Slappy and Patricia in particular.

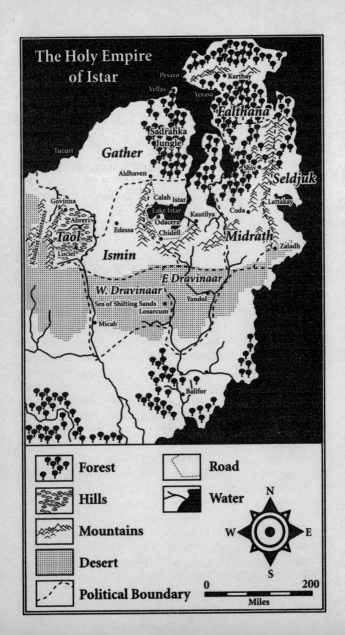

PROLOGUE ▼

The Lordcity of Istar was the center of the world around which all else revolved. Capital of an empire vaster than any other Krynn had ever known, it sat upon the shores of the sapphire lake that shared its name, its high, white walls encircling it like a mother's arms. Half a million souls—more than mighty Palanthas and Tarsis to the west combined—dwelt within that embrace. It outmatched other cities not only in size, however, but also with splendor. There was a legend that the great statues that stood atop its gilded gates had wept at the city's beauty when they were first raised, though they were crafted of solid marble.

Everywhere one looked in the Lordcity, there were wonders to behold. Vast manors and churches lined its wide, tree-lined streets, roofed with domes of gold and alabaster, and smaller buildings gleamed in the light of sun and moons alike. Broad plazas held gardens where a thousand different colors of flowers bloomed, and fountains sent water spraying high into the air, to glitter like diamonds as it plunged back to earth. Silken sails filled its harbors, overlooked by the God's Eyes, twin towers where beacons of polished silver blazed day and night. Idols of the gods of light stood watch from the city's heights, more than ten men tall, hewn of lapis and serpentine, sard and chalcedony. Its marketplace bustled with noise and laughter and a riot of trade riches: spices and satin, wine and pearls, brightly hued songbirds and the skulls of long-dead dragons.

Even in such a marvelous city, some wonders stood out. In the western quarter was the School of the Games, a vast arena draped in banners of silk, where gladiators had once fought and died and mummers now played out tales of wars long won, kingdoms long since conquered. In the north stood the Keep of the Kingfisher, a huge, strong-walled fortress that served as headquarters for the Solamnic Knights within the empire. To the east, high above the domes and treetops, surrounded by an enchanted grove of olive trees, rose the crimson-turreted Tower of High Sorcery, where the wizards dwelt.

All of these, however, were nothing beside the Great Temple. Sitting in the Lordcity's midst, the marble-paved streets radiating out from it like a wheel's spokes—or a spider's web, some said—the Temple was the most resplendent edifice ever built. Those travelers lucky enough to have seen the halls of the elven kings spoke of them as mere shadows of the Temple's glory. A wide plaza, the *Barigon*, surrounded it, large enough that nearly every soul in the Lordcity could stand within it and look upon its graceful, buttressed walls and seven golden spires that reached up like fingers clutching at the heavens. Within, amid lush gardens and pools filled with jewel-hued fish, stood more than a dozen buildings, each more glorious than the last. Among them were the entrance hall, itself larger than most cities' cathedrals, and the towering, silver-roofed cloisters where the clergy resided. The imperial manse, where the Kingpriest dwelt, surpassed even these, and at the eye of the Temple was the true heart of the city, the center of the world. There, grandest of all, was the basilica, a vast dome of frosted crystal that shone with its own holy light, like a star plucked from the heavens and set upon the earth.

This night First Son Kurnos glowered at the basilica from the steps of his cloister. A stocky, powerfully built man with thinning red hair and a bushy beard frosted with silver, he was the head of the Revered Sons of Paladine, the most powerful of all the world's orders, and adviser to the Kingpriest himself. He was also shivering with cold. The sky was dark, and though a month still remained until autumn's end, snow danced in the air above the Temple. It dusted the paths of crushed crystal that wound through the church's grounds and lit on the moonstone monuments of the Garden of Martyrs, which bore the names of those who had died serving the church. It was a rare thing—the Lordcity's winters were known for rain, not snow—and another time, Kurnos might have found it beautiful. Now, however, his thoughts were elsewhere.

"Quickly, boy," he growled, cuffing the ear of the acolyte who stood beside him. "I haven't got till sunrise."

The younger priest, clad in a gray habit that seemed all the plainer beside Kurnos's embroidered white robes, hurried past, down to the garden path. The same lad had woken Kurnos half an hour ago and given him the missive. It had come in a tube of platinum, inlaid with amethysts: a single sheet of vellum, scented with rosewater. Its seal was azure wax, bearing the triangle-and-falcon signet of the Kingpriest. It bore only Kurnos's name and three words in blue ink, written in the church tongue: *Tam fas ilaneis.*

Thou art summoned.

Kurnos felt uneasy. He had been First Son for five years and a lesser member of the imperial court for another ten before that. In that time, he had received numerous imperial summonses—but never in the middle of the night. Never, not even once, written in the Kingpriest's own hand.

Before him, the acolyte raised his hands to the cloud-heavy sky. He began to speak softly. "*Cie nicas supam torco,*" he murmured, "*Palado, mas doboram burtud.*"

Though I walk through night's heart, Paladine, be thou my light.

As he finished the orison, a soft glow, as of silver moonlight, rose around him. The First Son felt a twinge of jealousy. The boy's powers were minor but more than most priests could wield—Kurnos among them. In ancient times, when evil was rampant in the world, the clergy's holy might had been vast. In Holy Istar, however, centuries of holy war had left the forces of darkness weak and scattered, and the power to work miracles had dwindled along with the need for them. The god, the church's doctrine taught, was sparing with his gifts.

"The way is ready, *Aulforo*," murmured the acolyte.

Kurnos nodded, stepping out into the magical moonlight. "Go," he said, waving the boy away.

The acolyte retreated into the cloister as he set forth across the garden, past the graven monuments. The moonlight followed him over ornamental bridges and up marble steps, past almond and lemon trees, where nightingales sang. He turned aside from the basilica, making instead for the imperial manse. A pair of Solamnic Knights stood guard outside, clad in polished, antique armor; they dipped their halberds as he approached and stepped aside without a word.

The manse's doors were huge, made of beaten platinum. They swung open silently as he approached and stepped through into the vestibule. The entry hall, like everything in the Kingpriest's private residence, was richly appointed, with the finest furnishings from the empire's many provinces: mahogany panels from the jungles of Falthana on the walls; gold-threaded arrases from sun-drenched Gather; carpets woven by the desert-dwelling folk of Dravinaar. Columns, crowned with rose-petal capitals, ran down its length, and in its midst stood seven onyx pedestals, bearing alabaster statues of the gods of light.

Paladine, the supreme god of Good, loomed above the others, a long-bearded warrior in armor shaped like dragon-scales. Kurnos genuflected to the idol, kissing the platinum medallion that hung at his throat then pressing it to the god's glistening feet.

A door opened as he knelt there, and an old, bald cleric in a white cassock emerged. Kurnos recognized the man: Brother Purvis, the Kingpriest's chamberlain. His eyes were bleary as he bowed to the First Son.

"Your Grace," he said. "You are expected."

Kurnos rose without reply and handed the old man his fur-lined cloak. Together they walked down a broad, marble hall and up a stairway to a door of polished silver. It opened at Purvis's touch, and the chamberlain stepped aside to reveal a well-appointed waiting room.

"Revered Son," said a gentle voice.

Loralon, Emissary for the elves of Silvanesti, rose from a cushioned seat on the room's far side. As he did, he signed the sacred triangle—one palm atop the other, thumbs extended to a point beneath—that was the holy sign of Kurnos's order. It was a courtesy, for the Silvanesti took the pine tree, not the triangle, as their gesture of blessing. Kurnos nodded in reply, stepping forward as Purvis shut the door behind him.

The elf gestured toward another chair, and Kurnos sat, regarding him carefully. Loralon was as always: calm, reserved, eyes sparkling in the glow of the lamps that lit the room. He was old, even for his long-lived people, having seen more than five hundred years. Though his face remained unlined by age, his hair had turned silver, and a snowy beard—rare among the elves, found only among the most ancient—trailed down his chest. He was clad in full raiment, from the golden circlet on his head to the jeweled slippers upon his feet. He looked neither tired nor annoyed, and Kurnos wondered, not for the first time, if the elf ever slept.

They exchanged pleasantries, then sat in silence for a while, sipping from jeweled goblets of watered claret, mixed with spices from Karthay. In time Purvis returned, leading a tall woman, whose long, raven-black hair was pulled back into a severe bun that made her look older than her forty years. She wore robes of pearly satin trimmed with lavender and silver jewelry at her ears, wrists, and throat. Her dark eyes swept the room.

"It seems," she declared, signing the triangle as Loralon and Kurnos rose, "that I'm the last to arrive."

"First Daughter," the elf said, smiling kindly. "You were always the deep sleeper."

Ilista, leader of the Revered Daughters of Paladine—companion order to Kurnos's own—folded her arms. "What is this about?" she asked. "Is something wrong?"

Kurnos and Loralon exchanged tight-lipped glances.

"I think it likely," the elf replied, "but as to why His

Holiness has called us here at this hour, milady, I fear neither of us know any better than you."

Purvis stood aside while the Kingpriest's advisers greeted one another. Now he stepped forward, making his way to a pair of gold-chased doors at the room's far end. Engraved upon them was the imperial falcon and triangle—the one, symbol for the empire, the other for the god. The doors opened at his touch, letting white, crystalline light spill through; then he turned to face the three clerics, bowing low.

"His Holiness bids you welcome," the chamberlain intoned. "*Gomudo, laudo, e lupudo.*"

Enter, behold, and adore.

The audience chamber was smaller than the great throne room that occupied most of the basilica, but it was still far more opulent than those of other sovereigns. It brought gasps from those beholding it for the first time, but to Kurnos it was a familiar place. He scarcely noticed the mosaic of interwoven dragon wings that covered the floor, the strands of glowing diamonds that hung from the ceiling, the platinum triangles and lapis falcons that adorned its walls. Instead, his gaze went directly to the marble dais at the far end, beneath a violet rose window. Atop the platform stood a golden throne, wreathed with white roses and flanked by censers of electrum that gave off tendrils of pale smoke. His eyes slid past these, focusing at last on the man on the satin-cushioned seat.

Symeon IV, Kingpriest of Istar, Paladine's Voice on Krynn, was not a physically imposing man. Nearly sixty years old, he was small and plump, pink-cheeked and beardless. At first glance, he looked almost like a child, though there was sharpness in his black eyes that left no doubt he was the most powerful man in all Ansalon. Many men, expecting him to behave in the manner of a eunuch, had quailed and broken before that unrelenting gaze. His golden, jeweled breastplate and the sapphire-studded tiara on his brow gleamed in the white light. He raised a hand that sparkled with precious stones.

"*Apofudo, usas farnas,*" he said, beckoning.

Come forward, children of the god.

Obediently, Kurnos moved to the dais with the others and mounted the first step. They bowed their heads as the Kingpriest signed the triangle over them, murmuring a soft benediction. Symeon sat back, smoothing his silvery robes.

"You have questions," the Kingpriest said. "Here is my answer. I have called you here because the time of my death is near."

Kurnos started, surprised. Beside him, Loralon's brow furrowed, and Ilista's eyes widened.

"Sire?" the First Daughter blurted.

Symeon was a hard man—not cruel, but distant. All knew that while Istar honored him, there was little love for the Kingpriest among the common folk of the land. His midnight eyes glinted, and Ilista looked away, unable to meet his stare.

"Holiness," Loralon ventured, drawing Symeon's gaze away from the First Daughter. "How can you know this? Has something happened?"

"Yes," the Kingpriest replied. "Something *has*. Tonight, as I was reciting my midwatch prayers before taking to my bed, a visitor came to my chambers. A dragon."

"What?" Kurnos said, and all at once the imperious glare was on him. He weathered it, though he could feel his face redden. "Pardon, Holiness, but there *are* no dragons left in the world. All know that Huma Dragonbane banished the wyrms of evil a millennium ago, and Paladine himself bade the good dragons leave soon after."

"I *know* the history, Kurnos," the Kingpriest declared coldly. "Nevertheless, the dragon was here. Its scales shone like platinum in sunlight, and its eyes were diamonds afire. It spoke to me, in a voice of honey and harpstrings. I knew at once it was Paladine himself, taken flesh.

" 'Symeon,' said the dragon, 'most beloved of my children. Within a twelvemonth, I will call you to uncrown. From that day, you shall dwell evermore at my side.'

"And so, my children, I have called you here to share this news. The coming year shall be my last."

The audience hall was utterly still. Kurnos and Ilista stared in shock. Loralon stroked his beard, lost in thought. The rose window made the only sound, hissing as snow pattered against the glass from outside.

Finally, the First Son cleared his throat. "How can this be?" he asked. "It's only seven years since you were crowned, Majesty."

The Kingpriest nodded. "Yes, but Paladine's word will not be denied. Soon I shall be with him."

"There is precedent," Loralon added. "A century and a half ago, the god appeared to Kingpriest Ardosean I as he lay dying." The elf regarded Symeon evenly. "You are fortunate, Holiness. Most clerics live their entire lives without beholding such a sight."

"Our luck is as poor as yours is good," Ilista added. "It is hard not to envy Paladine for taking you from us."

The Kingpriest nodded, accepting the compliment as his due. "There is another reason I have summoned you three here," he said, his gaze falling upon Kurnos. "If I am to go to the god, I must name my heir."

For a moment, the First Son blinked, not understanding. Then he saw the way the dark eyes glittered, reflecting the gems of Symeon's tiara, and he felt his throat tighten. His skin turning cold, Kurnos tried to speak, but his voice failed him. He looked down, unable to meet the imperial gaze any longer.

"Yes, *Aulforo*," Symeon said. "It is my wish that you take my place upon the throne. When I am gone, you shall be the next Kingpriest of Istar."

———◆———

The rest of the audience passed in a blur. Later, Kurnos dimly remembered the rite of succession that followed the Kingpriest's pronouncement: a long liturgy by Symeon, to which he responded at the proper times, like a man half-awake. Loralon and Ilista both served as witnesses, vowing before Paladine and Symeon alike they would support Kurnos's rule. Finally, the Kingpriest recited the final *"Sifat"*—*Be it so*—and the ritual ended.

After, Purvis escorted the imperial advisers from the audience hall, then out of the manse and back into the night. Loralon and Ilista took their leave, returning to their quarters to find some rest before the new day. Kurnos didn't retire, however—sleep was the furthest thing from his mind. Instead, he lingered in the Temple's gardens, wandering the snowy paths about the gleaming basilica. This time he hardly noticed the chill in the air, and he also took no notice of the monks and knights who passed him as he walked. His mind roiled, the thoughts coming back and back again to the same four words:

I will be Kingpriest.

It had always been a possibility—in Paladine's church, he was second in stature to the man who sat the throne—but he had never truly credited that it would happen. The Kingpriest usually chose a patriarch from one of the empire's provinces to wear the crown after him, as a way of maintaining the peace. Symeon himself had been high priest of Ismin, to the west, until his own coronation. Anyway, Kurnos was past his fiftieth year and had been sure he would grow into an old man by the time the Kingpriest died.

All those assumptions had crumbled now, replaced by a thrill that plunged through him like a silver arrow. He was the heir. Before long, the powers of church and empire would be his to wield. It was an intoxicating thought, arousing a hunger that had lain dormant in him for many years. He thought of the power that came with the Kingpriest's sapphire tiara and felt giddy. All the things he could accomplish!

A glimmer of light caught his attention, and he stopped in his tracks, looking up. The sky was clearing now—the snow had stopped, he wasn't sure when—and through the garden's trees the velvet black of night was giving way to violet. The red and silver moons hung low in the east, both razor-thin crescents, and beneath them, the clouds were glowing saffron. He blinked. Dawn had been hours away when he'd left the manse. Had he truly wandered the Temple's gardens so long?

As he was wondering, a dulcet sound arose from the basilica: the chiming of silver bells within the Temple's tall, central spire. The crystal dome caught the sound, ringing to herald the coming dawn, and the Temple grounds suddenly burst into life as priests and priestesses spilled out of the cloisters, answering the call to morning prayer. Many exclaimed in wonder at the unexpected snowfall, and Kurnos watched as they made their wide-eyed way past him to the basilica.

Suddenly, he began to weep.

He tried to hold it back at first, but soon his cheeks were wet. The tears he shed were not born of sorrow, however, but of joy. He even laughed, his heart singing along with the music of the bells. Smiling, he wiped his eyes, clearing his vision—and stopped, sucking in a sudden breath.

Down the path, in the shadow of a great ebony tree, was something that did not belong in this place: a tall, grim figure swathed in black. It was a man, his dark hood covering his face save for the tip of a thick, gray beard. He stood motionless, and though he couldn't see the man's eyes, the First Son was sure the dark-robed figure was looking at him. The chill in the air seemed to sharpen as he met the man's gaze.

Yes, hissed a cold voice. The hooded head inclined slightly. *It will do.*

Suddenly terrified, Kurnos cast about, searching for one of the Knights who patrolled the Temple grounds. There was none nearby, though—and what was more, none of the other clerics bustling past seemed to see the shadowy figure at all. Swallowing, Kurnos turned back toward the tree, intending to do something, perhaps cry out . . .

And stopped. The dark figure was gone.

He stepped forward, peering deeper into the shadows, but there was no sign of the man. Kurnos swallowed, shaken. *Perhaps I imagined it*, he told himself. *I'm tired—jumping at shadows, that's all.*

In his mind, however, the dark figure remained, lurking and watching as he turned toward the basilica to greet his first day as the Kingpriest's heir.

CHAPTER 1 ▾
FOURTHMONTH, 923 I.A.

The drums of war hadn't sounded in Istar for years.

The empire had not known peace in all that time, of course—goblins and ogres still lurked in the wildlands, for one thing, despite repeated Commandments of Extermination from the Temple, as did cults that worshiped dark gods. And while most realms paid homage to the Kingpriest, some— notably the distant Empire of Ergoth—refused to do so. It was enough to keep the imperial armies from growing idle, but Istaran hadn't fought Istaran in over half a century, since the end of the Three Thrones' War.

The *Trosedil*, as the church tongue named the war, had arisen when three different men, each with their own fol- lowings, laid claim to the throne. Such factional splintering had happened before, when a Kingpriest died with no named heir, but this time it was particularly tragic. For two decades the dispute had bloodied the empire's fields, until Ardosean IV, also known as Ardosean the Uniter, had defeated his rivals, beheading Vasari II and imprisoning Theorollyn III, thereby becoming the one true sovereign.

With the war's end, prosperity returned to the empire. Gold flowed freely, filling the coffers of castle and temple alike. By the time the Uniter died, ten years after the

Trosedil's ending, the realm was almost completely healed, the old divisions forgotten.

Not everyone shared in the bounties of peace, however. Taol, westernmost of Istar's provinces, had no spices, no silks. Its hills yielded copper and iron, not rubies and opals. Its people had been barbarians at the empire's dawning, until the priests came to pacify them and teach them the ways of Paladine. Even now, they remained simple borderfolk, and though they were poor compared with people who dwelled in the lands to the east, they had long been content with their lot.

Ullas obefat, the old saying said. *All things change.*

The troubles had begun the previous autumn, with a blight that devastated harvests all over the borderlands. Famine followed, and with it came plague, a terrible sickness called the *Longosai*—the Slow Creep—that started at the provinces' fringes and worked its way from town and town as winter came on. When they saw the troubles their people faced, the Taoli nobles had acted quickly, sending riders to the Lordcity to plead for help. Before the messengers could reach the lowlands, however, the snows had come, vicious blizzards that buried the lands and choked the roads. The riders vanished into the storm and were never seen again. The food and healers the borderfolk needed never came. The *Longosai* spread, made worse by starvation.

Even then, however, matters might have mended, had the first travelers to ride into the highlands when the thaws came been traders, priests, or even Solamnic Knights. Instead, however, it was the Kingpriest's tax collectors who sojourned to Taol when the roads cleared at last. They came as they always did, at the dawning of springtime, to collect the annual tithe from the borderfolk to bring back to the holy church. What they found instead, however, were sickness, empty larders, and men and women made desperate and angry by suffering.

Inevitably, it came to bloodshed. The *Scatas*, the blue-cloaked imperial soldiers who accompanied the tax collectors, killed several bordermen who tried to fight. The highlanders struck back, slaughtering soldiers and clerics alike. The survivors fled back to the Lordcity, bringing word of a peasantry risen in revolt. The Kingpriest closed the roads that led to Taol and issued an edict demanding the heads of the rebels' leaders. By the time the last snows melted, the borderlands were dry tinder, awaiting a spark.

The war drums hadn't sounded in Istar for years. They wouldn't remain silent much longer.

———◆•◆•◆———

Tancred MarSevrin thrashed and thrashed, fighting with all his might. He was too weak, though, and his struggles soon began to weaken, his cries grew silent. Finally he slumped, defeated, his wild, fearful eyes staring at nothing. His legs kicked one last time, then were still.

Cathan kept his hand over the dead man's mouth, counting slowly to ten and fighting the urge to scream. Finally, knowing it was done, he pulled back and stood above the bed, staring at the body. He ran a shaky hand over his face, then reached down and closed Tancred's eyes. Sucking in a shuddering breath, he drew a blanket over the pinched face.

"Farewell, brother," he whispered.

The bedchamber was plain, stone below and thatch above, a closed, wooden door leading to the front room. A second blanket hung over the lone window, drenching the room in shadows. The furnishings were spare: a straw bed and two wooden stools, a foot chest with no lock, a clay chamber pot crusted with filth. The only ornament was a sacred triangle of white ceramic hanging on the east wall. No one had changed the rushes on the earthen floor in some time, and their sweet smell had long since yielded to the sour reek of sickness.

Cathan looked down at the shrouded corpse, feeling hollow. When the tears came, he let them flow.

The *Longosai* was a terrible way to die. It began as an innocent-looking rash on the hands and feet, but that harmlessness didn't last long. It steadily worsened, erupting into weeping sores that crawled up arms and legs and blossomed on swollen groins and throats, wasting away the flesh and turning its victims into skeletons wrapped in loose folds of corrupted skin. As the end came on, so did madness, bringing a wild sheen to the eyes of the dying and bloody froth to their lips. Death soon followed.

The plague had missed the village of Luciel as it raged across Taol, somehow leaving it untouched all winter while ravaging the hamlets nearby. Oveth, Fliran, even Espadica only two leagues away had all succumbed, but when the snows finally began to melt, Luciel remained intact. The townsfolk had sighed, thanking the gods they had survived such a harsh season . . . then, on the third day of spring, they'd begun to die.

Drelise had been the first victim. A priestess of Mishakal the Healing Hand, she had been an old woman—the winter just past her ninetieth—and her goddess hadn't been able to spare her from the Creep's killing touch. Both her apprentices soon followed, leaving the village with no one to mix balms and poultices, or bleed the dying to purify their flesh. A week later, twenty folk were dead; after another, the toll had risen to a hundred. Soon blue mourning cloths hung by the doors of nearly every house in Luciel's valley, and more than a few stood as empty as old skulls, derelict and silent.

Before the *Longosai*, the MarSevrin clan had numbered five. Utham, its head, was a weaver, his wife Luska a midwife. Tancred, the eldest of their children, had been twenty-two, a quick-fingered lad set to inherit his father's loom. Cathan, four years his junior, seemed his brother's twin, sharing his shaggy brown hair and clever eyes. Wentha, their younger sister, was a pretty, golden-haired girl who had just begun to catch the fancies of the village's young men. The MarSevrins had been happy, content to live in a land that, though sometimes hard, lay nonetheless beneath Paladine's blessing.

Luska had been one of the first twenty victims. Utham had followed a few days later. Cathan himself developed the telltale rash a few days later, but he had fought it off, as some did, and it had left only a few pockmarks on his skin when it waned. Tancred hadn't been so lucky: For the past ten days, Cathan had tended to him, bringing his brother water to drink, porridge to eat, and bowls to puke in, while his life ebbed away.

Cathan had woken at dawn that morning, curled up on the floor by the bedside, to find Tancred staring at him. He'd looked a stranger—once tall and strong, he was as thin as one of Wentha's old twig-dolls, his face gaunt and sallow. His bloodshot eyes had gleamed unpleasantly as he raised a bony hand to beckon Cathan near.

"Brother," he'd rasped, sounding like a whetstone on rusted iron. Cathan gave him a swallow of water, most of which dribbled down his chin. "How is Wentha?"

"She's well," Cathan had said, his throat thick with tears. Their sister, though devastated by the loss of their parents and Tancred's decline, had yet to show any sign of the plague. She lived across town now, with Fendrilla, an old woman who had lost both her daughters to the Creep.

Reaching out, Tancred had taken Cathan's hand. His once iron-firm grip had been sweaty and feeble, and his eyes shone like embers. Cathan had seen that look in his mother's eyes and then his father's. He'd known that, before long, Tancred would begin to rave. He'd known, too, what he had to do and had wondered if he could carry through with it.

"Promise me," Tancred had hissed, his breath stinking. "Swear you'll not die like this. Neither of you."

Coldness twisting his guts, Cathan had looked away.

"Swear!"

Cathan had squeezed his eyes shut, grinding his teeth to keep the sobs at bay. Finally, he'd managed a nod, Tancred had smiled, a horrible rictus filmed with blood.

"Very well, then," he'd said and settled back to wait.

They'd made the pact together, as they stood by the pyre where their parents had burned. They knew what the *Longosai* did in its last days and had sworn that neither they nor Wentha would suffer so. Cathan kept his word: as Tancred lay still before him, he had covered his brother's face and smothered him. It was merciful, but that didn't stop the tears from coursing down his face as he looked down on the unmoving form in the bed, so wretchedly small after the Creep's ravages.

Later, he would find a wagon and haul Tancred to the pyres at the edge of town, as he had his mother and father. By nightfall, his brother would be ashes, gone. How much longer, he wondered, before I follow him?

He turned and looked across the room, at Paladine's sign on the wall. He'd prayed before it every day, at the proper times—dawn, midday, sunset, even midnight—while Tancred lay wheezing behind him, his life draining away. He'd begged the god to spare his brother's life, to drive off the disease. Now, his mouth hardening, he strode over to it, tore it down, and flung it across the chamber. It smashed against the gray stone, shards pattering down among the dirty rushes.

"Damn you, Paladine," he spat and stormed out of the room.

A fortnight later, Cathan crouched in a gully as cold rain dripped down from the branches of pines above. Shivering, he drew his brown cloak about him, but it was already soaked through, along with the stained tunic he wore underneath. A cough tickled his throat, and he fought it back with a grimace.

Another man stirred beside him in the ditch, turning a hooded head his way. Within the cowl, a smile lit a plain face, beneath a downy blond moustache.

"You look," Embric Sharpspurs whispered, "like you'd rather be some place else."

Cathan coughed shaking his head ruefully. "Wouldn't you?"

The gully was one of many that cut through the stony ground, deep amid Taol's hills. The land around them was gray and barren, rocky crags fringed with scrub bushes and oaks not yet come into spring leaf. The clouds above were low and leaden, giving off a maddening drizzle so fine it was almost mist. Thunder muttered somewhere far away.

Embric shrugged. "Could be worse," he said, his mouth crooking into an almost-grin. "Could be sleeting."

Cathan shook his head and was opening his mouth to reply when a hand touched his shoulder. He twisted, reaching for the long dagger he wore on his belt. He had the knife halfway out of its sheath when he stopped, meeting the gray, flinty gaze of an older man.

"Easy, MarSevrin," said the man. He was small and wiry, clad in hunting leathers and a mail shirt beneath his gray mantle. A few white hairs dusted his dark beard, and an angry red crease ran from his left ear to the corner of his mouth. "A boy your age should know better than to play with sharp things. Both of you, keep quiet. If you give us away, I'll hang the both of you by your balls for the others to throw rocks at."

"Yes, Tavarre," Embric and Cathan said together.

"Good," the older man said. "Now sit tight, and wait for the signal." He patted Cathan's shoulder, then was gone, vanishing into the brush like a ghost.

Before the plague, Tavarre had been *Baron* Tavarre, the lord of Luciel Vale. He had seldom come down to the town in those days, keeping mainly to his keep, but Cathan's father had named him a fair man. He was also an avid hunter, often roaming the highlands in search of game. It was said he knew every tree, every rock, for miles around. Staring at the bushes where Tavarre had disappeared, Cathan believed it.

The *Longosai* hadn't left the baron's keep untouched, so folk said, though Tavarre never spoke of what had driven him to flee its halls and take to the wilds. Others had joined him, men and women whom the sickness had spared. They were bandits now, roaming the hills in search of prey. Embric, a boy of twenty who had been a childhood friend of both Tancred and Cathan had been one of the first to join Tavarre's band, and he'd urged them to join up too. They'd refused, however, not wanting to leave their family.

That was before.

Cathan had gone to the bandits as soon as Tancred's body was burned, demanding to be brought to Tavarre. The baron had looked him over carefully, then nodded, agreeing to take him on. Since then, they had kept to their camp, hidden in the wilds, waiting. There was more waiting to banditry than Cathan had thought, and his restlessness grew to anxiety, even with the training at arms his fellows gave him. He needed someone to lash back at, a target for his grief.

Finally, the chance had come. The day before yesterday, Tavarre's scouts had ridden into the camp with news. A party of *Scatas*, soldiers of the imperial army, were riding through the wilds nearby. There were a dozen of them, but they didn't interest Cathan as much as the other who rode with them: a cleric of Paladine.

So they'd set out, two dozen men with Tavarre in the lead. The baron had chosen a likely spot for an ambush, along the road the *Scatas* traveled, and the'dy settled in and begun to wait anew. That had been last night, with four hours still lacking before dawn; it was nearly midday now, and Cathan was beginning to wonder if there really *were* soldiers nearby.

Just then, though, he heard the sharp, trilling song of a bluefinch. It wasn't an unusual sound in the wilds, but Cathan's muscles tautened anyway. Tavarre had taught his men several calls to use for signals, and the bluefinch was one of the most urgent. It trailed away, then came a second time, closer and shriller. He bit his lip as he reached beneath his cloak, feeling for the leather sling he kept looped through his belt. When he had the weapon in hand, he reached for a pouch he kept at his belt, and pulled out a jagged, white lump—not a stone, but a bit of broken ceramic. He'd taken the remnants of the holy symbol he'd smashed before his brother died. Now he rolled the shard in his hand, his mouth a hard line.

"Tancred," he whispered, "be with me."

He could hear them now: the thud of hoofs on the muddy road, a dozen paces away. Beside him, Embric loaded a battered crossbow, and together they turned to peer over the gully's edge, at the road below. Cathan sneered as he saw the *Scatas*, their blue cloaks soaked, clouds of breath-frost blossoming from within their plumed, bronze helms. Behind them, beneath a canopy carried by a pair of drenched acolytes, rode the cleric. He was a fat man, his satin robes stretched tight where his prodigious belly pressed against them.

Hating him immediately, Cathan tucked the shard into the pouch of his sling and prepared for the attack.

———◆———

Revered Son Blavian sniffled, loathing the accursed weather. It wasn't like this in the lowlands. True, it was the rainy season in the Lordcity now, but at least there it was *warm*. Despite the covering his servants carried, and the warm, vair-trimmed vestments he'd brought with him, he was cold to the bone. He blew on his pudgy hands, trying to warm them.

"Paladine's breath," he grumbled. "What manner of man would *want* to live in this place?"

He expected no answer. The *Scatas* had spoken little since they'd set forth from the Lordcity for Govinna, Taol's highland capital. They bore several coffers of gold coins and orders for Durinen, the province's patriarch, from the Kingpriest himself. Blavian wasn't sure just what the message said, but he had a good idea. Before he'd left, First Son Kurnos had spoken to him about the brigands who had absconded to the hills. No doubt the Kingpriest meant for Durinen to fight back against the robbers. That would explain the gold: waging such a campaign would not be cheap.

Whatever the reason for his journey, though, Blavian was proud the First Son had chosen him. Kurnos was the imperial heir, after all—it was good to have his favor. Hopefully, that would make up for having to slog through this damp, frigid country . . .

He heard the strange, trilling song again. He frowned, looking up to call out to the soldiers—*pray, what bird makes such a call?*—and saw something, just for a moment: a dark shape, moving behind a pine-dotted hummock. He gasped, and was drawing breath to shout a warning when the hillsides came alive.

It happened so quickly, it seemed over almost before it began. The *Scatas* had time enough only to lay their hands on their swords before more than a score of cloaked figures rose from the bushes to either side of the road, crossbows loaded and ready. A few others held slings, whirling them slowly above their heads. Blavian cast about, a cold stone deep in his gut as he realized quite a few weapons were trained on him.

"Show steel, and you'll be dead before you finish the draw," warned one of the ruffians, a wiry man with a scarred face. He perched atop a mossy boulder, a naked sword in his hand. He waved the blade, looking past the soldiers. "Let down His Corpulence's covering, will you, lads? Let him feel the weather."

Wide-eyed and white with fear, the acolytes tossed the canopy aside at once, and moved away from Blavian. The Revered Son winced as rain pattered down on his balding pate, then puffed out his chest as the man on the boulder laughed.

"What are you about?" he demanded. "Who are you?"

"I'd think that must be obvious." Grinning, the man hopped from the rock down onto the road. He nodded toward the soldiers, who were glancing at one another, fingering their weapons' hilts. "Tell your men to throw down their swords, Reverence, unless they want to leave this place with more holes in their bodies than they came with. It's all right—we only want to rob you."

"What!" Blavian exclaimed. He thumped a fist against his thigh, his voice rising to a roar. "This is preposterous! You have no right—"

Something hit him then, a mass that seemed to come from nowhere to slam into his collarbone. He heard a gruesome snap before he toppled from his horse, splashing down into the mud—then the pain hit, gagging him. He yowled, writhing, but his acolytes stayed where they were, too afraid of the bandits to move.

The lead brigand's smile didn't waver. "Reverence, you've seen what my men can do," he said. "Next time, they won't aim to wound."

For a moment, the only sounds Blavian could manage were small, pained grunts. After a few tries, though, his voice came. "You heard him. Swords down, all of you."

As one—some with visible relief—the *Scatas* unsheathed their blades and tossed them to the ground. The scarred man signaled to his fellows, and several dropped their crossbows and darted in, snatching up the swords. Another took the reins of the pack horses that carried the Patriarch's gold, and yet another pair emerged from a gully and came toward Blavian himself. One held a cocked crossbow, the other an unloaded sling. The Revered Son knew at once that the second man—no, a boy from the looks of him—was the one who had dared to strike him.

"Your purse, sirrah," said the crossbowman, "and your jewels."

Blavian goggled, reaching for the heavy golden necklace he wore as an emblem of his potency within the church. "You cannot do this!" he cried as the robbery continued around them. "I am a servant of the god!"

The slinger bent down, ignoring his protests, and plucked a small object up from the ground, a white chunk half the size of a clenched fist. Blavian thought the thing that had hit him had been a stone or perhaps a lead pellet. Instead, he saw it was a chunk of broken ceramic. The boy pressed it briefly to his lips, then tucked it into his belt. Then he turned to the cleric, his lip curling.

"This is for Tancred," he snarled.

The Revered Son had only a moment to wonder who Tancred was before the boy drew back his foot and slammed it into the side of his head, crashing his world down into blackness.

CHAPTER 2 ▼

They were arguing again in the throne room.

It wasn't Ilista's habit to arrive late to the imperial court, and the First Daughter could hear the buzz of voices as she dressed in her private vestiary. Most belonged to minor courtiers, but others she recognized: Kurnos's firm, clipped sentences, Loralon's soothing tones. Then, as her attendants helped her don a snow-white surplice over her violet-trimmed robes, another voice cut through the rest, silencing them. The Kingpriest normally presided over the court in austere silence, letting his advisers do the talking, but today he was clearly angry—not quite shouting, as he sometimes did when his temper broke loose—but with an edge to his words.

Ilista scowled impatiently as the servants set an amethyst-studded circlet upon her head. The velvet curtains that led to the throne room muffled Symeon's voice, and she couldn't make out what he was saying. She had half a mind to go into the audience hall in her sandals, but propriety stayed her long enough for her attendants to help her into her satin slippers. Hurriedly she genuflected toward the golden shrine in the vestiary's corner, then parted the curtains and stepped through.

"—will not stand!" Symeon snapped, his voice ringing throughout the hall. "If these varlets *dare* put swords to the throats of Paladine's servants, their heads should be mounted atop Govinna's gates!"

The Hall of Audience was enormous, as was only proper for the holiest and mightiest man in the world. It was a perfect circle, two hundred paces across, bathed in soft light from the crystal dome that arched overhead. The floor was rose-veined marble, polished mirror-bright; the walls were lacquered wood carved to resemble scarlet rose petals, so that the chamber seemed to rest within a vast, living bloom. Golden censers filled the air with the scents of spice and citrus, and platinum candelabra held hundreds of flickering white tapers. Garlands of spring flowers—starblooms, daffodils, and pink roses—hung everywhere.

Around the room's edges stood Istar's elite, clad in rich garments, the men and women alike perfumed and powdered, jewels glittering at ears and throats, fingers and wrists, ankles, brows, and even toes. Several Solamnic Knights stood in a cluster across from Ilista, splendid in their polished, engraved armor. Elsewhere, the First Daughter spied Marwort the Illustrious, the white-robed wizard who represented the Orders of High Sorcery at court. There were the hierarchs of the other churches, too: Stefara, the High Hand of Mishakal, in her sky-blue healer's robes; Thendeles, Majere's grand philosopher, in his faith's plain red habit; Peliador of Kiri-Jolith in gold, Avram of Branchala in green, and Nubrinda of Habbakuk in purple, and with them, the high clergy of Paladine—Kurnos, Loralon, and other human and elven priests, all in shimmering white.

Ilista looked past them all to the far side of the room, where a blue mosaic swept across the floor to surround a pure white dais and a golden, rose-wreathed throne, twin to the one in the imperial manse. The Kingpriest sat upon the throne, all in silvery robes, gem-encrusted breastplate, and sapphire-studded tiara. His cherubic face burned red as he glared at an aging Knight who stood before the throne. Ilista recognized Holger Windsound, Lord Martial of the Knights in Istar. Holger was a proud man and not easily cowed, but he bowed his snowy head beneath Symeon's wrath.

A bell chimed in the galleries above the hall, heralding Ilista's arrival. She gritted her teeth as a hundred heads turned to look at her—including the Kingpriest's. His black eyes glittered in the light of the crystal dome.

"*Efisa*," Symeon declared. "We are pleased you have chosen to join us."

Ilista had a good excuse for her lateness. One of her priestesses had come to her that morning, claiming she was losing her faith. The girl's mother had died suddenly the night before, and she had demanded to know how the god could let such a thing happen. Ilista had stayed with her, drying her tears and telling her Paladine was wise and good, and everyone had a time when the god called her to his side. Eventually, the girl had agreed to meditate on the god's grace; she might yet leave the order or she might not. It was the best Ilista could hope for—there was no point in forcing people to believe.

She said nothing of this to the Kingpriest, however. Instead, she bent her knee to him, signing the triangle.

"Holiness," she said softly. "I apologize for failing thee."

Symeon glowered at her a moment, then waved her forward. "Come, then. Join your peers."

Everyone watched as Ilista strode across the chamber to stand alongside Loralon and Kurnos. They nodded to her as Symeon turned back to the aging Knight.

"Lord Holger was just telling us of an . . . *incident* that has happened in the highlands," the Kingpriest stated irritably. "Tell Her Grace what has happened, man."

Holger bowed, turning to face her. His face was like steel and showed none of the weariness of age. His hoary moustache drooped over a mouth that had never, in the two years

Ilista had served as First Daughter, broken a smile.

"Banditry, milady," he said, all but spitting the word. "An ambuscade aimed at imperial funds bound for Govinna."

An outraged murmur ran through the assembly, even though Holger was repeating his news purely for her benefit. The others fell silent, however, at a gesture from the Kingpriest, and all eyes returned to the First Daughter.

"*Palado Calib*," Ilista murmured. *Blessed Paladine.* "What happened? Did the robbers succeed?"

The aging Knight nodded. "They took the soldiers by surprise, and forced them to surrender the gold, *Efisa*. After, the bandits turned them loose without horse or sword, and disappeared into the hills."

Kurnos stirred beside Ilista, his brows knitting. "What of Blavian? The Revered Son traveling with them?"

"He fared less well, Your Grace. The bandits beat him badly, and his injuries were grievous. He lives still," the Knight added as the court stirred. Kurnos's face had turned nearly as livid as Symeon's. "He is resting at a Mishakite hospice and will recover, though it will take time."

"And the funds?" Symeon asked.

"Gone, sire. I know not where."

The Kingpriest's rosebud lips whitened, as did his knuckles as he gripped the arms of the throne. The courtiers looked at one another uneasily. Ilista watched Symeon carefully, looking for signs. His fury could be terrifying, but she had learned it was usually short-lived and could be tempered by reason. That was her job and the other advisers'. Today would be difficult, however, for Kurnos was every bit as upset as the Kingpriest. She exchanged glances with Loralon, who nodded. The next few moments would be crucial.

Kurnos stepped forward before either of them could speak. "Majesty, if I might offer counsel?"

Symeon nodded. "Of course, *Aulforo*. We value your wisdom, as always."

The First Son wasn't looking very wise. His hands trembled, and his face had tightened into a fearsome scowl. When he spoke, his voice was like a drawn bowstring.

"These bandits have gone too far," said Kurnos. "Tax collectors are one thing, but to attack a member of the clergy . . ." He trailed off, shaking his head, then took a deep breath. "Sire, I believe we should strike back, with force."

Gasps rang out across the audience hall, followed by hushed whispers. Ilista stepped forward, her mouth opening, but Symeon stopped her with a look and turned back to Kurnos.

"Go on."

"It would only take a part of the imperial army," the First Son explained. "Perhaps a legion or two. They would make short work of these brigands."

Ilista could contain herself no longer. "These brigands are the folk of Taol," she interjected. "You recommend a military attack on our own people?"

Around the court, folk nodded in agreement or shook their heads dismissively. Ilista paid no mind to them, however. Her gaze was on the Kingpriest. He stared back at her, his black eyes glinting.

"You don't agree these villains must be punished, then?" Symeon asked.

"No, not in this fashion, sire," she replied. "You are right when you say this cannot stand, but to send in the army . . . if we do, we risk inciting open revolt. None of us want another *Trosedil*."

A flicker of anger crossed Symeon's face, and for a moment Ilista feared she had gone too far by invoking the Three Thrones' War. After a moment, though, he turned to Loralon. "And you, Emissary? What is your mind?"

Loralon raised his eyebrows. "Majesty, it is not my place to put my hand on the empire's tiller . . . but if you would hear me, I agree with Lady Ilista. Sending forth the army is a drastic choice and could make matters worse. I suggest we negotiate instead."

"Negotiate?" Kurnos snapped. "These are robbers, not diplomats!"

"Your counsel is known already, First Son," Symeon said curtly, and Ilista relaxed a little. He would come around. The Kingpriest sat in silence for a time, his fingers steepled in thought, then nodded. "You are right, Loralon—and you as well, Ilista. This is no time to be rash. I shall weigh what I have heard, and render judgment after midday prayer. This court is adjourned until then." He rose from his seat, signing the triangle. *"Fe Paladas cado, bid Istaras apalo."*

In Paladine's name, with Istar's might.

The audience hall quickly dissolved into excited noise as the courtiers fell to arguing with one another. Some withdrew to anterooms, where food and watered wine awaited. Others hurried toward the dais, seeking to offer their own advice. Symeon waved them off and strode toward the door to his private sanctum. An acolyte hurried ahead to hold open the door.

Ilista watched the Kingpriest leave then started toward Kurnos, who gone over to Lord Holger. The two were speaking together in hushed tones, along with several other hierarchs. As she approached, the First Son looked up, his gaze meeting hers. His blue eyes smoldered with anger: she and Loralon had quelled Symeon's fire, but not his. She faltered, flushing beneath his baleful glare, then turned and hurried out of the room.

———◆———

Ilista's private chambers were dim and silent as she finished her evening prayer. Wetting her fingers, she pinched out the violet candles that flickered on the golden shrine, then kissed her medallion and pushed herself up from the padded kneeling-bench.

The room was richly done, as befit one of her station—not as fine as the Kingpriest's golden halls and certainly much less vast, but there was nothing meager about the great, sprawling bed draped in shimmering samite or the walls of teak inlaid with lavender jade. A tall, silver harp stood in the corner. She didn't play but Farenne, one of her attendants, did, and often came to soothe Ilista into sleep with sweet strings. Tonight, though, Ilista had dismissed Farenne early, preferring to be alone. Now she moved about the chamber, dousing the lamps that glowed softly here and there, until only a single taper remained by her bedside.

That done, she turned to the window, whose silken curtains fluttered in the breeze. The scent of jasmine blew in from the gardens. The breeze was chilly, though, so she pulled the window shut, then went over to her bed to climb up onto it. Kissing her medallion again, she doused the taper and laid her head down on satin pillows.

Sleep didn't come right away; that was not her way. It had always been Ilista's nature to dwell on matters while she lay abed. Tonight, her musings drifted to the First Son.

She had long ago accepted that she and Kurnos would seldom agree. He was obviously a capable cleric—one didn't rise so high in the church without priestly gifts—but he was also a hot-blooded man, quick to act and slow to forget a slight. They had argued often enough in the past, but she'd never seen him as outraged as he'd been today. What was it, she wondered? Had the attack on Revered Son Blavian truly affected him so terribly? He had spoken in the past of the need to put down the bandits in Taol, but today was different. Sweet Paladine, he had been ready to send in the *Scatas*! If he had been on the throne today, she was sure Lord Holger and his troops would have ridden out tomorrow morning, with orders to fight. She and Loralon could manage Symeon's ill humors. What would Kurnos do, though, if she opposed *him* once he wore the sapphire crown?

Her mind drifted to the man who still sat the throne. It had been more than a season since that strange, snowy night when Symeon foretold his own death, and still he was healthy. Stefara of Mishakal examined him every Godsday, looking for signs of illness, but he hadn't even had so much as a cold all winter long. Morbidly, and not for the first time, she wondered how the god would take him. Accident? Assassination? She signed the triangle at the thought, whispering a prayer to forgive her dark thoughts.

The Kingpriest had, in the end, elected to follow her and Loralon's advice—Lord Holger would alert the army but give no orders to march. One day soon, however, Kurnos would reign, and war might be swift. Ilista wished—again, not for the first time—that His Holiness had chosen one more temperate to succeed him. She thought of Loralon, whose wisdom ran deeper than any she knew. What a Kingpriest he would make!

Then she chuckled, her eyes fluttering drowsily shut. An elf on the golden throne! Istar would sink beneath the sea before such a thing happened. No, the decision was made—when the time came, Kurnos would rule, and she would serve him. There was no other choice.

------◆-◆------

Cold wind caressed Ilista's cheek, rousing her from slumber. She brushed at her face, annoyed. She'd *told* herself to close the window. Throwing off her blankets, she got up and glanced across the room. Sure enough, the curtains were wafting in the breeze, aglow with Solinari's shimmering light.

Suddenly she stiffened, a deeper chill grasping her. *Solinari?* The silver moon had been just a fingernail crescent and setting when she went to bed. Now it hung fat and orange over the Lordcity's rooftops. She *had* closed the window— now that she reflected, she was sure of it. Touching her medallion, she reached out for the night table, and the taper she'd left there. Her fingers found nothing, however. The candle was gone.

Her heart beat wildly as she looked about. Perhaps she'd knocked it off the table in her sleep—but no, it wasn't on the floor either. Which meant either she'd gotten up and didn't remember, or—

Or someone else had been in the room.

Palado, me scelfud on ludras fe catmas, she prayed silently as she rose from her bed, the marble floor cold against her bare feet. *Paladine, deliver me from lurkers in the dark.*

"H-hello?" she stammered, glancing about the shadow-cloaked room. "Is anyone there?"

She could call for help. A guard might hear her—or might not. She needed to do something besides stand and shiver. Quietly, she crept to the window and glanced out but saw nothing strange—except the moon, shining full where it had no right to be. Her whole body tense, she pulled the casement shut, then latched it carefully. *Maybe I didn't do that before,* she thought. *Maybe I forgot, and the window blew open while—*

"Hello yourself."

She whirled, crying out. The monk sitting on the corner of her bed jumped up, letting out a yelp of his own.

Ilista shrank back, goggling at him. He was short, barely taller than a dwarf, and spectacularly huge—three hundred pounds, at least, his white habit spread like a tent on his massive frame. What hair there was on his tonsured head was silver. His eyes were small and brown in his pink, jowly face. He looked as incapable of stealth as a man could be—yet where had he come from?

"Huma's hammer!" he exclaimed, putting a sausage-fingered hand to his brow. "You scared the Abyss out of me. You're lucky I didn't keel over from fright, *Efisa*—you'd need at least ten strong men to carry me out of here." He chortled, slapping his belly.

The First Daughter stared, confused. "Who are you?"

"Oh, no one important," he answered, still smiling. "Just a messenger. Call me Brother Jendle—it's as good a name as any."

She could only stand there, blinking at him. He seemed no threat—how *could* he, when the effort of merely standing seemed enough to bead his face with sweat?—but still . . .

"You *are* the First Daughter of Paladine, aren't you?" the fat monk asked, squinting at her. "Or did I get the wrong room?"

"I—no, you didn't—" Ilista said, then stopped. "What?"

"Oh, dear." Jendle clucked his tongue, waddling over to pat her hand. "Mind's addled, is it? Poor lass. Well, I'll give you the message anyway. Have to, you see. Hold still."

Ilista tried to draw back, but she reacted slowly, and he was adder-quick, his hand darting forward to clasp her wrist like a manacle. She drew a sharp breath, and suddenly the room unraveled around her. Everything—the bed, the open window, even Brother Jendle—frayed and swirled, then vanished, becoming another place.

She stood on a clifftop among the hills, a cold wind gusting in her face. She heard the song of bluefinches, smelled the scent of fresh rain. In the distance loomed the walls of a city, all but lost in a pall of fog. Beyond its walls, many miles off, towering mountains limned the horizon. Grass grew in tufts from the hill's rocky soil, and plane trees towered above. In the far distance stood a cottage—a herdsman's or charcoal burner's, probably, its chimney smoking. The clifftop was a peaceful place, a spot where one might lie in the summertime, guessing the shapes of scudding clouds.

All at once, the peace shattered. The birdsong ceased, and a distant rumbling rose from down in the valley. She looked, following the noise, and caught her breath. Dust rose among the hills, a great brown cloud that smudged the sky. It grew as she watched, and soon there were thousands of soldiers marching in unison, armor and weapons flashing in the sun. They moved swiftly toward her, devouring the ground with long, relentless strides. She peered at the army, wondering whose it was, yet already knowing in a way, long before she saw the blue cloaks, the bronze helmets, the falcon-and-triangle banners fluttering over the soldiers' heads. It was the imperial army, marching at last, at the behest of Kurnos.

Kingpriest Kurnos.

"Stop!" she cried, rushing to the cliff's edge.

The slope was too sheer, though, the gravel that covered it too loose to descend. She could only watch as the army came on, inexorably, coming closer . . . filling the valley . . .

Something happened, then, in the corner of her eye. She couldn't see what it was at first, but when she looked harder, there was something coming out of the west, where the misty city stood. Craning to see, she fought to see what it was . . . then, all at once, she saw a figure of shining light, like silver in full sunshine. She could not make out anything of the man at the glow's heart, for every time she tried to look through the shining glare, it stung her eyes and she had to turn away. The sight was beautiful and terrible, and she began to weep without knowing why.

The soldiers in the valley saw the shining figure too. They slowed at its approach . . . stopped . . . then broke and ran, casting swords and banners aside. In what seemed only a few moments, they had fled the valley altogether, until only the figure remained, gleaming brighter than the sun.

After the army was gone the shining figure seemed to nod to itself for a moment, glanced around as if searching for something, then turned toward the clifftop where Ilista stood and looked directly at her. She caught her breath, staring back as it raised its lambent hands toward her.

"*Efisa*," it spoke, and the world vanished in a burst of blinding white.

When she could see again, Ilista stood in her bedchamber once more, exactly where she had been when Brother Jendle touched her. Of the fat monk, though, there was no sign.

She heard a sound—a dry scraping, like metal being dragged over stone, coming from behind her. She whirled—and saw, for just an eyeblink, the slender tip of a tail slithering out her open window. It was serpentine and pointed, covered with scales that shimmered like silver in the starlight. Like silver . . . or platinum.

Her mouth dropping open, Ilista sprinted toward the casement. As she ran, though, she caught her foot on the edge of an intricate Dravinish rug, and suddenly she was pitching forward, arms flinging outward, falling . . .

Ilista woke in bed, her stomach a chasm.

It took a moment for the world to stop spinning. When it did, though, she looked to the table nearby. The taper was still there, as she'd left it, bathed in red moonlight, not silver. She sighed. It had been a dream, nothing more, doubtless brought on by her own worries over Kurnos's eagerness to attack Taol. There had been no fat monk, no army, no figure of light. And certainly, no platinum tail, sliding out . . . sliding out. . . .

Out her window.

She sat up suddenly, knowing what the chill in the room meant even before she turned to look out toward the gardens. The window stood open, curtains fluttering in the breeze.

CHAPTER 3 ▼

In all of Ansalon, three libraries ranked above all others. The greatest was the Library of Gilean in Palanthas, a vast hall of lore dedicated to the God of the Book. Legend had it that a copy of every text ever set to parchment or papyrus—or even clay tablet—rested somewhere in its halls under the care of a select order of monks led by the renowned Astinus the Undying. Second-largest—with one hundred thousand tomes, a fraction of the Palanthian library's size—was the Scriptorium of Khrystann, in distant Tarsis, which ran beneath the streets of that bustling seaport and was nearly as renowned as the white-winged ships that sailed from its harbor.

The third was the Sacred Chancery in the Great Temple itself. It stood in a wing to the north of the basilica, five storeys tall, its windows made of crystal the color of honey, so that even the moons' light looked like sunset within its halls. It was a labyrinth, and even the scribes and scholars who toiled within had been known to get lost now and again. The shelves reached up and up its high walls, with woven baskets on winches giving access to the topmost levels. There were no frescoes or mosaics within its halls, no sculptures or tapestries, not even decorative plants. There were only the books, the great mahogany desks where the copyists worked, and the god's platinum triangle hung on the end of every shelf.

Bustling during the day, the chancery was a still place this night, silent but for the scratching of a single quill pen. The pen belonged to a young scribe, a scrawny man whose hands and sleeves alike bore fresh and faded stains of purple ink. Though barely past twenty, his scalp had already begun to show through his thinning hair, and the spectacles perched on his nose were thick, making his eyes seem disconcertingly huge. He bent over a page of fine vellum, his gaze flicking to an open text beside him as he wrote, pausing only now and then to dip his pen into an inkwell or to scatter fine sand on his writing to dry it. So intent was he on his writing that he didn't hear the clack of sandals on the marble floor, and when Loralon's hand touched his shoulder, he gave a shout of surprise and nearly leaped out of his robes.

"Eminence!" he exclaimed, turning to focus his enormous stare on the elf. He blinked, getting awkwardly to his feet. "I did not realize you were still about. It's . . . what . . ." He glanced at an hour-candle burning nearby. "Three hours till dawn."

"*Lissam, farno*," said the elf. *Peace, child.* Loralon was fully garbed, as always, his beard meticulous and his gaze keen. "I did not mean to disturb you. First Daughter, this is Brother Denubis."

Denubis looked past the Emissary, noticing Ilista for the first time. She stood beside the elf, looking his opposite: pale and red-eyed, her hair and cassock in disarray. The scribe blinked.

"*Efisa*, I am honored. I do not often see you here."

"No, Brother," she replied, smiling. "I've never had a head for books, I'm afraid. What are you working on?"

"Translating the *Peripas Mishakas*, my lady, into the Solamnic vulgate."

Ilista's eyebrows rose. The *Peripas*, the Disks of Mishakal, were one of the church's longest—and oldest—holy texts. The originals were painstakingly etched on hundreds of platinum circles, the words so dense that each disk filled dozens of pages. The text at Denubis's side was only one volume of many in the

35

Church Istaran translation, and an early one at that. The scribe might be working on this translation for years—perhaps all his life. Such was the gods' work.

"I beg pardon for interrupting your work, Brother," Loralon said, "but I need to get into the *Fibuliam*."

Denubis looked even more startled than usual. "The *Fibuliam*, Eminence?"

"Yes, Brother. Have you the key?"

"Of—of course." The scribe reached to his belt, producing a ring on which hung an intricate golden object. It was not shaped like a key but like a slender, two-tined fork. "If you'll follow. . . ."

Ilista had not waited until morning to tell Loralon of her dream. She had hurried across the temple grounds to the cloister of the Chosen of E'li, the elven order. He had been awake— of course—and when she'd told him of her dream, he had been genuinely surprised. Hearing of her strange visitor, he had smiled, his eyes sparkling.

"It seems, *Efisa*, the god has chosen to visit everyone in Istar lately except me," he'd said without a trace of bitterness and bade her come with him to the chancery.

No one knew the library better than the Emissary. He spent countless hours there, poring over its tomes, and some said he knew every word within the pages of its many, many books. Ilista herself had never had much interest. She could read and write in the common and church tongues, of course, but Loralon seemed to know almost every language ever spoken—even those of empires long dead and the secret dialects of the dragons. One learned many things when one lived for centuries.

Now Denubis led them deep into the chancery to a stout door of gold-chased alabaster. The door had neither latch nor keyhole and was engraved with warding glyphs that—according to lore—could turn flesh to stone. The acolytes whispered that some of the statues in the gardens had once been men and women who had tried to force the stout door open. Ilista didn't believe that tale, but she'd never heard anyone refute it either.

Whatever the case, Denubis did not lay a hand on the door. Instead, he brought out the golden fork and a tiny silver hammer. Signing the triangle, he struck the one with the other, sounding a high, soothing tone. The chime rang for a moment, then he struck again, and a third time. Each note was slightly different, and they merged into a chord of remarkable harmony.

Motes of violet light appeared on the latchless door's surface, running across it in streams and waves in response to the music, moving always from its center to its edges. After a moment the whole wall seemed to shudder, then the door swung outward, revealing a dark room beyond. A strange smell came from within—dry and sharp, yet enticing, like the dreampipes some men smoked in Karthay.

Loralon dismissed Denubis. The scribe bowed and withdrew, leaving the elf and Ilista alone. The two high priests exchanged glances, then entered the chamber.

Through Istar's history, the Kingpriests had declared certain books and scrolls works of heresy. When this happened, the clergy brought any copies they found to the Lordcity, where they burned them in great "cleansing pyres," pouring holy oil on the flames to drive out the evil they consumed. For each banned tome, however, the church always preserved a single copy, so a select few could study the words that corrupted the hearts of common men. These they kept in the *Fibuliam*.

Loralon spoke a word in Elvish, and the room filled with light. Ilista stared around in awe. The chamber was tall and circular, a tube of marble that ran up the full height of the chancery. Its shelves curved up the walls in rings, accessible by a spiralling ramp. At its apex, the sacred triangle looked down upon all.

The elf walked up the ramp, running his delicate fingers over one shelf, then the next.

"There is a grimoire here that might be of help," he said as Ilista followed him. "I read it a century ago, but I remember it well—a tome of prophecies from the empire's dawn, when warlords, not Kingpriests, ruled here." He smiled slightly. "They banned it because, unlike most prophetic works, some of it came unfortunately true. Ah."

He stopped a third of the way up the ramp and found a slender volume bound in basilisk skin. Pulling it from the shelf, he blew off a film of dust and carried it to a landing where a stone desk stood. Ilista watched as he opened the book. Archaic calligraphy covered the title page, along with crude illuminations of dragons, griffins, and other mystical beasts.

Qoi Zehomu, it proclaimed. *Psandru Ovrom Vizeva.*

"It's in High Dravinish," Loralon said in reply to her inquiring look. "Men once spoke this tongue in the southern provinces, when they were free city-states. The title means *What Shall Come: The Foresights of Psandros the Younger.*"

Gently he turned its brittle, yellowing pages. There were scores of verses within, all carefully inscribed and illustrated. He went too quickly for Ilista to note what most were about, but she did make out some illustrations: a building that could only be the Great Temple; a throne, broken in three parts; five proud towers, two in ruins; and a strange symbol that looked, to her eyes, like a burning mountain. Finally, he came to one near the end, and pointed.

VIZILOVIOS IHOMUA.

"*Advent of the Lightbringer*," the elf translated.

Ilista scanned the page. The prophecy was short, only two stanzas long:

Vesinua, yuzun horizua,
Bon drova bruvli, Isto gizua,
Vilo lush vevom su behomu,
Vizilovra, gavos avizua.

Ita deg dridiva so anevunt,
So gonnunt, sos volbua sivunt,
Su ollom viu nirinfo vesuu,
Ita muzaba susilva so gnivunt.

"What that means," Loralon explained, "is this:

"From the west, the setting of suns,
In troubled times, with Istar endangered,
Carrying lost riches he comes,
Lightbringer, bearer of hope.

"And though the darkness shall fear him,
Hunt him, seek his destruction,
He is the savior of holiness,
And the gods themselves shall bow to him."

Ilista shook her head. "It doesn't mean anything to me. It might as well be a lunatic's ravings."

"It is," Loralon said, smiling. "Psandros was quite mad, but time and again, his words have come true—the Third Dragonwar, the rise of the Kingpriests, the *Trosedil* . . . you see? Of course, some of it hasn't happened yet—Chaos has yet to walk the land again, thank the gods—but still, this is a dangerous book, *Efisa*, and your dream matches the prophecy. Didn't you say this man of light came out of the west?"

Ilista stared at the ancient words. The *Fibuliam* was warm, but she found herself shivering. "What does it mean? What should we do?"

Loralon smiled, closing the book again. He walked back down the ramp and slid it back into its place on the shelf, then turned, his hands folded within his sleeves. His eyes shone in the elf-light.

"Not *we*, Your Grace. *You*," he said. "The god wishes you to find the Lightbringer."

———◆———

The Kingpriest had adjourned his court for the day, and the three high priests had retired with him to his private audience room in the manse. Outside the windows, the clouds shone dusky rose, and the sound of someone playing a long-necked lute rose from the gardens. Soon the bells would summon the faithful to evening prayer. Out in the city, merchants were putting away their wares and linkboys were lighting the thousands of crystal lanterns that made the Lordcity seem a sea of stars at night. Before long, the folk of Istar would fill the wine shops, the concert halls, and the theaters, while young lovers strolled the gardens and byways, taking full advantage of the mild spring weather.

Kurnos had intended, that night, to go to the Arena. A troupe of mummers from bronze-walled Kautilya were performing there this week, and tonight's fare was a favorite of his: *The Death of Giusecchio*, a bloody tragedy of treason and regicide. Now, looking from Symeon to the First Daughter, he couldn't help but think there was enough intrigue in this very room to slake his thirst for such a drama. Ilista looked wan and weary, and whenever his eyes met hers, she glanced away and started fussing with the cuffs of her sleeves. Ilista had told them of her vision the night before, the fat monk who had appeared to her and proved in the end to be the platinum dragon. He could tell, though, that there was more she wasn't saying. Something was afoot—but what?

"A voyage?" Symeon asked, sipping watered claret from a crystal goblet. He regarded Ilista steadily from beside one of the golden braziers that flanked his throne. "Beyond the empire, no less?"

"Only to Solamnia and Kharolis, Majesty," she replied, eyes downcast. "Both lands pay us homage, and the Solamnic Knights guard this very Temple. I would ask a company of such men to escort me, as protection while I follow my vision."

Symeon's lips pursed. "All this to seek a man of light, glimpsed in a dream."

"A *god-given* dream, Holiness," Loralon corrected. "No different from the one you had last year."

Kurnos shook his head. He wasn't sure he believed any of it. Symeon was still healthy, after all, and he had long since begun to wonder if the Kingpriest had simply imagined Paladine's visitation. It rankled him, particularly after the past two days. If *he* were Kingpriest, several thousand *Scatas* would be marching toward Taol even now, to exact justice upon the bandits there. Symeon was a firm ruler when it suited him, but he relied too much on others' advice—particularly Ilista and Loralon. Even now, he was regarding the latter over the rim of his wine glass, weighing his words.

"That may be so," the Kingpriest allowed, and shifted back to Ilista. "This man of light, who do you think he is?"

"I do not know," she replied. "I will need to search for him. I am sure he will already have shown signs of the god's touch, though."

"If you find him?" Kurnos tugged his beard. "What then?"

"I will bring him here."

The Kingpriest nodded, but Kurnos didn't smile. He stared first at Ilista, his mouth a lipless scowl, then at Loralon. The Emissary returned his gaze with a mildness that made the First Son's ears redden. He is complicit in this, Kurnos thought. He's holding something back—they both are. If anyone had asked him to give a reason for his suspicion, he would not have been able to. He was sure, though, the man of light was a danger.

Symeon, however, did not share his mistrust. "That is well," he said finally. "I should like to meet this man, if he exists. Kurnos, send word to the harbormaster to ready a ship to carry the First Daughter to Palanthas. I shall contact Lord Holger and ask him to provide a Knight to lead the escort. *Efisa*, you will sail before the week is out."

———◆———

Ilista stood at the aft rail of the *Falcon's Wing* as the great galleon glided across Lake Istar's crystalline waters. The ship's white wake stretched out behind, and beyond it lay the Lordcity, a distant jewel sparkling on the shore. The gleaming beacons of the God's Eyes flashed at the harbor's mouth, even from miles away. The deck creaked and rolled, and gulls shrieked above, diving now and again into the surf to snatch up shimmering fish. Up high in the rigging, men shouted to one another as they scrambled about; below the deck, broad-chested minotaurs snorted and growled as they worked the twin banks of the vessel's oars.

The past three days were a blur in Ilista's mind. It had been a remarkably short span to ready for such a voyage, and she'd found time for little else, aside from prayers and a few hours' dreamless sleep each night. She had named Balthera, one of her most promising aides, to act in her stead while she was away and had instructed her attendants in packing her vestments and the other accouterments she would need for her travels. The rest of the time she'd spent writing: missives to high members of the Revered Daughters elsewhere in the empire, a few last decrees she needed to issue, and even a testament, declaring her wishes for her order, should some ill befall her while she was away.

Finally, this morning after prayers, she had gone to the basilica with the other high priests for the *Parlaido*, the benediction of Leavetaking. Symeon himself had daubed her forehead with seawater blessed by Nubrinda of Habbakuk and spoken the ritual farewell, and then she had left the Hall of Audience, bound for the harbor.

Her escort had been waiting on the temple's broad steps. Sir Gareth Paliost was a Knight of the Sword, a seasoned warrior of fifty summers, the gray hairs in his hair and moustache outnumbering the brown. He was to be her only companion as they sailed. Other Knights would join them in Palanthas. He was a taciturn man and had spoken perhaps a dozen words to her since this morning, half of them "*Efisa*" or "Your Grace." Otherwise, he kept to dour silence, his hand seldom far from his sword. Lord Holger gave him full commendation, however, so it was a comfort to have him at her side.

Loralon had been waiting on the jetty where the *Falcon's Wing* was moored, and had taken her aside while stevedores busily loaded her belongings into the hold. Smiling, the Emissary had given her a small, golden box.

"A parting gift," he'd said. "We can use it to speak, though you will be far, far away. Look into it and speak my name, and if I have the power, I will answer."

She had opened it and caught her breath at what lay inside: an orb of shining crystal, small enough to fit in one cupped hand. It was warm to her touch, though the day remained cool, and there was something in its weight that spoke to her of power. Imprisoned within the orb was a single rose, its petals an exquisite blue she had never seen before, even in the Temple's gardens. An elven flower, no doubt, for an elven artifact.

She had embraced the Emissary, kissing his downy cheek—and surprising him for the second time in recent days—then, with Sir Gareth beside her, walked up the ramp to the deck of *Falcon's Wing*. Less than an hour later, the ship had raised its golden sails, moving out onto the lake's open water. They were bound for the River Mirshan and thence to the sea. After that, a two-week sail awaited them before they made port in Palanthas.

That all lay before her, and Ilista was still looking back. She thought of Kurnos as she watched the Lordcity vanish behind her. The First Son had watched her suspiciously the past several days. She had felt his piercing gaze on her throughout the *Parlaido*, and no longer doubted he knew there was more behind her journey than the dream. She and Loralon hadn't mentioned Psandros's prophecy to anyone. If it came out that her voyage was, in part, an answer to a text from the *Fibuliam*, it could go against her—and the Emissary as well. For that reason, they had kept the full truth to themselves.

What *is* the full truth? she wondered, her hand going to her medallion. What if I *do* find this Lightbringer?

The Lordcity disappeared at last behind a rocky point dotted with cypress trees. Biting her lip, Ilista turned away from the rail, her gaze shifting to the waters ahead.

CHAPTER 4 ▼

FIFTHMONTH, 923 I.A.

Cathan's hand sweated in its glove as he stood at the edge of the training grounds, waiting his turn at sword drills. At the far end, Lord Tavarre was shouting at the youth before him, a lad named Xenos who had joined the bandit group scarcely a week ago. The baron was in a full-throated rage, calling the lad one name after another—*lackbrain, slackard, shitskull* . . . it got worse from there. Xenos, who could not have been more than sixteen, turned bright red, his eyes brimming with tears. If there were a way, he might have tunneled into the stony ground to escape. Instead he cowered, shoulders hunched, and rode out Tavare's wrath.

Early on, Cathan learned not to meet the lord's gaze when he was angry—it was best, he'd found, to look elsewhere, so he turned to gaze across the valley. The bandits' camp was well hidden, a cluster of hide tents covered in brush at the bottom of a steep-walled ravine. A stream ran through its midst, cold and clear, tiny fish darting up to snatch water-striders from its surface. Scraggly spruces clung to shelves on the rocky cliffs to either side. The bandits had watchers hidden on the higher purchases, scanning the road for signs of trouble, but they were hidden from below. The wind gusted through the canyon, chilly for this time of year. Cathan wondered if the summer would ever come.

Four weeks had passed since Cathan's first raid, and there hadn't yet been a second. The high road was quiet, devoid of the usual traffic of the trading season. Word from neighboring towns was the Kingpriest had closed the road to the merchants who usually traveled it, and while there were rumors of more *Scatas* massing in the neighboring province of Ismin, Cathan hadn't spoken to anyone who had seen them firsthand.

He hadn't been idle over the past month, however. To begin with, Tavarre had punished him for kicking the fat priest half to death, ordering him to cook his meals and polish his sword and saddle for two weeks, then putting him on patrol duty for a third. Roaming the cold hills, sleeping on the rocky ground and eating nuts and roots, had been thoroughly unpleasant, but better than emptying the baron's chamber pot. Now he was back, and had joined the other new hands—the bandits' ranks had swelled as more folk succumbed to the plague in Luciel. He and they were still in training. Cathan was good with his sling, but his blade work still needed practice.

"Left shoulder shot!" barked Tavarre. "MarSevrin, wake up!"

"Uh?" Cathan started, his attention returning to the other end of the bare patch of dirt that served as the bandits' sparring field. Xenos had skulked off, and now the baron was glowering at him from beside a much-abused straw dummy.

"Come on, you damned dullard!" snapped Tavarre. "Advance!"

Flushing, Cathan shook his head to clear it, then raised his weapon—an oaken rod, in place of the short, broad blade he'd taken from one of Revered Son Blavian's soldiers—and started forward. He moved briskly toward the dummy, his brow furrowed, gauging distance—six paces, five, four. . . . Finally, as he drew near, he made his move, bringing his blade around in a vicious arc, snapping his wrist at the last moment so the sword struck the dummy with a loud *thump*, squarely amidst the red mark daubed on its shoulder. Straw flew, and the other young men behind him cheered. Grinning, Cathan lowered his sword as he turned away.

"Hold! I didn't tell you to return to the line!"

Cathan stopped, gritting as teeth as Tavarre stalked forward, his cloak billowing. "I'm sorry, milord."

"Sorry's for bairns and priests, lad—not warriors." The scars on Tavarre's face deepened as he spat in the dirt. "Put your blade back where it was."

Cathan blinked, confused, but when the baron's scowl deepened he did as he was told. Raising the wooden sword, he brought it around so it touched the dummy again and left it there, glancing at Tavarre in confusion—he'd *hit* the target, hadn't he?

Reaching out, Tavarre grabbed the rod's tip with a thick gloved hand. "Do you see this?" he asked, pulling the weapon away from the dummy. "*This* is what you kill with—the last four inches of your blade. You struck three inches father down."

Cathan shook his head. "But milord—this isn't the sword I usually use. Mine's shorter."

"Sweet Jolith's horns, boy," Tavarre swore. He gave the weapon a hard shake, then shoved it away. "I don't *care* about your usual sword. *That's* the one you're fighting with today."

Cathan's face reddened, and the other young bandits laughed. Tavarre rounded on them at once, bellowing. "Stop that damned snickering! This is serious! *Always* know the weapon in your hand, even if it's not your own! A real battle's not always neat—you can break your sword or drop it, and you'll have to grab what you can find! You can bet a *Scata* won't wait while—"

A long, rising howl cut him off, echoing across the ravine. It was a wolf's call, but there hadn't been any wolves in the hills around Luciel since before Cathan was born. Tavarre reacted swiftly, spinning and jerking his own blade from its scabbard. He had taught the sentries that signal. It meant there was a rider approaching the camp.

Bandits came out of their tents and rose from where they had been playing at dice and sulla-sticks, pulling out blades and cudgels, axes and knives. Many loaded crossbows or nocked arrows on bowstrings. Cathan dropped his practice sword and went for his sling, delving into his pouch for the shards of his family's sacred triangle. The hills had a way of throwing sound, and already he could hear the thud of approaching hooves. He ran on Tavarre's heels to the camp's edge, where an earthen game trail led out into the wild.

The approaching rider rounded a bend a few minutes later and reined in hard as half a dozen quarrels hit the ground before him. His horse reared, eyes rolling, and he tumbled from the saddle, the breath *whoofing* out of him as he hit the ground. Tavarre's lieutenant, a massive, balding man-at-arms named Vedro, was on him in an instant, pointing a short-hafted spear at the man's throat.

"Wait!" the rider cried. "I'm not armed!"

Cathan looked the man up and down. Sure enough, he held no weapon, nor was there any sheathed on his belt. He wore a tunic of rough, undyed wool, not a soldier's armor or the robes of a priest, and he had an unruly mop of sandy hair. Cathan had been whirling his sling in a circle over his head. Now he let it slow and drop, the ceramic shard still in its pouch.

"Deledos?" he asked.

Several bandits looked at him, Tavarre among them. "You know him?" the baron asked.

Cathan nodded. Deledos was the son of the town chandler. His younger brother Ormand had been a childhood friend. The *Longosai* had taken father and brother alike. He was lame, his right leg twisted from a break in his youth, which had kept him from joining the bandits.

"It's all right," Cathan said. "He's come from Luciel."

Deledos nodded enthusiastically, staring at the spear's gleaming tip. For a long, moment, no one moved . . . then Tavarre lowered his sword. "Vedro," he said.

The man-at-arms pulled back, but his eyes stayed narrow and he offered no hand to help as Deledos struggled to his feet. Reboy had bitten his tongue in the fall and wiped blood from his lips.

"I'm s-sorry, milord," he stammered, eyes downcast as he bowed to Tavarre.

The baron waved him off. "What's this about, lad?" he demanded. "Why have you come?"

"To find him," Deledos replied, pointing at Cathan.

"Me?" Cathan asked, surprised. "What for?"

Deledos met his gaze for a moment, his eyes dark, then looked away.

Cathan's mouth dropped open as a cold, hard feeling settled in his stomach. "Oh, no," he moaned.

A spear of light pierced the gloom as the door swung open. The small room was dark and close, the windows covered over. There was no sound, save for the soft rasp of troubled breathing. Bundles of herbs hung from the ceiling to mask the sour, sharp smell. They weren't enough, however, and the odor brought a stab of pain to Cathan's heart as he looked upon the cot, and the figure huddled beneath the blankets.

He stood in the doorway, paralyzed. He'd come straight from the camp, sharing Deledos's horse. He swallowed as a woman came up beside him—an old, stooped crone, her gray hair cropped short in a widow's cut. Her face was pale and mournful, and she looked far older than her sixty years. She said nothing, only laid a frail hand on Cathan's arm.

"Fendrilla," he said. "How long?"

"Two days," she whispered. "It's early yet, lad. There's still plenty of time."

He shook his head, a bitter taste in his mouth. "For what?"

"For praying," Fendrilla replied, pointing.

Cathan's lip curled as he saw the triangle, hanging by the bed: a plain, wooden one, its white paint worn and faded with age. With a snarl, he shook off the old woman's grasp and strode across the room. Reaching the triangle, he pulled it down and turned toward the door. "What is this?" he demanded.

"Lad," Fendrilla answered, shaking her head. "The god—"

Livid, he hawked and spat on the holy symbol, then flung it to the floor. "*That* for the god!"

Horrified, Fendrilla hurried forward to pick it up.

"No!" he snapped. "Paladine's done enough harm already. I won't have his mark—"

"Cathan?"

The thin, quavering voice came from the bed. Cathan stopped, his insides lurching, then turned and knelt beside it. With a shaking hand he pulled back the blankets. "Wentha?"

She had been a boyish girl, scabs on her knees and her freckled face seldom free of dirt, but she had begun to change since her thirteenth name-day. Slowly, she had started to grow beautiful, to draw stares from the village's boys. She'd let her hair grow long, tumbling down over her shoulders in honey-colored waves, and the rest of her body had started to go from sharp angles to curves. Cathan had watched with pride, over the past year, as his sister changed into a woman.

Now she was changing into something else. It was early yet, the red blooms on her arms the only sign, but it wouldn't be long before the *Longosai* turned her into something wretched, as it had the rest of his family.

"Oh, Blossom," he began, then faltered, bowing his head. He *would not cry.*

"Where have you been?" she asked. She was pale, tired-looking, but not yet gaunt. That would come. "You stopped coming to visit, after . . . after Tancred. . . ."

He shook his head. She didn't know about the bandits. "I've been busy, lass, but I'm here now."

She smiled, and his heart nearly broke. Though it was the same lovely smile she'd always had, he saw only a terrible rictus. He looked away, and when he found the strength to turn back her eyes had fluttered shut again. He set her hand down, then laid his head on her chest, listening. Her lifebeat sounded horribly weak to his ears.

Paladine, he prayed silently, If you are the great god of good the clerics claim, do this one thing and I'll serve you the rest of my days. She's just a girl. Heal her.

For a moment, the beating of Wentha's heart seemed to strengthen, her breathing to lose its faint, whistling wheeze. Cathan pulled back, his eyes wide, wondering if Fendrilla had been right after all—had his prayer healed her?

When he looked closer, though, the rash was still there, angry red bumps running from wrist to elbow. The *Longosai* had her and would not let go so easily.

Slowly, he drew the blanket back over her and stood still, then, with a growl, he turned and walked away. Fendrilla moved to stop him but held back when she saw the wildness in his eyes. His thoughts roiling, he stormed out of the old woman's cottage, into the half-light of sunset.

He walked for hours, first through Luciel's cluster of thatched cottages—many of them dark now, emptied by the plague—then up the rutted road, climbing the ridge that marked the edge of the valley where he'd lived all his life. He didn't look back but kept on, the shadows of pines and boulders lengthening around him. Somewhere he found a fallen branch, and swiped at imagined foes: *Scatas*, fat priests, Paladine himself. Always he made sure to hit them with the last four inches. That was what killed.

In time—he wasn't sure how long, but it must have been hours—he stopped walking. The sun had set, and the red moon was rising, the hue of its light matching his mood. He'd gotten off the road sometime and had been wandering the wilds. Now, looking around, he saw things he recognized: a boulder shaped like a man's face, a familiar stand of birches. Ahead, a narrow ravine cut through the crags. Without his mind to tell them where to go, his feet had brought him back to camp.

I'm coming home, he thought. Sighing, he cast aside his branch and walked on.

Cresting one last hill shoulder, he came to a halt again as he looked down at the gorge below. There was something different about the camp: cautious about lighting too many fires, the bandits tended to bed down early. Only the watchers remained awake for long after dusk. Now, though, the ravine was bustling, men calling out to one another as they hurried about. Some bent by the stream, filling skins with water. Others were saddling the horses, or pulling down tents. Amidst it all, Lord Tavarre stood on a grassy hummock, snapping orders and shouting curses.

Cathan stared in amazement. He'd only been away from camp a few hours. What was going on? He hesitated, not sure he wanted to know—he could go back to Luciel, no one would miss him—but finally he clenched his fists and started down into the ravine.

A wolf howled before he'd gone very far, and half a dozen cloaked men met him halfway down the slope. One stepped forward, sword in hand. "Halt!" he barked. "Name yourself before I give you a new hole for breathing."

Hearing the man's voice in the dark, Cathan couldn't help but chuckle. "Thanks, Embric, but I've all the holes I need," he said, raising his hands to show they were empty.

The shadowy figure hesitated, then lowered his weapon, pulling back his hood to reveal his scruff-bearded face. Embric asked with concern, "What are *you* doing back? Your sister—"

Cathan shook his head, scowling, and they stood there silently for a time. Embric looked at his feet, his face grim. Finally, Cathan blew a long breath through tight lips, and nodded toward the tents.

"What's happening down there?" he asked. "It looks as though you're striking camp."

"We are," Embric said. "Another rider came, a while after you left. He—"

"What in the blue Abyss is going on up there?" growled a voice from down the hill. "Six men, and you can't handle one intruder?"

Lord Tavarre hurried up toward them, Vedro at his side. His scarred face was set with anger and darkened even more when he saw Embric and the other bandits. Before he could say anything, though, his eyes fell on Cathan and widened.

"I came back," Cathan said. "Where are you going?"

The baron looked at him a moment, then ran a hand through his graying hair and turned to Embric. "Go back down and get to work. You too, Vedro. I'll be along."

The bandits hesitated, then withdrew, and Tavarre turned to Cathan, beckoning with his hand. "I would have bet against your returning. Walk with me."

Cathan glanced around, then nodded, and fell in beside his lord. Tavarre walked quickly for a short man, striding through the dark with a huntsman's sureness. They made their way through the night with the commotion of the camp falling behind as they went back the way Cathan had come. When they reached the face-shaped boulder Tavarre stopped, so Cathan did too. The baron regarded him quietly in the moonlight.

"What is it?" Cathan asked nervously, wondering why Tavare had taken him away from the others. "Embric said something about a messenger."

Tavarre nodded. "You know we're not the only bandits in the highlands, yes?" He went on without waiting for Cathan's nod. "Well, there's been talk for a while, of banding together. Now it's finally happening. There's a man named Ossirian, a higher lord than me—he's called us all to him, for something more than waylaying priests. Something bigger." He paused, his eyes glittering. "We're going to attack Govinna."

"What?" Cathan said, shocked.

"That's what I said, when I read the message," Tavarre said, grinning slyly. "I know Ossirian, though. He has a plan. We're to move out at once and meet up with the others at Abreri."

Cathan stood there, his mouth open, unable to think what to say. Govinna was Taol's largest city, walled and well-guarded. It was also a fortnight's march away—far enough that Cathan had never seen it. The bandits had joked about sacking it, more than once, but that was all it was—jests.

"Listen, lad," Tavarre said, putting a hand on Cathan's shoulder, "you don't have to come. I see where your heart is. Stay with your sister."

Cathan held his breath, considering. He could remain here in Luciel, with Wentha—but to what end? She would waste away, like his parents, like Tancred, and nothing he could do would stop her death. On the other hand, Govinna was where Durinen, the borderlands' high priest and ruler, lived. He couldn't save his sister, but he could help bring down the god's servant. That was something.

Slowly he exhaled, lips tight against his teeth. "No," he said. "I'm with you."

CHAPTER 5 ▼

SIXTHMONTH, 923 I.A.

The day began for Symeon as it always did, with Brother Purvis waking him by ringing a chime made from the wingbone of a silver dragon. It still lacked nearly two hours before dawn, and he lay awake for a time, listening to the nightbirds' final songs. Dust danced on the silver moonlight streaming through the windows of his chamber. It was nearing summer, and the room was already warm. In the Lord-city, late spring was a time of humid days and cool nights, punctuated by lashing rainstorms that swept in off the lake. Smiling, the Kingpriest pushed off his white, silken sheets and rose from his golden bed for the last time.

The morning passed quickly, following the usual routine. Purvis brought him a mug of honeyed wine, and he drank it in his private bath while blind servants scrubbed his pink, soft skin. After, barbered, powdered and perfumed, he passed to his vestiary, where still more acolytes helped him into his ceremonial raiment: robes of Lattakayan satin, bejeweled breastplate, rings and slippers, and the sapphire tiara that had graced the brow of every Kingpriest since the end of the Three Thrones' War. Last, he donned his medallion, kissing the platinum triangle and murmuring the god's name before slipping it over his head.

He was late today, as it happened, and the dawnsong bells were already chiming in the Temple's central spire as he left the manse. He crossed a rose-covered bridge from the palace to the basilica, taking little notice of the fingers of mist that rose from the gardens below, or the clerics that hurried, answering the call to prayer. A scarlet butterfly with wings an arm's length across fluttered close to him, curious, then rode the drafts away.

The Temple's priests—most of them, anyway—already had gathered when he arrived in the basilica, more than a thousand men and women in all. They were from all over the empire: almond-eyed Dravinish, Falthanans with forked, dyed beards, even a few Solamnians and swarthy Ergothmen, each wearing white robes in the styles of their homelands, and of course, the Silvanesti, tall and beautiful, led by Loralon and his aide, a slim, golden-haired elf named Quarath. A choir of elven priestesses sang a hymn of heartbreaking beauty as the Kingpriest ascended his dais, the hall resounding with their song.

As he had every day for the past six years, Symeon spoke the *Udossi*, the Blessing of Sunrise, a half-hour liturgy in the church tongue that he knew as well as his own name. He scarcely heard the words as they passed from his lips, so familiar were they, and before he knew it the censers that flanked his throne issued gouts of white smoke, and the priests dispersed, returning to study and chancery, office and prayer room. Symeon retired to his private sanctum within the basilica, a chamber with flamewood walls and an alabaster fountain whose waters smelled of lavender. There his servants brought his morning meal—honeycakes, bloodmelon, and cheese made from mare's milk.

He scanned scrolls as he ate, his eyes gliding over reports from the hierarchs, as well as missives from the provinces. Most of them he stopped reading after a dozen words or so, making certain none of the tidings were particularly dire before setting them aside: his underlings would deal with most of these matters. As Voice of Paladine on Krynn, he could not trouble himself with every one of his subjects' needs. When he reached an epistle marked with Taol's golden-bear sigil, however, he stopped and read it carefully. Revered Son Durinen sent reports weekly, with the precision of Karthayan clockwork, and Symeon read every word the highland patriarch set to parchment.

This week's message was nothing unusual, to the Kingpriest's disappointment. The banditry in the hills continued, the robbers sacking occasional caravans that dared to break the ban he had placed on trade with the Taoli. The patriarch's men caught some, mounting their heads on gatehouses and at crossroads, but the bandits' losses were few. Durinen wrote about the plague too, this *Longosai* that continued to ravage his holdings. It had spread farther north, encroaching on Govinna itself. Symeon shook his head as he read about the hundreds who had died, and the thousands still sick, but only for a moment did he dwell on the *Longosai*. No healer—not even Stefara of Mishakal—had the power to stop it. He only hoped it would run its course before it spread to the lowlands. Clucking his tongue, he set the missive aside with the rest and went to hold court.

He remained in the Hall of Audience the rest of the morning, hearing more word from the Lordcity's various nobles and merchant princes. It was tedious work, and by the time the basilica bells sounded the midday, his head had begun to ache. Adjourning court, he returned to his sanctum, where he sat in silence, rubbing his temples. He barely touched the buttered lobster his servants brought for his midday meal and only drank one of his customary two goblets of watered claret. When the noontide passed and the audience resumed, the ache had become a stab, flaring behind his left eye with every heartbeat.

It soon proved too much, and he withdrew more than an hour early and forewent his usual appearance on the Temple's front steps, where it had been his habit to pronounce blessing on the folk who gathered in the *Barigon*'s wide expanses. Instead, he retired to his private rose garden to while away the rest of the day. He lay on a cushioned bench in the sunlight, listening to the distant, muted murmur of the city outside the Temple's walls as servants fanned him and fed him golden grapes. A hippogriff, a winged horse with the head of a raptor, cropped clover nearby and drank from a pond whose bottom was made of crushed amethyst.

Around sunset the pain abated again, becoming a low throb he could nearly ignore. He rose and waved to a waiting servant, who brought over two violet apples. Symeon fed these to the hippogriff, the docile beast taking the food from his hand, then wended his way back toward the basilica. It was twilight, and the bells tolled the evensong.

When the *Opiso*, the Sunset Prayer, was done, he returned at last to the manse for the evening banquet. Most of his inner court attended, as always—among them Loralon and Quarath, First Son Kurnos, and Balthera, the acting First Daughter. Symeon's banquets were something folk tried not to miss, every night a different delicacy from Istar's many and various provinces. Last night it had been peacock in a spicy sauce favored in Lattakay. Tonight it was *seshya*, a stew of shellfish and rice from the seaport of Pesaro. More watered claret accompanied the meal, and milk sweetened with palm sugar.

The conversation remained light, though the hierarchs whispered of brigands and borderlands when they thought he wasn't listening. When the courtiers began to leave after the meal was done, he let them go, until only Kurnos remained.

He and the First Son retired to an open balcony, where fireflies bobbed lazily on the night breeze and golden cats with six legs slumbered on the cool marble floor. Someone was reading poetry in the garden below, a soothing ode whose words Symeon couldn't quite make out, as he and the First Son sat down at the *khas* table.

Khas was an ancient game, and folk played it in all Ansalon's realms. It was one of the pastimes Symeon enjoyed most, and his set was one of the most remarkable in the world. The board was made of ivory, lapis, and moonstone, interwoven and shining in the moonlight, but it was the pieces that made it so unusual. Where most *khas* men were carved of wood or forged of metal, the Kingpriest's were something altogether different.

They were alive.

It wasn't quite the right word, but the right word didn't exist outside the spidery language of wizards. The warriors and knights, viziers and wyrms that stood upon the board, none more than six inches high, were creatures of magic, not flesh. They stood frozen most of the day, seeming nothing more than exquisite crystalline sculptures—half white, half black—but when the Kingpriest and his heir sat down they shuddered to life, one by one, and began to move—heads turning, tails twitching, lances dipping to salute the foe.

Symeon took the white pieces—he always took the white—and they set to playing. When their respective turns came, they leaned forward to whisper to their pieces, which moved in response, marching, galloping, and slithering across the table according to their commands. The game passed quickly, mostly in silence, as they sipped *moragnac* brandy and ate almond-paste sweets.

"Aha!" the Kingpriest declared after they had been playing a while, as one of his pillar-shaped Fortresses rumbled forward on creaking wheels, crushing one of Kurnos's Footsoldiers beneath it. The soldier let out a tiny cry as it died, then vanished and appeared, twisted and broken, in front of the First Son. His side of the table was littered with little black corpses, and the remnants of his shattered forces huddled defensively in a corner of the table, surrounded by the white army.

"You see, Kurnos?" Symeon asked. "You left your flank open again."

Kurnos grunted, scowling at the board and stroking his beard while the Kingpriest sipped his *moragnac*. Swallowing, the First Son leaned forward, whispering to one his champions, a tiny, perfect replica of a Solamnic Knight. Crystal armor rattling, the Knight bowed and gave ground, moving close to his Emperor, then brandishing his needle-sized sword at the foe.

Symeon chuckled at this and leaned forward at once to murmur to his Guardian, a coiled gold dragon that hissed and slithered forward. Talons and sword flashed for a moment, and then the wyrm caught the champion in its jaws and bit it in half. Kurnos shook his head in disgust as the remains of his Knight vanished from the board.

Four moves later, pinned down and unable to move, the First Son sighed and spoke to his Emperor. With a resigned sigh, the grizzled Emperor rose from his jet throne, drew a dagger from his belt, and plunged it into his own breast.

"*Rigo iebid*," Kurnos declared as the Emperor crumpled in a heap. *The realm has fallen.* "A fine game, Holiness."

"Yes," Symeon agreed, plucking a sweet from the plate. "I'm improving, I think. Perhaps one day, you won't need to lose . . . deliberately."

Kurnos stiffened, flushing, as the Kingpriest nibbled his confection and smiled. He opened his mouth then shut it again, shrugging. "Sire, I don't know what to say."

"Then say what's on your mind." Symeon chased the sweet with a swallow of *moragnac*. "You're thinking overmuch of Lady Ilista, aren't you?"

The First Son's face darkened even more, and he coughed into his hand. On the table, the *khas* pieces rose from death and shuffled back across the board, revivifying themselves and jostling one another as they resumed their positions. Down below the balcony, in the rose garden, Symeon's pet hippogriff made a sound that was half-whinny, half-skirl.

Two months had passed since the First Daughter's departure. Ilista had sent reports as regularly as the patriarch in Taol, first when she reached Palanthas, then as she and the Knights who guarded her made their way south across Solamnia. At first, the messages had been hopeful, expressing her certainty she would find the one she sought in the next town or monastery. When the later messages came, however, it was always the same—the man of light from her dreams was not there. Lately, the hope in her previous missives had darkened to discouragement. In her most recent one, two days ago, she wrote of leaving Solanthus, Solamnia's southernmost city, still with nothing to show for her quest. She would cross the border from the Knights' lands to Kharolis within the week, and everyone who read her words could tell she was losing energy and heart.

"It must be difficult to fail and fail again," Kurnos said, swirling his brandy. "What if she doesn't find him?"

Symeon rubbed his brow. The headache was worsening again. It made it hard to think, but he fought through the pain.

"Then she comes home," he said softly. "That's not what's troubling you, though, is it? You're not wondering what we'll do if Lady Ilista fails—you want to know what happens if she *succeeds*."

Kurnos bowed his head. "Sire, your perception humbles me."

"Quite." Symeon reached down, plucking his Guardian from the board. The tiny dragon writhed a moment, then stiffened, becoming cold crystal in his hand. "Who is to say what will happen? If this man truly does wield Paladine's power, he may rise high within the church—perhaps even to the throne."

"A Kingpriest from beyond the empire?" Kurnos asked.

Symeon shrugged. "It wouldn't be the first time."

That much was true. A century and a half ago, the dying Kingpriest Hysolar had chosen Sularis, then the High Clerist of the Solamnic Knights, to succeed him. It had been a controversial choice, though, and only Sularis's reputation for impeccable honor had won over a skeptical church and laity. Whoever Ilista's man of light was, he wasn't likely to have such a fine pedigree. Kurnos's scowl spoke more than words.

All at once, Kurnos vanished from Symeon's sight—as did the *khas* board, the balcony, and everything else, swallowed by an angry red flash as the throb in Symeon's head became an inferno. He heard himself grunt in agony and tasted bile as sweets and brandy tried to force themselves back up his throat—but the strange thing was the smell. For some reason, the aroma that filled his nose was that of baking bread.

"Majesty?" Kurnos asked, sounding very far away. "Sire, are you all right?"

Symeon wasn't all right. The pain didn't subside as before. Instead it grew stronger, stronger, until it felt as if a second sun had kindled amidst his brain. His right hand went suddenly slack, dropping into his lap. The Guardian tumbled from his limp grasp, and he felt it spring to life as it fell, imagined its wings spreading to fly back to its place on the board. The dragon he saw, however, wasn't made of white crystal—it was platinum, shining in the sun.

So beautiful, he thought.

The sun in his head burst, and he knew nothing more.

Kurnos leaped to his feet, his eyes wide, as the Kingpriest slumped sideways in his chair, then fell to the floor. The sapphire tiara tumbled from Symeon's brow as he lay on his side, twitching. The twitches slowed, and he was still.

It happened so quickly that Kurnos could do nothing at first but stupidly stare. Then, shaking himself, he ran to the Kingpriest's side and grabbed him by the shoulders, trying to pull him upright. Symeon sagged in his grasp, his face the color of cold ashes. Desperately, Kurnos fumbled at his throat, seeking the a lifebeat. He found it, weak, faltering.

Nausea gripped the First Son. He glanced around, looking for help, but there was no one. Even the servant who had poured their brandy was gone. Fear ran through him, then, and his eyes darted toward Symeon's snifter—*poison!* his mind cried—but a moment later he dismissed the notion. He'd been drinking the same *moragnac*, eating the same sweetmeats. No, something else had struck the Kingpriest down—a fit of some sort, swift and deadly.

No, not deadly—not yet. If a healer came soon, Symeon might survive. Kurnos turned toward the manse, opening his mouth to cry out—

Let him die.

Kurnos caught his breath. The voice sounded horribly close, as if someone had whispered in his ear, and there was something about it, a coldness and cruelty that made it sound familiar. He furrowed his brow, wondering, then his insides turned to water as memory came back to him. He was back in the garden, snow on the ground, looking at a dark hooded figure under an ebony tree. He glanced around, seized with panic, but there was no one to be seen. There were many shadows on the balcony, though, and more still in the gardens below. The dark hooded man was near.

Let him die, the voice said again. *You will be Kingpriest.*

He held his breath, suddenly afraid of the noise that might come out of his mouth if he tried to speak. The voice was right—if he stayed silent, Symeon would be beyond help in moments. No one would know—no one would even question. The throne would be his. All he had to do was wait. He stared at the sapphire tiara, glittering where it had fallen. . . .

"No," he gasped. A shiver wracked his body. Then, easing the Kingpriest back down, he ran back into the manse, shouting for the servants.

------◆◆◆------

Three hours later, Kurnos stood outside the Kingpriest's bedchamber, his mind roiling. Symeon was within, in his bed, with Stefara of Mishakal at his side. Brother Purvis had sent acolytes to fetch the high healer as soon as he heard of the attack, and she had taken the Kingpriest into her care at once. Before she began her ministrations, though, she had insisted he and Purvis leave the room. Now Kurnos paced back and forth across a small, comfortable salon, his eyes moving again and again to the bedchamber's golden doors.

A door opened, but not the golden one. At the other end of the chamber Brother Purvis appeared—the man looked wretched, his face contorted with grief—and waved in Loralon. The elf signed the triangle as he strode forward, the door clicking shut behind.

"The hierarchs have been informed," the elf said. "No one else knows."

Kurnos nodded. Symeon's illness would remain secret for now, until the court prepared a proper proclamation. Nearly two hundred years ago, half the Lordcity had burned when Theorollyn I fell to an assassin's dagger, and since then the imperial court had taken great care when misfortune befell a Kingpriest. *Triogo ullam abat*, the saying went.

The mob rules all.

The candles burned lower. Finally, after what seemed half the night, the golden doors opened and Stefara emerged, beckoning them in. She was exhausted, her plump face pale and shining with sweat as they followed her toward the golden bed. No one spoke as they looked down on the figure lying among the sheets and cushions.

Symeon looked like a corpse. He was wan and haggard, and the right side of his face drooped in an unpleasant grimace, paralyzed by the attack. His chest rose and fell, weakly.

"There's nothing more we can do for now," Stefara said. She touched her medallion, the blue twin teardrops of the Healing Hand. "It is only by the grace of the gods that he still lives. He'll regain consciousness in time, but he won't live long. Autumn, perhaps, but no more."

She left them alone with the Kingpriest. The sound of the door shutting behind her echoed in the stillness. Kurnos swallowed, glancing at Loralon. He could see his thoughts reflected in the elf's sad eyes. Symeon's vision was true, after all. The god had called him to uncrown.

"You must rule now, Your Grace," Loralon said. "As heir, it falls to you to assume the regency."

Kurnos bit his lip, staring at the unmoving form in the bed. He considered telling the elf—about the strange voice, the dark figure, how close he had come to letting Symeon die—but set the impulse aside. Better that no one knew. Instead, he reached down, to brush the Kingpriest's left hand. On the third finger was a ring of red gold, set with a large, sparkling emerald. Swallowing, he pulled the ring off.

Loralon said nothing, only waited patiently, his hands folded before him.

For a long moment Kurnos hesitated, staring into the emerald's glittering depths. Finally, he sighed and slid the ring onto his finger. It felt strange—too heavy, too tight, still retaining the warmth of Symeon's body. His eyes shifted to the Kingpriest, lying weak and vulnerable in his bed . . . and then he heard it again, the voice, chuckling coldly in his head.

Very well, the dark man said. *That will do . . . for now.*

CHAPTER 6 ▼

The sun sank behind the Kharolis mountains, setting the clouds ablaze and flooding the valleys with shadow. On any ordinary evening, the town of Xak Khalan, a scattering of slate-roofed houses nestled in one of those valleys, would have been thriving: children playing beside the riverbank while their mothers stirred pots over outdoor cooking fires; rough, bearded woodcutters sharpening their axes for the next day's work; old graybeards sitting on logs and swapping tall tales about how, when they were young, they'd spied a band of centaurs or kissed a dryad in the wild woods to the west. Later, folk might have gathered about a fire to dance or gone to a nearby hollow to listen to a wandering poet, while the moons' red-silver light streamed down through the boughs of aspen and oak. It was a small town, and poor—particularly compared with the pillared, greenstone halls of the city of Xak Tsaroth two days to the south—but the people were happy with their simple lives.

Tonight, however, was no ordinary night.

Word had spread quickly when the First Daughter of Paladine came to town, accompanied by a dozen Knights from the fields of Solamnia to the north. That had been yesterday, and today the lumberjacks hadn't gone out into the forests, keeping near home to see what was afoot. It had been years since any priest higher than Falinor, the local Revered Son, had come to Xak Khalan, and talk had flown thicker among the villagers than the blackflies that hummed in the summer breeze. At last, as the westering sun began to dip behind the jagged peaks, the sound of silver bells filled the valley, and folk answered the call, flocking out of town until all that moved in Xak Khalan were a few stray goats and the creaking wheel of the mill. They went east, roughly six hundred in all, following a stone-paved path up the edge of the valley to where the church stood.

The town's houses and shops were plain, but its temple was not. When Kharolis adopted the Istaran Church as its faith more than a century ago, the people had abandoned the forest glades and stone rings where they once worshiped, choosing to build high, domed halls in Paladine's name. Xak Khalan's church was nothing beside the cathedrals of Xak Tsaroth and downright tiny compared with the sprawling temples of the east, but it was still fine, its seven copper spires burning crimson in the twilight. Lush ivy crawled up its stone walls, and its tall, brass-bound doors stood open, beckoning. Within, its stained windows cast shafts of blue and green light through the worship hall, falling over oaken pews and frescoed walls, serpentine-tiled floor, and a triangular altar of white stone. Smoke from a dozen incense burners and scores of candles eddied in the glow, making it look as if the vaulted chamber were underwater. The bells chimed on, falling still only when the last of the pilgrims from Xak Khalan had taken their seats.

Ilista stood by the altar, clad in her ceremonial vestments—silvery cassock, white surplice fringed with violet, and amethyst circlet—and laving her hands in a golden bowl. She kept her back to the villagers, staring up at the domed ceiling. The mosaic there was crude by Istaran standards but had a primal force the eastern artisans lacked. It showed Paladine as the Valiant Warrior, a white-bearded knight astride a cream-colored charger, thrusting a lance into the heart of a five-headed serpent. She focused on the god's image, her lips moving in prayer.

"Please," she implored. "Let this be the one."

She had first performed the *Apanfo*, the Rite of Testing, in Palanthas, two days after she and Sir Gareth made port. The patriarch there had listened to the tale of her dream, and the figure of light, and told her yes, there was one among his clerics who might well be the one she sought. He was called Brother Tybalt, a middle-aged priest who could conjure water out of dry air. If anyone in Palanthas was the one she sought, the patriarch told her, it was him.

She had looked on as Tybalt prayed to the god, holding his hands over an electrum basin, and watched with amazement as the flesh of his palms opened and clear, cold water instead of blood flowed forth to fill the bowl. The miracle was one thing, however; the *Apanfo* was something else. The Rite of Testing had found him wanting, his character flawed with pride in his own powers. Ilista wasn't sure how the rite would reveal the Lightbringer to her, but whatever the case, by the time the prayer ended she had known it wasn't him. Disheartened, she had assured the patriarch that while Brother Tybalt was a fine priest, he was not the one she sought. After that, she had turned her eyes hopefully to the road before her.

So it had gone, as she and Sir Gareth's Knights wended their way across Solamnia's plains, from city to town, castle to monastery, never staying in one place for more than a day or two. Time and again, the clergy had brought forth its brightest lights, men and boys who could work all manner of wonders through their faith, and time and again they had failed. Always, there was something lacking. The old graybeard in Vingaard loved his wine too much; the young initiate at the abbey near Archester nurtured lustful thoughts about a girl in town. The tall, swarthy deacon at Garen's Ford doubted his own faith, questioning whether he'd chosen rightly in swearing his vows, and the cherubic scholar in Solanthus had once struck a novice in a rage. They were good men all, but the hoped-for revelation never happened when she spoke the Rite. None was the one, and each time it grew harder to look ahead with hope as she and the Knights set forth again.

Finally, they had left Solamnia, passing beneath the tall, white arches that marked its border. The fields gave way to hills, and then to mountains. That had been eight days ago, and she had tested no one in that time. Kharolis was a sparse kingdom, with only two great cities: Xak Tsaroth in the north and seaside Tarsis in the south. Other than that it was wilderness, deep forests and rolling grasslands where barbarian horsemen ruled. The hinterlands seemed an unlikely place to find the man she had dreamt of.

Then they had come to Xak Khalan, and things had changed. Revered Son Falinor, a bald, stoop-shouldered priest of more than eighty winters, had listened to her tale, then nodded, telling her of one of his charges, a young priest who could purify spoiled food with a kiss. As always, she had demanded proof of the boy's powers and watched, impressed, as he pressed his lips to a moldy ear of corn and the blight lifted from it, leaving ripe, golden kernels behind. So, here she stood in Xak Khalan's hillside church, ready to work the Rite one more time.

She removed her holy medallion and dipped her fingers in the bowl, dripping water on each of the amulet's three corners. "*Palado Calib, flina fo,*" she prayed in the church tongue. "*Mas auas fud, tus mubo fesum.*"

Blessed Paladine, I am blind. Be thou my eyes, that I may see.

She turned, looking out at the expectant faces of the townsfolk. She had looked at thousands of those faces, these past months, watched their anticipation change to disappointment again and again. Behind them stood the temple's clerics, three dozen in all, the bent form of Revered Son Falinor smiling toothlessly in their midst. On her left were Sir Gareth and his men: ten young Knights of the Crown, their armor gleaming in the turquoise light. To her right was an alcove, separated from the rest of the worship hall by a curtain of pale blue velvet. She could sense the man behind it, waiting as she signed the triangle over the assembly.

Merciful god, she thought. Let it be him. . . .

Among the holy items laid out on the altar was a chime of violet glass. She lifted it and flicked it with her finger, three times. Its pure tones filled the hall.

"*Aponfud, ti po bulfat fum gonneis,*" she intoned. "*Bridud, e tam bimud.*"

Come hither, thou who would be tested. Approach, and name thyself.

The blue curtain pulled back, and a stout, fair-haired man appeared, clad in heavy robes covered in gold embroidery. A murmur rippled through the onlookers as the young priest stepped out of the alcove and crossed to Ilista. His eyes were downcast and stayed on the floor as he knelt before her.

"*Fro Gesseic, usas lupo fo,*" he murmured. "*Praso me gonnas.*"

I am Brother Gesseic, beloved of the gods. I ask to be tested.

Ilista nodded, examining the young man's face. He was handsome, in a rough way—a woodsman's son who had heard Paladine's call. There was a humility about him that she hadn't seen often in Solamnia and rarer still in Istar. It was a good sign. She caught herself biting her lip as she set down the chime and took up a golden ewer filled with sweet oil. Carefully, she raised it, saluting the silver triangle over the temple's entrance, then poured a dollop on Gesseic's head. As it dripped, glistening, from his sandy hair, darkening his robes where it fell, she touched her medallion to his forehead and closed her eyes.

The church fell silent, the townsfolk watching in openmouthed awe as the *Apanfo* began, but Ilista didn't notice. A wizard could have cast a fireball in the middle of the room and she wouldn't have flinched. She turned inward, focusing, and felt her breath slow as she reached out, through the medallion. Gesseic's mind lay before her, many-layered, like the petals of a white rose. She had seen many such roses lately, all of them beautiful, but each hid a blemish—some small flaw that marked them as impure. Holding her breath, she reached out to peel back the first layer. . . .

. . . the rose vanished, and she was somewhere else: a mountaintop, mantled in snow, looming so high clouds scudded beneath her. The air was sharp, chilly, the sky dark and dusted with more stars than she had ever seen—great clouds of them, as dense as sand on a dune. She cast about, startled. This was new, different.

Something stirred in the corner of her eye, and she saw him, standing in the snow, watching her. Gesseic did not speak, but a glad smile lit his face as he stepped toward her.

It's him! she thought, triumph surging through her. After all the time she'd looked, she'd found the one. The Lightbringer. The god's chosen. She imagined him mantled in light, stopping armies with a wave of his hand. They would return to the Lord-city together, welcomed with song and laughter, the streets adrift with rose petals. She lifted her gaze to the starry sky. It's him, Paladine be praised, it's him, it's him!

When she looked again, her joy faltered. Gesseic had changed—shrunk, she thought at first, then she realized she was looking on him not as he was now, but as the child he once had been. She had peeled the layers all the way back to his boyhood memories—seven summers old, or about, though the eyes were still an adult's.

She was so intent on studying his face that it took her a moment to see the wasp. Ilista gasped—it was huge, the size of a hummingbird, its carapace the color of polished jet. She could see its stinger as it crawled along his arm, poised a hair's breadth from the skin of Gesseic's wrist.

She hissed, pointing. Gesseic looked, raising his arm. The wasp buried the stinger in his flesh.

The pain in his voice as he cried out made her wince, and her own arm flared in sympathy as he smashed the wasp. Then, his arm already swelling from its venom, he lifted its mashed form by a wing and stared at it, his face creased with agony. Though half-crushed, it wasn't dead, and the horrid thing writhed in his grasp.

His eyes darkened with anger, and Ilista felt hope slip away. "No!" she cried, already knowing what was going to happen. "Don't!"

Gesseic didn't listen. Reaching up, he grabbed another twitching wing and ripped it off. His lips curled into a vengeful grin. . . .

With a sudden rush, the mountaintop vanished, and she was back in the temple, staring at the young priest as a shudder ran through him. A groan burst from his lips as he remembered killing the wasp. It was the smallest of flaws, a flash of childhood meanness, but he knew, as well as Ilista did, what it meant. He had taken joy in tormenting another creature. He was impure.

With a sorrowing sigh she pulled back, lifting her medallion away. It left a red mark on his skin as he bowed his head and sobbed. A murmur of dismay ran through the congregation. Ilista bowed her head. She'd been so *sure*, for a moment.

"*Ubastud, usas farno*," she bade.

Rise, child of the god.

He did, tears in his eyes, and trembled as she bent to kiss him on both cheeks. She felt hollow inside, lost. Another failure, another hope come to nothing. Despair clutched at her, but she fought it back. The Rite wasn't yet done; she had to finish it.

"*Porud, Fro, e ni sonud mos*," she declared, signing the triangle over him. "*Sifat.*"

Go forth, Brother, and do no wrong. So be it.

"Forgive me," he said. Wet tracks ran down his cheeks. "I'm sorry."

She wanted to tell him there was nothing to be sorry for, that he was a good man and a fine priest, even though he wasn't the one she sought. She wanted to lay a reassuring hand on his arm or even to embrace him, hold him while he cried. It was against the ritual, though, and she could only stand still, watching with all the austerity she could muster, as he turned and walked, sobbing, back toward the alcove. The last thing she saw, before her own tears blinded her, was the desolation in his face as he drew the curtain shut.

She was still seeing his face at midnight, as she stood alone in the temple, putting away the instruments of the ritual. Gesseic wasn't the only one who felt betrayed—behind him stood a dozen other priests, the ones she had tested in Solamnia, and behind *them* were Revered Son Falinor and the folk of Xak Khalan. All of them stared at her in her mind, hurt and angry.

She had let them all taste, however briefly, the hope of true holiness, something beyond the mere piety of priesthood—and she had let them all down, proving they were merely human.

Who are you to judge? they asked her silently as she laid the glass chime in a padded, lacquered box. Are you so untainted yourself, to think you know purity?

Yet, she *did* know. She remembered the elation that had run through her when she'd dreamed of the Lightbringer. Brother Gesseic had come closer than the others, but even he had fallen short, hadn't given her the same feeling.

She looked up at the god on the mosaic. It was dark outside now, and the blue-green glow had yielded to the gold of candlelight. "Why did you choose me?" she asked. "I can't do this any more. I don't have the strength. . . ."

A cough broke the stillness, and she gasped, looking down. Even the clerics had left her alone—whether out of respect for her own sorrow, or resentment, she couldn't say. The noise was loud amid the stillness. Her hand went to her medallion as she backed into the altar, staring at the figure framed in the doors. For a moment she thought it might be some villager, angry enough to seek revenge upon her, but when the figure stepped forward she saw the light glint on antique armor, and deepen the hard lines of Sir Gareth's face. He had been waiting just outside, she knew, watching for trouble.

"*Efisa?*" he asked. "Are you well? I heard voices—"

She shook her head. "It was just me. Come in, Gareth."

He did, looking uncertain as he shut the door. He strode toward her, armor rattling, then stopped a respectful distance away and stood erect, hands clasped behind his back.

"My men have secured provisions," he said. "We stand ready to march at your word."

"Very good," she replied. "We shall leave for Xak Tsaroth at dawn." There was no point in lingering here when she was unwelcome. She sighed, tugging her sleeves. "Tell me, Gareth—do you think me a fool?"

The Knight's moustache twitched. "*Efisa?*"

She waved her hand, taking in the whole hall. "You saw what happened here," she said. "That boy could have been a great priest. The god is in him—but after today, I'm not sure I'd blame him if he quit the clergy."

"Ah," Gareth replied, looking uncomfortable. She hadn't spoken like this to him before.

"You know what I'm searching for. Am I a fool for doing so?"

"My lady, Draco Paladin himself bade you undertake this quest," he said slowly, choosing each word with care. "The god doesn't send his servants on fool's errands."

Ilista shook her head. "You're a man of great faith, Gareth."

The Knight shrugged.

He remained as she finished packing her trappings, then they left the temple together, making their way down the path to Xak Khalan. They left the accouterments behind. Gareth's men would come later to fetch them. He did his best to guide her around the town, keeping to its perimeter and out of sight, but even so she could feel the stares of those villagers who were still awake, the resentful looks that always seemed to follow her when she left a place. She repeated Gareth's words, telling herself she was working Paladine's will, but it didn't make her feel much better.

They had made camp on a hilltop overlooking the town, pitching tents amid the crumbling, vine-choked walls of what once—centuries ago, from the looks—had been a small keep. Two Knights met them as they climbed the path to the ruins and fell in alongside, carrying torches to light their way. Most of the others were still awake amid the cluster of tents and campfires, sharpening their swords and polishing their shields. They stood and bowed as Ilista passed.

The feeling that something was wrong struck her as soon as she saw her tent, but she didn't know why. She frowned as she regarded it: a pavilion of white and violet silk, the sacred triangle mounted on a pole before it, another hung above the . . .

She stopped suddenly, catching her breath. "The flap. It's open."

The Knights snapped to a halt, and Gareth stepped forward, sword half-drawn. She had pinned the flap closed that afternoon, before setting forth to perform the *Apanfo*. Now it hung loose, waving in the evening breeze.

One of the younger Knights swore under his breath. The other coughed softly. Gareth glared at them both. They were the same pair he'd set on guard duty while the rest attended the ritual, newly dubbed boys who couldn't be much more than twenty.

"Jurabin, Laonis," he growled. "If any harm has come to Her Grace's belongings, I'll have both your spurs. Get the others."

Their faces pale, the Knights turned and hurried away. In moments they were back with the rest of the Knights, bare swords in hand. Half fell in around Ilista, forming a ring about her. The rest gathered by Gareth, awaiting his orders. He dispatched them quickly, sending two to watch the tent's other side, and putting two more to either side of the entrance. His face grim, he crept forward. His blade rasped free of its scabbard, and he used it to flip the flap wide, then stepped inside. Jurabin and Laonis followed, torches in hand.

Ilista tensed, waiting for the sound of ringing steel. Instead, all was silent for a long moment, then the flap flew aside again and Gareth emerged. He still had his sword, but in his hand was something else.

"There's no one within, *Efisa*," he said, Jurabin and Laonis still searching behind him, "but I found this."

He held it up, a roll of rough parchment, tied with plain hempen cord. It bore no seal. She stared at it, swallowing, then reached out and took it from his hand. Her fingers trembled as she untied the cord and unfurled it. It was two sheets, in fact, not one. The first, she saw, was a map of some sort. She gave it a quick, frowning glance, then turned to the second page, and her breath left her in a rush.

You have traveled far, First Daughter, it read, *but your journey nears its end. Go not to Xak Tsaroth but into the mountains. Follow the map.*

I have been awaiting you. I am the Lightbringer.

CHAPTER 7 ▼

The orb caught the candlelight, gleaming as she opened the box's golden lid. There was something else to it, though—a faint, blue-white shimmer that owed nothing to the tapers burning within the tent. Ilista held her breath, watching the ghost-light dance. Like most Istarans, she found sorcery strange and a little frightening—even the magic of the elves, whose wizards wore the White Robes as a rule. Her apprehension had been enough, so far, to keep her from using the orb. Now, though, was different.

She looked at the scroll, resting in her lap, and the simple words on it. The Knights had searched and searched but found no trace of whoever had left the message. She practically had to beg Sir Gareth not to stand guard within her tent, and she knew he was just outside, even now, in case of trouble. She'd read the scroll fifty times, its words chilling and exciting her all at once. Loralon had to know, as soon as possible, so she reached into the box and lifted out the flickering orb.

It was lighter than it looked—perhaps hollow—and cold as snowmelt. The bluish light swelled as she cupped it in her hand, swallowing the candles' dim glow and making her shadow huge upon the tent's wall. She caught her breath, glancing toward the flap, but Sir Gareth didn't burst through as she feared.

The Knights didn't see the witchlight, which was good. Istarans mistrusted magic, but the men of Solamnia loathed it. Ilista swallowed, gazing into the orb. Its shimmer caught her gaze and held it. She muttered a quick prayer, asking Paladine's forgiveness for meddling in sorcerous ways, then drew a breath.

"Loralon," she whispered.

For a time, nothing happened, and she began to wonder if she'd done it wrong, and the spell hadn't worked. As she was looking up, though, the magic took hold, so quickly she nearly dropped the orb. The crystal warmed in her grasp, and the light began to spin and swirl, making a sound like a mad flautist's song. She peered into its depths when she recovered, trying to make out shapes within the boiling glow—and slowly they emerged, resolving into a blurred image, like a fresco painted in bad plaster, then sharpening until it became Loralon's bearded face. It was past midwatch now, morning closer than sunset, but the Emissary looked neither tired nor disheveled. Instead he smiled at her, a little sadly. Her skin rose into bumps at the sight of his disembodied visage, resting in her hand. She would have to say a long cleansing prayer, when this was done.

"First Daughter," Loralon said. "I have been hoping you would contact me. I have grave tidings."

He told her about Symeon's illness, and though the Kingpriest had seldom been warm toward her, she found herself weeping all the same. The Kingpriest still could not speak, and his right arm and leg remained paralyzed. The people of the Lordcity, on hearing of his condition, had gathered in great numbers outside the Temple to pray for him, but no one in the church believed he would survive.

As for Kurnos, he was proving more assertive. Already he talked of sending the army into Taol after all, but Loralon had stayed him thus far, still counseling caution. The bandits had not struck in the highlands in some time, and the chance that they had stopped altogether was enough to curb the First Son. Loralon seemed to think it a hopeful sign that Kurnos listened to reason, but Ilista was less sure. The First Son's temper was short, and she feared the slightest flare-up would give him the excuse to wage war on the Taoli.

In her mind, she saw an army advancing through craggy hills, and she shivered. Her dream on the night Paladine had appeared to her was coming true. She hoped she could complete her quest before the *Scatas* marched.

"You did not use the orb because of His Holiness, though," Loralon said, his eyes glittering. "What has happened? Have you found the one you seek at last?"

Her free hand strayed to her medallion. "Not exactly. I think he may have found me."

She told him of the mysterious scroll, reading its message to him. His eyes widened.

"Whispering limbs and leaves," he said when she was done, surprising her. She had never heard him swear before. "The message truly says *Lightbringer*? Have you mentioned the prophecy to anyone else?"

She shook her head. "Have you?"

"Not even the Kingpriest." He stroked his beard, the shock smoothing out of his face like ripples from a still pond. "What of the map?"

She held it up, tracing along its lines with her finger. "These are the mountains near here," she said. "Sir Gareth has traveled to Xak Tsaroth before, and he knows the roads. There is an old monastery this way—it belonged to monks of Majere once, he says, but it's been abandoned for years."

"Not any more, evidently." A smile ghosted Loralon's lips. "*Efisa*, the choice is yours, but I think you should follow the map."

Ilista nodded. It would mean turning from her planned path, true, but what good had that path done her so far? Who was to say that it led to anything but more failure? Looking again at the scroll, she could barely keep her hopes from spilling over. *I am the Lightbringer*—how could it be anything else?

She and Loralon spoke a while longer, of smaller matters, then bade each other farewell. Within the orb, the elf spoke a word, and his image flickered, then faded back into the maelstrom of the orb's light. That dimmed as well, returning to the ghostly glimmer she'd first observed when she picked up the crystal. The orb turned cold again, and she signed the triangle over herself to ward off ill fortune as she put it away.

She lay awake in her bed after, staring at the pavilion's silken roof. It was some time before she slept.

The day dawned gray, the mountains shrouded by fog, and a light drizzle fell as Ilista and the Knights rode south, away from Xak Khalan. The peaks loomed on either side of the road, jagged and steep, more barren with every mile. Their snowy summits disappeared into the cloudrack. Ashes and firs clung to the rocks, and creeping brambles Sir Gareth called Hangman's Snare. Here and there, stones littered the path from where they had broken free of the slopes above, and once they even heard the crack and rumble of a not very distant slide, echoing amongst the crags.

Well after midday the road forked, a smaller path breaking off and running deeper into the wilds. An obelisk of white stone leaned among the bushes, overgrown with ivy. At its crown was a copper spider, now green with age—the holy symbol of Majere, the god of thought and wisdom. Ilista paused before the monolith to study the strange map, then bit her lip, looking from one fork to the other. In the end, though, she had little choice. They could rest the horses and themselves at the monastery and continue in the morning. So they turned from the main road to follow the spider. She prayed it wasn't leading her to a web.

The going from there soon grew harder, the path rougher and steeper, cracked and littered with scree. Bracken covered it over in places, so they had to dismount and lead their horses through. Cave mouths yawned in the slopes above, like the eyes of skulls. The Knights eyed these warily, their hands on their swords. Kharolis was a wild country, and Gareth knew many tales of terrible creatures that lurked in the mountains, preying on goats and lizards . . . and now and then unwary travelers. Goblins, in particular, were rife in some places. Ilista had never seen a goblin outside a bestiary, but she still shuddered as she imagined the squat, twisted creatures shrieking down upon them from the caverns above.

Drizzle gave way to downpour. The horses grew skittish, tossing their heads and whinnying, and the Knights did too, several drawing their swords. Ilista hunched low in her saddle, her sodden robes weighing her down. The clouds sank lower still, hungrily devouring the mountains. They changed color, too, first darkening to near-black then shifting to a sickly green. The wind grew strange—utterly still one moment, then hammering the next—and the gold of lightning flashed in the distance. Thunder muttered in reply.

Gareth's blade wasn't out, but his hand strayed to its hilt as he rode up alongside Ilista. Water streamed off his winged helmet as he lifted its visor, and he shouted for her to hear him above the wind.

"The storm will be on us soon, *Efisa!* Have to find shelter before it breaks!"

Ilista frowned, glancing up at the anvil-shaped clouds, towering above the mountains like a great wave. The way they boiled and flashed, they almost seemed alive. Her gaze dropped again, to the path ahead. She wanted to go on, yearned to reach the monastery. It was only a few more leagues—surely they could cover that ground before things grew too hard.

Lightning flared close by, making her jump as it struck a wooded outcropping only leagues ahead. Trees became torches, and the stone burst, sending rubble and burning wood pouring down the hill. The thunderclap that followed, a heartbeat later, made the ground tremble beneath them, and set Ilista's ears ringing. The horses reared and snorted, the Knights struggling to keep them calm.

Hopes of further progress dashed, she nodded to Gareth. "Go."

A few barked orders later, the party had reined in, and all but two of the Knights were off their horses, clambering up the slopes toward the caves. They climbed around boulders and scrabbled across gravel, grabbing tree trunks to steady themselves as they went. Soon they disappeared, swallowed by the rain and gloom.

A small mace hung from Ilista's saddle. She hadn't wanted to carry it, being untrained in arms, but Sir Gareth insisted. Now she thanked him silently as she reached down and pulled the weapon free. She gripped it tightly, heart hammering. Though Gareth was near—his sword finally unsheathed—and the two Knights who held the horses hovered close by as well, she felt horribly helpless beneath the looming thunderheads.

The wind howled. The rain became icy knives. Thunder's growl rose into a bellow. The Knights did not return.

Worried, Gareth guided his horse to the path's edge and called out, but the storm smothered his words. The horses were near mad with fear, and the Knights fought to keep them from bolting. Ilista twisted her own reins, repeating a warding prayer over and over as she stared at the thunderheads. *"Palado, me ofurbud op to me bulfant bronint . . ."*

Paladine, be my shield against those who would do me ill. . . .

Out of nowhere, something appeared in the sky, streaking down out of the seething clouds. Ilista gaped as she watched it plummet and saw it glint as lightning flashed nearby. Armor, she thought, but couldn't find her voice. A heartbeat later, it struck the rocks with a horrible crash and tumbled down the slope to stop on the path.

Ilista's horse bawled, nearly throwing her. By the time she got it under control again, Gareth was off his steed and sprinting toward the tangled ruin on the ground. Feeling ill, she coaxed her mount forward as the Knight knelt down on the ground, raising his visor to see. He looked up as she came near, his face ashen, and raised a hand to warn her off. It was too late, though—she could already see.

It was Sir Laonis—or had been, once. Now she recognized the young Knight only by the etchings in his armor. The rest was a ruin, battered and ravaged, a few jagged slashes even tearing through his breastplate. His left arm was gone, and the rainwater pooled around him was pink with blood, darkening as she watched.

She swayed in her saddle, wanting to vomit, and Gareth was beside her in an instant, steadying her with a firm hand. When the tide of nausea ebbed, she fought for her voice. "What—what did that to him?"

Gareth shook his head.

"There!" cried one of the other Knights. He stabbed a finger skyward.

They turned to look, squinting against the slashing rain. At first, Ilista saw nothing amid the darkness, but then a flash lit the sky and there was something there, silhouetted against the coruscating clouds: a huge, serpentine shape thirty feet long from its head to the tip of its tail. It flew on broad, leathery wings, its body twisting as it banked high above them. Thick, stone-grey scales covered the rest, pale as death on its underbelly. Long, wickedly curving horns swept back from its head, and its narrow eyes gleamed green. Fangs the length of a man's hand filled its snarling mouth, and its dangling legs sported talons like scythe blades. At the end of its tail was a wicked, bony barb. Its mouth stretched wide, and a shriek like tearing metal rose above the storm's din—then, as quickly as it had appeared, it was gone, wheeling and disappearing back into the clouds.

"*Palado Calib*," Ilista croaked. "Was that a dragon?"

Gareth shook his head. "No, Your Grace—the dragons are gone from the world, as the legends say. That was a wyvern."

Ilista had heard tales of wyverns. They were kin to the long-vanished dragons, but were smaller and much more stupid, though every bit as cruel as the wyrms that had once filled Krynn's skies. They possessed no fiery breath, nor did they use magic as true dragons did, but they were still deadly. The barb on the creature's tail was a stinger filled with venom that could kill in moments. They fed on anything they could find—Gareth's goats and lizards leaped to Ilista's mind—and while they were usually too vicious to hunt in packs, they sometimes gathered in swarms.

The Knights cried out again, and sure enough, a second wyvern swooped out of the clouds. This one's scales glistened black, but other than that it resembled its brother in every way. There was something odd about it, though, Ilista noticed— something in the way it moved. It struggled rather than soared, moving slowly, jerkily.

"Huma's silver arm," Sir Gareth swore. "It's carrying something."

Lightning blazed, and they saw it: another young Knight clasped in its claws, arms and legs dangling. As they looked on, the monster's tail shot down, driving its stinger into the man's body. Then it pulled up, opening its talons and letting the remains plunge earthward like a giantling's discarded toy. The body smacked into a cliff face, then rolled down in a tumult of stones and broken bones until it stopped, tangled in a mass of Hangman's Snare.

High above, the black wyvern screeched, tucked in its wings, and dove.

Ilista watched in sickened fascination as it plunged straight toward her, its mouth a forest of fangs, its eyes blazing orange. Her mace fell, unnoticed, from her grasp. Beside her Gareth raised his sword high, shouting and slamming his visor shut. He brought the flat of his blade down hard on her horse's rump.

The mare leaped forward at once, plunging down the path with Ilista clinging to the reins. Glancing back, she saw Gareth dashing toward his stallion, sword flashing in his hand. The wyvern was too fast, though, and he had to throw himself on the ground, rolling over and over as its talons clutched at the air, missing him. Instead, it snatched up his steed and lifted it off the ground, beating its wings furiously as it fought to rise.

The horses were all wailing with terror, but Gareth's screamed loudest of all, struggling mightily as the black-scaled monster bore it away. Its stinger drove into the horse's flesh once, twice, three times, then the animal gave one last thrash and sagged, twitching. Gareth struggled to his feet, stunned and glaring as the wyvern let his steed drop, then he raced to the other horses and leaped astride one. Above, the wyvern banked and disappeared back into the storm as Ilista reined in again.

There was shouting now from the hillside. Several men were scrambling down the slope—the Knights, or what remained of them, five now instead of ten. Sir Jurabin limped behind the rest, his right leg ripped bloody, scowling against the pain as he stumbled and nearly fell.

Another cry sounded from above, and Jurabin turned toward a third wyvern—this one the color of rust—as it bore down on him. A lesser man would have fled from such a sight, but Jurabin was a Solamnic Knight and trained to meet an honorable death. Bracing himself, he brandished his blade and faced down the beast. Ilista, Gareth, and his fellows could only watch as the monster swooped in.

It hit him hard, claws furrowing his armor, spattering blood across the stones. Somehow, though, the brave Knight didn't drop his sword, even as it lifted him off his feet; instead he stabbed wildly, the beast's scales turning away his blade once . . . twice. . . .

The third mad thrust drove home, as Jurabin buried his blade into the flesh beneath its wing. The wyvern's triumphant cry became a shriek of pain, and it wavered, sinking as the Knight managed to twist the sword, working it deeper. Finally, it stung him and let him go—and his sword snapped, leaving two feet of steel lodged in its flesh.

Jurabin was dead before he hit the ground. The wyvern, however, had a moment of struggle before it plummeted as well, crunching down atop a broad, flat boulder. The surviving Knights cheered at its death, but Sir Gareth shouted them down, waving his sword at the sky. Ilista looked up, and her mouth went dry. Five more wyverns circled overhead.

"Ride!" Gareth roared. "Ride, all of you!"

Ilista was already moving, digging her heels into her horse's flanks. It hurled itself down the pass, terrified by the storm and the smell of blood, leaping recklessly over stones and bracken alike. She heard the rumble of hoofs behind her as the Knights charged after. She pulled on her reins to let them catch up, but the panicking mare wouldn't slow. All she could do was hold on and pray as the horse flew down the trail.

She heard a wyvern shriek above her and looked up to see one of them bank and begin its dive, streaking straight toward her. It was the same gray beast she'd first spotted, its eyes blazing and jaws agape. Its talons and stinger glistened red. Gareth was bellowing in Solamnic somewhere behind her, but the wyvern paid no notice, arrowing toward her—the one unarmored morsel in the lot. She threw herself forward, flattening herself against the mare's neck and laughing madly. She'd been afraid of *goblins!*

Her breath blasted from her lungs when the beast struck, and for an instant there was no sound but a howling roar, no sight but red mist, no taste but blood in her mouth, no feeling at all. Then she came back to herself, and the pain came with it, her shoulder bathed in liquid fire where the wyvern's claws grazed her, plunging through skin, sinew, and bone alike. The other talon missed her flesh altogether, snagging her robes instead and clutching her. She felt herself lifted in the air. She stared at the ground as it fell away beneath her, her stomach lurching. There was Gareth, gazing up at her in horror, there were his Knights, mouths agape. She tried to call out to them, but it hurt too much to draw breath.

The wyvern wheeled, and her companions disappeared from view. She rose higher and higher, the wyvern soaring toward the raging stormclouds, and Ilista closed her eyes, waiting for the stinger to strike, the burning poison in her veins. Please, she prayed silently, let death be quick.

The stinger didn't strike. Instead, there was a deafening *boom*, and the wyvern lurched sideways, jarring her and sending fresh spikes of pain through her body.

The stink of roasting flesh flooded her nostrils, and she opened her tearing eyes. The wyvern's right wing was on fire, the membrane curling like burning paper. It screeched in agony, its tail whipping about, as it began to whirl and flutter.

Merciful Paladine, she thought as the ground started rushing toward her. Lightning struck it!

That was when she saw him, standing on a ledge beneath her: a lone figure in a gray cassock, his hood pulled low against the wind. He was too far away, the storm too fierce, the pain too great, to make out any more details. She watched as he raised his arms, head thrown back, shouting at the storm. Thunder roared again, making her skull buzz, and a blinding lightning bolt flashed down, ripping through the wyvern's other wing. Shrieking even louder, it dropped like a meteor and let her go.

All at once, Ilista was tumbling free, spinning as she fell, now looking at the storm-wracked sky, now the wyvern, all aflame, now the ground rising toward her with sickening speed.

Suddenly, it stopped—or rather *she* stopped, her shivering body slowing, then halting in midair as the blazing wyvern slammed into the ground below. She gasped, astounded, as she hovered there, then looked down and saw the man in gray again, the one who had summoned the lightning to kill the beast. He was looking at her now, hands outstretched, and she knew he was the one holding her aloft. He moved his arms, and she moved toward him, floating through the air like a leaf on a stream . . . then he lowered her, slowly, onto the rocky ledge beside him.

Firm stone pressed up against her, and she lay wheezing, trembling with pain as she stared up at him. She tried to make out his face, but shadow hid his features.

"Welcome, *Efisa*," he said.

The world went black.

CHAPTER 8 ▼

I star was a land of grand cities. Besides the Lordcity, there was Karthay in the north, with its tiered gardens and many-colored rooftops; Tucuri at the mouth of the River Gather, all towering minarets and latticed windows; Kautilya, the Bronze City, its sprawling baths shrouded in mist; Lattakay in the east, known for its sprawling wharf and Street of White Arches; and a dozen more that put such exemplary western cities as Palanthas and Xak Tsaroth to shame.

The borderlands had only one true city of note: Govinna. It was small and dense, standing on twin hills, the two halves surrounded by walls of granite. Arched bridges crossed the gorge between, while the River Edessa frothed far below. Within, it was a maze, its stone-and-plaster buildings leaning over the narrow laneways so far that in some places they nearly touched. Here and there, open squares broke up the closeness, wide expanses with fountains or statues in their midst. Markets sprawled along the gorge's edge, where great winch-lifts and long stairs led to the unquiet waters below. It was a gray town, with few trees and many rooftops shingled with stone, but it was not plain. It could not have been, with its temples.

Govinna had a surfeit of churches, more than a score in all, looming well above the rest of the city. The borderfolk had built them in a fashion that resembled the worship-halls of Solamnia, more than those of Istar—sharp peaks in place of domes, dragon-shaped gargoyles instead of delicate spires, green-aged copper where gold or silver might have gleamed. Strong-walled and solid, they might have appeared fortresses, had it not been for their stained-glass windows and the god's triangle mounted above their doors. In the midst of Govinna's western half, at the crest of the hill, was the Pantheon, the grandest temple of all. It was one of the few churches in Istar that would not have looked tiny beside the Great Temple, though it looked utterly unlike that church, all sharp corners and dark hallways instead of arches and open spaces. Within, in tapestry-hung apartments atop its highest tower, dwelt Revered Son Durinen, the Little Emperor.

The name had nothing to do with Durinen's stature, for he was in fact a huge man, nearly seven feet tall and built like an ogre. Rather, it was an inherited title, one his predecessor had borne, and others before him, going back some eighty years, to the time of the *Trosedil*. In the year 842 the reigning Kingpriest, Vasari the Lion, had died suddenly in his sleep, heirless. In the confusion that followed, two rival hierarchs had vied for the throne. One, Evestel, took the name Vasari II and claimed the throne in the Lordcity. The other, Pradian, fled with his followers to the borderlands, and set up his rival church in Govinna.

Amid the confusion the *Miceram*—the ruby-encrusted crown of the Kingpriests—vanished. Scholars argued over the means of its disappearance. Some said Pradian stole it, while others claimed the old Kingpriest's ghost took it north and flung it into the sea. Still others believed Paladine himself had claimed it, appearing in his form of the platinum dragon and flying away with it clutched in his talons. According to this telling, the god was keeping it in his realm beyond the stars and would return it to Krynn when the need for it was greatest. In its place, Pradian had adopted an emerald diadem instead and Vasari a circlet of topaz. Thus began the War of Two Thrones, which later gained a third when Ardosean IV emerged in the desert city of Losarcum, wearing a tiara of sapphires.

In Govinna, Pradian won the favor of the powerful, cleric and noble alike, and ordered the Pantheon built. Scholars agreed he was the mightiest of the three warring Kingpriests, a lord of fire and fury, yet pious as well. Even a century later men claimed, sorrowfully, that had fate moved differently he would have won the war. Instead, however, he died untimely, shot by an archer during the Battle of Golden Grasses. Though a successor, Theorollyn III, rose in his place, the Govinnese faction never recovered from the loss, and so, when the *Trosedil* ended, it was Ardosean who marched into Istar and beheaded Vasari on the Great Temple's steps. Theorollyn, denounced and discredited, was imprisoned the High Clerist's Tower, far away in Solamnia's northern mountains. From then on, the Kingpriests had worn the sapphire tiara, and those who wore the emerald diadem bent their knees to the east and called themselves Little Emperors, in memory of what might have been.

Tonight was the Night of White Roses, the midsummer rite that commemorated the death, a thousand years before, of Huma Dragonbane, the greatest Solamnic Knight who ever lived. Huma had martyred himself while using the fabled dragonlances to drive Takhisis and her dragon hordes from the world, and ever since, temples all over Ansalon had thrown their doors wide so the faithful could pay him homage. Even now, the Pantheon's gates stood open, and chanting processions bearing icons of Huma and his lance wended through the city's narrow laneways, toward the great church.

Durinen stood on the parapet of his tower, draped in silvery robes, his brow aglimmer with emeralds. He tugged at the braids of his long, black beard as he looked out over the city. It was a clear, cool highland night, the sky starry and purple, devoid of cloud or moon. The sounds of hymns rose from below, and candles burned in the night. He scowled, folding his arms across his bearish chest. No, he didn't like it at all.

The night's peace set him on edge. It had been weeks since he'd heard aught of the bandits who were causing so much trouble to the south, and most folk were glad for it, but the quiet only made him worry. His people were still hungry, the *Longosai* still ravaged the land—a plight he sympathized with, particularly since the plague was beginning to appear within Govinna's walls, but which he had no power to remedy. The province's larders were bare, and there was no cure for the Creep. The Lordcity was no help either. With Symeon ailing, Kurnos had taken a hard stance against the borderfolk. Luckily, rumors the imperial army was on the march had proven false, but that would change, if the bandits resurfaced. They *would* resurface, he was sure, and what better place and time than here and now, with the Pantheon's doors standing wide open?

He summoned the captain of his guard, an aging man in polished scale mail, and told him of his worries. The captain ran a hand over his shaven head, listening patiently.

"I could order the city gates shut," he said, "and I'll put more men on the roads, watching for trouble. If anyone tries to ride on the city, we'll know."

"Do so," the Little Emperor said, "and be quick about it. Report back to me when you're done."

With a curt nod, the captain turned and headed back down the stairs into the Pantheon. When he was gone, Durinen turned back to the city, shining with rivers of tiny lights beneath the darkening sky. Govinna's walls had never been breached, even at the end of the *Trosedil*. Once the gates were shut, the bandits would never get in.

He shook his head, leaning against parapet's iron rail, and wondered why that common wisdom didn't make him feel any better.

The answer, of course, was that the bandits were already in the city and had been for days.

They had gathered in a wooded dell near Abreri, a town not much bigger than Luciel, now all but emptied by the plague. A dozen bands, each the size of Lord Tavarre's, answered the call, and their leaders bent their knees to the local lord, a burly, grizzled man named Ossirian who had spoken to the rabble from atop a mossy boulder, explaining his plan. The Night of White Roses was near, and the faithful were flocking to Govinna to observe the rites at the Pantheon. Rather than storming the city—a fool's errand, with only five hundred men under his command—Ossirian meant to take it by surprise.

The bandits, then, hadn't set out in a large group, or even in their smaller bands, but rather in little gangs, none more than six men. They had made their way north to Govinna, disguised as pilgrims, their cheeks smudged with soot in remembrance of the dragonfire Huma had faced in his last battle. The first had entered the city three days before the holy night, and others followed, a few every hour. By the time the captain's orders reached the gatekeepers that evening, it was too late. When the city's massive gates rumbled shut, they sealed Ossirian and his men inside.

Each gang of bandits had its own orders, a task in the coming plan of attack. Some waited in key places, ready to cause distractions for the city guard. Others—Ossirian and the other leaders among them—entered the Pantheon with the pilgrims, slipping past the guards in the pressing mobs of the faithful, and took up positions within the temple, waiting for the signal. Still others lurked at crossroads and courtyards, watching for trouble.

Cathan was one of these last, and he wasn't happy about it at all. He fidgeted as he crouched in the mouth of an alley, looking out into an empty plaza. He pulled his hood low, tugging at his sleeves. For the third time in a minute, his hand reached beneath his cloak to the hilt of his sword.

Huddled in the shadows beside him, Embric Sharpspurs snorted. "You might try being a little more obvious," he muttered. "A guardsman still might not notice you, provided he was blind and an idiot."

"What guardsman?" Cathan snorted, gesturing at the courtyard. It was deserted and had been since well before sunset. They weren't even on the right side of town. The plaza was on

Govinna's eastern hill, away from the temples. When the attack happened, the trouble would be on the other side of the river.

"We've been here how many hours, and what have we seen? One mangy cat. I bet there isn't a single guardsman in this entire half of the town." He shook his head angrily. "We're going to miss it all."

"Suits me," Embric replied, shrugging. "If I can get through this without drawing my sword, count me glad."

Cathan ground his teeth. He'd left his sister in Luciel, traveled all this way, spent night after night training at swordplay— for what? To stand in an alley while all the fighting happened elsewhere? It made him want to spit. I should leave, he thought. Let Embric stay here—if I hurry, maybe I can get to the Pantheon in time to join Lord Tavarre and the others. . . .

Before he could do more than push to his feet, though, a sound cut through the night, echoing across the river from the temples: a chorus of long, low notes, blown by priests on curving dragon horns. It was the traditional call to the believers, summoning them to the liturgy in Huma's honor—but it was something else, at the same time: the prearranged signal the bandits had been waiting for, all across the city.

Hearing the blare of the dragon horns, Cathan cursed. He was too late. The attack had begun.

———◆◆◆———

As it happened, the chaos started on the east hill only a few blocks from Cathan and Embric. While the horns were still sounding, a gang of bandits used axes to break down the doors of one of the city's great wineries, then laid into the massive storage tuns with their hatchets, flooding the area with Govinnese claret. Moments later, another mob set fire to a clothworks across the river. Along the gorge's edge, men with knives darted from one great winch to the next, cutting the ropes that held up the river-lifts. Baskets and wooden platforms fell like autumn apples, splashing into the Edessa or smashing the boats and docks below. In the north, three mountain-sized brigands laid into one of Govinna's most beautiful monuments, the Fountain of Falling Stars, with heavy sledges, smashing it to rubble in less than a minute. Those few true pilgrims who remained in the streets panicked, fleeing through the narrow streets and crying for help.

Faced with such sudden, random destruction, the town guards reacted as Ossirian had hoped—with utter confusion and disarray. They scattered in every direction, their numbers thinning as they tried to respond to every incident at once. The bandits refused to give them a fair fight, though, running away rather than standing their ground, leading the guards into alleys where more of their number waylaid them, surrounding the watchmen with crossbows and swords. Most of the guards surrendered. Knights and even *Scatas* might fight on against unfavorable odds, but Govinna's sentries valued their lives much more than their honor. Caught flat-footed, they threw down their arms.

Things happened just as quickly within the Pantheon. The moment the call to prayer sounded, Ossirian, who had been kneeling in the hall of worship with the rest of the faithful, rose and raised to his lips a horn of his own—made of a ram's horn, not a dragon's. At its harsh blast, more than fifty men rose, throwing off their cloaks and drawing swords. Most had positioned themselves near the guards within the temple, and overcame them easily, setting blades to throats before the watchmen could react. A few scuffles broke out, and two guards and a bandit died, but for most there was little bloodshed.

Ossirian had the advantage, but he knew it wouldn't last. The city's defenses were in a shambles, yet it wouldn't be long before those guards who remained regrouped and tried to counterattack. He turned to Tavarre and the other lords, barking orders

"Seal the doors! Find Durinen! Half a thousand imperial falcons to the man who brings me the Little Emperor!"

The bandits scrambled to comply. Some rushed to the church's apse, barricading its doors with pews, fonts, and whatever else they could find. The rest spread out through the Pantheon, surging through its halls as clerics fled, sandals flapping, or cowered, begging for mercy. They moved from vestiary to antechamber, copy room to meditation hall, breaking down doors when they found them locked. Ossirian himself led the main charge up the stairs of the Patriarch's Tower, shoving priests aside as he sought the unmistakable, huge bearded form of Durinen.

The Little Emperor's servants had barricaded his private apartments at the tower's top, but the wooden doors didn't stand long against the bandits' long-handled axes. Splinters scattered across rich carpets as Ossirian and his men broke through, and the bandits pushed past the trembling acolytes into the patriarch's study, his bedchamber, the innermost sanctum where his personal, golden altar glimmered with candlelight. They were all empty.

"Damn it!" Ossirian roared, his gray-bearded face livid. He grabbed Tavarre's arm, pulling the baron to him. "He must be someplace!"

Tavarre shook his head. "He isn't. We've looked everywhere."

Snarling a vile curse, Ossirian swung his sword at the altar, scattering candlewax everywhere. They had failed. The Little Emperor had escaped.

———◆———

In a courtyard near the Edessa's western bank, amid a patch of yellow-flowered bushes, stood a bronze statue of a rearing horse. Once a sculpture of Theorollyn had sat astride it, but the church had torn it down and melted it long ago. The courtyard was little used. The folk of Govinna considered it an unlucky place, and it was deserted most of the time, except for occasional gangs of children who took turns climbing up and riding the false Kingpriest's steed. Thus tonight no one heard the soft crack that came from the statue nor saw the air shimmer around it, as it might in summer's heat.

The surface of the pedestal rippled for a moment as the magic that affected it lifted away, then a section of stone flickered and faded, becoming an open hole leading into darkness. A man poked his shaven head out through the opening and glanced about, then nodded and climbed out, sword in hand. The captain of the guard looked around the courtyard more carefully, then turned to the statue and hissed a soft word.

Durinen scowled at the distant clamor of fighting as he emerged from the statue. He was livid—with the bandits for daring to attack the Pantheon, with his guards for letting it happen, and with himself for not seeing it coming. His only satisfaction came from having outwitted Ossirian and his men, who would be scouring the temple for him, looking in vain, even now. A wolfish smile tightened within the thicket of his beard.

The bandits were well organized, that was certain. Durinen had read Rudanio's *Shapes of War* and knew good tactics when he saw them. They had made a mistake, though, assuming they knew everything there was to know about the Pantheon. It was a reasonable belief, he supposed, since the lords who led the brigands had spent enough time in the temple, but it sheltered some secrets even they didn't know. The most important—today, at least—was a particular old wine-cask in the cellar beneath the refectory. It, too, was an illusion, like the side of the riderless horse's pedestal; in fact, it was a doorway to a passage beneath the city's streets. Now, as Ossirian was cursing in his tower, the Little Emperor looked back at the Pantheon and chuckled with small satisfaction.

"We should cross the river, Worship," offered the captain. "There will be less trouble that way."

Durinen considered this, then nodded. If they could get to the east gates and out of the city, they could find a place where he could be safe until the guards recaptured the city.

"Go on, then," he bade.

The captain led the way, his bald head glistening as he crept from one lane to the next, constantly watching to make sure the way was clear. Finally they reached a narrow bridge, lined with pear trees, that arched above the Edessa. On the far side, the east hill looked quieter than the west, though smoke still rose above the rooftops here and there. Kissing his sword for luck, the captain darted across the span, keeping down as he went. Durinen hurried after—though with his bulk, it was hard to stay low—and they reached the far side together. They ducked into a doorway for a moment while the captain made sure no one had seen them, then stepped out again, darting through the streets of Govinna's eastern quarter.

"Sounds like things are quieting down," hissed Embric, glancing west. "Think it worked?"

"How should I know?" Cathan snapped. His mood had grown steadily darker as the shouts and clashes of swords rang out across the city. They still hadn't seen a single person. "The bloody Pantheon could be burning and we'd only find out if the wind—hammer and lance!"

Embric looked up sharply at Cathan's sudden oath. He caught his breath. They were no longer alone. Two other figures had emerged from the mouth of a street across the plaza, and stood by a cistern, resting while they caught their breaths. One was a bald swordsman in a fine suit of scale, but Cathan and Embric only glanced at him, staring instead at the other man. He didn't have his emerald diadem, but even so there was no mistaking the man. Ossirian had described him in detail, back in Abreri—the huge, bearish body, the long, braided beard.

"Branchala's balls," Cathan breathed.

Embric nodded silently.

The Little Emperor stooped over the cistern, scooping water to his mouth with a cupped hand while the swordsman looked around. Cathan pulled back deeper into the shadows, reaching for his sword again. This time he didn't let go.

"Think we can take them?" he asked.

Embric shrugged, reaching for his own weapon. "Have to try. Ossirian wants him caught."

"Right, then."

They paused a moment longer, tensing, then bolted from cover, swords ringing clear of their scabbards. Durinen started at the sound, his mouth dropping open as he stumbled back from the cistern. He cast about, looking for a way to escape as the bald man raised his sword, stepping in front of him to head off Cathan and Embric.

It was two against one, but even so, Cathan knew they were outclassed from the moment the jeweled sword came out of nowhere to parry Embric's first wild slash. The guard captain was a veteran fighter and could have given Lord Tavarre a challenge. Against two untrained bandits, he barely needed to expend any effort. He ducked easily under Embric's return swing, stepped sideways, and twisted, his blade flicking hard against Cathan's to turn it aside. The ring of steel on steel echoed off the walls surrounding the plaza, and Cathan's hand went numb for a moment. The captain spun to follow through, kicking him in the stomach and sending him stumbling back.

Alone, Embric fought frantically, giving ground as he went on the defensive. The captain came on, his mouth a firm line as his sword flashed again and again and again. Somehow, Embric managed to block the attacks, but each parry came slower than the last, and one stroke left a red line across his face. Blood beaded from the cut, dripping down Embric's face. He wiped it away with the back of his hand, casting about while the captain stepped back, looking for an opening.

"Cathan!" he shouted, terrified. "Help!"

Cathan, though, was down on one knee, still trying to get his breath back and could only watch as the captain resumed his attack. The bald man's mouth twisted into a wolfish smile as he lunged, stabbing at Embric's groin. Frantically, Embric moved to parry—then swore suddenly as the swordsman reversed the feint, twisting and raising his blade to drive it through leather and flesh.

It happened so fast, Cathan didn't realize at first what had happened. It was only when the captain jerked his bloody sword free and Embric sank to his knees, his tunic dark under his right arm, that he saw. Embric fought to get back to his feet, knowing already it was too late.

With cold efficiency, the captain's sword flicked out and cut Embric's throat.

An inarticulate cry erupted from Cathan's mouth as his friend collapsed, the cobblestones awash with red beneath him. A star of rage exploded in his head, and he forgot the Little Emperor altogether, bolting toward the captain with his sword slashing the air. The bald man fell back a pace from the storm of savage blows, but he turned each slash aside, sidestepping and circling—and suddenly lost his footing as he slipped in Embric's blood.

The captain's eyes widened as he staggered, flinging out his arms to keep his balance. The predatory smile vanished from his lips as, maddened with grief, the young bandit brought his sword down with a shout. Despite his rage, Cathan remembered his training. The last four inches of the blade struck the man's shaven head, hacking through his skull with a sickening crunch. The captain blinked, then his eyes rolled over and he crumpled, yanking Cathan's sword from his hand.

Cathan's hands shook as he stumbled back, each short breath a stab of pain. He had never killed a man before—except Tancred, and that had been mercy, not violence. He stared at the two bodies sprawled on the cobbles for a long moment, then turned away and vomited.

He was sobbing and wiping his mouth with his sleeve when he remembered the Little Emperor. With a jolt he turned, expecting Durinen to be gone, but the priest was still there, backed up against the wall and gaping at the captain's corpse. He looked up, his eyes meeting Cathan's, and turned to run.

It was pointless. His strides were long, but he was a heavy man, and Cathan was young and quick. Any borderman who had ever seen a mountain cat fight a bear and win would have nodded in recognition as Cathan pounced on the hulking patri-arch, knocking him sideways then dragging him down onto the ground. Cathan landed on top of Durinen, and his fist slammed into the bearded face before the Little Emperor could recover—once, twice, three times, feeling the nose shatter, teeth splinter, blood spray. Durinen cried out, trying to rise, but a fourth punch hit his cheek, slamming his head back against the paving stones, and he went silent and still at once.

Cathan knelt beside the patriarch, not moving for a long time. Finally he leaned forward, his face gray, rolled Durinen onto his stomach, and tore a long strip off the fine, silvery robes. He used it to tie the man's wrists together, tight enough that the cloth dug into his flesh. Then he bound the Little Emperor's feet and pushed himself to his feet. He stopped at the captain's body long enough to jerk his sword free, then—with one last, sickened glance at Embric—sprinted off toward the river, looking for help.

Lord Ossirian looked from Cathan to Tavarre. "He's one of yours?"

The baron nodded proudly. "Yes, lord."

They stood within the Pantheon, in the patriarch's private antechamber, adjacent to the main worship hall. It was a plain room, all of stone, with a silver shrine in the corner, gold-threaded hangings on the walls, and brass lanterns burning in wall-mounted cressets. Durinen sat on the floor in the room's corner, his face a swollen, bloody mess, flanked by sword-armed bandits. He glowered but didn't seem apt to move any time soon. Ossirian regarded him, scratching his head. He didn't seem sure whether to be amused or annoyed that a whelp of a boy, not he, had caught the Little Emperor.

Finally, though, a smile split his lips, and he clapped Cathan's shoulder. "My thanks to you, MarSevrin. I promised a reward for this prize, and you shall have it."

Cathan swallowed, staring his boots. They were stained

with blood. He wondered whose. "Sir," he murmured, "might I ask a favor instead?"

Ossirian's eyebrows rose. He glanced at Tavarre, who shrugged. "Very well," he declared. "Name it, and we'll see how magnanimous I'm willing to be."

"Actually, sir, it's two things," Cathan replied, then pressed on before Ossirian could object. "First, a—a friend of mine died today. I'd like him to be buried proper."

"That," Ossirian replied, "you didn't have to ask for. We'll see to him, don't worry. What's the second thing?"

Cathan drew a deep breath and held it, steeling himself. He'd been working himself up to this, but it still wasn't easy. His eyes shone with tears as he looked up at Ossirian. "I want to go home. My sister has the *Longosai*. I thought I could avenge her, coming here, but I was wrong. I should be with her."

At first, Ossirian didn't answer. He continued to glare at Durinen, his eyes narrow.

"Cathan," Tavarre cut in, "you don't know what you ask. We need every man here, to secure the city. You can't just—"

"No." Ossirian held up a hand. "The boy can go. I need men out there to watch the south road, in case the regent sends his *Scatas*. He may well, after tonight. I can spare a band—your band. It needs to be someone I can trust."

Tavarre met his gaze, frowning. Finally he nodded. "If you think it best."

After Ossirian ordered his men to take Durinen away, he turned to confer with his lords about how best to hold the city, now that the Little Emperor was theirs. Forgotten, Cathan left the antechamber, walking out into the worship hall, a long, vaulted chamber with shadowy corners and high windows that gleamed rose and azure in the moonlight. He made it as far as the first stone pew before his legs gave out, and he sank down onto the seat with a moan. He stared up at the great platinum triangle on the wall above the altar, thinking of Wentha, Embric, and the man who had died on his sword today. Then he bowed his head and wept.

CHAPTER 9 ▼
SEVENTHMONTH, 923 I.A.

There was no pain. Am I dead? Ilista wondered. Is this how it happens? Like waking from sleep?

Through the ages, sects had disagreed—often violently—about the afterlife. Traditionalists said it was a shining city on a mountain, while certain scholars in the church claimed it was simply Paladine's eternal presence. Some heretics in Istar's southern deserts believed there *was* no hereafter, only oblivion. In none of these beliefs, however, did the dead know hunger or thirst, heat or cold.

Ilista's stomach growled. Her lips were parched. She shivered in the chill.

She let her eyes flutter open, adjusting to the light. She lay in a small room of gray stone. Daylight streamed through the narrow, open window, sparkling with dust. The only furnishings were the simple pallet where she lay, a clay chamber pot, and a wooden triangle on the wall. A monk's cell, she realized. Somehow she had made it to that monastery.

Her packs were in the corner. Stiffly, she rose and walked to them, amazed that she didn't feel pain or appear to suffer any wounds. Beside her packs were a clean white cassock and a pair of leather sandals. She put them on quickly, genuflected to the wooden triangle, then headed slowly toward the door. It opened before she reached it, letting in more light, along with a low, rumbling sound. Sir Gareth stood in the opening.

"*Efisa!*" he exclaimed. "You're awake!"

"Sir Knight," she replied, signing the triangle. She hesitated, unsure what to ask him. Finally, she settled on the simplest question. "What is that noise?"

Gareth smiled. "Come," he said simply. "It's best you see for yourself."

———◆———

The monastery stood on a ledge surrounded by snowy peaks, at the end of a steep, narrow trail. It was a small, simple place, having once been home to the monks of Majere. Even in Istar, the Rose God's clerics were ascetics, spending their days in quiet meditation. Their temple stood out in the Lordcity for its gray plainness. Here, the abbey consisted of only a few low buildings surrounded by a stone wall. It featured no gardens, save for a few ornamental stone piles arranged in circles and spirals. There was a cloister, a stable, a refectory, and a chapel, all simple as peasant's hovels, lacking even glass in their shuttered windows. The only adornment was a whitewashed wooden triangle atop the church's roof. The Majereans might have built the monastery in their god's name, but it belonged to Paladine now.

The rumbling grew steadily louder as Ilista followed Sir Gareth across the yard. They passed several clerics along the way, clad in simple gray habits, their hooded heads bowed. The shapeless garments made it hard to tell if they were men or women. A few turned to watch as she passed but glanced away when she looked at them, and none of them spoke a word. Ilista frowned, puzzled, as they reached the abbey's southern wall. A flight of mossy stairs led to its top, and, beyond, a plume of white mist rose into the air, curling with the wind. She looked questioningly at Gareth, but he only started up the stairs, motioning for her to follow. She did, then stopped, stunned, when they reached the top.

"*Palado Calib*," she gasped.

The Majereans disdained man-made finery, but they had always cherished nature's beauty. Here, they had found a wonder. A river ran foaming past the monastery, then plunged over the ledge, thundering to a pool a thousand feet below. Fog veiled the waterfall, sparkling with rainbows as it rose into the sky. Used to the slow, wide streams of Istar's heartland, Ilista could only stare at the rushing torrent in awe.

"Did you bring me here?" she asked the Knight after a time. She had to shout over the waterfall's roar. "To this place, I mean?"

"No, *Efisa*," Gareth replied. "When the wyvern carried you off, we were sure you were lost. Then the other beasts fled, and when we rode on we found the one that grabbed you dead near the road. We searched for you all night and finally came to this place. The monks took us to you, showed us you were safe. We buried our dead and have been here since, waiting for you to wake."

"How long?" she asked.

"A week, milady."

Ilista's eyes widened. "What happened to my wounds?"

Gareth shrugged. "When we found you, you were already healed, and the monks do not speak. I think they've taken a vow of silence."

"Just so," said a voice.

Ilista jumped. So loud was the waterfall that neither she nor Gareth heard the old monk approach. He stood behind them, robed and cowled, bent with age. He bobbed his head, signing the triangle, then drew back his hood to reveal a wizened, spotted face with only a few wisps of hair. His eyes were clear, however, and glinted in the sunlight.

"Pardon," he said. "I didn't mean to startle you, First Daughter. I am Brother Voss. I was sent for you."

"I thought you didn't speak," Gareth said.

Voss smiled toothlessly. "Usually, yes, but the master gave me permission, so I can take you to him."

"The master?" Ilista asked.

"The one who brought you here, *Efisa*." The old monk gestured back toward the chapel. "Come. He wishes to meet you."

———◆·◆·◆———

The chapel, like the rest of the monastery, was austere in the extreme, its floor bare stone, its walls and ceiling free of mosaic or fresco. The columns that ran down its length had no ornate capitals, and no carvings marked the wooden pews. The candles were made of raw beeswax, and even the triangle above the stone altar was made of silver, not platinum. It was everything the Great Temple was not, yet it was still a house of the god, and Ilista genuflected just the same as Brother Voss led her across the threshold. Silent again, the monk stepped aside and waved her in.

She started forward, Gareth at her side. The chapel was empty. No one sat at the pews or knelt at the simple shrines along its walls. Behind them, Voss shut the doors with a boom, shutting out the light, save for the sharp spears that jabbed through the shadows. Ilista glanced back, then exchanged looks with Gareth and went on to the altar. They stopped there, kneeling, and she reached to her throat, searching for her medallion.

It was gone. Someone had removed it while she slept. She cast about, her heart beating savagely in her breast.

"Are you looking for this, *Efisa*?" asked a soft voice.

She turned, startled. A young monk stood between the pews, his hood drawn low. He raised his hand. Ilista's amulet dangled from his fingers.

Gareth was on his feet in an instant, his hand on his sword. The monk did not flinch, didn't even glance at the Knight. Though she couldn't see his face, Ilista could feel his eyes on her. The medallion swung slowly in his grasp as he extended it.

"Do not fear, *Efisa*," he said. His voice was like honey poured over harpstrings. "I watched over you while you slept and thought it best to keep your holy medallion with me. Now that you've woken, though, it belongs in your possession."

Gareth stepped forward, but Ilista touched his arm, stopping him, and moved toward the monk herself. Reaching out, she took the medallion from him, pressed it to her lips, and pulled it over her head. She stared at the monk, who stared back.

"What is your name, Brother?"

"I am called Beldyn, milady."

"What of your vow of silence? Has your master given you leave to speak?"

He nodded. "In a way." Reaching up, he pulled back his hood. "You see, I am master here."

Ilista's eyes widened as the cowl came off. The face beneath was thin and beautiful. His skin was smooth, beardless. He could not have seen more than seventeen summers. Where most monks went close-cropped and tonsured, his hair was long, brown locks tumbling down over his shoulders, and then there were his eyes. She had never seen such eyes before—not the color, though their pale, glacial blue was striking, but rather the way they seemed to shine with an inner light as they regarded her, boring into her. They had the look of a man wracked with fever but without the sheen of illness. Caught, she found herself unable to look away.

"You," she said dully. "You're the one who killed the wyvern."

Beldyn nodded, his eyes sparkling. In the distance, the waterfall rumbled on.

"You healed my wounds?"

"I did. Also I sent the message that brought you here. I am the one you seek, *Efisa*."

He is, she thought. She could feel it, see it in his strange, bright eyes. A moment later, though, she forced herself to look away in doubt. She'd thought the same of Brother Gesseic and the men before him, and she had been wrong. While her wounds were gone, neither she nor the Knights had seen him heal her. She shook her head warily.

"Any man can call himself holy," she said. "It must be proven."

"Of course," Beldyn replied. "I will have your regalia brought here, and you may use this chapel for the Rite. You shall have your proof, First Daughter, before the silver moon rises."

———◆———

Three hours later, as the sun set behind the mountaintops, Ilista was laving her hands at the altar while the monastery's brethren watched from the pews. As before, the Knights stood watch to the left, their armor shining. They were only six now. She thought of Laonis and Jurabin, and the others who had died, now lying beneath stone cairns in the mountains. If she had chosen to ride on to Xak Tsaroth, rather than coming to this place, they would still be alive.

Palado, sas bolias loidud ni calonn, she prayed, glancing at the curtained alcove to her right.

Paladine, let their deaths be not in vain.

Biting her lip, she turned to face the monks. They watched her expectantly with their cowls thrown back—twenty men and women, all older than the man they called master, their faces taut with anticipation and belief. She saw Brother Voss sitting in the foremost pew, and there was such faith in his gaze that for a moment the ritual's words failed her. She shut her eyes, forcing herself to doubt. It was Paladine's place to decide, not her. Swallowing, she lifted the ceremonial chime from the altar and struck it.

"*Aponfud, ti po bulfat fum gonneis,*" she intoned.

The curtain—rough wool instead of satin or velvet—pulled back, and Beldyn came forward, moving with a quick, sure step. He wore the same plain, gray habit as before, his long hair tied back. His eyes glittered as he took his place, kneeling before her. "*Fro Beldinas, Paladas lupo fo,*" he declared, gazing up at her. "*Praso me gonnas.*"

I am Brother Beldyn, beloved of Paladine. I ask to be tried.

Ilista hesitated, surprised. The other petitioners had all lowered their eyes as they spoke, but Beldyn gazed at her directly. There was no arrogance in his mien or voice, only certainty that he was whom he claimed to be. Caught by his gaze—brighter, it seemed, than candlelight could explain—Ilista had to fight back the urge to kneel before *him*. You are First Daughter, she told herself sternly. It is right he should bow to you.

Her hands shook as she anointed him with the golden ewer. He did not blink as the oil ran down his face. She paused, swallowing. Took off her medallion and raised it. Drew a deep breath, let it out. And touched the platinum triangle to Beldyn's forehead.

With the others, she had needed a moment to push her way into their minds. Beldyn *pulled* her in, drawing her down like the sandwater pools of the Sadrahka jungle. The rose of his mind bloomed, revealing all that lay within. His dreams, his hopes, his memories all but leaped out at her as she looked at them. There was no pride in it, though, but simply the force of certainty.

This is what I am.

She studied all of his facets, pushing deeper, her mind clenched with dread as she sought the inevitable flaw, the thing that would prove Beldyn fallible. Her breathing grew sharp, hitching in her chest, and she could feel the eyes on her, monks and Knights alike watching rapt as she delved deeper into the young monk's soul. Farther, farther, now crying, now laughing, each breath a shuddering gasp . . .

Suddenly she was on the mountaintop again, snow beneath her feet, the stars glittering like jewels above. The sea of clouds was roiling around her, and the cold wind tugged at her robes, billowing them. She staggered and nearly fell as the rapture lifted from her, leaving her weary and dazed. Her heart skipped and leaped, and she felt tears freeze on her cheeks as she turned and saw Beldyn.

He stood nearby, in the place where Gesseic had been. His

hair had slipped free of its bonds and blew behind him like a banner. His eyes were twin blue suns, blazing in the night, and looking into them she felt her insides quiver and churn. He was the one. He had to be. She could feel the truth of it, radiating from him like heat from a fire.

No, she told herself. *No*. Not yet.

"Who are you?" she whispered.

He smiled at her but made no reply. Instead, he turned and walked away, farther up the slope to the peak's sharp summit. His feet glided effortlessly across the snow as he went, but she struggled, sinking shin-deep with every step. By the time she caught up with him, he had turned around and was staring at the sky, his hands outstretched and open at his sides. Smiling, he shut his eyes, reached up into the night and pulled down a star.

Ilista gasped, her mind reeling. It was impossible. High as they were, the stars were much higher still, certainly too far to touch. Yet she saw it, his fingers pinching shut around one of the countless glittering motes, then plucking it down, tiny as a pebble and bright as its brothers above. He held it before his eye, studying it as a gemcutter might study a diamond, then smiled and clenched it in his fist. Light flared briefly between his fingers and was gone—as was the star when he opened his hand once more.

His eyes seemed to shine even brighter than before as he studied her. He flung his hands upward and brought down the heavens.

The stars moved so slowly at first that Ilista didn't notice it until she saw the emptiness at the sky's rim and realized they were drawing away from the horizon. They sped up as she watched, now flowing like a river, now darting like meteors, now so fast they made white streaks against the dark. Bit by bit, the constellations came apart. The sky over Beldyn grew brighter and brighter still, until it seemed a second sun shone where all the stars gathered. His face aglow with bliss, he lowered his arms.

The pool of light fell and washed over him, each star flaring bright when it touched him, then winking out. The stars didn't simply disappear, however, but added their light to his own, making him shine brighter with every heartbeat—first his eyes, then the rest of him, until starglow swathed him like a mantle, obscuring him from view. By the time the last stars had fallen, the glare was so bright that Ilista had to turn away.

She heard the whisper of his footsteps, felt him draw near, but she didn't look, tears crawling down her cheeks as she stared away into the starless night. He was the man she had dreamed of, the figure of light the god had revealed to her.

"Do you still doubt, *Efisa*?" he asked.

She shook her head, not trusting her voice.

"Then take my hand."

He held it open before her, each finger a bright comet's tail. For a moment she balked, afraid his touch might burn her to ashes, but the light gave no heat. Swallowing, she raised her hand, reaching out and touching his luminous flesh.

Rapture flooded her at his touch. Her back arched . . . her eyes pinched shut . . . the warmth of blood flooded her mouth. Oh Paladine, she thought, so this is how purity feels . . . please, it's too bright . . . it *hurts*. . . .

As abruptly as she'd left it, she was back in the chapel, her face damp with tears, her robes with sweat. With a gasp she let go, and her medallion fell from her grasp to clatter on the floor. Beldyn was looking at her, no longer cloaked in light but his eyes still shining.

For a moment, the words of the rite eluded her. When she spoke them at last, her voice quavered and nearly broke. "*Ubatsud, usas farno*," she bade, tears rolling down her face, "*e bidud Paladas gonam fas.*"

Rise, child of the god, and know thou art Paladine's chosen.

Beldyn stood, and Ilista bent forward, ritually kissing his cheeks. As she did, two words circled in her mind. Around and around they went, a bright certainty that drove away her doubt and despair:

The Lightbringer . . . the Lightbringer . . . the Lightbringer!

The waterfall was even more beautiful in Solinari's glow. The silver moon rode high, and the mist of the torrent caught and trapped its light, becoming a vast, brilliant serpent that sparkled as it writhed on the wind. The Majereans had chosen rightly when they made their monastery plain. Beside the shining mist, even the Great Temple itself would have seemed small.

Ilista was accustomed to living amid power and splendor in her place at the Kingpriest's side, but today she had been humbled. She remembered how Beldyn's mind had felt as she delved into it, and she shuddered at having seen something so bright, as if her own thoughts might have polluted its existence.

She had been standing alone on the abbey's south wall since the *Apanfo* concluded, staring at the mist and remembering the ecstasy that had flooded her at the touch of the glowing hand. Now, somehow, she heard the scuff of sandals on stone above the waterfall's bellow. She turned, already knowing it was Beldyn. He signed the triangle as he came near, and she bowed her head, spreading her hands contritely.

"Please, *Efisa*," he said. "I am but a simple monk."

She looked up, shaking her head. "You're more than that."

"Perhaps."

Ilista swallowed, gathering her thoughts. "How long have—have you known?"

"I don't know," he replied, gazing out at the shimmering mist. "I remember little of my childhood and nothing of my parents. I was an orphan in Xak Tsaroth when I met Brother Voss."

"Voss? The monk you sent for me today?"

Beldyn nodded. "Most of the monks here were once clerics in the city. Voss sometimes went among the poor, giving them what aid he could, and one day he saw me lay hands upon a woman dying of the gray fever and heal her sickness.

"Yes," he said as Ilista's eyes widened, "the god's power was in me even then. Voss brought me back to the temple of Paladine and told the patriarch what he had witnessed. That was a mistake—the patriarch called it blasphemy to think an untrained child could perform such miracles when ordained priests could not." He shook his head. "There are many in the church who would not believe in my powers."

Ilista bit her lip, thinking of other hierarchs who would react like this patriarch—perhaps even Kurnos himself. "What happened then?"

"Voss, may Paladine bless him, wasn't so easily daunted. Instead he took me in and taught me the church's ways in secret." Beldyn's eyes danced with memory. "He even consecrated me as an acolyte. When the patriarch found out, he nearly ordered us both stoned as heretics. Too many people loved Voss, though, so he banished us instead. Voss asked his brethren to come with us." He nodded down into the courtyard, where the monks were emerging from the refectory, their supper done. "As you see, a few listened."

"We traveled deeper into the mountains," he went on, "and found this place. The Majereans were long gone, so we restored it and made it our home. We've lived here ever since . . . six years now."

"Now *you're* the master," Ilista said.

He nodded. "A year and a half ago, Voss named me a full Revered Son and appointed me his successor. The others accepted it—they have long known and trusted me. I became head of the abbey, and since then I have been waiting."

"Waiting?" Ilista's brows knitted. "What for?"

"For you, *Efisa*." His eyes were silver pools in the misty light. "The night before I became master, I too had a dream. In it, a woman rode out of the north, pursued by beasts on shadowy wings. She said to me, *Pilofiram fas*—you are the Lightbringer—and then I woke. I told Voss, and he said it was a vision from the god. One day I would meet the woman, and my life would change forever.

"Ten days ago I had the dream again, and I knew it must be time. I sent one of my monks to Xak Khalan, with a message—which, of course, you found. A few days later, when I saw the wyverns had taken wing in the storm, I knew someone had roused them, so I went to help you. I only wish I had been quicker, so others might have lived."

They stood together silently. Silhouetted by the mist, Beldyn looked as he had in Ilista's dream, and in her vision during the *Apanfo*. I found him, the priestess thought, overjoyed. I truly found him.

"Your wait is over," she said softly. "The time has come for you to leave this place."

"Yes," he replied. His eyes shone. "Have you dined, *Efisa*?"

Ilista blinked, taken aback. She had been too excited to eat earlier, but now her stomach growled hungrily. "No, Brother."

"Nor have I," he said, extending his hand. "Will you join me?"

She hesitated, suddenly afraid. A jolt of fear ran through her as she remembered what his touch had done to her earlier. She wasn't sure she could bear the feeling again. A moment later, though, she shook herself, thrusting the thought aside. This was a man of flesh, not light. Biting her lip, she laid her hand upon his wrist. He was solid, warm, human. Smiling, she walked with him down to the courtyard, the mist ablaze behind them.

CHAPTER 10 ▾

The gray stallion was frothing and dust-caked, blowing hard as it galloped toward the Lordcity's western gates. The rider astride it seemed in even worse shape, her billowing blue cloak torn and dirty, her hair pasted to her scalp with sweat and grime. She was pale with weariness, her eyes red-rimmed, and she seemed apt to fall from the saddle at any moment. She wore no armor or helm, no sword or bow, though her livery resembled that of the *Scatas* who made up the empire's armies. Instead, what she clutched in her hand as she pounded up the broad, stone-paved road was something much more dangerous: an ivory scroll-tube, bearing the insignia of the Little Emperor.

The empire of Istar was vast, and sending urgent messages required a network of post-houses, where riders could stop and change horses to speed them on their way. Even so, the woman on the frothing gray had been riding for four days and nights since she'd left the highlands, and by the time she reined in before the tall, gilded gates, in the shadow of the statue of Paladine that crowned them, she could barely keep her head up long enough to present the silver scepter that identified her as a member of the Messenger's Guild to the sentries. The guards regarded the scepter, with its winged horseshoe crown, for a long uncertain moment, then nodded and handed it back, waving her into the city.

It was mid-afternoon, and the streets were quiet. Istar sweltered in the summer, and its folk repaired to the wine shops and baths during the hottest part of the day, emerging as the sun dipped toward the horizon. Rather than the press of robed bodies that filled the city in the mornings and evenings, the rider encountered only a few people on her way to the Great Temple—soldiers, clerics, and a long-bearded Holy Fool who leaped and threw pebbles at her as she thundered past. The broad, tree-lined avenue led straight from the gates to the great arch that let out onto the *Barigon*, then on to the sprawling church. Galloping across the plaza, she clattered to a halt before a Revered Son and half a dozen acolytes who had come to receive her. They took the reins from her shaking hand and thrust a goblet of watered wine at her once she'd swung down from the saddle. She gulped it down quickly and ate a snow peach another youth offered, which invigorated her enough that she could at least walk without leaning on anyone—for now, at least.

The priest asked her for whom her message was intended, and she looked at him sourly.

"The chief of the imperial kitchens," she snapped, holding up the scroll-tube. A silken ribbon dangled from it, bearing the imperial triangle-and-falcon. "Who do you think?"

She went in through a side entrance, the priest puffing along beside her as he kept up with her long, quick strides. The Kingpriest was still ailing, he told her, and not taking visitors. The regent, however, would be glad to receive her at his first convenience. She nodded at this and pressed on, scattering several squalling peacocks as they made their way through the gardens to the basilica. Within, the Revered Son bade her wait in a bright, pillared antechamber. She washed the road's grime off her face with a basin of cool, lemon-scented water while she bided. Presently the cleric returned and led her down a hall hung with red roses to the Kingpriest's private study.

First Son Kurnos sat behind a desk of polished mahogany, poring over a set of ledgers. He was not in a good mood. The papers tallied the yields of the gold mines the empire maintained in its newest colonies, far to the south on the frozen islands of Icereach. He scowled, running his fingers down the columns. Ore production was down considerably from last year. He didn't notice the courier at first when she entered, and when he finally looked up his forehead creased with annoyance.

"Bring it here," he snapped.

The rider strode toward him then dropped to one knee and proffered the tube with both hands. Kurnos took the tube and opened it, leaving the messenger on her knees while he removed the parchment within and broke its crimson seal. Unfurling the scroll, he scanned its words—then stopped, his eyes narrowing, and read it again.

Your Holy Majesty, it proclaimed.

Be it known that on the twenty-eighth day of Sixthmonth, this year 923 I.A., a force of Taoli patriots conquered the city of Govinna. As you read this, we hold Revered Son Durinen and have posted watchers along our borders. Those in the Lordcity have ignored our plight too long. While you recline in perfumed halls, we die of plague. While you dine at grand banquets, our children starve.

We do not demand much; only aid you, with your vast wealth and power, can easily provide. Send us food and healers to cure the Longosai, *and we shall release the Little Emperor. Ignore our plea, and may Paladine have mercy on him—and on you.*

Kurnos's face darkened as he stared at the scroll. Slowly, he crumpled the parchment in his fist, then threw it in the kneeling courier's face.

"Leave," he growled. "Now."

Seeing the fury in his eyes, the messenger rose and hurried from the room. Kurnos pushed to his feet, glaring after the rider, then whirled and flung the scroll-tube across the room with a curse. It struck the wall and shattered, ivory splinters clattering onto the floor. He'd warned the others that something like this would happen, but Symeon had listened to the First Daughter, not him—to Ilista, who was far from here, in Kharolis. Meanwhile, he had to face the fruit of the Kingpriest's inaction against the bandits, while—

"Your Grace?"

Kurnos turned slowly, his nostrils flaring. "What is it?"

An acolyte had opened the door. Now he paled and drew back, seeing the anger on Kurnos's face.

"I—heard a noise, *Aulforo*," the boy stammered. "Is all well?"

A laugh barked from Kurnos's lips. "No, boy. All is *not* well." He paused, thinking quickly. "Send word to Loralon and Lady Balthera. I must meet with them in the Kingpriest's chambers at once. Go!"

Flinching, the acolyte withdrew. Kurnos had to force himself to breathe slowly to quell his rage. It took a while. Finally, though, he shook himself and turned from his desk. The trouble in Icereach forgotten, he strode out of the office, bound for the manse.

———◆———

Symeon's condition had improved somewhat in the weeks since his seizure. His right arm and leg were still lifeless, and his drooping mouth made him seem to scowl all the time, but he had some of his old strength back, and his speech too. Words came haltingly and badly slurred, but he was intelligible most of the time. He could rise from bed, too, if someone carried him, and this afternoon he sat in a highbacked chair on the balcony where he'd fallen ill. The breeze that blew in off the gardens was warm, and smelled of saffron. In his good hand, he held the scroll, the left side of his mouth twitching as he read.

"Un . . . fortunate," he mumbled.

Weakly, he raised the parchment. Loralon took it from him. A small, dark line appeared between the elf's brows as he read the missive, then passed it on to Revered Daughter Balthera.

"Holiness, this is a difficult situation. We must treat it with care."

"Bah," Kurnos scoffed. "That was your counsel the last time we discussed Taol." He waved his hand. "You see where it led."

Loralon spread his hands. "In that case, I recommend we send the provisions they need."

Symeon's good eye widened. "Cap . . . capitu . . ." he began, stumbling, then gave up with a frustrated grunt.

"Capitulate?" Kurnos finished for him. "Preposterous!"

"I prefer to call it mercy," Loralon said.

Kurnos shook his head, digging his nails into his palms to keep his temper in check. "Sire, we have thousands of *Scatas* near the Taoli border. If they march now, they could crush these rebels and take back Govinna before winter."

Symeon considered this, the thumb of his left hand rubbing his medallion. "That may . . . be," he mumbled at length, "but . . . I will . . . not . . . go before Pal—Pala—the god . . . with . . . bloodstained hands."

Kurnos snorted, furious. The Kingpriest had recovered physically, but he was not the same man. The old Symeon might have been weak-willed, but he could be ruthless when the situation warranted. Since he'd recovered his speech, however, he had shown all signs of having turned soft.

"No!" Kurnos protested, pounding his palm with his fist. "We can end this now! We cannot just sit by and let—"

"You . . . can," Symeon interrupted, his good eye blazing, "and you *will*!"

Kurnos opened his mouth to argue, then closed it again, seeing the resolve in the Kingpriest's face. Instead, he turned to look out over the balcony at the gardens below. The lemon trees were in full fruit, and bees hummed about the roses. For a time, no one spoke, so that the only sound was the growl of the hippogriff and the distant murmur of the city. The folk of Istar had emerged from the wine shops, ready for the evening's trade.

The moot ended soon after, when Symeon dozed off in his chair. Kurnos considered waking him but knew it would be of no use. The Kingpriest slept often these days and didn't wake easily. They would have to wait, until tonight at least, for him to rouse from his dragon-haunted dreams and decide what to do.

Kurnos quit the manse soon after, returning to his study in the basilica. There, he issued a terse order to the lord of Icereach: if he didn't return the gold yields to their former levels by spring, he would pay with his lands and title. The empire had many ambitious nobles who would gladly take his place.

Evening prayers came and went, and Kurnos retired to his private quarters in the Revered Son's cloister. He stared at a supper of goose stuffed with forest mushrooms until it was cold, then bade the servants take it away. By then it was dark outside, the red moon bloodying the city's alabaster walls. Pouring a snifter of *moragnac*, he retired to his parlor to brood.

He had meant to go into the city tonight. The poet Abrellis of Pesaro was at the Arena, reciting his new work, the *Hedrecaia*, an epic about the ancient wars between Istar and the city-states of Seldjuk. Kurnos's anger still smoldered, however, so he threw himself down on a cushioned bench and sat silently in the gloom.

The more he thought about Govinna, the more it infuriated him. If Symeon bade him treat with the rebels, it would set a dangerous precedent. It was well for Loralon to speak of mercy, for he wouldn't have to face the outcome from the throne in the coming years. Taol might be the only province in turmoil right now, but there were many places where unrest could flare up—particularly if word spread that the Lordcity met uprisings with anything but the point of a spear. The savages in Falthana's jungles, for instance, might decide the city of Shiv was ripe to pluck. Or the Dravinish nomads might start harrying caravans in the southern deserts. In every corner of the empire, some militant faction would see concession with the borderlands as a weakness to be exploited.

"It *is* a problem."

Kurnos stiffened, his blood turning to ice. Slowly, he rose from his seat, turning to gaze across the parlor. The room was dark, lit only by a single electrum lamp beside his chair, and there were shadows everywhere. The voice—the quiet, cold, *familiar* voice—had come from the shadows.

"Who's there?" he demanded. He wanted to sound furious, but his voice shook. "Show yourself!"

A soft, mocking chuckle floated out of the dark. Kurnos had never heard laughter so devoid of mirth.

"Very well," the voice said. "If it will please you. *Kushat.*"

At the strange, spidery word, the lamp rose from the table where it stood and floated slowly across the room. Kurnos's eyes widened as the lamp glided to a dim corner near an arras depicting the building of the Great Temple. Beneath the tapestry, its light fell on a tall, slender figure cloaked in robes of blackest velvet. A deep, dark hood covered the man's face, obscuring all but the tip of a gray beard. Only his hands were visible, waving as he directed the lamp to hover near him. They were withered things, bony and spotted with age.

Kurnos's heart thundered in his chest. He knew the figure; it had haunted his dreams since he'd first seen it, months ago.

"Wh—who are you?" he breathed.

The robed man stepped out of the corner. Kurnos backed away as he came forward, stopping only when he bumped into a wall. The man came on, relentless, until he stood an arm's length away, and though the night was nearly as hot as the day, the air around him was cold enough to raise webs of frost on a nearby window. Kurnos shivered.

"Well met, First Son," said the voice from the hood's depths. "Perhaps you have heard of me. I am Fistandantilus."

CHAPTER 11 ▼

To the people of Istar, wizards were objects of contempt and suspicion. Even those who wore the White Robes of Good won a wide berth when they walked the Lordcity's streets. True, one of their number attended the imperial court, but they were still the only powerful cadre in Istar who didn't bend knee to the Kingpriest. They wielded powers beyond the ken of pious men and counted the evil Black Robes as allies, rather than with the enmity they deserved. Of the five Towers of High Sorcery, two stood within the empire—one in the Lordcity itself.

While they abhorred wizards, however, Istarans did not fear them. The Orders remained within the empire's borders because of the Kingpriest's forbearance. A word, and the might of both the church and the imperial army would descend upon them—and, before the might of the Kingpriest, no wizard could stand.

No wizard, except one.

For most, Fistandantilus was a legend, a bogey invoked to frighten willful children. Few had ever seen the man, but tales abounded. He was unspeakably old, folk whispered, having discovered magic that helped him outlive even the ageless elves. He could travel across the whole of Krynn in an eyeblink. If he twitched his little finger at a man—even a mighty archmage—the man would die in agony, his blood set aflame. He drew out the souls of younger wizards and devoured them to fuel his strength.

Unlike most bogeys, though, the tales about Fistandantilus were true. Even the Conclave who ruled the Orders of High Sorcery feared him. While the holy church didn't make an exception for him in its avowal that all Black Robes were beyond the god's sight, people whispered he kept one of his many dwellings within the Lordcity. No one spoke his name, lest he hear; instead, folk simply called him the Dark One.

Looking upon the tall, black-robed figure, Kurnos shivered from more than just the preternatural cold. His throat was so tight he could barely breathe, and he might have fled, provided he could convince his legs to move. Instead, he stood statue-still, his back flat against the wall, and trembled.

Fistandantilus let out a rasping chuckle. "What, Your Grace? No pleasantries? No idle talk? How disappointing." Though Kurnos could not see his face, the curl of his lip was plain in his voice. "But then, you are a busy man. You have your empire to run, so I shall be brief. I wish to offer my help."

He moved his hand as he spoke, and though his terror did not lessen, Kurnos felt himself almost relax. His mouth moved, but it took a few moments for words to come out.

"H-help?"

The dark wizard nodded, the tip of his beard bristling against his chest. "Hard to believe, I know. As it happens, though, we share a common interest, you and I—putting you on the throne."

"What?" Kurnos blurted. "Symeon has already named me heir. I am destined to rule."

"Perhaps, but there is another who could take your place, one who would be a terrible danger for those of us who walk the shadowed path."

The First Son furrowed his brow, confused—*who?*—then suddenly, he caught his breath.

"The one Ilista has found," he murmured. "The one she was looking for, but . . . Ilista never said aught of making him Kingpriest."

"She did not mean to," the Dark One answered. "Still doesn't, actually, but that changes nothing. This boy, the one called *Lightbringer*, must be stopped, if you are to rule. I am offering you the power to stop him."

He gestured, speaking spidery words. His aged fingers wove through the air. Green light flared, bright and unhealthy, and when it faded something hung in the air above his hand: a loop of red gold set with a large, glittering emerald. Kurnos gasped, then looked down at his own hands. The ring he'd taken from Symeon's finger when he became regent was gone, his skin itching where it had been. As he stared at the jewel, Fistandantilus twitched his fingers, and the ring started turning slowly in the air.

"What—what are you doing?" Kurnos demanded.

Fistandantilus inclined his head. "A fair question. Within the gem, I have imprisoned a . . . *being*. A spirit, if you will."

Kurnos drew back. There was something disturbing about the way the way the light played across the emerald's facets.

"A demon, you mean," he breathed.

"If that is what you wish to call it." Velvet-cloaked shoulders rose and fell. "Whatever word you choose, though, this creature is beholden to the one who wears the ring. Its name is Sathira. Speak and it will do your bidding, whatever you ask."

The dread of what might lurk within the ring was second in revulsion to Kurnos's yearning to reach out and take it. There was something seductive in the way it sparkled, and he heard the low hiss of whispering in the back of his mind. He knew, if he listened closely, he would hear his own name. He shuddered, forcing his hands to remain at his aides.

"If I refuse?" he asked.

"Then I shall find another who won't."

Kurnos had thought the sorcerer's voice could get no colder. He now realized he'd been wrong. The words came rimed with frost, leaving the afterthought unspoken. *And you shall never take the throne.*

A shudder ran through him. Treating with dark wizards was a sin in the church's eyes. Treating with demons was worse. He could always atone later, though, he mused—and he must take his rightful position as Kingpriest, the god's power his to wield. Otherwise, what? The rest of his life spent as First Son, the crown always beyond reach? Or worse, banished from the Lordcity, to the dimmer lights of the provinces? Fistandantilus was right—there were hundreds of male priests within the Great Temple's walls, and thousands more beyond them. One of them would take the ring if he didn't first.

Without thinking consciously about what he was doing, he reached out, plucking the jewel from the air. It felt like ice against his skin as he slipped it back onto his finger.

"Very good, Your Grace," Fistandantilus said, nodding. "The rest is up to you. You know what to do."

With that, he vanished.

There was no light, no magical aura—only a faint shimmer in the air and a dull sound like a gong being struck in reverse. One moment he was there, and the next he was gone. The frost began to fade from the windows at once, but the sense of disquiet that had surrounded the Dark One remained.

Kurnos gaped at the place where the mage had been standing, then turned his gaze downward to the ring itself. The emerald sparkled, almost mischievously, but there was something else, too. He had once heard a sea captain speak of hideous creatures, gliding beneath the water's surface, sinister shapes one could never quite make out. Whatever lay behind the gem's lambency, the darkness in the ring, refused to lie quiet.

It was looking back at him.

Take it off! his mind screamed. Go to the harbor and throw it from the God's Eyes into the depths. Find a blacksmith and burn it in his forge. Use two stones and smash it. Scatter the pieces to the winds!

He did none of these things. Instead he stood still and silent, gazing into the jewel's dark depths until an acolyte knocked on the door and entered, bowing.

"*Aulforo*," the boy said when Kurnos looked up, "you should go to the manse at once. Emissary Loralon has a report to make, word from the First Daughter in Kharolis. His Holiness bids you attend."

His Holiness, Kurnos thought, shivering. He could feel the ring's power tingle throughout his body. All he had to do was speak one word, one nonsense name, and the title would be his to claim.

No, he thought. Not yet.

Scowling, he made his way out of darkened study, into the hot evening air.

◆────◆◆◆────◆

"They have . . . set out for . . . home, then?" Symeon asked. "They've left . . . the mon—monast—" He broke off with a wince, breathing hard.

Loralon bowed his head. The four heads of the church had gathered on the balcony of the manse again. The city glimmered beyond the Temple's walls, a sea of golden lights.

"Yes, sire," the elf replied. "They rode out this morning. Only—they are not sailing back to Istar. Lady Ilista has chosen to travel overland."

"Overland?" Balthera echoed, her voice rising with dismay. She was a small woman, thin and birdlike, with hair the color of straw. "They'll need to pass through Taol!"

"Yes," Loralon replied. "Under the circumstances I cautioned her against it, but she insisted. It will take less time than riding all the way to Tarsis, then taking a ship back here—and they will be passing through the southern part of the borderlands, far from Govinna."

Balthera's frown deepened, but Kurnos spoke before she could.

"Why is it so important she arrives quickly?"

Loralon looked at the Kingpriest, who sighed.

"Because," Symeon said, "she wants . . . to get here . . . while I still . . . live. She thinks this . . . young monk . . . might . . . heal me." He slumped, breathing hard, as the other high priests looked at one another. When he had his wind back again, he chuckled. "Well. I doubt . . . the god's . . . will shall be so . . . easily thwarted, but . . . we should . . . still pray for . . . Ilista's safe . . . return."

"*Iprummu*, Holiness," Balthera said solemnly. *I shall.*

"As will I," Loralon agreed.

Kurnos hesitated, his gaze lowering to the marble floor. He sighed. "I as well, sire," he muttered. As he spoke the words, however, his fingers strayed to his left hand, to the emerald ring.

The Garden of Martyrs was quiet tonight, save for the chirping of crickets. Kurnos stood in its midst, looking out past the moonstone monuments toward the manse. Light glimmered from the high balcony, where he had left the Kingpriest. Symeon had been dozing quietly when he and the other hierarchs departed the manse. Soon Brother Purvis and his servants would come to bear him to his bed.

What if it really happens? he wondered, fists clenched at his sides. What if this Brother Beldyn's powers *do* heal him?

He could see it now, unfolding like the plot of an Ismindi high tragedy. The throne, nearly his, slipping from his grasp. Symeon's reign would continue, and his weak will might well be Istar's undoing. Symeon would not send the army to Taol, and rebellion would spread, flourishing throughout the provinces. Before long, it might well spiral into civil war.

No, Kurnos thought. It cannot happen. It *will* not.

He looked down at the emerald ring and shivered despite the evening's warmth. The moons were hidden now, behind clouds red with the Lordcity's glow. The gem sparkled with alluring light anyway. He held it up to his eye, peering within. He could see nothing there, save for the vague flicker of a shadow, but he could *feel* it—a presence trapped in the crystal, longing to be free. He could feel its eyes upon him.

Do it, a voice seemed to whisper. *Say the name* . . .

He took a deep breath, his lips parting. "Sathira," he whispered. "Come forth and heed my words. . . ."

Green light flashed within the ring, making him squint and turn away. It washed out in waves, the white obelisks around him reflecting its gangrenous glow. The ring grew warm, then hot, until he felt his skin begin to blister beneath it. Kurnos clutched his hand, groaning in pain and wondering if the Dark One had tricked him. Was this just some elaborate ploy to destroy him? Would the ring's green flame consume him, burn him to ashes?

Just as the heat threatened to wrench a scream from his lips, however, the emerald's glow flared sun-bright, then died with a noise like cloth tearing, only deeper. Like a pall of smoke, shadows billowed from the gem. They poured forth in a great gout, devouring what little light there was in the garden, surrounding Kurnos in blackness. The shadows eddied and swirled around him, colder than the frozen gales of the southern sea. Wisps broke free, dancing like witchfire, utterly soundless.

Kurnos stood amid it all, shuddering and biting his lip to keep from crying out. The iron taste of blood mixed in his mouth with coppery fear.

At last, the final shreds of shadowstuff flowed out of the ring, and their churning began to slow. Bit by bit, they coalesced, pulling inward and condensing until they seemed to take on physical form . . . arms . . . hands . . . fingers. Kurnos's mind told him that pure black could get no darker, and yet the shadowstuff did just that, becoming so thick that it drained the light out of the world around it. The air in the garden grew freezing, so cold it burned, and the leaves of nearby bushes turned brown and withered.

The shape the shadows took, at last, was that of a woman, but only by the barest of margins. The shadow-woman was legless, dissolving into inky wisps where her hips should have been, and her fingers were far too long, ending in sharp points. Her body wove back and forth in a way that resembled a snake more than a human, and tiny, pointed wings sprouted from where her shoulder blades ought to have been. Worse of all, though, was the head: long and narrow, bald and featureless, save for two slits of venomous green light in place of eyes. These moved back and forth, taking in the garden, then widened, flaring brightly when they settled on Kurnos.

"Master," Sathira said. Her voice was the snarl of jackals, the hiss of vipers, the mad buzz of wasps. "I hear and obey. What is thy will?"

Kurnos couldn't find his voice. More than anything, he wanted to stop, flee, order the horrid creature back into the ring. He knew, though, that it was too late. He couldn't say why, but he was sure Sathira would not retreat until she had tasted blood. She waited, staring at him with the unblinking flatness of things that lived under stones.

Palado Calib, he prayed. Forgive me for this. It must be done. It *must*.

He beckoned and tried not to cringe as the shadow-thing moved nearer. Unable to meet its cold gaze, he drew a deep breath, shaking all over, and spoke.

"Listen to me," he said. "There is something you must do. . . ."

———◆———

Symeon sat alone in his bed, a book propped in his lap. His illness had robbed him of many pleasures—strolling his gardens, playing *khas*, attending banquets—but his love of words remained. Tonight, as with every night of the past week, he sat up late, poring over the *Reflections* by the philosopher Pendeclos of Majere. His mind was elsewhere, however, so though his eyes slid across the words on the page, he barely noticed what they said.

The dilemma he faced was one Pendeclos, who had loved theological quandaries, would have enjoyed. On one side of the coin, Paladine himself had foretold his death. Even many months later, Symeon recalled the dream vividly, the god's honeyed voice telling him to uncrown. On the other side, though, was the young monk Ilista had found, this Beldyn. If he indeed had the power to heal, did that not also come from the god? What if the boy came to Istar and offered to cure his ailment? What then?

There was a proverb, oft-quoted by Pendeclos: *Usas supo munam fat. The god's mind is one*. That applied to Paladine as well as Majere. It was sometimes hard to understand the dawn-father—otherwise, why would men need clergy?—but Paladine did not contradict himself. There were only three possible solutions the Kingpriest could see, then: first, the boy's powers might not be as great as Ilista hoped; second, they would not reach Istar; and last, he would die too soon for Beldyn to help.

"Let it be that," he murmured, sliding an ivory marker between the pages and setting the book aside. His hand went to his medallion. "Take me, Paladine, if it is your desire. Better that than the others."

He frowned, then, shivering. The room had grown cold. He glanced at the window, but it was shut—and besides, it was still summer. Still the flesh on his good arm rose into bumps, and his breath became a plume of mist in the air. A deeper chill ran through him as he watched ice form on the goblet of water he kept by the bedside. This was no freak chill—something was causing it to happen. What?

He didn't have to wait long for the answer. As he shrank back, feebly tugging at his blankets to cover himself, the shadows in the room's corner shifted. They moved like a living thing, undulating and swelling, then darkening and growing solid . . . more and more solid. His heart beat erratically and he held his breath as he watched the darkness take form—a lithe, feminine form that shifted and coiled like smoke. Finally, two glowing slits appeared in its face, combing the room, then blazing with green fire as they settled on him.

With a soft hiss, the creature broke away from the darkness, gliding across his bedchamber. He watched it with horrible fascination—the way its body floated above the floor, the wintry glare it fixed on him, never once wavering as it drew near his bedside. He wanted to slip away, to get up and run, but his enfeebled body wouldn't let him. He wanted to shout, but his throat tightened until it was hard even to breathe.

Watching the monster draw near, he had a thought that terrified and amused him, both at once. He'd asked for death, only moments ago. Evidently, someone had been listening.

The . . . *thing* . . . hovered before him, poised like a coiled serpent. Its blazing eyes bored into his own. Black talons like scimitars reached out, inches from his flesh. In that moment, with death at hand, all fear left Symeon IV, and he nodded, his rosebud lips relaxing into a smile.

Palado Calib, he prayed silently, *mas ipilas paripud. Mas pirtam tam anlico.*

Blessed Paladine, forgive my wrongs. I give my soul to thee.

Aloud, he said, "Very well. Come on, then."

Snarling, the demon lunged. Its talons plunged into his breast, piercing him without breaking the skin. Cold pain surged through him, worse than any he'd ever known before. Then it went away.

Chapter 12 ▼

Ninthmonth, 923 I.A.

Wentha lived in darkness now, her windows shuttered, the candles gone from her bedside. Silence filled the room, broken by the thin wheeze of her breath. Her body was wretchedly thin—a skeletal girl now, rather than the blooming young woman she had been—and she shivered no matter how many blankets covered her. The herbs hanging from the rafters could no longer mask the sour reek and the drier, mustier scent beneath.

Autumn came early to the highlands, tinting the trees with flame. Watching his sister from the doorway, Cathan knew she would be gone before the leaves fell.

He'd returned from Govinna with the rest of Tavarre's band more than a month ago, setting camp in the same gorge as before. He'd meant to go to Luciel immediately, truly had, but something had stopped him. Fear, probably—to see his sister again would have made her illness real. He'd spent his days in other ways, practicing swordplay or taking watch over the broad, winding highroad. The rest of the time, he'd roved the hills, thinking dark thoughts—but always staying away from Luciel.

Finally, last night, Tavarre had drawn him aside as he sat by the fire, casting dice with the other bandits. "We came back here for your sake, lad," the baron had said. "Keep hiding from her, and you'll wake one morning to find it's too late."

Bolstered by Tavarre's words, Cathan had taken one of the horses this morning, and ridden back to town. Now, standing at the entry of Wentha's sickroom, he found he could go no farther. He knew what she would look like—he'd seen his parents die, and Tancred too—but still he couldn't face her. That wasn't his sister in the bed anyway. His sister was gone. Sighing, he shut the door.

"She's a valiant girl," said Fendrilla. The old woman stood near him, grave and ancient. She had aged ten years over the summer. "She fights."

Cathan nodded, not wanting to hear it. "You'll keep looking after her?" he asked. "Until—until—"

"You know I will, lad." She rested a bird-bone hand on his shoulder. "I wish you'd let me pray for her."

Shaking his head, he stepped away from the old woman. The gods had abandoned him, abandoned Wentha. Paladine was far from Taol. The *Longosai* was all over the north now, spreading even within Govinna's walls, and neither Kingpriest nor regent had replied to Lord Ossirian's demands. The *Scatas* would come any day now, and the god would do nothing to stop them.

The thud of hoofbeats on the dirt road outside brought Cathan back to the present, and he heard the creak of leather and a grunt as a man jumped down from his saddle. Mail rattled as booted feet hurried toward the house, and Cathan went to the door and flung it open, a hand on his sword. It was Vedro, his stubbled face red from the hard ride. He wore a crossbow across his back and an axe at his belt.

"There you are," he said, and glanced around, at the rocky land around Fendrilla's cottage. "Where's the horse? Tavarre needs it."

"The horse? Why?"

Vedro scratched his neck. "The scouts came back," he said.

"There's a group of riders near here, couple leagues south."

Cathan paused, glancing over his shoulder. Tavarre had asked for the horse only. He ought to stay here. Wentha might live out the week, but she also might not last past the morrow. He knew he didn't have the strength to see her. He'd tried, and his courage had failed.

"All right," he said, hating himself as he spoke the words. Jaw squared, he pushed past Vedro, on toward the spot where he'd tied the gelding Tavarre had given him. "You can have it—but you're taking me, too."

———————◆———————

Taol's hills had a way of channeling the wind. One moment the air was completely still, holding the ghost of summer's warmth, then, suddenly, the pines would bend and gusts would pummel between the crags like a hammer of ice. It was doing this now, and Ilista sat hunched in her saddle, pulling her hood low. Tears froze on her cheeks, and despite her woolen gloves, she could no longer feel her fingertips.

She looked up at the rest of the party. Sir Gareth and his men bore up with typical Solamnic stoicism, their armor and visored helms keeping some of the cold at bay. They glanced this way and that, watching the slopes for trouble. Her eyes drifted past them, to the figure who rode beside her. Beldyn sat erect on his brown palfrey, his head bare, his hair whipping behind him. If the wind troubled him at all, he gave no sign.

They'd left the monastery weeks ago, Beldyn bidding his brethren farewell then riding away without looking back. Turning north, they had crossed the golden grasses of the Schalland Plains as the sun beat down upon them, then endured torrential rains as they threaded their way through the Khalkist mountains. The young monk remained untroubled through it all, his piercing blue eyes always fixed on the horizon before them.

At last, five days ago, the Khalkists had given way to craggy foothills, and the party passed between a pair of white, ivy-covered obelisks that marked the empire's border. Ilista had signed the triangle as they passed, whispering a prayer of thanks, but Beldyn had done more, reining in to stare at the standing stones. She'd watched as he dismounted and walked over to one, running his fingers over its smooth edges. His eyes had seemed to shine even brighter than usual when he returned to his saddle.

She'd asked what was wrong, and he'd shaken his head.

"Nothing—a feeling. As if I were coming home."

They would be at the Lordcity in a fortnight, if they kept pace. Ilista shut her eyes, picturing it—riding with Beldyn through Istar's streets, then on to the Temple, where the Kingpriest lingered on the edge of death. She'd spoken to Loralon a few times over their journey, using the enchanted orb, and the news he'd given her was grim. Symeon had suffered a second seizure, and it was a miracle he still lived at all. Brother Purvis had found him near death, slumped over in his bed, and Stefara had saved him, but just barely. His mind, the healer said, was all but gone. The Kingpriest lay senseless, taking water and food. He would live a few more weeks, then Paladine would take him. Nothing could stop it now.

Ilista smiled, as she had smiled then. Stefara didn't know about the Lightbringer. She pictured it in her mind: Beldyn kneeling at Symeon's bedside, praying to Paladine for help. Then the Kingpriest would awake, his shattered body and mind whole once more—

Gareth stopped suddenly, raising his hand. "Hsst!"

Snapping out of her reverie, Ilista reined in her horse. Hands on their hilts, the Knights formed a protective ring about her. Amid it all, Beldyn looked about, his brows knitting with confusion. After a moment, he nudged his horse over to Gareth. Ilista joined them, her fingers brushing the new mace she'd taken from the monastery.

"Trouble?" she whispered.

Gareth raised a finger to his lips, and Ilista fell silent. Nerves tingling, she glanced up at the slopes. They were steep, dotted with mossy boulders and swaying trees. Plenty of shadows in which to hide. Up ahead, a narrow cataract foamed down several layers of rock, making noise enough to drown out the whisper of boots on stone, or steel sliding against leather.

Beside her, Beldyn nodded slowly, his face smooth and his eyes closed. "It begins," he murmured.

Ilista blinked. She was about to ask what he meant when the sound of hoofbeats rose ahead, echoing among the hills, growing steadily louder. She looked up and saw one of the Knights, a tall, silent youth named Reginar who had been riding point, gallop around a bend. He reined in, his horse snorting as it tossed its head.

"Road's blocked," he panted, pushing up his visor. "A tree, some rocks."

Gareth made a face, looking up the hillside. "A barricade. Like as not, we're being watched."

"We are," Beldyn said.

Ilista looked at him sharply, but his gaze was far away, looking north, beyond the hills. He still appeared unworried, his face holding the satisfied look of a man who just figured out a clue to a troubling riddle. Before she could ask him anything, Gareth leaned close, his eyes stone-dark.

"*Efisa*, we should turn back."

Her eyes lingered on Beldyn, however, and the Knight had to touch her arm to rouse her. "Uh?" she asked, then his words sank in and she nodded. "Very well. There's another pass to the south. We can—"

She never finished. Beldyn jabbed his heels into his horse's flanks, and suddenly he was galloping forward, past the startled Knights and on down the road.

"Beldyn!" Ilista cried. On instinct, she spurred her own mare after him.

Gareth grabbed for her robes, but he didn't catch hold of her, and she heard him swear behind her. A moment later, the clatter of mail told her the Knight was giving chase, his men with him. She kept her eyes on Beldyn as he rounded the shoulder of a hill. Her mare snorted, hooves thumping against the stony ground. They were heading into a trap—he had to know it, as well as she did. Why—

She came upon the tree so suddenly, she barely had time to pull up, saving her horse from spearing itself on the broken stubs of branches. It was an oak, its leaves fringed flame-orange, its trunk wide enough to crush any hopes of jumping over it. Beldyn stood his palfrey just before it, looking about. The young monk was calm, his eyes gleaming as he looked up the hillside, as if awaiting someone.

"What are you *doing*?" she asked, grabbing his arm. "We have to get away from here *now*!"

"Too late," said a firm voice.

Ilista started, twisting in her saddle to follow Beldyn's gaze. On an outcropping partway up the northern slope stood a short, wiry man in a mail shirt and hooded cloak. He cradled a crossbow in his arms, a quarrel on the string. He nodded to her, and turned his head west, toward the clamor of the approaching Knights. Then he lifted his head and let out a raptor's shriek.

To either side of the road, the hills came alive as more than a score of cloaked figures appeared. They rose from the shadows, stepping out of the undergrowth or from behind boulders, armed with crossbows and slings. Their armor was lighter than the first man's—leather breastplates, mostly, some with metal studs—and all had shortswords or axes at their belts. Ilista knew at once they were trapped. Gareth and his men could put up a fight, but they would never overcome them all. Even so, she reached for her mace, her blood pounding in her ears.

"Yield!" called the bandits' leader. "Throw down your arms, and this will end without bloodshed!"

Everything seemed to slow. Ilista held her breath. Beside her Gareth's horse danced sideways as he drew his sword. He was a Solamnic Knight. It went against his honor to surrender without a fight. Beneath his raised visor, his moustache twisted into a warlike snarl. The other Knights yanked their blades from their scabbards.

The bandit chief raised his hand while the ring of steel echoed among the hills, then brought it chopping down. Ilista heard the snap of crossbow strings, and a steel quarrel buried itself in the ground before her. Her horse reared, whinnying, as more bolts narrowly missed the Knights as well. Ilista hauled on her reins, trying to control her mare. Beldyn did not budge.

"That was a warning," the lead bandit proclaimed. "Next time, we won't aim to miss."

Ilista was still staring at the quarrel when a hand touched her arm. Startled, she turned to meet Beldyn's cool, assured gaze.

"Do as he says," he said.

Caught by his penetrating eyes, Ilista found she had no choice but to obey. Her mace thumped on the ground.

"At least the Revered Daughter has a brain," the bandit declared, and chuckled. "Now. The rest of you do the same."

"Never!" Gareth cried, brandishing his sword. "We do not give to highway—"

"MarSevrin," the bandit said.

Something white flew down from the hillside, and the Knight's fierce glare vanished in a red spray as it struck him, just beneath his open visor. He slumped against his horse's neck, then toppled from the saddle with a crash. His sword skittered from his hand, and he lay still, his face covered with blood.

Ilista looked at him, aghast, then turned to the younger Knights, as they began to raise their own blades. "No! Enough!" she shouted. "Stop this, before you get us all killed!"

The Knights looked at her, then at Gareth, then at one another. One by one, they dropped their swords.

"Very wise," the lead bandit noted. "Now dismount, all of you, and don't move."

Beldyn moved first, a strange smile curling his lips. He hadn't flinched, even when Gareth fell. Ilista and the Knights followed, keeping their hands up. Several ruffians half-climbed, half-slid down the slope while the rest kept their crossbows trained on the party.

Ilista looked at Beldyn as they approached. "What now?"

He shrugged, unafraid. "We go with them," he said. "Fear not, *Efisa*. We are in the god's hands."

She would have asked him more, but just then one of the bandits grabbed her and pulled a sack over her head, blocking out the world.

———◆———

Night fell as the bandits rode back to camp. They covered the last few miles by torchlight, leading their blindfolded captives up a winding game trail. At last, as the gibbous red moon was rising, they passed sentries and rode down into the gorge to where the rest of the gang waited. A great cheer went up as they led the hostages into the camp.

Cathan moved quickly to the camp's central yard, watching as his fellows forced their captives down onto their knees upon the dusty ground. His eyes settled on three figures in particular amid the cluster of Solamnic Knights. One was the Revered Daughter who had first surrendered her weapon, the group's leader, apparently, her white robes fringed with violet. The second was her companion, a monk who seemed too young for his gray cassock. He was a strange one, carrying himself with such assurance that but for the sack covering his head, he might have been an honored guest rather than a prisoner.

The third, the one to whom Cathan's gaze kept returning, was the commander of the Knights, the man he'd felled with a single, well-aimed piece of his family's broken holy symbol. The man hadn't regained consciousness and had made the journey slung over his saddle. Now, as the bandits untied the cords securing him to his horse, he slid limply to the ground. Cathan felt sick as he looked upon the Knight's senseless form, the face crusted with dried blood. His thoughts harked back to the guard captain in Govinna.

You've killed again, a cold voice said in his head.

One by one, the bandits pulled off their captives' blindfolds, laughing as the Knights winced in the bright light of the camp's fires. Tavarre unmasked the priestess last of all, bowing as she squinted in the glare.

"Welcome, Your Grace," he said, his scar deepening as he grinned. "First Daughter Ilista, isn't it? I remember you from the last time I attended His Holiness's court. I am Tavarre, fourteenth Baron of Luciel. These are my loyal vassals."

He gestured to the bandits, who laughed again. Ilista blinked at him, then her eyes widened. Beneath his shaggy beard and grime-streaked face, Tavarre was still recognizable as the nobleman she'd once met.

"Baron . . . ?" she began. "But why? To fall in with common ruffians—"

The bandits rumbled at this, but Tavarre silenced them with a look. "Pardon, *Efisa*," he said, "but these are no mere ruffians. Most were my subjects not long ago, and I lived in a keep, not a hollow in the hills." He glanced around, shrugging. "Things change, but now, I tire—as do you, I'm sure. We will talk more on the morrow."

He signaled to his men, who started forward. Before they could take two steps, however, the priestess raised her hand— an imperious gesture that gave the bordermen pause, even though she was their captive.

"Wait," she said. "What about Sir Gareth?"

Cathan followed Tavarre's gaze to the fallen Knight, then watched as the baron knelt down and eased off his helmet. Gareth's forehead was livid, the flesh puffy and dark where Cathan's shot had struck. The blood had clotted in his receding hair.

Tavarre probed the wound with his fingers, then looked up and shook his head as the Knight groaned. "His skull's cracked," he said. "The swelling's pushing the bone into his brain. It's a wonder he survived this long. I'm sorry, Your Grace—no one can help him."

"I can."

Everyone turned at the sound of the soft, musical voice. The strange young monk was looking at Gareth, his ice-blue eyes gleaming. Now he looked up, sweeping the crowd with his strange gaze. Cathan caught his breath as their eyes met. There was something in Beldyn's serene expression that made hope leap within him, just for an instant. I believe him, Cathan thought, wondering. Huma's silver arm—who *is* this monk?

Tavarre met Beldyn's look with skepticism, though. "I've seen wounds like this before," he said. "Even a Mishakite healer would have trouble with it."

"Maybe so," the monk said, "but I am no Mishakite."

Silence settled over the camp, punctuated by coughs among the bandits. Cathan glanced at them, and saw their brows furrowed as well. They had seen something in the monk's face too.

"Let him try," the First Daughter said. "What have you to lose?"

Tavarre frowned, scratching his beard. He gave the monk another long, hard look, then shrugged. "Very well, but no trickery."

Smiling, Beldyn got to his feet. He walked to Sir Gareth and knelt beside him, bending low to examine the gruesome ruin of his face. His fingers came away red. Tavarre shook his head again but said nothing as Beldyn signed the triangle over the Knight's motionless form. That done, the monk cupped his left hand over the wound, then pressed his right over his own breast. His expression blank, he took a deep breath and began to pray.

"Palado, ucdas pafiro, tas pelo laigam fat, mifiso soram flonat. Tis biram cailud, e tas oram nomass lud bipum. Sifat."

Paladine, father of dawn, thy touch is a balm, thy presence ends pain. Heal this man, and let thy grace enfold us. So be it.

A deep silence settled over the camp as Beldyn waited. Even the usual sounds—the whisper of the pines in the breeze, the chatter of night-birds, the crackle of the campfires—fell away, and the world seemed to constrict, pulling tighter and tighter until there was nothing but the place where the monk's hand touched the Knight's broken skull. No one breathed. No one dared. A minute passed, then another.

Nothing happened.

Cathan shook his head. He should have known better. The god was far from this place. Looking at Lady Ilista's stricken face, he couldn't help but smirk. She'd truly believed the monk could do it, believed with every bit of faith in her, and now that faith had failed her. Cathan chuckled to himself, knowing how she felt.

"Well," Tavarre said. "I think we've wasted enough—"

"Mother of Paladine!" one of the bandits gasped, pointing. "Look!"

Cathan turned back to Beldyn, his eyes narrowing—then they widened into a stare of amazement. The young monk still hunched over Gareth, but now there was a silvery shimmer, like sunlight on water, where he touched the Knight's wound. Cathan blinked, afraid his eyes were playing tricks, as the shimmer became a gleam, then a glow, bathing Beldyn and Gareth both in its radiance. The monk squeezed his eyes shut, his face lined with concentration. Sweat beaded on his forehead, his lips pulled back from clenched teeth, muscles tightened in his arms and neck . . .

Light flared, as bright as the sun.

CHAPTER 13 ▼

The light flowed outward, flooding the courtyard and casting sharp shadows from the tents and trees beyond. Horses shied, and the bandits and their captives alike turned away, throwing up their arms to ward off the blinding glare. Vedro growled, his sword rising as he stepped toward the light, but Tavarre grabbed his arm before he could get near the young monk, shaking his head. Eerie, musical sound, like a carillon of glass bells, filled the air.

When the light finally faded, it took the music with it, leaving the camp utterly silent. Blinking against the green ghosts it left in their eyes, the bandits leaned in, crowding closer and murmuring in wonder at what they saw.

Sir Gareth didn't move, nor did he wake, but the light had cleansed the blood from his face and smoothed the lines of pain around his mouth. Of the horrible, purple swelling that had marked his forehead, only a faint white scar remained, fading as the bandits watched. Beneath his breastplate, his chest rose and fell steadily. Moments ago, he had been dying. Now he looked like a man who had just fallen asleep.

The silvery glow continued to shimmer around Beldyn for nearly a minute after. He knelt amid it, eyes still closed, his cheeks tracked with tears. His skin had turned fever-pale, and his lips trembled. Finally, the wisps of light clinging to him died, and he sat back with a shuddering sigh. His head drooped wearily, his chin touching his chest.

Ilista's wondering gaze went from him to Gareth and back again. She had known he was capable of this—her vanished wounds from the wyvern attack had made that clear—but seeing it with her own eyes was different. She had watched Stefara and other Mishakites work their healing arts many times before, but Beldyn possessed greater power than any of the others by far.

She signed the triangle, then looked at the bandits. They shook themselves, blinking blearily, as though waking from a dream. Tavarre and Vedro stood side by side, wearing matching looks of wide-eyed awe.

"Do you believe now?" she asked.

Tavarre swallowed, then raised his hand and scratched his beard. His men tensed, waiting, and Ilista knew that whatever the baron said, they would follow. He met the gaze of a young bandit, the one who had felled Sir Gareth with his sling, who nodded slowly.

"I nearly think I do," said the young bandit. "Can he do it again?"

<hr />

Cathan hurtled up to Fendrilla's cottage at a gallop, leaping out of the saddle before his horse even stopped. He hammered on the door, calling the old woman's name. She opened it, holding a candle and peering at him tiredly. It was still three hours before sunrise.

He barged past her without a word, ignoring her questions as he strode through the common room to the smaller chamber where his sister lay. Fendrilla plucked at his sleeve, trying to stop him, but he shook her off, grasping the door's latch and creaking it open. He stuck his head into the gloom within.

"Wentha?" he whispered.

The shape beneath the blankets stirred, moaning. She tried to speak, her voice so thin, then fell into a fit of coughing—wet, tearing hacks that wouldn't stop.

Cathan was at her side in two steps, on one knee by her bed, holding the hem of his cloak to her lips until the spasm passed. It came away flecked with blood, putting a chill in his heart, and he reached out to stroke her face. Her skin was hot and sweaty, drawn taut over her cheekbones. A sheen of sweat covered everything. Her eyes rolled, the pupils huge as she tried to focus on him.

"Hush, Blossom," he said. "It's me. I've brought someone."

"Cathan?" Fendrilla called from the common room. "Cathan, there are riders outside!"

Rising, he turned and hurried to the door. "It's all right," he told the old woman. "Light some candles. I'll be back in a moment."

Tavarre was already afoot, striding toward the cottage. A pair of bandits lingered behind him, minding the horses, and a few more stood near the white- and gray-robed forms of Lady Ilista and Brother Beldyn, keeping their crossbows ready. When the baron saw the anxious look on Cathan's face, he motioned for the clerics to follow him inside.

"The girl," Beldyn said as he came close. The pallor and weakness that had afflicted him after he'd healed Sir Gareth were gone, and his eyes glittered in the moonlight. "She is your sister?"

Cathan nodded.

"Take me to her."

Fendrilla shrank back as Cathan led the others inside. He took a candle from her hands, nodding reassuringly, but his heart was hammering as he entered the sickroom again. A gasp burst from his lips as the taper's glow fell over Wentha's face. The *Longosai* had nearly run its course. Her wasted skin was covered with blotches and sores, some weeping, others crusted over. Her thin hair—once honey-hued, now colorless—clung to her scalp in patches. Her staring eyes were bloodshot, her lips dry and cracked, her throat swollen and black. Turn away! his mind screamed. Instead, though, he forced himself to look at her, gaze at her with love, through stinging tears.

Then Beldyn was there, looking down at the bed. He didn't shy from her plague-ravaged features. Instead he smiled, reaching out to brush a stringy lock from her eyes.

"It's all right, child," he said. "I am here."

She stared back at him, eyes wide with confusion and fear. There was madness there too, and Cathan felt ill, his thoughts going back to their brother. Tancred had looked that way, in the end. It was all Cathan could do not to break down in tears.

Beldyn's smile didn't falter, though. Instead, he signed the triangle and rested his hand on her brow. Shutting her eyes, he began to speak, softly at first.

"Palado, ucdas pafiro . . ."

Cathan knew to expect the light this time and shut his eyes as it blazed from the monk's hand. Even so, it still surprised him, coming on quicker than before, then flaring brighter than it had with Sir Gareth. It filled the room, stabbing out through windows and gaps in the thatch above, silver knives cutting through the night. The light blazed around Cathan, but there was no heat to it at all. In fact, it was cool against his skin, soothing. Even from a distance, he felt the day's aches lift away, taking his grief with them and leaving a delicate hope behind.

All at once, the light was gone. Darkness flowed out of the room's corners again.

The first thing Cathan noticed was the smell. The stink of disease was gone, and in its place—though faint—the attar of roses hung in the air. Half-afraid of what he might see, he opened his eyes to look.

Beldyn had fallen back from the bed, and Ilista bore him up, grasping his arms, as he gasped for breath. His face was the same ashen color as his travel-stained habit, and his breath whistled in his chest. The light clung to him, reluctant to leave now that the miracle was done. It flickered stubbornly, like a candle flame fighting the wind. The god's power had taken more out of him this time—but that didn't surprise Cathan. The Knight had been dying, but he hadn't suffered for weeks beforehand, as Wentha had.

It was harder to look at Wentha. Cathan could hear the change that had come over her—her breathing had lost its harshness, no longer halting. It was evening out into a slow, soft rhythm, but he still feared what his eyes might see. If she was still wasted and frail, he thought he might go mad. He touched his sword, not sure who he would use it on if his sister was still dying: Beldyn or himself. Before long, though, the not knowing became too heavy to bear. Swallowing, he let his gaze drift to the bed.

He saw a little girl asleep, golden hair pooled about her head. She was still thin, weak from her illness, but her cheeks were pink again, the lips no longer twisted into a grimace. Her sores were gone, as was the swelling in her throat. But for her frailty, the *Longosai* might never have touched her— and the frailty would soon disappear as well. Though she slept, her thin lips were curled into a smile.

It was too much. Oblivious to Beldyn or anyone else, Cathan fell forward onto the bed, buried his face in the blankets, and sobbed.

———◆—◆◆—◆———

Wentha MarSevrin was only the first. Ilista and Beldyn spent the rest of the night in Luciel, and all of the following day. There were only a few dozen people left in the village— the rest lost to the plague, fled, or gone to join the bandits— and the young monk insisted on visiting them all. More to the point, so did Lord Tavarre, and as he held their lives, and the Knights' in his grasp, the baron had final say. He and his men led Beldyn from home to home, and again and again the holy light fell upon the wretched forms of men, women, and children. Each time, when it faded, all traces of disease were gone, and the once-doomed fell into a peaceful, life-giving sleep.

Beldyn weakened as the hours passed, falling into a deeper trance every time he invoked the god's power. Each time it took him longer to regain his strength, and each time the glow that hung about him afterward seemed to linger longer. By midmorning his debility lasted an hour with each healing. By the afternoon it was two. Ilista pleaded with Tavarre to put a halt to it, but the baron refused. So did Beldyn. Stubbornly he pressed on, spurning food and drink, intent only on healing everyone that he could.

Finally, as the sun set behind the distant Khalkists, the light did not die as he lifted his hand from an old man who had once been the town weaver. Even as the man—the tenth he had seen since he began—lay slumbering peacefully, a smile on his swarthy face, Beldyn collapsed, slumping to the ground without a sound. Ilista hurried to his side, probing his wrist for the lifebeat, then turned on the baron, her mouth a hard line.

"Enough," she said, and to her surprise the lord of Luciel agreed.

The silver moon rose at midwatch that night. Its light found Ilista in an upper room of the village's sole tavern, dozing on a stool beside the chamber's simple bed. Beldyn lay beneath the blankets, his face drawn and wan, his eyes moving rapidly beneath their closed lids. The light had finally begun to fade, but it still surrounded him like a mist, its eerie glow making her shadow loom large on the wall.

The door's latch rattled, rousing her with a jolt, and she turned to see Tavarre come in. In his hands were two steaming mugs. The aroma of tarbean tea filled the air. He crossed to her, glancing at the plate of cabbage and rabbit meat that sat untouched on the floor next to a full cup of watered wine, then offered one of the mugs. She took it gladly, cupping her hands around it to warm herself. The autumn nights were cold in the highlands.

The baron stood silent beside her, drinking his tea and gazing at the young monk. He made no apologies for slaving Beldyn until he passed out, and Ilista knew he might well do it again as soon as the monk regained his senses. She couldn't blame him either. These were his people, and finally he had a chance to save them. Would she do the same, in his place? Probably, she thought.

"This changes things," he said after a time. "I had hoped to keep you captive. The First Daughter of Paladine would make as fine a hostage as the Little Emperor—perhaps better. Now, though. . . ." He broke off, sighing, and brushed a hand across his eyes. "I only wish you had come sooner."

He has lost someone dear to him, Ilista thought, studying his stricken face. That's why he threw in with the bandits.

"What will you do now?" she asked.

Tavarre came back to himself slowly. "Keep you here," he said, "until the last of my people are healed. I must do that much. After that you can go, but. . . ." He trailed off, looking at the floor.

"But what?"

He shrugged. "We're not the only village in the highlands, and the *Longosai*'s all over Govinna now, from the messages I've gotten." He shook his head. "It seems a terrible waste for one with such gifts to go to the Lordcity, where all is well."

Ilista shook her head firmly. "All is *not* well in the Lordcity. The Kingpriest is dying, and *his* power can save him." She gestured at Beldyn, who lay still, the strange light diminished to a few glittering motes. "If we can heal Symeon, I can convince him to send help to Taol. If he dies, Kurnos will take the throne—and I fear all he'll send are soldiers."

Tavarre made a face, clearly not liking any part of that, but he was a practical man, and nodded. "Another few days," he said. "Then you can go. I hope that, when the Kingpriest is cured, one of the things he sends back to us is *him*."

They drank their tea in silence, both lost in thought, until gradually the light around Beldyn went out. He stirred, shifting in the bed, then his eyes opened. They pierced the dark, bright and clear in the moonlight. Seeing them, Ilista felt an unreasoning stab of fear. There was something new in the bright gaze, a zeal she hadn't seen before, and at once she knew why. He had spent much of his life in the monastery. Now, out in the world, he could use his powers as he never had before. He was helping people, and he reveled in the act, as some men lived for drink or the dreamseed they smoked in Karthay.

He sat up, pushing off the blankets. "I am ready," he said. "We can begin again."

Tavarre gave him no argument, and while Ilista had a mind to, she didn't get the chance. Beldyn was on his feet already, straightening his habit as he made his way to the door. Both she and the baron had to hurry to keep up with him as he headed out into the hall, then down the steps.

The baron's hulking man-at-arms was waiting in the dim common room. When they appeared, he leaped to his feet, striding quickly toward them. Ilista drew back, grabbing Beldyn's sleeve and pulling him back, but Vedro ignored them, drawing close to Tavarre instead and whispering in his ear.

"They are?" Tavarre asked, scowling. "Who?"

"MarSevrin, of course," Vedro replied. "A few others. I told them to shove off, but—"

"What's the trouble?" Ilista asked.

Tavarre and Vedro glanced up, their eyes sliding past the First Daughter, to Beldyn.

"Nothing," the baron replied. "A few of the lads are waiting outside, is all."

"Waiting . . . for me?" the monk asked. His eyebrows rose. "Why?"

"To thank you, they say," Vedro replied.

Though she couldn't say why, Ilista suddenly felt cold. She didn't think the bandits had harm in mind. Tavarre and his man didn't seem worried about that, and besides, it would make no sense. Nonetheless, a shiver of apprehension ran through her.

"Don't," she told Beldyn. "I don't like this. We can go out the back."

The monk looked at her, though, and her protests died before his glittering gaze. He smiled at her. "No, *Efisa*. If they wish to show gratitude, I will not deny them."

When they emerged from the tavern, they found a small crowd standing in the street. Most were bandits, although there were also villagers—those who had been spared the plague. At the fore was Cathan, whose sister had been the first Beldyn healed. He smiled when he saw the monk, wearing a look of utter admiration.

"All right," said Tavarre. "What's this about?"

Cathan's face all but glowed as he stepped forward. He reached across his body and started to draw his sword.

Hissing between his teeth, Vedro leaped forward, and Tavarre followed a heartbeat later. Beldyn raised his hand, however.

"Be easy, my friends," he said. "He means no harm. Do you, my son?"

The young bandit had stopped in his tracks, taken aback by the sudden movement of the baron and his man. He shook his head, and warily Tavarre and Vedro drew back. Despite Beldyn's assurances, however, Ilista held her breath as Cathan's blade rasped from its scabbard. It flashed in the moonlight as he raised it, pressing its quillons to his lips. Carefully, he laid it on the ground before Beldyn's feet, then dropped to his knees in the dust.

"I give you my oath," he said, bowing his head. "You gave me back my world last night. You've shown me the god's true face, when I had sworn never to look upon it again. My life is yours."

Tavarre's mouth dropped open as the others—bandits and villagers alike—followed suit. These were his subjects, and they were pledging fealty to another. He made no move to stop them, however, and when he recovered from his initial shock he nodded, understanding.

Beldyn stepped forward to lay his hand on Cathan's head—a curiously fatherly gesture, between two men of such tender age—and his musical voice rang out. "I did not ask for your life, my friend," he said, "but I accept your loyalty just the same. It may be that I have need of it one day."

Suddenly, he changed. For a moment the monk swam before Ilista's eyes, and he was a monk no more. His cassock was gone, and in its place were robes of pearly satin, shimmering with more light than the moon alone could explain. Jewels adorned his fingers, wrists and throat, and a familiar jeweled breastplate glittered over his vestments. It was the imperial raiment, but the crown on his brow was not the sapphire tiara Symeon wore. It was heavier, older, encrusted not with sapphires but with rubies.

Great god, she thought. It's—

Just as suddenly, the vision was gone. Beldyn stepped back from Cathan, and he was as before, his habit smeared and frayed. Ilista blinked, looking at Tavarre and the others. None of them had seen what she had.

You didn't see anything, either, she told herself. You're overtired, that's all. Too many false visions have come from men who simply needed sleep.

Still, as Beldyn moved among the other bandits, touching each in turn, she found she couldn't shake the chill that lodged deep under her skin.

The next night, at her request, Tavarre agreed to let her have Loralon's orb. Beldyn, who had spent the day healing the folk of Luciel, slumbered in his room at the tavern, shrouded with sparkling light. For the first time since the bandits captured them, she was left alone, and she crept into another darkened room to invoke the crystal's magic. She spoke the elf's name, and soon, his face swam before her.

Loralon frowned, listening carefully as she spoke of the ambush and what had happened since. She didn't mention her vision, having decided it was only a hallucination brought on by fatigue, but she told him about everything else—including the oath Cathan and the other bandits had sworn to Beldyn.

At last he stirred, his eyes narrowing. "How many, would you say?" he asked.

"About a dozen," she replied. "There might be others, though, once the word spreads. Emissary, what should I do?"

Loralon paused, stroking his beard. He was silent a good while, then his shoulders rose and fell. "Nothing, yet. There is a purpose to this, I believe—though what, I don't know. Put your faith in Paladine, *Efisa*—all things have a purpose."

A sound came from his door. She saw Loralon look over his shoulder, and the door of his chamber swing open. Quarath, his aide, stepped in and silently proffered a scroll.

Frowning, Loralon held up a slender finger to Ilista. She watched as he turned and took the missive from the younger elf. Quarath bowed, then departed as the Emissary broke the seal and unfurled the parchment. He scanned down its length, then stopped, his already pale complexion turning almost translucent as he read it again. When he rolled it up and turned back toward the orb, he looked every one of his five hundred years. Ilista caught her breath. In all the time she'd known him, she'd never seen Loralon so distraught.

"Your Grace, I'm afraid I must go to the manse at once," he said, his voice hollow. He paused, and she could see it in his eyes before he licked his lips and spoke the words she dreaded to hear.

"The Kingpriest is dead."

CHAPTER 14 ▼

For three days, the Revered Daughters took over the manse and shut out all others, including the imperial servants. It was their task to see to the Kingpriest's body, performing secret rituals to protect him from decay. They washed him ritually, painted the sacred triangle on his forehead, and removed his innards, burning them and placing the ashes in an urn, then pouring holy oil on top and sealing it with red wax. Some said they added their own blood to the ashes, but only the priestesses knew for sure. Others said there was sorcery involved, but none could prove it. The only light that burned in the windows of the manse came from funerary candles, and the only sound was the Daughters' voices, raised to a high, keening wail.

While the priestesses went about their secret rites, the Revered Sons saw to the people. Priests of the god rode through the city on golden chariots, accompanied by squads of Knights and *Scatas*, stopping at every crossroads and plaza to make the official pronouncement. "*Binarud, Istaras farnas, usas stimno ruhat,*" they proclaimed, their deep voices echoing among the arches and domes.

Mourn, children of Istar, for the god's voice is silenced.

In the past, the folk of Istar had sometimes rioted after the death of the Kingpriest. Folk still told the tales of the burning that followed Theorollyn's murder, and the Night of Ten Thousand Spears, when the imperial army had moved in after five days of unrest following the passing of Ardosean II. With Symeon, though, it was different. The hierarchs had made it known he was ill, and besides, he had named an heir. Folk were not yet calling Kurnos the Kingpriest, for he had not yet taken the throne, but they had already begun to argue in the wine shops over what sort of ruler he would make. Most prayed at shrines and hung blue cloths outside their homes, but a few still followed the old ways, wailing, rending their garments, and smashing pottery in the streets. The priests frowned upon such practices but did nothing to stop them. This was not the time to arrest folk for heresy.

The Great Temple fell into mourning. The basilica's crystal dome, which ordinarily shone brilliant white, shifted to somber azure during the grieving time, and the song of the bells in the central spire turned doleful. The statues in the Temple's courtyards wept real tears, it was said, and the blooms in the Kingpriest's private rose garden withered and fell to dust.

At last, on the fourth day, the Revered Daughters emerged from the manse to bear the Kingpriest's body to the basilica. There it lay upon a rose-marble bier within the Hall of Audience, surrounded by wreaths of blue roses. Much of the clergy spent the next three days in prayer near the Kingpriest's body, while noblemen, merchant princes, and dignitaries came to pay homage. All who visited left some token—opals and pearls, spices and scented balms—upon the bier, for Symeon to bear into the afterlife.

At last, at twilight on the sixth day, the funeral began. The faithful gathered in the Lordcity's midst, the mighty filling the basilica, the common folk packing the wide expanses of the *Barigon*, while choirs of elves sang a solemn paean. In the Hall of Audience, Balthera, still acting as First Daughter in Ilista's absence, laid a shroud of spun silver over the bier, kissing the triangle on Symeon's forehead before she covered his face forever. Then, as the mourners bowed their heads but Kurnos—

wearing the Kingpriest's jeweled breastplate but not yet his crown—stepped forward to stand before Symeon's body. His face grave but proud, he began the liturgy for the imperial dead.

"*Aulforam ansinfamo*," he prayed, "*Symeon Poubirta, gasiras cilmo e usas stimno.*"

We send forth our sovereign, Symeon IV, lord of emperors and voice of the god.

Within the Hall the mourners stirred, the response rising from them like distant thunder. The crystal dome caught the words and rang with them, so those in the square outside heard and spoke it as well, tens of thousands of voices rising into the deepening sky. "*Ansinfamo.*"

The liturgy went on, with Kurnos reciting the deeds of the Kingpriest's life and reign and entreating Paladine to spare him the torments of the Abyss and give him comfort beyond the stars. Again and again the basilica, and then the *Barigon*, rumbled with the responses. Finally, two hours after he began, Kurnos walked around the bier, pausing at each corner to sign the triangle, then stopped again at its head to deliver the final benediction.

"*Oporud, Symeon*," he intoned. "*Palado tas drifas bisat.*"

Farewell, Symeon. May Paladine guide thy steps.

"*Sifat*," murmured the Lordcity.

At that, a silver gong sounded from the balcony overlooking the Hall, and the bier burst into flame.

Those who didn't know the ritual and who hadn't been at the funeral of Symeon III eight years before gasped as fire rose from the Kingpriest's body. Ghostly white limned with blue, the flames leaped from the bier, twining like dancers or lovers as they rose higher and higher. No one moved to flee, for the mourners knew these flames did no harm. There was no smoke, so smell of burning, no heat to bake the air. It was a cleansing, holy fire, and though its tongues licked close to his body, Kurnos did not flinch as it blossomed up and up, finally brushing the crystal dome.

A ringing filled the air, loud and pure, as the sacred fire bathed the dome. Out in the city, folk exclaimed in wonder as the blue light that had shone above the basilica for the past six days flared star-white, then settled back to its familiar silver. Within the Hall of Audience, the flames surrounding the body flickered, then vanished, leaving no scorch marks behind. The lords and clerics who filled the vast chamber stared at the body beneath the silver shroud, signing the triangle. The god had shown his favor and claimed Symeon's soul. The Kingpriest was gone, and now all eyes turned to the figure at the bier's head.

Kurnos turned and strode across the Hall, the crowds parting as he headed for the dais and the golden throne. He paused to genuflect at the foot of the steps, then ascended slowly, stopping on the second-highest stair. No man, save the Kingpriest himself, could mount the topmost. Raising his hands in entreaty, he turned to face the mourners.

"*Ec, Kurnos, lufo e Forpurmo, ceram fecapio,*" he proclaimed. "*Pelgo me biseddit?*"

I, Kurnos, heir and First Son, lay claim to the crown. Will any speak against me?

The hall was silent, save for the occasional quiet cough. Folk looked at one another nervously. It had been at this point in the ritual, with Vasari II on the verge of donning his new topaz crown, when Pradian had appeared in his emerald diadem to challenge him. Today, however, no one said a word, and a smile split Kurnos's red beard.

"*Sam gennud,*" he declared, "*tus stulo loisit nispitur.*"

Then bring it forward, so the throne shall stand empty no more.

The mourners turned as the golden doors opened at the room's far end. Loralon emerged, clad not in funereal blue but in the god's silver. Quarath walked a pace behind him, bearing a white satin cushion. Upon this lay the Kingpriest's sapphire tiara. The crowd parted as the two approached, striding past the bier at a slow, steady pace, then bowing before the dais. Quarath stopped, proffering the cushion, and the elder elf took the tiara and climbed the steps.

"*Kurnos, usas farno,*" Loralon spoke, "*gasiro brud calfos bid iridam e oram?*"

Kurnos, child of the god, will you rule this empire with justice and mercy?

Eyes shining, Kurnos nodded. "*Ospiro.*"

I swear.

"*Sas ladad smidos, tair sifi ponfos?*"

Will you smite its enemies, wherever they are found?

"*Ospiro.*"

"*Usam motilos, e sas bollas somli?*"

Will you speak for the god and work his will?

"*Ospiro.*"

"Very well." Loralon raised the tiara, whose sapphires sparkled in the dome's light. "*Fe Paladas cado, bid Istaras apalo, tam Baham agito.*"

In Paladine's name, with Istar's might, I name thee Kingpriest.

With that, he set the crown upon Kurnos's head. Regent and First Son no longer, Kurnos raised his head, signing the triangle to the court as its ruler for the first time. Then, amid cries of "*Sa, Kurnos Porsto!*"—Hail, Kurnos the First!—he mounted the dais's highest step and walked at last to his throne.

Far beneath the Great Temple, carved out of the bedrock, was a vast, dark crypt known as the *Fidas Cor Selo*, the House of Old Emperors. The *Selo* predated the temple itself, for Istar's old warlords had originally built it beneath their great palace at the Lordcity's midst. That palace had long since vanished, torn down by the first Kingpriest, but the ancient sepulcher remained. Within lay the remains of every true ruler of Istar, on slabs of marble within great pillared vaults. Alabaster reliefs more than twenty feet tall covered the doors of each tomb, sculpted into huge, lifelike images of the men interred within. The old warlords' faces had worn away over the years and now stared facelessly out into the gloom, but the Kingpriests' remained as sharp as the day they were sculpted—protected, some said, by the god's grace—staring into the gloom with eyes of stone.

Walking through the sepulcher, one could gaze upon centuries of Istarian rulers: the hard visage of Theorollyn II, who had been a gladiator before turning to the priesthood; the benevolent countenance of Sularis of Solamnia; the aged features of Quenndorus the Conciliator, who had quelled the violence following the assassination of Kingpriest Giusecchio; and more than a score of others, many forgotten by all but scholars. These, however, accounted for only a few of the vaults within the catacombs. Beyond them, the tunnels went on and on, lined by tombs that remained open, stone mouths yawning wide, awaiting those who would rule in the centuries to come. Even in its earliest days, Istar's rulers had known their realm would last for thousands of years.

Kurnos stood in a pool of candlelight before one of the empty vaults, surrounded by deep silence. Reaching up to touch the sapphire tiara, still strange-feeling on his brow, he peered into the shadows within.

This is mine, he thought, shivering. One day, I shall lie here.

He looked to his left, at the vault that had been empty only hours ago. After the funeral, the Revered Daughters had borne the body down here—again in secret—and placed it and the offerings his subjects had brought within the tomb. Now it was shut forever, its edges sealed with lead. Nevorian of Calah, one of the empire's greatest sculptors, had already begun work on the cherubic face that would grace the gray-stone door, but for now, there was only a bronze plaque, bearing the name of Symeon IV.

A shiver ran through Kurnos as he read the name. Oh, Holiness, he thought. I put you there.

He tried to forgive himself. It had been Symeon's heart that finished him in the end. Weakened by his illness, it had finally given out while he slept. A gentle passing, Loralon had called it, but Kurnos knew better—yes, the Kingpriest likely wouldn't have recovered from his sickness, and yes, Sathira hadn't killed him outright, but the demon had done damage enough to speed the end along, and she had done it at *his* bidding.

His eyes went to the emerald ring on his finger, and he cringed, as he had every time he'd looked at it, in the weeks after first summoning the demon. Even down here, amid the darkness, he could sense her shadow within the stone. Waiting. With a snarl, he reached for the ring and tried to pull it off. He'd tried to remove it nearly every day since that terrible night, but it didn't budge, though he twisted and twisted it until his finger bled.

"You won't be rid of it that easily."

Kurnos started at the sound of voice. Turning, he peered down the rows of empty vaults, gray shadows in the gloom. There were tales of ghosts—the *Selo* was a burial place, after all—but the cold voice belonged to no spectre. After a moment, he caught his breath, seeing it: a deeper shadow amid the murk. A cold wind seemed to blow through the catacombs as he looked upon the dark hooded figure.

Kurnos had to try a few times before his voice came. "Why not? I am Kingpriest now. I have power."

"Indeed." Fistandantilus inclined his head. "Much good it will do you, though, if another usurps it."

"Usurps it?" Kurnos asked, his eyes narrowing.

"The First Daughter's pet. The monk. He already wields great power, with no crown on his brow." The dark wizard chuckled softly. "You don't know, do you? You don't even know where Lady Ilista and this Brother Beldyn *are* right now, do you?"

Kurnos glowered, shaking his head . . . then it came to him, and he caught his breath, looking sharply at the sorcerer. "The borderlands. He's in Taol?"

"Just so," Fistandantilus said. "If you doubt me, ask your adviser, the Emissary. I have been using my magic to listen to his private conversations with the First Daughter. They scheme against you, Holiness—nothing spoken aloud yet, but that will come. Unless you *use* your vaunted power rather than merely talking about it."

With a croaking laugh, he stepped back and was gone, vanished in the darkness.

Kurnos stood silent, trembling as he stared at the emerald on his finger. The shadow within danced, mocking him, and he looked away. At once he wished he hadn't, for his eyes turned back to the empty vault, where one day he would find eternal rest. Now, with Fistandantilus's laughter echoing in his mind, he wondered if that time might come sooner than he hoped.

◆━◆━◆

When he held court the next morning, Kurnos found everything, everyone, in the Hall of Audience looked different from the top of the dais—smaller, somehow, like Symeon's enchanted *khas* pieces. The pieces were his now, though, as was the manse . . . the Temple . . . the empire. He was Kingpriest, and when the courtiers spoke to him, there was true reverence in their voices and in their eyes.

His first act was to get rid of part of his court. Power bases always shifted after a new Kingpriest's coronation, and this would be no exception. There were certain hierarchs Kurnos favored more than the ones who had served Symeon—priests more inclined to support him—and so he dismissed Avram of Branchala and Thendeles of Majere, sending them back to their home temples elsewhere in the city. That done, he also named a new First Son: a young, raven-haired cleric named Strinam, who had vowed to support Kurnos at court, no matter what. Balthera he kept around for now. She was malleable and not the true First Daughter anyway. He had his plans for Ilista.

Finally, after Kurnos finished arranging his human *khas* pieces to his liking, he smiled. Shifting on his throne—it wasn't as comfortable as it looked, and the armrests were too high for his liking—he raised a bejeweled hand for silence and made his first move.

"On my first day as Kingpriest," he began, the dome ringing

with his voice. "I make this declaration. I am not Symeon. I will not sit idly while my empire frays."

The courtiers glanced at one another, murmuring. A few, like Lord Holger, nodded approvingly. Others frowned. He paused, noting the dissenters. They would soon follow Avram and Thendeles. He took a deep breath, steeling himself, and went on.

"I speak, of course, of the traitors in Taol," Kurnos continued. "Had we acted early, we could have hunted down these brigands easily. We didn't, though, and now they hold Govinna and the patriarch, and matters are worsening.

"This shall no longer stand. I will *not* brook rebellion in my lands. Thus, I call upon Lord Holger to ride forth to Ismin. There he will meet up with the second and fourth *Dromas* and march to the borderlands at once."

An explosion of voices erupted, jangling the crystal dome. A *Droma* was one of the largest divisions in the imperial army—some ten thousand men strong. Cities had fallen to a force that size, and now Kurnos was ordering *two* into the field. Not once in his reign had Symeon taken such bold action against his own people, and the courtiers quickly began to exclaim and argue with one another, everyone talking at once.

"*Rubudo!*" Kurnos bellowed, surging to his feet. *Silence!*

The noise stopped at once, all eyes turning to the dais. Symeon had never risen from his throne, either.

"I will have *order* in this court!" Kurnos barked. His face was florid, his nostrils flaring. To his left, he saw Loralon step forward, bowing, but he gestured sharply to stay him. "The time for conciliating with our enemies is done. I command the empire's armies now, and I mean to use them. By Year-Turning, every Taoli who has taken up arms against this throne shall swing from a gibbet. Is that understood?"

Loralon blinked, then bowed his head and stepped back, a frown creasing his ageless face. Kurnos glared at him, then turned back to Lord Holger to give further orders. Even as he spoke to the Knight, however, he felt the ancient elf's eyes on him.

He allowed himself a wolfish smile. There would be resistance from Loralon, he knew. He was planning on it.

The smile returned an hour later, when a soft knock sounded on the door of his private dining chamber. Kurnos ignored it, lingering over his midday meal—cockatrice stuffed with figs and a salad of Falthanan greens—until the knock sounded again. Sipping watered claret, he looked up at last.

"Enter, Emissary."

Loralon stepped in, signing the triangle. His slippers whispered across the Tarsian carpets. Kurnos drank from his crystal goblet, watching him approach.

"Holiness," the elf said, "I must ask you to reconsider—"

Kurnos slammed the goblet down on the tabletop with a noise that would have made most men jump. Loralon only blinked, but he did fall silent.

"I am Kingpriest now," Kurnos growled. "I have *made* my decision. I will not always heed your counsel, as Symeon did."

Loralon hesitated then clasped his hands before he went on. "I understand that, but there is something else you must know. Lady Ilista is in Taol, in the army's path."

"I am aware of that, Emissary," Kurnos said, sipping his wine. "I am also aware—as you are—of *why* she's there."

"Sire?" The elf's eyebrows rose.

With a sweep of his arm, Kurnos knocked his goblet across the room. It smashed against the wall, making a crimson stain on the white marble. "Don't play the fool with me, Emissary," he snapped. "I know she and that monk of hers are consorting with the bandits even now! For that duplicity, Ilista is no longer a friend to crown *or* church."

Loralon might have argued, but instead he sighed, looking at the floor. "And the monk?"

"I will cast him out as well. You are to have no further contact with either of them. If I learn you have disobeyed me in this, I will send you back to King Lorac."

Loralon withdrew shortly after, his face drawn with worry. Seething, Kurnos turned back to his meal—and stopped, his eyes falling on the emerald ring.

It shimmered on his finger, reflecting the light that streamed in through the room's high windows. Within the light, the shadows wavered seductively. He grimaced, feeling its band tingle against his skin, and tried to look away. To his horror, he found he couldn't. The gem and the dark shape within caught his gaze and held it.

Use me, said a voice in his head. It wasn't Fistandantilus this time but Sathira's harsh hiss. Two green pinpricks flared within the stone, watching him.

What harm will a second murder do, when you've already had me kill once?

She was right, he knew. Sathira had slain Symeon—not right away, perhaps, but killed him slowly just the same. She would do the same to anyone he named. All he had to do was speak her name and bring her to life. If he used the demon for the good of the realm, as he had the first time, would it be truly evil? He opened his mouth to speak, and the presence in the gem crouched, poised to surge out in a gout of shadow and hate.

Suddenly, he stopped. He was *Kingpriest* now, for Paladine's sake. He had the clergy, the Knighthood, and the imperial army at his call. What were Ilista and Beldyn beside that, even if every bandit's sword in Taol backed them? How much could the demon do that Holger and his *Scatas* could not?

"No," he hissed. "I don't need you."

The glinting eyes within the gem narrowed to slits, and he felt a stab of fear. Then, however, the sound of soft, mocking laughter filled his mind, and his fright changed to gnawing dread.

Ah, Holiness, the demon said. *You will. You will.*

CHAPTER 15 ▼

Cathan drew his hood down, trying not to shiver in the autumn wind as he twisted his sling in his hand. Deep in the highlands south of Luciel, he crouched on a ridge thick with mountain ashes, their branches heavy with scarlet berries. Below, the imperial highroad snaked through the craggy hills. From his vantage, he could see two leagues of the broad, stone-paved path, all of it empty. In the two days he'd been perched on this outcrop he'd seem no other living being. He was alone in this place, save for his horse—tethered downhill and contentedly cropping at patches of tough grass—and a lone hawk that circled hungrily beneath the pall of gray clouds.

He hadn't wanted to go on watch duty and resisted at first, telling Lord Tavarre he wanted to stay near Wentha. She had returned from the edge of death, but she was still weak and frail. Even more than that, he didn't want to leave Beldyn. In the week after he swore his oath, he kept near the monk, watching for trouble with a hand on his sword, and he balked at the notion of leaving to go out into the hills. He argued about it with the baron, and things might have come to shouting if Beldyn himself hadn't intervened, drawing him aside and speaking to him quietly.

"This is a dangerous time," the monk had said. "I need to know the men on watch are trustworthy."

So here he was, with a only horse for company, watching the hawk soar over the hills. As he did he let his mind wander, going back to that night in Farenne's house, when the light had poured from Beldyn's hands and banished the *Longosai*. Part of him still didn't believe it—it must be a trick of some sort—but there was no denying that Wentha was well again, and dozens of others as well.

Swearing the oath had been far from an easy decision. He'd forsaken Paladine and come to hate the clerics who worshiped the god. Bowing to any god had seemed a betrayal. In the end, though, it had come down to the simple fact: Wentha lived, and Beldyn was the reason.

Now he was one of many. When he'd left for sentry duty, more than fifty men and women had already knelt at the monk's feet. The number surely had grown, and soon word of the miracle at Luciel would spread to the neighboring towns. *A holy man has come. Bring your sick, your suffering, and he will cure them.* How many folk would swear to Brother Beldyn then?

Suddenly he sucked in a breath. He'd heard something: the tread of a foot in the grass behind him. He reached for his sword, starting to turn—then stopped as the edge of a blade touched his neck. His skin turned cold as the steel pressed against his skin—not hard enough to draw blood but holding him completely still, not even daring to breathe.

"Daydreaming," said a gruff voice. "A watchman should pay attention, or he might lose his head."

The sword lifted away. He spun to his feet at once, jerking his blade from its scabbard with a ring that echoed down in the valley below. He stupidly took a step toward his assailant before he recognized the etched armor the man wore and stopped.

"Sir Gareth?"

The Knight raised his sword in salute, then nodded at Cathan's own blade. "What's this, boy?" he asked. "Do you mean to attack me again?"

Flushing, Cathan lowered his weapon. He'd carefully avoided Gareth thus far, afraid the Knight might find out whose slingstone nearly killed him. Apparently, he had. "I didn't mean—"

"Easy, lad," Gareth said, sheathing his sword again. "I seek no satisfaction for what you did. There is no honor in holding grudges—and besides, I survived. Now, if I'd died, that would be different. I would have been furious."

Cathan frowned, not sure if Gareth was joking. The Knight's face might have been made of stone, as stern as ever.

Awkwardly, Cathan slid his sword back into its scabbard. He ventured a tentative grin. "What are you doing here?"

"I tired of your village, to be honest," the Knight replied, stepping forward to peer down at the highroad. "So I asked Her Grace's leave to ride out here. It might help if someone attentive was on lookout. You're lucky I wasn't an imperial scout, lad, or I'd have—" He broke off, his eyes going wide as they ranged past Cathan, then whispered a curse. "Huma, hammer and lance."

Cathan turned, his heart lurching as he followed Gareth's gaze. At first he didn't see anything, but when he squinted he made out what the Knight had spotted. Faint and distant above the hills to the east, the sky had turned dark, a gray-brown cloud rising from the road.

"What is it?" he hissed, already suspecting.

Sir Gareth reached to his sword again, brushing its hilt. "The last thing I wanted to see."

All they could see of the body as they climbed was one arm, dangling over a ledge halfway up the slope. There was blood on the fingertips, already beginning to dry, and a lone fly had lit on the hand, perched as if wondering what to do with such a feast. Cathan felt his stomach twist as he stared at the corpse, wondering who it was, and nearly lost his footing, grabbing the root of a nearby tree as his feet slid out from under him. Gravel rattled down the cliff beneath him. The noise drew a fierce look from Sir Gareth, and they stopped for a moment, listening, before the Knight nodded and started toward the top of the hill again.

They had ridden here at a gallop, nearly five miles to the next vantage—a looming tor fringed with furze. When Cathan had whistled and no reply came from above, he and Gareth had exchanged hard glances. Perhaps the sentry Tavarre posted here had dozed off. Or perhaps not.

Unburdened by armor, he got to the body first and soon wished he hadn't. The man was sprawled on its stomach, the moss beneath him dark and damp with blood. At once, Cathan saw what had killed him: a pair of long, deep gashes in his back, deep enough to show the white of bone and the drab colors of the man's insides. More flies crawled on the open wounds. Cathan retched and spat.

Gareth came up beside him, looked at the body, then reached down and rolled it onto its back. Cathan tasted bile when he saw the man's battered face. He'd hit the ledge head-first, and it took a moment for Cathan to recognize him.

"Deledos," he groaned. "The chandler's son."

"They cut him down from behind." Gareth's voice was thick with disgust. "Then threw him over the edge." He waved his sword at the precipice above. Turning away from Deledos's corpse, he started up the hill again.

Cathan grabbed his arm. "What if they're still up there?" he asked, wondering who *they* were exactly.

Gareth gave him a look, then shook off his grasp and kept climbing. Cathan followed, his arms and legs burning as he pulled himself up the slope.

They stopped again just short of the hilltop, and Gareth peered over the crest. A heartbeat later he ducked down again and started tightening the straps of his shield around his arm. His sword hissed as he drew it.

"What is it?" Cathan breathed.

"Four of them," Gareth replied. "*Scatas*. Blood on their swords."

"*Four*? But—"

Before Cathan could say more, however, Gareth rose and strode up the last few paces to the tor's scrubby crown. Swallowing, Cathan unsheathed his own blade and hurried after.

There they were, standing beneath a stand of cone-heavy pines, talking together in hushed, clipped voices. There were indeed four of them, clad in riding leathers and the blue cloaks of the imperial army. Their bronze helms glinted, plumes fluttering in the wind. So intent were they on their conversation that they didn't look up until Gareth raised his sword and clanged down his visor. When they saw him they glanced at one another, not sure what to do.

Gareth rushed them while they were still making up their minds, leaving Cathan stunned behind him. The four *Scatas* drew themselves up in surprise then ran forward as well, swords held high.

Cathan had seen Lord Tavarre spar with Vedro and others. He had seen the captain of Govinna's guard cut Embric down. Now, though, as he watched the Knight storm into battle, he knew he was looking at something else entirely, a man who fought with precision and grace, even when weighted down with mail. Gareth spun to his left, letting two of the men barrel past, then smoothly ducked beneath the lashing blade of a third and raised his shield to block the fourth. The clash of metal filled the air and was still ringing among the hilltops when Gareth shoved the fourth *Scata* back, neatly driving his sword into the man's stomach. The soldier screamed and crumpled as Gareth jerked his blade free.

Taken aback by their comrade's sudden demise—it had taken little more than a heartbeat—the other three *Scatas* fell back, watching Gareth with narrowed eyes. As they did, Cathan stepped up beside the Knight, his sword-hand sweating inside its glove. Gareth gave him a nod.

"You take the one on the right," the Knight said. "The others are mine."

"But—"Cathan began, but it was too late to argue.

The soldiers attacked again, and then he was parrying, turning away a blow aimed at his knees, pivoting aside as a sword point flashed toward his eyes, catching another stroke that would have cut him in half. The smash of blade against blade rang up his arm, numbing his shoulder as he shoved his attacker back.

Beside him, Sir Gareth fought two men at once, lunging away from one man's clumsy stoke while he batted the other man back with a sweep of his sword's flashing blade. The man stumbled, then regained his footing and hurled himself back into the fray. Gareth raised his shield, hammering the charging man in the face with its rim. The *Scata*'s head snapped back with an awful sound—neck or skull, Cathan wasn't sure— then dropped in a heap on the ground. Gareth kicked him, making sure he wasn't faking, then turned to his last foe, both men with bloody swords at the ready.

Cathan's opponent lunged in again, stabbing at his heart— a good, quick blow he couldn't parry in time. Instead he twisted, rocking on the balls of his feet, and a hot line of pain raced across his back as the blow scored him. He gasped, his tunic tearing, then felt a tug as the blade snarled in his cloak. Instinct taking over, Cathan whirled, tearing the weapon from his opponent's grasp. Pulled off-balance, the *Scata* staggered to his knees. Cathan turned back, afire with pain now, and slid his sword between the soldier's ribs. The man choked, spitting blood, his wide eyes fixing in his head as he slid off the blade. Gasping, Cathan wheeled to go to Sir Gareth's aid.

Sir Gareth needed none. He had laid into his opponent, driving him back with a flurry of swift, measured blows. The *Scata* gave ground frantically, looking for somewhere to run, but Gareth didn't relent, battering away until finally the soldier missed a beat. Steel met the man's neck, and his head flew free, an expression of shock frozen on his face as it tumbled into the furze. Blood sprayed as the rest of him made a wet, terrible sound and collapsed.

The Knight saw to the other *Scatas*, making sure they weren't playing at being dead, then inspected the cut across Cathan's back, peeling back his bloody tunic. He prodded at the gash, bringing a groan from Cathan's lips.

"You'll live," he said, then nodded at the bodies. "Outriders, them—dispatched to clear away lookouts. Now let's go see what's raising that dust." He waved his bloody sword at the cloud that hung in the air, very close now and drawing nearer every moment.

Crouching low, they hurried across the hilltop. The pain in Cathan's back flared with every step, and he had to bite his lip to keep from crying out as they wormed along on their stomachs. Closing his eyes, Cathan took a deep breath, then raised his head, looked out into the valley below, and gasped.

He'd been expecting a large patrol—maybe five hundred men—but the force on the Highroad was much greater, a mass of footsoldiers clogging the path as far as he could see. There were thousands of them, an ocean of blue cloaks beneath a forest of glinting spears. Among them, here and there, he made out the colors of clerics—the gold robes of Kiri-Jolith's war-priests, the blue of Mishakite healers, and the white of Revered Children of Paladine. Horn players and drummers walked with them too, though from here the wind's howl drowned out the music. Standards bearing the triangle and falcon floated above the rest, leaving no doubt: this was the Kingpriest's army, marching to war.

"Mother of the gods," Cathan breathed.

"Indeed," Gareth replied, beside him. The Knight didn't seem the slightest bit surprised by what he beheld. "A *Droma*, at least. It seems Lord Kurnos wants a war."

Cathan continued to stare at the army below. He'd never seen so many fighting men in one place. The rebels who had taken Govinna were a rabble beside this great mass. The pain in his back disappeared. He was too numb with fear to feel it.

"Wh-what do we do about them?" he stammered.

"Do? Nothing, yet," Gareth replied, pushing himself up and striding back the way they'd come. Cathan hurried after. "We must return to Luciel at once. Lady Ilista and your baron will want to hear about this."

CHAPTER 16 ▼

Ten mounds of earth disturbed the courtyard of Luciel's keep where Lord Tavarre had once lived. It overlooked the town, perched on a cliff that plunged hundreds of feet to the jagged rocks below: small fortress, invisible from the town below. Its simple, stone curtain wall surrounded a stable, a granary, and a two-storey manor, which had housed a dozen people, before the plague came.

Ilista hesitated as she emerged from the manor's upper doors, standing on a bridge that led to the battlements. The baron had given the keep over to her and Beldyn, and to Sir Gareth and his Knights as well. He himself refused to sleep within its walls any more, and Ilista couldn't blame him. There were too many ghosts there, for the ten mounds had once been his household, of whom only he and his man Vedro remained. The rest were victims of the *Longosai*, from its earliest days. Most were servants and retainers, but two graves stood out among the rest, marked with stones where the others were bare. In one lay Ailinn, once baroness of Luciel and Tavarre's beloved wife; in the other, his son Larris, who would have been ten years of age that summer.

The baron stood before the mounds, his head bowed, as Ilista made her way down to the courtyard. His shoulders shook, and though he heard the First Daughter's tread on the stairs, he did not turn to greet her.

No wonder he took to the hills, she thought as her eyes flitted to the mounds. She thought of the others that filled Luciel's graveyard and of the scorched patches of earth where pyres had burned. No wonder they *all* did. If only . . .

If only what? a voice asked in her head. Symeon may have ignored the plague, but even if he hadn't, what could have been done? The Mishakites couldn't have stopped it. No one could—or so she would have said, not long ago. Now things were different, though. Now there was Beldyn.

The monk was not at the keep right now, but rather stayed in Luciel, as he had every day since they'd come to the town. It was slow, healing all who suffered from the *Longosai*, but finally he was nearing the end of the task. A dozen men and women had remained ill this morning. By nightfall they would be half as many. When the morrow ended, the plague would be gone.

After that, Ilista didn't know. Symeon's death and Kurnos's coronation had surely changed the situation, but she didn't know how. She had tried repeatedly to contact Loralon, but to no avail. No matter how many times she spoke the Emissary's name, the crystal orb remained dark, empty, her own reflection mocking her from its depths. Something had changed to keep Loralon silent, and not knowing what it was infuriated her. Tavarre had sent out riders to learn what news they could. Now, seeing the leather scrollcase tucked in the baron's belt, she knew one had returned.

He straightened, signing the triangle, and though he did his best to blot them, tear-tracks still glistened on his scarred face when he turned to face her.

"*Efisa*," he said, his voice hoarse.

"Your Honor," she replied, then faltered, seeing something in his eyes, beneath the sorrow—a deeper unhappiness as his gaze met hers. "What's wrong? Is it Beldyn?"

He shook his head, pulling forth the scroll-case. "I'm sorry."

Ilista took the scroll-case from him and undid its lacing to remove a sheet of parchment. The wind tried to snatch it away, but she held on, unfolding it with trembling fingers. *Something's happened*, she thought. *To Loralon? Was that why he'd turned silent?*

That wasn't it. It was much worse, and as she read her skin turned cold.

There were three degrees of censure in the Istaran Church. The first, *Bournon*, was a simple reprimand for minor sins, easily lifted with an atonement tithe and three nights of fasting. The second, *Abidon*, was an official reproach and not so easily removed. It took a patriarch or a hierarch of the Great Temple to do so. The church bestowed it upon those who committed some great affront to Paladine, and while it was in effect, the condemned could receive no sacraments, nor could he set foot on consecrated ground. The clergy declared hundreds of folk *Bournon* each year, and perhaps a few dozen *Abidon*.

The third degree was different. *Foripon* was a full declaration of anathema casting the condemned out of the church. Often it led to inquisition and death. Only the Kingpriest himself could revoke such a denunciation, and none had ever done so. In her years at court, Ilista had only seen Symeon cast out a single man, a soldier who had pissed on a roadside shrine and refused to do penance for it.

Kurnos's reign was only days old, and he had already doubled that number. Written on the parchment were two names—hers, less the title of First Daughter, and that of Brother Beldyn. *For black heresy and consorting with traitors*, it declared—and beneath their names, a promised reward of a thousand gold falcons.

Tavarre reacted quickly, rushing to catch her as her knees buckled, but he couldn't stop the parchment from dropping from her hands. The wind caught it, sending it soaring over the keep's walls. She watched it spin away.

"No," she murmured. "It has to be a mistake."

The baron didn't reply, but his grip tightened. It was a familiar gesture, one of kinship. They were both outlaws, now. She shuddered at the thought.

Then another occurred to her. "Beldyn. Does he know?"

"No, *Efisa.*"

She nodded, then took a deep breath, and pushed away from Tavarre to stand on her own. "Come on, then," she said, turning. "We'd best—"

A sound rose, eerily filling the air as it echoed among the hills: the mournful howl of a wolf. Hearing it, Tavarre stiffened and muttered a curse.

"What was that?" Ilista asked as the howl died away.

"A signal," the baron replied. "The sentries have returned."

He whirled, his cloak flapping, and hurried up the steps to the battlements. Ilista followed, hardly breathing as she looked down from the keep into the vale below. In the distance, two frothing horses were galloping along a trail to the village. One was a bandit, cloaked and leather-clad, but the midday sun's light glinted off the other's armor, and she knew it was Gareth, come back early from his sojourn to the highroad.

Ilista swallowed as the riders charged toward Luciel. Already she knew what they were going to report, and she saw her knowledge mirrored in Tavarre's pale face as well. The *Foripon* seemed silly now. War had come to the highlands.

<hr />

They met down in Luciel, and gathered inside the tavern— Cathan and Gareth, Tavarre and Vedro, Ilista and Beldyn. Caked in road-dust, the Knight drank a flagon of raw wine to moisten his throat, then told what he had seen. Cathan nodded breathlessly as the others stared in shock.

"Well," Tavarre said when he was finished, and sighed.

"Perhaps they won't come here," Ilista said. "This is a small town. . . ."

"They'll come," Vedro growled.

Everyone looked into the room's corners, trying not to meet one another's gaze. In the end, it was Beldyn who coughed softly and spoke.

"We must leave, then," he said. "All of us."

Tavarre looked up, meeting the monk's burning gaze. After a moment, he nodded and turned to Cathan. "Did they see you?"

"No, but they'll find the bodies of their men," Cathan replied, "and we left tracks."

Vedro cursed, slapping his thigh in frustration. "It'll have to be tonight, then. They'll send riders ahead and have our heads if they find us here."

"Where can we go?" Gareth asked.

"Govinna," said Tavarre, running a hand through his dark, curly hair. "Ossirian will take us in—and he has to be told the army's in Taol."

Ilista cleared her throat. "You're all forgetting the *Longosai*," she said. "Beldyn, how many still have to be healed?"

"Only eight," he replied.

Vedro swore again, and the others slumped, looking defeated. They looked at one another hopelessly, and Ilista could tell they were all sharing the same terrible thought. The sick couldn't make the journey, but sunset was only three hours off. Already Beldyn looked tired, and wisps of holy light clung to him like clouds to the peak of a mountain. His strength was leaving him. No one wanted to say the words that flashed through their minds, though it was the only choice left. They had to leave the eight sick people behind, if the rest of Luciel were to live.

Beldyn's mouth hardened into a line, however, and he pushed away his mug of wine, untouched. "Bring them," he said. "I'll take care of it."

"What?" Ilista asked as everyone turned to look at him. "Beldyn, don't be ridiculous. You don't have the strength right now—"

He glared back at her, and her voice failed her. There was something terrible in his gaze, a ferocity she hadn't seen before.

"I said I'll take care of it," he declared. "We're not leaving anyone."

Ilista wanted to protest, to talk sense into him, but the blaze of his eyes stilled her tongue. It was a fanatic's look, and it made her uneasy.

Glancing around the room, she saw the rest of them watching her hopefully. They wanted to believe—and who was she to deny them? Looking back at Beldyn once more, the fierceness in his eyes, she could only nod and sigh.

"Very well, then," she said. "Do as he says."

———— ◆ ————

The rest of the day passed quickly. From the wall of keep Tavarre winded a long brass horn, sending its clarion blare ringing out across the vale. Men and women came running, emerging from houses and shops throughout the village. The bandits and Gareth's Knights took control of the situation, gathering the villagers in Luciel's central yard, sending runners to fetch food and blankets and fill skins with water from the town well. The scant survivors of the plague, barely two hundred in all, looked around nervously, not sure what was happening.

Clad in chain mail and a long riding cloak, his sword hanging at his side, Tavarre strode into the midst of his vassals and stepped up on a tree stump, waving for silence. He got it at once, though many darted glances about, searching for Beldyn. The monk had disappeared that afternoon, and no one had seen him since. Now the sky was red, the sun gone behind the distant Khalkists. Night would come soon, and Luciel's folk whispered fearfully as they turned listen to the baron.

He'd barely finished explaining about the army and the need to flee when the murmurs turned into a rumble of outrage.

"Leave!" shouted an old man, his bald head wrinkling with worry. "I've lived in this vale all my life!"

A young woman stepped forward, shifting a squalling baby on her hip. "Govinna is too far! We'll never get there with winter coming!"

"What about them?" demanded a stout, severe-looking matron. She stood near a cluster of bodies near the middle of the yard: the plague's eight remaining victims. They were an awful sight, gaunt and wasted, four men, three women, and one child, coughing and shivering where they lay atop bedrolls the bandits had spread out for them.

"They can't make the journey!"

Standing near Tavarre, Ilista swallowed, knowing the woman was right. The sick were too many. Beldyn might be able to lay hands on three of them, maybe four, but *eight?* It was more than he could handle. Though she knew there was no hope, one thing kept her from shouting it out—Beldyn's eyes, the stubborn ardor shining from them.

He appeared then, even as the villagers clamored and Tavarre tried to calm them down. At first, only a few folk saw the monk, standing at the yard's edge with his hands folded inside his sleeves, but when he stepped forward the mob grew silent and turned away from their baron to stare in awe.

Beldyn made his way through the crowd, which parted for him gladly. A few people dropped to their knees, while others whispered to one another, their voices tinged with wonder. As she watched the adulation in the borderfolk's eyes, Ilista had the feeling of having started something she could no longer control. They might balk at Tavarre for saying they had to leave Luciel, but she knew they would follow Beldyn across Ansalon, if he asked. Ilista's hand strayed to her medallion as the monk stepped up to the dying on their pallets.

Please be right, she thought, not wanting to consider what might happen if Beldyn proved wrong.

"Hear me, my children," he declared. His voice was stern, the music all but gone from it, leaving cold authority behind. He raised his chin, and his youthful features hardened before her eyes. "I know this is a hard thing, but it must happen. There is no shelter here, and Govinna's walls will keep us safe. As to these people . . ." he added, gesturing at the fever-wracked bodies, " . . . watch."

As he knelt before the eight pallets, the only sound in Luciel was the ever-present rush of the wind. He looked out upon the bodies, spreading his hands over them. Ilista stopped breathing without realizing it as he closed his eyes and began to pray.

"Palado, ucdas pafiro . . ."

The light, when it came, grew bright so fast that all around the yard, folk cried out, shielding their eyes against the glare. The chiming noise that accompanied Beldyn's healing rituals was louder and deeper, filled with strange echoes that came from nowhere. The autumn chill vanished, turning warm as the holy light engulfed Beldyn, then snaked out into the crowd in tendrils of silver fire. Ilista found herself trembling at the monk's power.

"Be right," she whispered, clutching her medallion until its sharp corners dug into her flesh. "Merciful Paladine, let him be right. . . ."

At last the glow rippled and began to fade, bleeding away into the gathering night. One by one it uncovered the bodies on the pallets, washing away like a sunrise in reverse. Each time it left a healthy person behind—clear skin, brows no longer damp with fever, breathing easily again as they slumbered. Only Beldyn remained, all but lost amid the radiance, his eyes burning blue through the god's white light. Ilista also saw the red gleam of rubies—then it was gone, swallowed by the brilliant whiteness.

The villagers who hadn't already knelt did so now, their faces aglow with belief. Atop his stump, Tavarre shook his head, his mouth crooking into a wry, wondering grin. Ilista stared, fingering her medallion worriedly. Beldyn, gazing out upon the doting folk of Luciel, closed his eyes, smiled, and crumpled to the ground.

CHAPTER 17 ▼

Everyone stared as Beldyn fell, dropping first to his knees, then slumping backward in a senseless heap. Some gasped, a few put their hands to their mouths, but coming so soon after the healing, his collapse took everyone aback.

With a cry. Cathan shoved his way through the mass of villagers, hurrying to the monk's side. The holy light continued to burn, rippling silver and making soft, crystalline sounds, but Cathan didn't balk. Holding his breath, he knelt hurrying and reached into the glow. It was a strange feeling, like putting his hands in a cool stream on a hot day, and the hairs on his arms stood erect, but there was no pain. Feeling around inside the light, he found Beldyn's head, pillowed on one outflung arm and lifted it, propping it in his lap. The monk's skin was clammy, and for a heartbeat Cathan feared he might be dead, but then he felt the body stir and the faint hiss of breath, and he sighed in relief.

Others were crowding close now, and the townsfolk parted to let them through. Ilista, Tavarre, Sir Gareth. Wentha was there too, somewhere—she had been standing beside him. Cathan heard their voices, taut with worry, but he didn't listen; his attention fixed on Beldyn, his hands moving within the light to brush hair from the monk's brow. The glow was already beginning to fade. Through it, he could see Beldyn's youthful face, pale and slack, the lips parted, keeping a bit of the smile they'd held before he fell.

Cathan patted Beldyn's cheek. "Reverence," he asked. "Can you hear me?"

Beldyn stirred, moaning, and his eyelids trembled open. The blue fire in his eyes was banked, but it flared a little when he saw Cathan. His smile widened.

"You kept your word," he said. "You came to my aid."

Nodding, Cathan continued to stroke his cheek. "How can I help?"

Beldyn considered this. Letting out a shuddering breath, he glanced not only at Cathan, but the others as well.

"Help me up," he said.

Cathan hesitated, looking at Ilista. The First Daughter bit her lip, unsure.

"Do it," Beldyn insisted. "The Kingpriest's warriors won't wait for me to gather my strength."

It was true, Cathan knew. Even now, the soldiers were heading for Luciel. Time was dear. So with a swallow, he grabbed Beldyn under his arms and rose, lifting the monk's weight. In a moment, Beldyn was on his feet again, though he leaned much of his weight into Cathan's shoulder. They exchanged looks, and Beldyn smiled.

"Thank you, my friend," he said.

They left Luciel an hour later with whatever they could carry. The sun set soon after that, but they kept on, moving well into the evening. Finally, when it was full dark and they had put two leagues of wilderness between themselves and the town, they stopped and spent the night huddled and shivering in the shelter of a stand of aspen. They lit no fires, for fear of the *Scatas*.

Hours later, they woke—more tired, it seemed, than when

they'd made camp—to the sight of ruddy light smearing the horizon. At first they thought it was dawn, but the glow was to the south, not the east. They stared silently, knowing what it meant but not daring to speak of it. The Kingpriest's men were burning their homes. Whatever became of them, no more maps would bear the name of Luciel.

The *Scatas* would not be so easily sated, however. Soon the riders would pick up their trail, if they hadn't already. As the villagers watched the fireglow, some of them weeping, Tavarre and Sir Gareth drew the leaders of the band aside to talk.

"We'll never make it," Gareth said, studying a map of Taol. Scowling, he traced his finger along the distance to Govinna, still many leagues away. "We can't outrun imperial cavalry."

"Can we hide from them?" Ilista asked.

Tavarre glanced at the villagers and shrugged. "Where? There's two hundred of us."

"We're done, then," Vedro said, and spat.

"No."

Everyone stopped, turning to look in surprise. Last night's healing had left Baldyn pale and weak, but he was recovering, and the silver light dimmed to a glimmer around him. His eyes blazed, silencing questions. Half the bandits and more than one of the Knights couldn't meet that unsettling gaze at all and looked away.

"There is a way," he said, pointing at the map. His finger marked a spot ten miles to the north, where the old road passed over the River Edessa. "This crossing. Is it a ford or a bridge?"

Tavarre leaned in, scratching his beard. "Bridge. That's high ground there—the river flows through a gorge."

"Good!" Gareth proclaimed, his eyes glinting. "We can cross, then burn it behind us."

The baron shook his head. "We could, if it were made of wood. That bridge is stone."

Everyone looked at one as the spark of hope they had felt

faded. Beldyn, however, still stared at the crossing.

"Then we'll knock it down," he said.

"How?" Tavarre pressed. "We have no tools, and even if we did, it would take days—oh."

He stopped, seeing the look in Beldyn's crystalline eyes. Everyone who saw knew what he had meant. Healing was not the only power the god had given him. Looking at him, the others felt some of his conviction flow into them. Besides, they had no other option but surrender, and that path surely led to the gibbet for them all.

After dispatching riders to trail behind and serve as watchers, the folk of Luciel—all of them cold, hungry and tired—broke camp and set forth, through the morning mist. Behind them, the distant glow of Luciel's death vanished in the brightening dawn.

* * *

They first saw the bridge late that morning, as the road humped over a hill-shoulder. The refugees halted at its crest. Less than a league away, the trail wound up to the lip of a chasm, where a narrow arch of white stone spanned the gap. Huge figures, carved from streaked granite, loomed at either end: statues of warriors, wearing old-fashioned, banded armor and holding oblong shields and tall spears. They had been four, once, but one had crumbled to pieces with the passage of years, and another was missing its head and shield arm. The others stared out, their beardless faces grim.

The villagers were exhausted from hours of hard marching, but now a ragged cheer broke out as they beheld the bridge. A few bandits joined in, raising their swords in the air.

"Is that it, Cathan?" Wentha asked. "Are we going to be safe now?"

He looked up at where she sat, astride his horse. He'd given it to her to ride, jogging alongside the whole time. He wanted dearly to tell her yes, everything would be all right, but glancing at Beldyn, he couldn't quite bring himself to believe it. The monk's face was drawn, weary. Even if the god *had* given him the power to destroy the bridge, would he have the strength to wield it? Cathan bit his lip.

Now he heard it, a new sound, rising above the murmur of voices and the wind's whistling: a low, ominous rumble coming from behind them. Hoofbeats. Freezing with dread, he turned and looked back down the slope, half-expecting to see hundreds of blue-cloaked *Scatas* bearing down on them. He didn't, although what he did see did little to raise his spirits either: the bandits' lookouts, lashing their horses as they thundered up the hill.

Tavarre and Gareth wheeled their steeds, cantering back to meet them, so the villagers wouldn't hear their breathless report. It was needless, though. The scouts' flushed faces and the glisten of blood on one man's arm told them enough. An uneasy murmur rippled through the mob as the baron came around and started back toward them. His scars seemed like canyons, cutting through his glowering face.

"Get to the bridge," he told them. "Move!"

The villagers didn't need to hear more. Their weariness forgotten, they surged forward again. Those with the strength broke into a run. Others glanced back, but still there was no sign of pursuit. Cathan could feel it now, though, shaking the ground beneath him: the hammering of hundreds of hoofs, and the shrill of war-horns with it.

Legs burning, he looked up at Wentha. His sister was white with fear, clutching the saddle horn. Then he looked at the distance to the bridge, and clenched his teeth. They still had nearly two miles to go. Swallowing, he drew his sword.

"Cathan!" Wentha shouted. "What are you doing?"

"I'll be all right," he said, hoping it wasn't a lie. "Blossom, listen. I want you to ride ahead without me. Don't stop till you're past the bridge."

She shook her head, her eyes filling with fear. Before she

could say a word, though, he slapped the horse on its rump with the flat of his blade. Whinnying, it pelted down the path as Wentha clung to its reins. Cathan's throat tightened as he watched her go.

The bridge crept closer, the slowness of it terrifying him. Despite shouting from Tavarre and Gareth to move faster, many of the refugees could only manage a limping walk. They were too spent to manage more. The armored statues loomed, frowning at them. They dwarfed the first riders—Wentha among them—as they passed them by, clattering over the arch as fast as their horses would carry them. Cathan tried to keep focused on them, but his gaze kept drifting back over his shoulder, seeking some sign of the soldiers. The hammer of their horses' hooves grew to a roar, echoing among the hills. Again and again, though, he didn't see them.

Until, finally, he did.

He faltered, his skin growing cold as he looked back up the hill-shoulder. A row of blue-caped riders stood their horse atop it, their bronze helmets glinting in the sun. As he watched, they raised their swords and spears, shouting a chorus of wild war cries, and then they plunged down the slope toward the refugees' poorly guarded rear. Cathan turned back to the bridge. The first few villagers on foot were crossing now, urged along by Beldyn and Lady Ilista. The span was narrow, though, and quickly a mob formed, shoving and clamoring to be the next across the gorge.

They would never make it, Cathan realized. The riders were too close. He spat a curse.

"*Baravais, Kharai!*" roared a voice just then. "Men of Solamnia, to me!"

Turning, Cathan saw Sir Gareth waving his sword, riding back through the press of villagers. Hearing his call, the other Knights converged on him, forming a small knot at the rear of the throng, their armor gleaming in the sunlight. Gareth spoke to them, then as one they nodded, lowered their visors, and rode back toward the *Scatas*.

"Wait!" Cathan cried. He stopped in his tracks, turning to run after the Knights. "What are you doing?"

Hearing him, Gareth twisted in his saddle and shook his head. "This isn't your fight, lad."

"But . . . there's only six of you, and there's—" Cathan broke off, waving at the onrushing horsemen.

"Yes," Gareth said, "and Draco Paladin willing, it will be enough."

Their eyes met through the slits of his helmet, and Cathan saw a determination that made him pull up short. He had never seen a man glad to die, but here it was. He couldn't know for sure because of the helmet, but he felt certain the Knight was smiling. Eyes stinging with tears, he turned around again and ran back toward the bridge.

———◆◆◆———

Ilista was standing beneath a looming statue, urging villagers across the chasm, when she heard the first clash of steel on steel. She turned, already knowing what she would see. She'd heard Gareth call to his men, and had known his intent. Even so, a gasp racked her throat when she beheld the Knights.

They had spread out across the path, the thinnest of floodwalls against the torrent. Now they fought, their blades flashing as they met the *Scatas'* vanguard. Sword rang against sword, scraped across shield, glanced off armor as they braced themselves, holding back the deluge. As she watched, several soldiers toppled from their saddles, badly cut or run through, and the rest stopped, held back by the Knights' furious onslaught.

It couldn't last. The *Scatas'* officers bawled at them, shouting furious orders, and quickly the soldiers firmed up, their ranks closing once more. They came on again, swords rising and falling, spears thrusting with vicious precision. Gareth's men held firm, but even so they soon suffered their first loss: a red-haired Knight of the Crown who took a spear through his breastplate, then collapsed with a crash. His fellows didn't pause, though: quickly the Knights spread out further, evening the spaces between them

Watching, Ilista felt a rush of emotion—admiration, dread, sorrow, guilt. Another Knight went down, his neck pouring blood where a *Scata*'s sword had nearly severed it. The others spaced out again, spreading even further. It was too little now, though, and the line started giving ground, fighting with redoubled fury as they backed their horses toward the bridge.

Someone caught her arm, snapping her back to her senses: Tavarre. His eyes were alive with stubborn fire. "Your Grace!" he exclaimed. "You must get across! I'll keep people moving here—go with Beldyn!"

He pointed, and she looked. While she'd been watching the battle, the young bandit—what was his name?—had gotten to Beldyn and was escorting him across the bridge, surrounded by throngs of villagers. Swallowing, she signed the triangle over Tavarre. He pushed her away, propelling her after the monk.

Quickly she reached the bridge and began to follow Beldyn and the young bandit. Halfway across, she looked over the bridge's crumbling rail, then quickly away. The gorge was deep, the foaming Edessa so far below that it seemed a white line tumbling among the stones. The wind gusted across the bridge, flapping her robes, threatening to fling her out into the void. She shut her eyes a moment, taking deep breaths, and pushed on to the chasm's far side.

When she reached it, she glanced back. Only three Knights remained, fighting furiously as they backed toward the gorge. She shook her head at the sight, wondering how Gareth and his men could stand before the press at all.

Beldyn was to her left, waving from where he stood with young Cathan—that was his name!—at the foot of the statue that had completely fallen to ruin. Bits of rubble overgrown with moss and ivy lay scattered about the carved warrior's feet. He gestured, beconing, and she went. Beldyn's eyes were shut, his face blank, and he clutched his medallion in his hand.

"You must be my eyes, *Efisa*," he said. "Tell me when to act." Bowing his head, he began to pray.

Ilista wasted no time. Hitching up her robes, she climbed onto the shattered statue's pedestal and looked back. The last of the refugees were on the bridge now, clumped together as they made their way across. Tavarre and Vedro brought up the rear, shouting obscenities and waving their arms as they herded the villagers along.

Farther on, she saw a flash of sunlight on armor as Sir Reginar fell before the *Scatas*, dropping to his knees with a sword wound in his side, then vanishing into the press. Sir Gareth, the bravest and stoutest, was alone now, almost at the chasm, battling furiously. His horse was gone, and his armor was awash with blood, though she couldn't tell how much was his enemies' and how much his own.

"Be ready!" she called to Beldyn.

Somehow, Gareth held the bridge. His sword snapped as he parried a slash from a *Scata*, and the blade glinted as it tumbled into the gorge. He didn't seem to notice—undaunted, he fought on with the weapon's broken stump. His shield, battered and gashed, finally split in two. He flung the pieces at the riders then drew a dagger from his belt.

"For the Lightbringer!" he bellowed, and hurled himself at the soldiers with the last of his strength.

Then he was gone.

Ilista stared, horrified, as Gareth disappeared among the *Scatas*. Shaking, she looked to the bridge. The last of the refugees were stepping off the span now, Tavarre and Vedro shoving them onto solid ground. The first of the *Scatas* started across, a thicket of spearheads extended before them. Ilista swallowed, touching her medallion.

"Now, Beldyn!" she cried.

At once, the young monk opened his eyes. Blue fire danced within them as he flung out his right arm, then he raised his voice in a shout that lashed the air like a thunderclap.

"*Pridud!*" he cried. *Break!*

A rumble shook the ground, startling the villagers and making the *Scatas*' horses rear. The bridge shuddered, dust and chips of stone showering into the chasm. The noise of the tremor echoed among the hills, like the growl of some long-vanished dragon.

Sparks flared from Beldyn's fingertips as he turned his outstretched hand palm upwards. "*Pridud!*"

The earth trembled again, louder and harder. On either side of the chasm, men drew back, shouting in terror. The headless statue collapsed altogether, tumbling into the gorge, and spider-web cracks spread across the bridge, shaking flagstones loose. The soldiers on the span turned, desperate, trying to flee to their fellows.

With a snap, Beldyn's fingers curled into a fist.

"*PRIDUD!*"

The silver light flared around Beldyn, blossoming from his hand to engulf him, then flashing outward in a rippling wave that struck the bridge like a dwarf-smith's hammer. As it did, the ground shook so violently Ilista had to clutch to the ruined statue's ankle to steady herself. Everywhere, men and women stumbled and fell. The bridge bucked, twisting horribly as more and more cracks widened all over it. The *Scatas* all but hurled themselves back toward solid ground beneath Beldyn's holy fire.

With an awful rending sound, the bridge burst asunder, sending stones and soldiers and horses alike thundering into the frothing river below. At the same time, Beldyn began to fall as well, his knees buckling as Cathan reached out and grabbed him, easing him to the ground.

The refugees walked on as the sun disappeared behind the Khalkists, the first stars agleam in the darkening sky. They moved slowly, their pursuers left behind, stranded by the bridge's collapse. The deaths of the Knights weighed heavily on them all.

The villagers looked to Beldyn with deeper awe than before. They had seen him heal; now they had seen him destroy. Too, they had seen what it cost him, for the shrouding light did not go away. It still shone brightly, like a second silver moon come to earth. He rode in a daze, head bowed, and did not look up. Several times he slumped and would have fallen, had Cathan not been at his side to bear him up.

Still he rode, refusing to stop, and so the borderfolk followed him, fighting through their own weariness to keep going well into the night, finally halting in a narrow cleft, out of the frigid wind. Huddled around smoldering fires, they ate a meager supper, then fell into restless slumber.

Not everyone found rest, however. Ilista sat alone on a boulder outside the camp, staring skyward, where dark clouds scudded, blurred by her tears. She had tried to sleep, but every time she closed her eyes she saw Sir Gareth, standing defiantly before the bridge, his broken sword ablaze with sunlight. Again and again she watched him fall, the Lightbringer's name on his lips. He had given his life, died with honor, but only the people in her ragged band would ever know. The word that went back to Istar would be that he'd fallen protecting traitors and bandits from the iron weight of the law.

Who is to say that isn't true? she wondered, shaking her head. Kurnos is the crowned Kingpriest—Symeon named him so. Who am I to act against him?

"You are my servant," said a voice, "doing my will."

Starting, Ilista rose to her feet. There was someone there, in the darkness, a shadow against the night. She drew back, reaching for her mace—then stopped, realizing she'd left the weapon at camp.

"Who is it?" she hissed. "Show yourself!"

He did, stepping close enough that she could make him out in the moonlight, a fat man in a white habit, a smile brightening his florid face. It was Brother Jendle, the monk she had dreamed about, these many weeks ago, in her room in Istar.

"I apologize, Your Grace," he said. "I didn't mean to startle you."

She didn't—couldn't—move, but only stared with her mouth open. His eyes sparkled with starlight.

"You're having doubts," he noted, "after what happened today."

She blinked back tears. "Sir Gareth—he was sworn to protect me."

"He did. If he hadn't held the bridge, the soldiers would have caught you. I wish things could have been different, but Sir Gareth did what was right. We should not mourn those who die fulfilling their purpose in this world,"

Ilista looked away, out into the dark. *What* purpose? she wanted to rail. What are we doing? What are we? A small, hungry band of ruffians, with both the church and the imperial army arrayed against us. How can we stand against the might of Istar? How do we know we're even right to try it?

"Damn it, Paladine," she whispered, "*what do you want of me?*"

When she looked back, though, the monk was gone.

She stayed on the boulder until the silver moon set. Then she returned to camp. When she slept at last, Ilista did not dream.

CHAPTER 18 ▼
TENTHMONTH, 923 I.A.

The hippogriff cocked its head as it peered at the hunk of raw meat, its raptor's eyes peering intently in the light of late afternoon. Its feathered tail twitched as it pawed the grassy earth with a forehoof. Its hooked beak opened and closed hungrily.

"That's right," Kurnos murmured. "Supper's here. Now come take it, you blasted wretch."

He'd had the meat torn from the hindquarters of an antelope his cooks were preparing for the evening banquet. Its bloody scent filled the air as he stood within his rose garden—bloomless still, more than a month after Symeon's death—facing off against the hippogriff. Since his coronation, the beast had steadfastly refused to come near him, though he knew it to be docile. The old Kingpriest had fed it from his hand, but around Kurnos it held back, no matter what he did. Now it finally seemed to be overcoming its reluctance and took a step toward him as he stood still, the meat dangling from his hand.

It ought to have. He'd been starving it for days.

He couldn't say why it was important that the hippogriff accept him, but that made it no less true. Certainly the imperial court had accepted him—once he'd gotten rid of the last dissenters, of course—and the folk of the Lordcity shouted his name in praise whenever he emerged from the Temple. When he'd attended a recital by a renowned Dravinish dulcimist last night at the Arena, the citizens had applauded louder for him than they had for the musician. Indeed, all the empire seemed to have little objection to his fledgling rule—except the bandits in Taol, of course, and the army would deal with them soon enough.

The hippogriff was another matter entirely.

It edged closer, head held low. He shook the meat a little, and the beast froze, watching him warily. Kurnos held his breath, leaning forward. Take it, damn you, he thought. Take it, or we'll be dining on more than antelope tonight.

Nothing moved. Somewhere in the gardens, someone laughed at an unheard joke. A gobbet of fat dropped from the meat into the grass. He looked down, watching it fall . . . then, in the instant of distraction, the hippogriff made its move.

Its wings—clipped since it was a foal to keep it from flying away—spread wide, and it reared back on its hind legs, letting out a whickering hiss. Kurnos gaped as it towered above him, at the forehoofs churning the air. He envisioned them coming down on him, breaking bones, maybe even cracking open his skull. With a shout he leaped back, tripped over his robes, and fell, sprawling in the grass as the hippogriff came down again. The meat fell from his hand, and he reached for it quickly—but not quickly enough. The beast's head darted forward with the speed of a striking snake, and it snatched up the morsel in its beak, then wheeled and galloped away to the far side of the garden.

Kurnos watched it go, hate brimming in his eyes. If he'd had a bow at hand, he'd have shot the animal dead. Instead, he took off his sandal and hurled it, but the throw fell far short. The hippogriff pranced, wolfing down the meat with three quick bites. Kurnos growled a curse as he pushed himself to his feet. At least no one had seen the humiliating scene, he told himself. He was alone in the garden.

No sooner had he thought that, however, than he saw the dark hooded figure. It stood in the shadows beneath a barren rose trellis, its shoulders shaking with silent laughter. Kurnos flushed with anger and froze with fear all at once.

"You!" he breathed.

Still chuckling, Fistandantilus stepped out into the reddening sunlight and crossed the garden. Seeing him, the hippogriff let out a terrified squeal and edged back into the garden's far corner. He glanced at the creature, shrugged, and turned back to the Kingpriest.

"Smart beast," he said. "It knows evil when it sees it."

Kurnos heard the double-edged meaning. "I am not evil," he snapped. "I am Paladine's voice."

Fistandantilus shrugged again.

Kurnos glowered, rubbing his fingers. The emerald ring had grown warm against his skin, and it was all he could do to keep from looking at it.

"What do you want?" he growled.

The wizard's beard—the only part of his face visible within his hood's shadows—moved as he smiled. "That is what I like about you, Holiness. You're very direct. How does your war proceed?"

A scowl creased Kurnos's face. He'd received his first report from Lord Holger only yesterday. They had entered Taol and were subjugating its southern fiefs even now. The Lord Knight had been concerned, at first, about the coming winter, but now he was certain the army would reach Govinna before the snows started falling. The Kingpriest said nothing of this, though. He remained stonily silent.

"Very well," Fistandantilus said. "I am here because I have information you might find interesting."

"Information?" Kurnos echoed. "From where?"

"Your own Temple, as it happens." The archmage's head shook as Kurnos's eyes went wide. "You see, I've been thinking about this Brother Beldyn, the ones the rebels are calling 'Lightbringer.' The name was familiar to me, you see, and just last night I remembered from where. It was in a book I read, a long time ago, so I went to the chancery to get it. Don't worry, Holiness—no one knows I was there. I had to charm one young lad, though—Denubis, I believe his name was—to let me into the *Fibuliam* so I could get this."

The mage gestured, and a swirl of orange light appeared in the air, halfway between him and Kurnos. With a sound like a great iron gong, the light slowed its spinning, then took on physical form. It resolved into a book—an old, slender volume, bound in basilisk hide—that hung in the air for a heartbeat, then fell to the ground with a thump. An ivory plaque protruded from between its yellowed pages, and peeling, gold-leaf runes marked its cover. Kurnos leaned closer, peering at it.

Qoi Zehomu, the runes read.

Kurnos licked his lips and swallowed, then looked up again. "Is that all?"

Fistandantilus shook his head. "You're eager to be rid of me, I know," he said, "but no—there's more."

Again he waved his hand, and this time Kurnos let out a gasp of pain as the emerald ring grew unbearably hot. He clutched at it, and—in spite of his misgivings—looked to see the gem was glowing, the same unpleasant green as the eyes of the demon within. Its shadows whirled like a maelstrom.

"You must use her again, Holiness," Fistandantilus said.

The pain was almost unbearable as Kurnos clenched his fist. The mage was right—the demon was the answer. All he had to do was speak her name, and his enemies would die. He looked at the hippogriff, still cowering and shivering in the garden's corner, and faltered. The beast thought he was evil. Would a good man use the ring?

"No," he declared. "I will win this war by my own terms."

Fistandantilus drew himself up, his beard bristling. "*You* would defy *me*?"

"I am Kingpriest of Istar!" Kurnos snarled back. "I will not bend to another man's will."

The chill that surrounded Fistandantilus became biting cold, and beneath him the grass turned white and withered before Kurnos's eyes. For a long moment, the mage didn't speak—when he did, each soft word hung in the air as if made of ice.

"Yes," he hissed, "but it is my doing that you sit the throne now, Holiness. Do not forget that. I can end your reign just as easily."

Suddenly his hand came up, and he snapped his fingers. Kurnos flinched, expecting agony, but the spell was not directed at him. Instead, a horrible sound rang out across the garden—a horse's scream, mixed with the shriek of a bird of prey. Kurnos turned, saw the hippogriff and immediately wished he hadn't. The animal was on the ground, its flesh burning, wings aflame and hoofs kicking as it squalled in pain. Kurnos could only watch in sick fascination, tasting bile. At last the beast gave one last great thrash and was still, save for the feeble twitching of its legs. The flames snuffed out, leaving the air thick with the stench of singed hair and flesh, but though it was dead, there was no sign of burning on its body. It seemed to have died naturally.

When he raised his horrified gaze from the dead hippogriff, Fistandantilus was gone. The sound of the mage's laughter remained, though, lingering cruelly in Kurnos's ears.

Later that night, Kurnos sat alone in his private audience hall atop his golden throne. The chamber was dark, save for the glow of braziers to either side of him. He had the *Qoi Zehomu* in his lap, open to the page Fistandantilus had marked. He did not move, save for the rise and fall of his breath, and the deepening of the frown upon his face. He had read Psandros's foretelling three times now—slow going, for his Old Dravinish was rusty at best—and he could not remember being so furious in all his life.

He was still staring at the mad prophet's words when a knock sounded from the golden doors at the chamber's far end. He took several deep breaths to quell his simmering rage before he spoke.

"Enter."

The doors cracked open, and Brother Purvis appeared. "Sire," the old chamberlain began, "the Emissary has arrived."

"Show him in."

Bowing, Purvis withdrew, then appeared again with the ancient elf behind him. Loralon was clad as always, in full raiment, neatly arranged. His ageless face aloof, he signed the triangle and glided silently forward to kneel before the throne.

"Holiness," he murmured. "How may I serve thee?"

Kurnos waited until Purvis had gone again, and the doors were shut. Then, calmly, he lifted the *Qoi Zehomu* and hurled it at the elf.

The book struck Loralon in the face, knocking him sideways, then hit the ground, cracking its fragile spine. Several pages came lose, torn from their binding. The ancient elf stared at it, his hand going to his mouth. Blood trickled from his lip.

"You conniving bastard," Kurnos growled as the elf stared up at him, an altogether alien look of shock in his eyes. "Get up."

He rose as the elf pushed himself dazedly to his feet and descended from the dais to stand before Loralon. His face was as red as his beard. His gaze smoldered.

"Majesty," Loralon said, "I did not—"

"I said *be silent!*" Kurnos roared and cracked the back of his hand across the elf's mouth.

Loralon's head snapped back, and he stumbled. The trickle of blood stained his snowy beard. "Majesty . . ." he began again.

Kurnos wanted to strike Loralon again and again. It took a great deal of effort to hold back, his fists trembling at his sides. "No!" he snapped. "I will not hear it, Emissary. You've been plotting against me all along—you and Ilista. Trying to bring this . . . this Lightbringer to the Lordcity to usurp my rightful throne!"

"Holiness, the prophecy says nothing about the throne," Loralon said. When he caught the look in the Kingpriest's eyes, however—rage, tinged with the glimmer of madness— he fell silent and looked at the floor.

For a time, Kurnos didn't speak. When he did, his voice was a razor, glittering in the dark. "If you were my subject, Loralon," he said. "I would summon the guards and they would take you away in chains. Tomorrow, you would burn at the stake for this betrayal, but," he went on, raising a finger as Loralon opened his bloodied mouth, "unfortunately, you belong to King Lorac, not me. I cannot kill you without breaking the peace between our peoples. Therefore, I'm doing the only thing I can—sending you back to the Silvanesti in shame.

"I have sent men to your chambers, with orders to seize all imperial property—as well as the crystal you've been using to conspire with Ilista. You will leave the Lordcity at dawn and return at once to Silvanost. If you do not—if you go to the borderlands, to help this wretched Lightbringer—things will go poorly for your people here. Do you understand?"

Loralon stared at him, stunned. Kurnos took a certain delight in his amazement and the defeat that crept into his eyes. The elf had meddled in imperial affairs, and now he was caught. Slowly, he nodded.

"Very well, Holiness," he said. He gestured toward the book. "But the prophecy cannot be denied."

"The prophecy is *heresy!*" Kurnos barked. He took a step toward Loralon, then checked himself, turning away. "Get out."

There was a silence, then the whisper of the elf's slippers across the marble floor. The golden doors boomed shut, and Kurnos was alone once more.

He slumped, putting a shaking hand to his brow. His head and stomach both ached, his right eyelid was twitching. He stood where he was for a time, a dull roar filling his head, then whirled with a snarl and grabbed up the book. He weighed it in his hands, staring at it with equal parts fear and anger. He knew of the prophecies of Psandros the Younger. They did have an unfortunate tendency to come true.

"Not this one," he whispered. "Not as long as I rule." Turning, he walked to one of the braziers by his throne. Giving the book one last, scornful glance, he tossed it into the fire.

The flames leapt, crackling hungrily as they devoured the *Qoi Zehomu*—first its pages, then its cover. As they charred the basilisk skin they changed color, turning bright green and leaping high above the golden vessel.

He felt no surprise at all when, as he was staring at the green flames, the ring began to burn his finger once more. As if pulled there, his gaze dropped to the emerald. It caught the fire's eerie light and magnified it, the shadows dancing within. The twin slits of the demon's eyes glared out at him, blazing with bloodlust.

It was wrong, he knew it. Sending the army after his foes was one thing, but what he meant to do went well beyond that. Still, he told himself, it had to be done. This Lightbringer was dangerous. He was as sure of it as he had ever been of anything in his life. He had to be stopped for the good of the empire.

Kurnos closed his eyes, took a deep breath. Forgive me, Paladine, he thought. This thing must be done.

"Sathira," he whispered.

A horrible howling filled the hall as the shadows came billowing out of the ring. The air around him became wintry, losing the heat of the brazier's flames. The ring seared his flesh, but he knew it would leave no mark, just as Fistandantilus's killing spell had left the hippogriff unscarred. Stefara of Mishakal had examined the poor creature's corpse, and though the signs of starvation troubled her, she had determined it had died naturally. The servants would burn the body tonight.

Kurnos felt a presence near him, the malevolence that poured from it drawing him back from his thoughts of the hippogriff. All at once he couldn't breathe, and he gasped, opening his eyes.

The demon was in front of him, her long, shadowy face barely a hand's breadth from his. Their eyes locked, as a long, thin talon rose and stroked his cheek. It burned where it touched him. He held his breath, trying to keep his mind from fraying at the demon's caress.

"Master," she growled in her jackal-wasp voice. "I had hoped you would free me again. I longed for it. What is your will?"

Kurnos hesitated, fear overcoming him at the last moment, then swallowed, putting the terror out of his mind. He had loosed Sathira. She would not return to the ring until he had given her a task. If he was certain of one thing, it was that he wanted her far, far away as soon as possible. He lowered his eyes from her scorching gaze.

"There is a place to the west," he said softly. "It is called Govinna."

———◆———

Dawn was breaking over Istar when Loralon left the Great Temple to face his exile. He did not go by ship, however, nor did he ride out through the gates. His people had their own way of traveling.

Ages ago, when even ancient Silvanost was young, the elves had tamed griffins as mounts. The Chosen of E'li kept a small aerie in the hills outside the Lordcity, where a dozen of the proud beasts awaited their call. Loralon still rode from time to time, traveling to his homeland to report to King Lorac. Now, as he stepped out of his cloister into the Temple's gardens, he closed his eyes, sending out a silent call.

Quarath, his aide, came out and stood beside him while he watched the sky. The younger elf's face was expressionless, his mien composed, but the sorrow in his eyes was unmistakable. He would be Emissary from this day forward, and it weighed on him to lose his master so suddenly.

It weighs on me too, Loralon thought, sighing.

"It will be a fine day," he said.

Quarath looked up, nodding. The sky was cloudless, the hue of ripe plums. He coughed softly. "*Shalafi*, I have spoken with some of the others, and we have all agreed. We want to leave with you."

"Leave?" Loralon echoed, taken aback. He shook his head, his beard wafting in the breeze. "No, Quarath! Our people need a presence here. These humans must be watched. You must make sure we keep our power in Istar."

Quarath nodded, bowing his head. "As you wish."

A distant sound—an eagle's cry, with a rumbling roar beneath—sounded from above. The elves looked skyward. There, circling above the city, was a large, odd shape, a great bird of prey with a lion's hindquarters. It wheeled slowly, riding the winds, and began to descend. Loralon eyed its features as it dove: the golden-feathered head, the sharp talons that could rend a man to pieces, the trailing, leonine tail. In some ways it resembled the hippogriff that had died mysteriously in Kurnos's garden just yesterday, but griffins were proud beasts and wild—never docile, like the other had been. Majestically the griffin swooped down, flapping its great wings to slow itself, and lit on a wide lawn, its claws digging furrows in the earth.

Loralon met its bright, amber gaze, then turned and kissed Quarath on the forehead. "Farewell, Emissary," he said.

Elves never wept in the presenc e of humans, but there were tears on Quarath's cheeks when Loralon stepped back. "Farewell, *shalafi*," he replied, interlacing his fingers to sign the sacred pine tree. "May E'li grant you fair winds."

The ancient elf nodded. "May he grant them to us all."

Turning, Quarath strode back toward the cloister. Loralon

watched him go, his lips pursed, then walked to the griffin, which tossed its head at his approach. He clucked at it, running his hand over its feathered neck, and it purred, nudging him with its beak. Smiling, he hitched up his robes and climbed onto its tawny back, settling himself between its massive shoulder blades, and whispered a word in elvish.

With a mighty roar the griffin leapt, spreading its wings to catch the morning wind. They were airborne, rising above the Temple. Loralon looked down, watching the Lordcity drop away beneath him, the basilica sparkling diamond-bright at its heart. The waters of Lake Istar glistened as the sun's first rays washed over them. The other cities of the empire's heartland dotted the wide, golden grasslands.

For a time, he looked to the west, considering. He longed to go to Govinna, to join Ilista there and give guidance. Above all, he yearned to see the Lightbringer with his own eyes, but he had to think of his own people. The Kingpriest had made it clear the elves in Istar would be in danger if he did anything so foolish. Kurnos might carry through with that threat, or he might not, but Loralon dared not take the risk.

Another voice called him now, from the south. The virgin woods of Silvanesti lay beyond Istar's southern deserts, cool and serene, swathed in mist and threaded with silver rivers. They were too far away to see, but he heard them just the same, beckoning with the voice of an old friend.

Come home, they called. *You have been away too long.*

With a sigh, Loralon patted the griffin's neck, then bent forward to speak a word in its ear. The beast shrieked in reply, then wheeled and soared away through the morning air, bearing the ancient elf back toward the land of his birth.

CHAPTER 19 ▼

The man was crying openly well before the Revered Sons were done with him—great, hitching sobs racking up his raw throat. Still they kept at it, three hard-eyed men in the red-fringed robes of inquisitors, taking turns asking questions while the bound villager—a man of perhaps fifty summers, bald and brawny, stripped to the waist and bleeding from a cut across his cheek—strained against the bowstrings that bound his hands and feet.

"Again," said the lead inquisitor, in a voice that matched the frigid highland wind. "Where are the other bandits? How many are they?"

"What of your lord?" demanded the cleric to his left. "Is he here or in Govinna?"

"Tell us about the one they call Lightbringer," growled the third priest. "Have you seen him?"

The man didn't answer; he simply kept weeping, broken, past the point of endurance. Tears ran down his face, mixing with his blood to drip on the stony ground. "I don't—I can't—please . . . mercy. . . ."

Standing nearby, Lord Holger Windsound turned away, his lip curling in distaste. He looked back across the valley, where the ruins of the village of Espadica still smoldered, capped by a pall of smoke. A few fires still burned here and there, but the worst was done. *Scatas* moved through the ashes, rounding up the last of the borderfolk and marching them away into the hills. A few bodies lay sprawled here and there. Not everyone let the army burn their homes without putting up a fight. It was a dreadful thing, razing a town, and one Lord Holger found distasteful but necessary. They had found bandits near Espadica, and the Kingpriest's orders were clear: all such towns were to be put to torch, the survivors moved to other towns—after thorough questioning, of course.

The man the clerics were working on had been an iron miner—most of Espadica's men dug ore—but he was also one of a gang of bandits the *Scatas* had caught in the hills near town. Of that gang, he was the only one they'd taken alive, and the priests had been at him for more than two hours now. He wasn't giving them any answers, though, and Holger suspected it was because he didn't know any. That didn't stop the inquisitors. Holger had seen them do this again and again in towns all over the south. Espadica was hardly the first village the *Scatas* had burned since they arrived in Taol.

They had been combing the southern fiefs for a month now, scouring the hills to little avail. Again and again, it was the same story: no brigands, only a scattering of common folk and grave-yards filled with plague-dead. The few men they caught knew nothing of import. Indeed, Lord Holger might have thought Kurnos's fears about the bandits were unfounded, except for two things. The first was the many hidden camps his men had uncovered among the hills. Long abandoned, those camps told the tale better than any prisoner might. There were many more bandits out there, but they had all streamed north to Govinna. That was where the real battle would be, but Holger wasn't about to march there until he knew the lands behind him were secure.

The second thing was Luciel.

The stories the riders he'd sent after the fleeing villagers told were wild ones, to be sure, and he'd decided they must be exaggerations. His *Scatas* claimed half a hundred Solamnics had fought them at the Edessa bridge, holding them off to make good the villagers' escape, but they had only brought back the bodies of six Knights. One of those had been Sir Gareth Paliost. Holger had burned the men with a heavy heart, building stone cairns to mark their graves. He had known Gareth and was sure the Knight had died valiantly, fulfilling his oath—no matter what—to protect the First Daughter.

No, Holger reminded himself. Balthera was First Daughter now, and Ilista was disgraced, *Foripon*. That made her a traitor, as much as the men who had taken up arms and captured the Little Emperor. Part of him still couldn't believe she had turned against the Kingpriest—she had always seemed devout, in the time they'd attended the imperial court together—but there it was. She and this young monk of hers, this Lightbringer, were beyond the god's sight now. That they cast their lot with the rebellious Taoli only proved it.

The wind blew a rope of smoke in his face, and he coughed, turning away from Espadica's remnants. The inquisitors were still working, pounding the borderman with questions. They were asking him about the Bridge of Myrmidons now, where Ilista and Beldyn had escaped the *Scatas* with the folk of Luciel. The man shook his head, denying any knowledge of what had happened, as Holger knew he would. The only men this side of the Edessa who knew what had happened were his own riders, and he didn't give their tales much credence. A sorcerer might be able to destroy a stone bridge with a word, but a monk barely old enough to shave?

Preposterous.

Finally, Holger lost his patience. The inquisitors might have kept going all night, given rein, but he didn't let them. "Enough," he declared. His snowy moustache drooped above a deep scowl. "You won't get anything out of that one."

The lead inquisitor, a gray-maned Revered Son named Rabos, glowered for a moment, as if he might challenge Holger's orders and carry on anyway. Instead, though, he exchanged looks with his fellows, then rose, nodding. The three priests stepped back, heads bowed, and signed the triangle. Holger walked forward, drawing his sword.

For all the weeping he'd done, the bandit met his death bravely, bowing his head and whispering a prayer to Paladine before the blade descended. Holger made sure it was quick, a single stroke lopping the man's head from his shoulders. It was a grim duty and one he chose not to shirk by ordering another man to do it. More than a dozen men had died by his sword over the past month. Now, as the blood poured from the brigand's body—it was always surprising, how much spilled forth—Holger wiped his blade clean with a handful of dry grass and decided this man was the last. He had spent enough time in the south. The land was secure, or near enough as made no difference. The time had come.

Half an hour later, he was back at camp, summoning his officers to him. An hour after that, riders galloped forth, bearing messages for the squads he had dispatched throughout the southern fiefs. It was time to gather again and march. Govinna awaited.

———————◆◆———————

Lord Ossirian leaned against the railing atop the Pantheon's highest tower. Beneath him Govinna drowsed in the morning light, smoke drifting from a sea of stone chimneys dotted by the green islands of temple roofs. His men walked the walls, bows and crossbows ready, and patrolled the city's streets, watching for trouble. His grim gaze went past all that, though, on to the hills to the south. His brows lowered, his bearded jaw tightening as though he could see the enemy through sheer will alone. The imperial army, however, steadfastly refused to appear.

It was out there, though. He could sense it, like a spoor on the wind. War was coming, and he was going to lose.

He'd first realized things had gone wrong when he learned of Kingpriest Symeon's death. Ossirian had been to the Lordcity many times, as recently as a year ago, and he knew enough of the imperial court to understand what the power shift meant. Symeon, he'd been certain, would negotiate, but Kurnos was a different matter. With the former First Son on the throne, Ossirian had the sickening suspicion that everything, all he had done, would come to nothing.

Then the soldiers came, and suspicion turned to certainty.

Riders had been arriving from the south for a week now, more every day. The tidings they brought were always the same. The *Scatas* had arrived in a town—one day Oveth, the next Espadica, even his home fief of Abreri—looking for signs of bandits. Sometimes they found none and quit the town in a rage. Other times they did, and people died.

He'd received word from Luciel, too. He'd dreaded what might happen if the soldiers discovered Tavarre and his men, but somehow the villagers had fled before that could happen. As if that were not wonder enough, they had managed to escape the *Scatas* and were marching north even now.

He'd heard the stories of the refugees' flight from men Tavarre had sent ahead, the tales of the monk who had destroyed the Bridge of Myrmidons. It was hard to discount them as fancy when they came from the lips of men who claimed to have seen the span collapse, but he told himself it had to be. Myths abounded of priests who could do such things, but they were hoary tales, dating back a thousand years to the Third Dragonwar and before. No cleric wielded that kind of power these days—and likely no one ever had. It was all stories, legends made up by the church. Ossirian might want them to be true, but that didn't make it so.

The same went for the other tale that preceded the so-called Lightbringer, of how he had cured the *Longosai*. Ossirian had heard the same story many times over the past few days. It had spread quickly through Govinna, folk speaking in hushed voices of how their neighbor's cousin or the uncle of a friend had felt the healing touch of Brother Beldyn. People listened to the stories with hope, for the plague had come to Govinna as well. It was still spreading slowly, but already a hundred were dead, and five times that many were sick, with more falling ill every day. In the crowded city, it wouldn't take long for the *Longosai* to rage out of control, like a flame in summer-dry brush. Folk knew it, too, and fear lurked in their eyes as they wondered how long it would be before they, too, lay wasted and feverish in their beds, coughing, vomiting and waiting for death. With that spectre hanging above them, it was small wonder so many wanted to believe the stories about the Lightbringer.

Plagues and miracle-working monks, however, were far from Ossirian's main worry this morning. Neither, in fact, was the imperial army, though he knew that would change once word came of its progress. Today, of all the things that troubled him, the foremost was the Little Emperor.

Ossirian never truly intended to harm the patriarch. Even when he'd taken Durinen prisoner, the threats he'd sent to the Lordcity were little more than a bluff. Perhaps another man might have been able to kill a hostage in cold blood, but Ossirian could not. He'd gambled, though, that the church hierarchs wouldn't guess that and would bargain with him—at least that was his hope, before Symeon had died.

He cursed, a bitter taste in his mouth. None of that mattered any more. The Little Emperor was going to die anyway.

It had been an amazingly stupid thing for Durinen to do. Last night—a scant few sleepless hours ago, in fact—the Little Emperor had tried to escape. Unable to face confinement in his own church any longer, he had attacked his guards when they brought the evening meal to the tower where they held him. The Little Emperor was a strong man, and he'd overcome the guards, leaving one man unconscious and the other with a broken arm. That gave him enough time to slip out and flee into the Pantheon's halls, seeking a way out into the city.

Before he could flee the temple, however, the guards had raised the alarm and sealed the building. He'd tried to hide, but one of Ossirian's men tracked him down in the Pantheon's servant's wing. The man had had a crossbow, shouting for the

Little Emperor to surrender. Foolishly, Durinen had tried to flee, and just as foolishly, the man had shot him.

Ossirian was no stranger to battle or to injured men. He knew a mortal wound when he saw it and could tell if it would kill a man fast or slow. He'd taken one look at the quarrel lodged in the patriarch's belly—too deep to pull out without taking half his insides with it—and bowed his head. Durinen might last days, even a week, but it would not be pleasant, and the end would come just the same. The prayers and medicines of the Mishakites Ossirian summoned wouldn't change that, any more than they could stop the *Longosai*. Now the Little Emperor lay back in his tower cell, drugged into a stupor with bloodblossom oil, awaiting the end—whenever it came. With gut wounds, you could never tell.

The tread of feet echoed up the tower steps, faint from far below, and Ossirian reached for his sword. In time a young man appeared, breathing hard. Ossirian recognized him—it was a lad from his own fief—but he still didn't lift his hand from his weapon. The boy bowed, wheezing after his climb. It was more than three hundred steps to the top of the tower.

"What is it now?" Ossirian snapped, his patience frayed.

The boy drew back at his anger, stammering. "I was looking—that is, I wanted to—you told me to tell you—"

"Tell me what?" Ossirian pressed. He knew it already—Durinen was dead, he was sure of it. He'd lost the last thin hope he had of saving his people from the *Scatas*. "Out with it!"

"Lord," the boy said, more composed now. "It's Baron Tavarre. The outriders spotted him and his lot on the road, about a league south of here. They'll be at the gates within the hour."

Ossirian blinked, surprised. He glanced over his shoulder, out across the hills once more, then, without another word, he pushed past the boy and dashed downstairs to the Pantheon below.

CHAPTER 20 ▼

W ord the survivors of Luciel had come spread through
Govinna with remarkable speed. By the time the city's
massive gates creaked open, folk were pouring out of homes,
taverns and shops to fill the narrow streets. Some came because
they had family or friends in the south and wanted to know
if they still lived; others because the First Daughter—*former*
First Daughter now—was with the refugees. More than a few
young women turned out in the hopes of catching the eye of
Lord Tavarre, a widower now and heirless. Most of those who
packed the winding roadways, however, did so for none of
those reasons. They came to see the monk, the miracle-worker,
who cured the *Longosai*.

Ossirian went out with an armed escort, watched over by
archers on the city's battlements, and met Tavarre and his
men just beyond bowshot of the walls. The two lords embraced
each other roughly, and there were tears on both men's cheeks
when they parted. Scratching his grizzled beard, Ossirian
looked past Tavarre to the mob of refugees. They were scrawny
and exhausted, shivering in their dirty clothes. Nearly three
weeks had passed since the fall of the Bridge of Myrmidons,
and the folk of Luciel had not borne it well. They were well,
though, with no sign of the *Longosai* among them.

Ilista sat her horse nearby, looking grave and troubled, and behind her—also ahorse—were two young men. The first wore fighting leathers and shared his saddle with a skinny, golden-haired girl. The other was clad in a dirty gray habit and had eyes like blue diamonds. The sun's light was pale, muted by the gray sky above, but around him the air seemed brighter, glittering like the snow on the hilltops did.

"You must be the one we've heard about," Ossirian said, "the one they call Lightbringer."

"I am," said Beldyn.

"The stories are true? You healed these people?"

"They aren't stories," insisted the young bandit beside the monk.

Ossirian recognized him then, beneath the road-grime and the scraggly whiskers that patched his cheeks. MarSevrin, the one who had brought him the Little Emperor, and begged leave to return south, so he could be with . . . with his dying sister. Ossirian paled, looking at the girl who rode with him. She was frail with hunger, dark smudges under her eyes, but as for the *Longosai*, there was no sign of the disease. Ossirian's lips parted as Wentha met his gaze, then blushed and lowered her eyes.

Catching his breath, he looked back at Beldyn, who smiled quietly within his radiance. For a moment all he could do was stare, caught by the monk's piercing gaze, then he eased his steed aside and waved toward the city, the green roofs of its temples rising above the walls.

"Come on, then," he said. "We have need of you."

When they first entered the city, the crowds were so thick, they could barely get out of the gatehouse. Folk pressed in on all sides, jostling and craning to see the newcomers. Many were sick or maimed. The blind, the lame . . . men afflicted with palsies, women stricken by barrenness . . . and here and there, those whose hands and throats showed the first darkenings of the Slow Creep. Those with the plague numbered more than the population of Luciel at its height, and they were only the beginning. In sickbeds all over the city, the people of Govinna were dying, their bodies ravaged by the *Longosai*.

When they saw the refugees for the first time, a great cheer rose from the crowd, hands rising to punch at the sky, a few throwing flowers or copper coins as Tavarre and Ossirian's men formed a wedge and started shoving their way into the throng. A mighty shout rose from the mob's midst, a cry that spread so fast that suddenly everyone seemed to take up all at once.

"Beldinas!" they cried. "Beldinas! Praise to the Lightbringer!"

Ilista stared in amazement as the party inched its way into Govinna, pushing slowly up the street. She had seen mobs like this before, in the Lordcity. It was the sort of crowd that had greeted Symeon on those rare days when he set foot outside the Great Temple. Looking out upon the sea of smiling faces—even those marred by sickness—she felt the lurking disquiet again. It was one thing for the people of Luciel to adore Beldyn, for what he had done for them, but this . . . these people had never glimpsed him before, yet they cried Beldyn's name in the church tongue, as if he were a Kingpriest himself. She shuddered at the fanatical fire in their eyes. If this was how they looked on him now, how would they react when he cured *their* sicknesses?

Beldyn did nothing to quell her apprehensions. He hadn't been in a city of any size in years, had lived in a crumbling monastery since he was a child. He should have blanched at the sight of so many shouting people—particularly when what they shouted was his name—but instead he looked about, tall in his saddle, and nodded to the swarming throngs, signing the triangle over them. Somehow, a young woman pushed through and threw herself at him, clutching at his cassock, but when Cathan moved to shove her back, Beldyn shook his head and clasped her hand in his, then gently nudged her away. She melted into the crowd again, her face glowing with joy.

They adore him, Ilista thought. Do people throng and yell for Kurnos this way?

She shook her head, shivering.

It took more than an hour at such a slow pace, but finally they reached the Pantheon, its high towers and slanted, copper roof looming at Govinna's heart. There they dismounted, leaving the folk of Luciel, under the watchful eyes of Tavarre's men. The baron, meanwhile, walked beside Ossirian leading the way to the temple, while Beldyn followed, still smiling, Ilista at his side. Cathan paused to kiss his sister, then left her with the other refugees, laying a hand on his sword hilt as he fell in protectively alongside the Lightbringer.

The mob filled the courtyard before the church—a plaza not as large as the *Barigon* in Istar but nearly so—even spilling up the long, broad stair leading to its great, dragon-carved doors. Only after those doors boomed shut behind them, shutting them inside the temple's dim, cool halls, did the shouting fall away and the press of bodies stop. Ilista pressed her medallion to her lips, her ears ringing.

The Pantheon's vestibule was dim and cool, the frescoes and tapestries on its walls all but lost in shadow. Clouds of pungent incense filled the air, glowing ruddy about the flames of candles. At the far end, another pair of doors gave onto the main worship hall, a vast, pillared space lit by stark shafts of light from high windows. Gold and silver gleamed all about, and though it bore little resemblance to the basilica in Istar—the hall was oblong, not round, and an altar, not a throne, stood at its head—its opulence still brought a pang of homesickness to Ilista's heart. After so long in the wilderness, she was back in the church's embrace. It was nearly enough to make her forget she was *Foripon*.

Beldyn looked around, eyes shining, and nodded to himself.

Ossirian led them out of the worship hall—the priests within watching with raised eyebrows as they passed through —and down a carpeted hall to a long circular stair. Up they went, through an archway marking the entrance to the Patriarch's Tower, past parlors and prayer rooms, up and up and still higher up, until at last they stopped before a pair of brass-bound doors, where two men in chain jacks stood watch. The guards dipped their spears to Ossirian, then stared at Beldyn as they opened up and let the group pass through. Ilista heard them whispering to each other as the doors thudded shut again

They entered a study with a broad snowwood desk, velvet-cushioned chairs and shelves lined with dusty books. A door opened on the far end, letting out an old, haggard woman in blue vestments. Ilista watched, thinking how long it had been since she'd seen a Mishakite healer. The woman spoke softly with Lord Ossirian, shaking her head at his questions. Finally she stepped back, her face grave, and led the way into the Little Emperor's private bedchamber.

The smell of bloodblossom hung heavy in the room. Its heady, soothing scent told Ilista all she needed to know. The Mishakites were sparing with the precious oil, for it was both expensive and dangerous. More than one rich lord had become addicted to the smoke that came from burning it, lost in a blissful haze while the gold vanished from his coffers. If the healer was using so much, Durinen's pain must be terrible indeed.

"He sleeps," the old Mishakite said. "He was screaming earlier, so I eased his suffering." She kissed her fingertips, then pressed them to the corners of her eyes to sign the goddess's twin teardrops.

The room was well appointed, jewels glistening on its walls, silken curtains hanging across a walk to a balcony outside. Mosaics of wild animals cavorted on its ceiling. The bed was a mound of furs and cushions in its midst. Once more curtains had surrounded it, but they were gone now, torn down and cast into a corner. There was blood on them and in the bed as well. Looking at the Little Emperor, Ilista caught her breath.

Durinen was shirtless, his bare skin white and shining with sweat that soaked his graying hair as well. His proud face was smooth, unlined by pain—the bloodblossom's work, surely—but muscles still jumped in his neck, and his fingers clutched the blankets like talons.

Worst of all, though, was the wound itself. The quarrel still lodged in his belly, surrounded by bandages that bloomed scarlet where his blood soaked through. The quarrel moved as he breathed, rocking back and forth with each exhale, and the drug's fumes could not hide the bilious stink coming from it.

Calmly, Beldyn reached to the neck of his cassock and withdrew his medallion. He brushed his fingertips across the patriarch's brow, then reached out and touched the bolt's iron shaft. Durinen's face tightened, a gurgle of pain bubbling up his throat.

"Don't," the healer warned, grabbing Beldyn's wrist. "That quarrel's the only thing keeping him from the gods."

Beldyn regarded her, his eyes piercing, until she paled and drew back. Head bowed, he went to stand at the head of the bed and gazed down on Durinen's face. Then, shutting his eyes, he tightened his grasp about his medallion and began to pray. His lips moved silently, and the air about him shivered then began to glow. A spasm of discomfort passed over his face, the corners of his mouth tightening as he reached out to touch Durinen's face. A groan escaped his lips, and he swayed like a drunk man, sweat beading on his forehead and running down his face. The nimbus around him flickered and began to fade. Blood welled between his fingers as he squeezed his medallion tighter and tighter still.

Too much time passed.

Merciful god, Ilista thought. He can't do it. Something's wrong. . . .

With a shuddering groan, Beldyn's knees buckled, and he began to sway.

Ilista tensed, but someone was quicker. In a heartbeat Cathan was at his side, catching his arm and holding him up. "Master," he said. "Wait. You have to stop. . . ."

"*No*," Beldyn moaned through thin, white lips. "Hold me. I must finish. . . ."

Cathan shook his head, his mouth opening to protest. Durinen's wound was too grievous. The wound was tainted, the contents of his bowels mixing with his blood, but something in Beldyn's face silenced his objections. Cathan tightened his grasp on the monk. Nostrils flared wide, Beldyn took a slow, deep breath to calm himself . . . and *spoke*.

The voice that came from his lips was not like any Ilista had heard him use before. It carried none of its usual music, no soothing undertone. Deep and firm, this voice filled the room at the tower's pinnacle like a thunderclap.

"*Abagnud!*" he shouted.

Awake!

The light flared around him, making Ossirian curse as it stung his eyes, flowing down over Durinen. With a grunt of exertion he let go of the patriarch's forehead and stumbled back, Cathan supporting him when he would have collapsed altogether. His shoulders slumped, but his eyes blazed as he continued to stare at the figure on the bed.

Despite the wound, despite the bloodblossom, the Little Emperor's eyes fluttered open.

He lay still, looking at the ceiling with confusion in his eyes. There was no pain in them and no drugged stupor. Instead they were bright, sharp. Brows knitting, he pushed himself up, propping himself on his elbows. He stared at the quarrel lodged in his flesh and frowned.

"What is this?" he asked.

"It's—it's all right," Beldyn gasped from behind him. "Take it—out."

Durinen nodded, looking dazedly at the quarrel. Then, with a motion so quick even the Mishakite had no time to do more than suck in a horrified breath, he reached up and yanked the bolt from his body.

Ilista cringed, expecting bright life-blood and entrails to gush from the wound. That didn't happen. Instead, barbed head and all, the bolt slid easily out of Durinen's belly, leaving behind only an angry weal on unbroken skin. As she watched, the red mark also faded—or rather, the rest of him brightened, his flesh turning healthy pink once more, rather than the sickly white it had been moments before.

Durinen turned the quarrel in his hand. There was not a spot of blood upon it. It shone with the light that streamed and coursed around Beldyn. Abruptly he flung it away, sending it clattering across the marble floor. Swallowing, he turned, his gaze seeking out Beldyn—then froze as he saw his savior, a gasp tearing from his lips. His mouth worked, but it took him several tries to find his voice.

"*You!*" he croaked at last.

Ilista looked up, shocked, and saw it too. Beldyn was as she'd seen him in Luciel, that first day when he'd laid his healing touch upon Wentha. Amid the mantle of light, bright enough that it brought stinging tears flooding from her eyes, she saw him clad in pearly samite and golden breastplate, jeweled rings and silk slippers. There, on his head, gleamed the crown. She stared at it: exquisitely crafted, all shimmering gold and sparkling rubies. She frowned, wondering what it was. It seemed so familiar. . . .

In a flash, it was gone, and Beldyn was a monk again, shrouded in shining light, his eyes fluttering closed as the effort of healing Durinen overcame him at last. Cathan kept him from crumpling, and Ossirian and Tavarre rushed to help him to a velvet-padded bench. None of them had shared Ilista's vision, nor had the Mishakite, who hurried to the bedside, gaping in shock at what just happened. Durinen had seen it, however. She felt certain she saw it in the Little Emperor's face . . . before, draining away to unconsciousness once more, he slumped back down among the cushions. He lay still, let out a slow breath . . . then began to whisper, his lips forming words Ilista couldn't hear.

"What's he saying?" she asked.

The Mishakite leaned close, listening, but frowned when

she straightened up again. "I don't know. It doesn't make any sense . . ."

With an irritated snort, Ilista rushed forward, pushing the healer aside to bend low. At first she heard nothing, so soft was his voice, but then, faintly, she made it out—the same four words, over and over—and her breath left her in a rush of wonder and terror.

"*Site ceram biriat, abat,*" the Little Emperor murmured. "*Site ceram biriat, abat . . .*"

Later that night, Ilista knelt alone in a chapel off the Pantheon's worship hall. The room held a small shrine blazing with white candles, atop which perched an icon of Paladine, coiled in his form as the platinum dragon. It stared down at her with topaz eyes that danced with light. She did not speak, made no entreaties of the god. Her thoughts were spinning too quickly for prayer.

Tavarre and Ossirian both pressed her, but she hadn't spoken to them of the Little Emperor's whispered words, nor had she revealed her vision of Beldyn in imperial raiment. Finally they had abandoned her to tend to the matter of finding places for the refugees from Luciel to dwell. First, though, they'd taken Beldyn down from the Patriarch's Tower, to a bedchamber in the cloisters and there laid him down to rest. Cathan remained with him, as faithful as any hound, and Ilista had come down here to be alone. It seemed like only a short time ago, but the candles on the shrine had burned down to waxy stubs, and her legs were numb from kneeling.

Hinges creaking, the door to the sanctuary opened behind her, and silvery light flowed in. She swallowed, feeling the presence in the entry.

"Brother," she said, turning. "Come in. I was just thinking of you."

Beldyn entered, chuckling. He had taken off his torn habit and wore a simple white robe, unadorned and unembroidered, in its place. He bowed his head as he shut the door, his bright eyes downcast.

"Forgive me, *Efisa*," he said. "I did not mean to interrupt."

Ilista shook her head, pushing herself up. Her knees popped as she got to her feet. "It's all right," she said. "I've been here too long. Besides, we must talk."

"Yes," he agreed. "We must."

They left the chapel together and went to a nearby apse, where they sat together on a marble window seat. Ilista looked out through the glass, at the city below. The red moon shone down on Govinna, limning the roofs of its temples with crimson fire. Though she couldn't see them, she felt the presence of people in the streets. They were out there still, holding candles and chanting—Beldinas, Lightbringer, Beldinas. . . .

"*Site ceram biriat, abat*," Beldyn said. "Whoever wears the crown, rules."

She started and turned to look at him.

"Yes," he said, running a hand through his thick, brown hair. "I heard him say it too, just before I passed out."

Ilista shivered, but said nothing. Fear ran through her like silver fire.

"He saw something in that room," he pressed, leaning closer. His eyes gleamed. "You did, too. You can't hide it from me, *Efisa*. What is it?"

She didn't want to tell him. She was too afraid of what it all portended. His glittering blue gaze caught her, transfixed her, and she found herself speaking the words anyway. "Beldyn, have you heard of the *Miceram*?"

He paused, catching his breath, then nodded. "The Crown of Power," he replied. "Brother Voss told me the tales when I was a boy. The first Kingpriests wore it, but Paladine took it away a hundred years ago, when the Three Thrones' War began."

"That's one tale," she said, shrugging. "No one is sure what became of it, to tell the truth. Whatever happened, though, no one has seen it since. Although many have searched, there is no trace of its whereabouts. After it disappeared, people began to whisper that it would return one day, when darkness ruled the land. The man who bore it would be the true lord of Istar."

"Whoever wears the crown, rules," Beldyn whispered. His eyes glistened in his own light. "I am to be Kingpriest, then."

Ilista jerked as if stung, the color draining from her face. She looked away. "I didn't say that."

"You've been thinking it," he replied, his hand grasping hers. "You saw me wearing the *Miceram*, up there in the tower, didn't you?"

She shook her head, pulling away from his grasp. "It can't be. Darkness doesn't rule the land. Kurnos is no friend of mine, but he is not evil."

"Isn't he?" Beldyn pressed. "He sent the army here to slaughter innocent women and men, burn their villages. When we helped them instead, he cast us both out of the church. Don't you think it's convenient the old Kingpriest died when he did? *Efisa*, Paladine only knows what dark pacts Kurnos has made—"

"No!" she snapped, rising from the bench. "I know Kurnos. He is hard man, but he serves the gods."

"Tell that to Gareth," Beldyn said, standing and gesturing out the window. "Tell that to the others who died needlessly in these hills. I will stop him, *Efisa*. You saw what happened out there today, in the streets. The people *will* follow me. I will be Kingpriest!"

Ilista threw up her hands. "The Crown is lost! How can it help you if no one knows where it is?"

He looked at her, then, and she shivered at the fervor on his face. His devoutness had always unsettled her a little, but there was something more awful about his certainty. "Someone knows, *Efisa,* and I think I know who."

She shook her head, trembling. "Who?"

He smiled, his eyes glowing with zeal. "The Little Emperor."

CHAPTER 21 ▼

The crowd that had greeted the refugees the day before had been large, hundreds strong. It was nothing, though, compared with the throng that gathered outside the Pantheon the following morning. As word of the Lightbringer's arrival spread throughout Govinna, more and more people poured into the plaza before the church, the hundreds becoming thousands, some bearing torches and lamps to warm themselves in the dawn's chill. As the numbers swelled, the noise they made grew as well, first a low murmur, then a buzz of muttering mixed with the occasional pious voice raised to sing a hymn. Finally, while rosy strands of the coming day reached out across the turquoise sky, the crowd picked up into a chant, low and steady, like drums beating an army's marching cadence in the church tongue:

"*Beldinas Cilenfo! Beldinas Nirinfo! Beldinas Pilofiro!*"

Beldyn the Healer! Beldyn the Savior! Beldyn the Lightbringer!

So it went as the sliver-thin silver moon rose above the hills, just ahead of the sun. Ossirian's men, standing guard outside the Pantheon, eyed the mob warily, hands twisting about their spearshafts. As with any place in Istar, the gathered masses were a fickle and dangerous thing. If their mood soured and they chose to move on the temple, even a full phalanx of warriors wouldn't be able to hold them back.

Suddenly, the tone of their murmuring *did* change. It wasn't anger that tinged their voices, however, but joy. Some waved their arms in the air, others fell to their knees, weeping, but most jabbed their fingers up toward the Pantheon's tallest tower. There, high above, several figures had appeared on a balcony. Though high above the crowd, there was no mistaking who they were. The hulking form of Lord Ossirian, the tall, austere shape of Lady Ilista, and standing between them, clad in robes the color of polished ivory and shadowed by the young bandit who accompanied him always now, was the one who drew the fiercest cheers. The Lightbringer had appeared.

Beldyn behaved as though he were Kingpriest already, thought Ilista, smiling and waving to the crowd, accepting their adulation as his due. Looking at him, then down at the shouting masses below, she wondered if he even needed the Crown.

Ossirian seemed to share that thought, for there was a glint of envy in his eye as he leaned over to speak to Beldyn. "They were never mine," he said. "Not truly. I held the city, but I didn't rule. They're yours now, lad—say the word, and they'll follow you to the Abyss."

Beldyn shook his head, still smiling. "It isn't the Abyss where I mean to lead them."

He stepped forward, raising his hands, and at once a hush fell over the crowd. Awestruck eyes stared up at him, from the courtyard and the terraces and rooftops around it. In the east, the clouds glowed golden as the young monk swept the crowd with his strange, glittering gaze. Ilista realized she could hear her own blood pounding, fast as a yearling foal's. She gripped the copper balustrade, her knuckles whitening as Beldyn drew a deep breath, let it out, and began to speak.

"You have suffered, my children," he proclaimed, his musical voice carrying out across the plaza. "Plague has come to you, and your church and empire do nothing to help. In the Lordcity they sup on honeyed milk, while you make do with scraps. The man who sits upon the throne, who should be aiding you, instead seeks to crush you by force. Even now, his *Scatas* advance upon this city, having burned their way across the southlands.

"War is coming, and the battle to be fought here will be a terrible one—not just because the enemy is vast, but because of who the enemy are. It is not the spawn of darkness who march toward the walls, not goblins or ogres, or those who follow the gods of evil. No, my children, those who come are our brothers, men like you, ordered into unjust battle by a Kingpriest corrupted."

A gasp ran through the mob at this, and on the balcony Cathan and Ossirian both looked sharply at Beldyn. Ilista's mouth dropped open as well. It was one thing to speak ill of Kurnos privately. Doing so in front of the better part of an entire city, even one stirred by rebellion, was something else. It was unwise. Before she could do more than frown, however, Beldyn went on.

"Yes, corrupted!" he bellowed. "How else to describe a man who sends soldiers to subjugate his own people, rather than bread to feed them? Istar is a holy place, the mightiest Krynn has ever known, and Lord Kurnos is a tyrant, unfit to rule. The god's voice, he calls himself. Pah! A lie, unless the god is the Queen of Darkness herself, working to rot the empire from within! Will you allow this to happen?"

The people of Govinna roared in reply, thousands of voices becoming one great, thunderous roar. "*No!*" they cried.

"Will you surrender to the troops he has sent to quell you? Will you kneel before a ruler who does not merit his crown?"

"*No!*"

"Then follow me!" Beldyn shouted, stretching out his arms. "I am the Lightbringer, foretold by ancient prophecy! Follow me, and help rid Istar of evil once and for all! Follow me, for *I* am the chosen of the gods, and with Paladine on our side, we must prevail!"

The sun broke over the horizon, spilling dawn's light across the city. It painted Govinna's walls and kissed the bridges that linked its two halves together, setting its high rooftops ablaze with coppery fire. It fell across the courtyard, making long shadows of the buildings to the east. When it fell upon the balcony and on Beldyn himself, the air about him came alive, sparkling in the golden morning, falling in shimmering waves from his body, in a cascade that poured down from the tower's heights.

The throngs remained silent a heartbeat longer, staring in awe, then bellowed in reply, louder than any dragon's cry, clapping hands and stamping the ground as the chant took over again. *"Beldinas! Beldinas! Beldinas!"*

Beldyn stood amid it all, bathed in the newborn sunglow, smiling.

Amid the furor, a lithe, dark shape huddled at the courtyard's edge, staring up at the balcony with eyes like green, burning splinters. No one came near Sathira. Though they didn't see her crouched in her native shadows, the cold that surrounded the demon kept people away. A few folk even signed the triangle, muttering warding prayers at the unnatural chill. She laughed silently, for she had no mouth, and her talons clenched as she glowered at Beldyn. Let the mortal folk believe in him, she thought. It will only make their weeping more bitter when it comes.

First, though, there was the day to get through, or what remained of it. The sunrise had thwarted her as she sought to cross the yard, but winter was near, and the days were growing shorter. In a few hours, there would be darkness to spare, and she could move freely again. Let Beldyn live one more day—it would only sweeten the taste of his soul.

Hissing in anticipation, she pulled back into the darkness, into shadows so thick that none could see her, not until she struck. Let them fear me, she thought.

Then she was gone, lost in gloom cast by the morning light.

The halo of sunlight vanished from Beldyn the moment he stepped back into the tower. By the time the sky began to darken again, though, the familiar silver glow had taken its place. All that day, he remained in the Pantheon's worship hall, receiving the folk of Govinna. Many came simply to kneel before him, bowing their heads to kiss his medallion while Cathan looked on with steely eyes. Though Ossirian's men made them yield their weapons at the temple doors, the young bandit kept one hand on his sword at all times.

Scattered among the supplicants came others, those who had been there to greet him when he arrived in the city the day before: the sick and crippled, some leaning on other men's shoulders as they drew near. Many were victims of the *Longosai*, but there were others, too, who did not bear the dark blotches that marked them as plague-stricken. The healing light flared for them all, as it had so often in Luciel, filling the shadowy hall again and again as Beldyn laid his hands upon the supplicants. Those with the Creep rose from their knees, untainted. A woman blind since childhood blinked back tears from eyes that could see once more. A man paralyzed from the waist down rose and began to walk. Some laughed for joy, but many others wept, murmuring tearful thanks while Beldyn sprinkled them with holy water and signed the triangle in farewell.

Ilista stayed near at all times, standing silently behind the altar. Beldyn was getting stronger, his powers holding up better than in Luciel. Then he had only been able to heal eight a day and one at a time. Today in the Pantheon, though, he touched more than a score of Govinna's folk before sending them away again, fully cured. Ilista watched as one by one

223

they rose, as healthy as if they had been well all their lives, and the light that hung around Beldyn grew from a flicker to a dazzling glare.

In the end, though, even the Lightbringer tired, and as the sunlight that lanced down from the hall's high windows shifted to evening crimson, Beldyn's endurance finally gave out. His shoulders slumped and his eyelids drooped as he pronounced Paladine's blessing upon a healthy young boy who, only moments before, had been covered with weeping sores. As the child's sobbing mother led him away, he gave a weary sigh and shook his head.

"No more," he breathed. "Tell them they can return on the morrow."

Cries of disappointment rang from the vestibule as the temple's clerics turned the rest of the people away, then the worship hall's dragon-carved doors boomed shut, blocking them out. Beldyn walked to a pew and slumped down onto it. Ilista watched as he spoke briefly with Cathan, then the young bandit bowed and withdrew, disappearing out a side door.

"His sister," Beldyn said when he caught her look. "He hasn't seen her all day. I told him he could stay with her tonight."

Ilista nodded, sitting down beside him. "You did great things today."

"Not enough." He shook his head, gesturing about the worship hall. "How many more are out there, for every one I helped today?"

She nodded, thinking of the mobs that had been in the courtyard this morning. Probably they were all still there. She rested a hand on his shoulder. "You can't ease the world's suffering in a day."

"Not without the *Miceram*," he whispered.

Ilista looked up at the mosaic of Paladine on the ceiling, her stomach twisting. Even when she'd heard Kurnos had declared her *Foripon*, she hadn't thought of herself as a traitor to the empire. Now . . . she had brought Beldyn here, had stood by as he all but named himself Kingpriest this morning.

What does that make me? she thought. Paladine, how am I to serve thee?

She didn't hear Ossirian come in, didn't see him until he was nearly upon them both, lowering his bearish form to genuflect toward the altar, then bowing to Beldyn as he came forward.

"What is it?" she asked.

"Durinen," the lord replied. "He's awake and asks for the one who healed him."

Beldyn nodded. "Very well," he said, rising from the bench. He smiled at Ilista. "There are things I wish to discuss with him as well."

———◆———

The Little Emperor would not receive guests from his sickbed, so he had moved from his private chambers to the study. He was still weak from his wound and leaned heavily against his desk, staring across at Ilista and Beldyn when Ossirian showed them in. His eyes narrowed, his mouth drooping into a grave frown.

"I hear," he said, "that you have been making my subjects your own."

Ilista's brow creased at the words, and Ossirian scowled as well, but Beldyn folded his hands politely.

"Pardon, Your Worship," he said from within his mantle of light, "but that is not quite right. They have come to me. I only received them."

"Hmph," Durinen replied with a shrug. "Well, I am a practical man. I know I have little power to stop you." He pressed his fingertips against his stomach, where the quarrel had been, and his eyes closed for a moment, remembering. "Besides, perhaps you are right to do so. There are things I know about you that even you have not yet perceived."

Beldyn nodded. "The *Miceram*, you mean."

The Little Emperor's eyes flared wide, and Ossirian let out a snort of laughter. Durinen glared at him, lips pursed, but

225

chuckled in spite of himself. His eyes flicked to Ilista, then back to Beldyn. "You *do* know, then. How much have you guessed?"

"Very little," Beldyn replied. "Only that, whatever the tales might say, you may know the truth of the crown's disappearance."

"Indeed," Durinen said, raising an eyebrow. "That is a great deal already."

He rose and shuffled across the room to a bookshelf where several scrolls lay. He peered at them for a moment before producing one, then walked back around the desk and handed it to Beldyn. He said nothing, standing back as the young monk removed the silken tie about the parchment and unrolled it. Ilista crowded nearer and Ossirian too, as Beldyn studied the scroll. The words it bore were in the church tongue, as was a well-rendered illumination of a man in rich finery—flowing white robes and jewels, an emerald diadem on his brow. His face was dusky, his hair close-cropped, his face shaven. His prominent nose and piercing eyes gave him the look of a hawk.

None of this caught their attention, however, so much as what he held in his hands. There was a second crown, wrought of gold and aglitter with rubies.

"Pradian," Durinen said. "The man who would have won the *Trosedil* had he lived, whose dynasty should be ruling the empire entire and not just this province." His mouth twisted bitterly.

Ilista shuddered as she stared at the image. The man glaring back out at her had dared to challenge the Lordcity from this very temple a century before. She felt a strange kinship with him. Both of us traitors to the throne, she thought. Her eyes went back to the ruby crown in his hands.

"The *Miceram*," she noted. "He stole it?"

"No!" Durinen snapped. "Not stole. *Claimed* it, as his due. He was at Vasari's side when he died. He held him in his arms and heard the Kingpriest name him heir, but there was no one to witness those words, so it came to war. Here he ruled until he died untimely, and Ardosean seized the throne. We Little Emperors have kept the truth alive, ever since. We alone know where he hid the Crown."

"Hid it?" Ilista pressed. "Why? Surely, if he'd used it—"

"Then people would have called him a thief, as you just did." The patriarch shook his head as Ilista flushed in embarrassment. "Whoever wears the Crown may rule, but Pradian wanted the people's respect. He meant to win the war on his own terms, then reveal the crown to affirm his claim. He would have done so, too, but for one killing arrow.

"Your next question," he added, raising a hand as Ilista's mouth opened to speak, "is why none of his heirs have simply donned the crown. You hold the answer in your hands. Read."

Beldyn and Ilista looked down the page, and Ossirian craned to see as well. There, written in archaic calligraphy, was a verse:

E Pradian Miceram nomid, e sam nouton aulcam si adomfrit cilid, beton 'tis cir boniit, bareis op onbordas. Bebo ninlugit attaid sam ih torpit.'

"And Pradian took the Crown of Power," Durinen recited, shutting his eyes, "and concealed it beneath the temple he had built, saying 'Let this remain here, guarded from the unworthy. Let the way not open until it is needed again.'

"We have all tried to bring it back, we Little Emperors," he went on, "and we failed. The door it lies behind did not open for Theorollyn, who was first after Pradian, and it has opened for none since."

The study was silent as Beldyn read the text again. His eyes settled on Pradian's hard countenance, then rose to meet Durinen's stare. "Where does this door lie?"

"In the catacombs," Durinen replied. "There is an old fane there, far beneath the Pantheon. Its location is written elsewhere in the text you hold. But beware. The door is only the first—"

It happened so fast, Ilista barely had time to note the sudden chill that bit the air within the study. The shadows in the corner nearest to the Little Emperor came alive, bleeding outward like ink spilled on a page. A horrible noise, like a hyena's mad cackle mixed with the droning of carrion flies, filled the air as they enveloped Durinen. Two green slits appeared within them, flashing like storm-trapped lightning. He stiffened in its nightmarish embrace, the color draining from his face.

Eyes wide with terror, the Little Emperor opened his mouth to scream.

The darkness tore out his throat.

Blood sprayed from Durinen's body, turning the front of his robes bright crimson in an instant. Ilista heard someone scream, then realized it was her own voice as warm droplets spattered her face. The Little Emperor stood erect a moment longer, making a ragged, gurgling noise as he clutched at the dark, wet smile that had appeared beneath his chin. Then the darkness let him go, and he toppled face-first to the floor.

No one moved. Ilista's mind cast about, trying to make sense of what had just happened. Her gaze rose from Durinen, lying in a spreading scarlet pool, to the shadow-thing that was changing now, taking on solid form—sinuous and wavering. Its poison-green slit-eyes narrowed on Beldyn.

She knew then, with a sudden rush that robbed her of breath—knew why it was here. It was no coincidence—the creature had been sent to kill the Lightbringer. What horrified her most, however, was the certainty of who had sent it.

Palado Calib, she thought. Kurnos, what have you done?

Time slowed as the shadow demon stared at Beldyn, tensing like a coiled serpent. It eyed him warily, wavering as it regarded the aura of light that cloaked him. He stared back, his eyes wide with fear for the first time since Ilista had known him.

A loud ringing filled the air, and time sped up as Ossirian jerked his sword from its scabbard. "Guards!" he barked. "To me!"

The door burst open at once, and the two bandits who had stood watch outside the room burst in, weapons at the ready—then stopped in their tracks, their jaws going slack as they saw the Little Emperor's gruesome remains and the shadow looming over the scene. They blinked, their faces turning the color of chalk.

The shadow didn't hesitate. Whirling, it rounded on the guards with a snarl, then flowed across the room with a grace that was at once beautiful and horrific. The men froze before it, transfixed. It ripped the first man apart with three quick sweeps of its claws, hurling the scraps aside in a gory shower. The man's partner screamed, panicking, turned to run—and died just as swiftly, a single talon of shadowstuff, as solid now as iron, punching through the back of his skull. He dangled lifelessly from the demon's claw, then went down in a heap when it jerked free.

Seeing his men fall, Ossirian hurled himself forward, swinging his sword as the shadow turned back toward Beldyn. He hacked at it viciously, a mighty two-handed blow that would have cleft a man in two from neck to groin, but the creature was no man. The weapon passed through it as though it wasn't there and bit into the wood-paneled wall behind it. Ossirian stumbled, thrown off balance, and barked a vicious curse.

With another shrieking laugh, the shadow grabbed his head in its claws and squeezed. Ossirian screamed, then a sickening crunch cut him off, and his arms and legs drooped. The demon let him go, and he fell beside Durinen, blood streaming from his nose, mouth, and ears.

It had all taken less than a minute.

The shadow hovered over the corpses, four ruined things that had once been men. Ilista thought, oddly, of Cathan, the boy from Luciel who had sworn to protect Beldyn. He would be a fifth, now, if he were here. A mercy, perhaps, that he was not—but neither was anyone else.

Except for her.

She watched, her whole body turning cold, as the demon turned toward Beldyn once more. It hissed, long blood-dripping claws flexing, and she knew she had to do something. Strangely, there was no fear—only sorrow that after all she had gone through, it came to this. She reached to her throat, drawing out her medallion from beneath her robes.

"Paladine," she murmured. "Please be with me."

The shadow leaped with a snarl, an arrow of darkness streaking across the room. Ilista was quicker, though, reaching out with her free hand to shove Beldyn aside. He stumbled back with a shout, slamming against the wall.

"*Efisa*, no!" he screamed.

Ilista ignored him. Instead, she yanked the medallion free, its chain snapping, and thrust it forward as the shadow struck her. Its claws sank into her flesh like spears of ice, and the pain was horrible, a hundred times worse than when the wyvern's talons had struck her, but she shoved the pain aside, pressing the medallion into the heart of the shadow demon as its talons ripped her open. The creature's laughter was all around her, sounding like a hundred leering madmen. Red mist fogged her vision, but she blinked it away, forcing her breath out in a shout, fearing she would never draw another.

"*Scugam oporud!*" she cried, her breath fogging in the shadow-born cold. *Demon begone!*

The laughter twisted, turned into a furious scream as silver light flared, filling the room.

Silence, darkness.

———◆◆◆———

"Open your eyes, child."

Ilista knew the voice. She did as it bade.

She stood in Durinen's study, surrounded by carnage. The Little Emperor and Lord Ossirian lay side by side like broken dolls. Before the doors, the bloody tatters that once had been the men who guarded the room, glistened red. At her feet . . .

She felt an awful rushing within her, like falling in a dream. The thing that lay before her was her own body, torn asunder by the shadow demon's talons. Beldyn sat beside her, his fine robes smeared with her blood, cradling her head in his arms. He had his own medallion in his hand and was praying over her, and with sick understanding she knew that he was trying to heal her. Even if he'd still had the strength, though, it was too late. Finally, after a long moment, he slumped forward, pressing his face against her lifeless forehead, and began to sob.

She felt a wistful ache at that. She had never seen him weep before.

"Here, child," said the voice again.

She looked up, at the bedchamber's window. It was open now, the silver moon glowing behind it. Standing before it was Brother Jendle. The fat monk smiled at her, his eyes shining.

Turning from her own corpse, she stepped toward him, then knelt on the blood-slick floor, bowing her head. "My god," she said. "I have tried to work thy will."

"I know, child." He rested a pudgy hand on her head. "It's time for you to rest now."

She looked up then, and sudden, joyful tears sprang to her eyes. Brother Jendle was gone, and in his place stood a great dragon, its scales gleaming like mirrors in the moonlight. Glancing around, she saw the bedchamber, too, had vanished. She was on a mountaintop now, bare stone and snow beneath the stars. There was something familiar about the scene, she thought, and then she knew. It was the same place she had seen when she tested Beldyn, months ago, when he had pulled the stars down from the sky.

"Come," said the platinum dragon. "We have a long way to go."

Ilista stared at the heavens a moment longer, then signed the triangle. "Farewell, Beldinas," she whispered.

She turned again and climbed onto the dragon's broad, glistening back. It vaulted into the air, rising up and away, toward the silver moon.

CHAPTER 22 ▼

Cathan shoved through the crowd outside the Pantheon, forcing people out of his way with shoulders and elbows, stepping on feet and drawing dark looks and curses. He didn't slow, though, didn't look back, even when he sent people sprawling. Nor did he shout, or even speak. He was afraid that if he opened his mouth the sound that came from it first would be an uncontrollable shriek.

He'd been with his sister only a quarter of an hour ago at an inn by the western lip of the chasm that split Govinna in two. A drab public house improbably named *The Ox and Grapes*, Ossirian and Tavarre had named it one of the places where the folk of Luciel could take shelter for now. Wentha had a room there she shared with three other girls. The others had left, giggling, when he arrived, and he and his sister had shared a light supper of bread and cheese, with cups of mulled wine to stave off the evening's chill. That was where the acolyte had found him, a boy of thirteen with plain vestments, panting with exertion as he burst in and told him the Lightbringer had been attacked.

He'd been running since, across an arching bridge and through the winding streets to the Pantheon. He was afraid of what he'd find, half-expecting the people there to have run wild, but the crowds in the courtyard were calm, and he soon realized they didn't know yet. That was just as well, he told himself. They would find out soon enough, anyway.

I should have been there, he thought as he neared the temple steps. I swore to guard him with my life. If I'd been with him . . .

You're no warrior, a cooler voice replied within his head, not like Tavarre and Ossirian are, or like Gareth was. You call yourself a protector, but you're not. You're just a boy playing grown men's games.

With a snarl, he shut that voice out, dashing up the stair. The guards outside the doors lowered their spears and let him pass into the shadows of the Pantheon. His footsteps echoed loudly as he sprinted down its halls.

He found Tavarre at the foot of the stair to the Patriarch's Tower conferring in hushed voices with a handful of the bandit leaders. They were all ashen-faced, he saw, and worse, a couple had been weeping. Cathan made for the knot of men, shoving past Vedro as the big man tried to hold him back.

"Where is he?" he demanded. His voice sounded strange to his own ears, like a harpstring tightened too far. "Is he dead?"

Tavarre looked up, surprised, as the bandits glowered at Cathan. "Who?"

"Beldyn!" Cathan pressed, waving his arms. "He's dead, isn't he?"

The baron's mouth twisted into a bitter knot. "No," he said, "but he's just about the only one."

Cathan felt a worse dread. "What do you mean?"

Tavarre told him. Ossirian. Durinen. Ilista.

"Gods," was all Cathan could say. "Oh, gods . . ."

"He's up there with her now," the baron said, nodding toward the stair. "He refuses to let us enter, but he has been asking for you."

Cathan blinked. "Me?"

Tavarre laid a hand on his arm, his scarred face pinching as he fought tears. "I think you're the closest thing he has to a friend, lad. Go to him."

Up he went. It was a long way, and he was breathing hard when he reached the gilded doors at the top. There was a smear of blood on one door and spatters on the landing as well. The stink of it was thick in the air, and Cathan fought back his rising gorge as he stepped forward and tried the door. It was locked. He knocked instead.

"It's me," he said.

For a time there was no reply. He heard a something at last, the soft click of the doors' bolt sliding back. With a soft groan, the doors swung inward, revealing the Little Emperor's study.

Cathan took one look at the remains of the men who had died in the room, then turned and vomited on the floor. His throat was raw as he turned back, looking past the bodies by the door. There was more blood pooled around the desk. The door to Durinen's bedchamber was open, and light flared within. Biting his lip, Cathan stepped over the corpses and went toward the glow.

The First Daughter lay upon Durinen's bed, her white face flecked with red, a blanket pulled up to her breast. Her hands lay folded atop the blanket, her eyes shut. It hurt terribly to see her dead, and he looked away toward the Lightbringer.

Beldyn sat on the bedside, his head in his hands. The god's holy light still glimmered silver around him, but within it his new, snowy vestments were crimson-wet. Cathan stepped toward him, his mouth opening, as he realized the blood was Ilista's. Hearing his footfalls, Beldyn looked up. His eyes were red and puffy.

"Who did this?" Cathan demanded, his face burning with rage. "Say the word, and I'll bring you his head."

"I nearly think you would." Beldyn's voice was thin, hoarse. "The one responsible is far away, and I need you here, my friend. There is something we must do, if Ilista's death is not to be in vain."

Cathan knelt, the marble floor hard beneath him. "Name it."

The Lightbringer nodded, then lifted something from the cushions beside him—a scroll, spattered with blood like everything else. He ran his hands over it for a moment, then unfurled it, looking up at Cathan.

"What do you know of the *Miceram*?" he asked.

———————◆◆◆———————

The red moon was high and half-full over Istar, washing the city with sanguine light. Midnight had come and gone, and while the Great Temple was never entirely still—there were always Knights on patrol and acolytes tending the gardens—it was as quiet as it ever was. Most of the lights were dimmed, and the only sounds were the chirping of crickets and the warble of night birds as they flitted among the almond trees. Cords of mist drifted across the lawns and pools. Beyond, the Lordcity slumbered as well. In another hour, the fishermen would meet their boats at the wharf, and the bakers would make the day's first bread, but for now Istar slept.

Kurnos did not.

He stood alone—Brother Purvis and the other servants had long since retired—on the high balcony overlooking the temple grounds. He leaned against the rail, his brow clouded, and looked down at the rose garden below. The flowers there still refused to bloom, and worse, since the hippogriff's death the grass had begun to die as well. He'd never caught anyone at it, but he knew people were whispering about the strange blight. Some called it a sign—but then, someone in the Temple *always* called such things signs. An apple couldn't fall in the orchard without some old priest claiming it was a portent of the god's displeasure.

Kurnos chuckled without feeling any pleasure. Every night, when he tried to sleep, his dreams tormented him. Symeon haunted them, his eyes accusing, his childlike face drawn into a snarl of pure hate. Always it was the same. The dead Kingpriest reaching out, fingers clutching like talons, and when Kurnos raised his own hands to ward him off, he saw his hands glistening with blood.

Mine, Symeon's voice rang in his ears, echoing in the darkness even after he woke, bathed in icy sweat. *Mine. You killed me....*

Kurnos shivered, shutting his eyes, and brought his fists down hard on the balustrade. It had to be done, he told himself, repeating the words like a mantra. It was for the good of the realm. I did what I had to do.

"Of course you did."

The cold voice didn't surprise him this time, nor did the chill in the air. That was the other reason he was still awake. He was waiting. Opening his eyes, he turned now to see the black-robed figure, standing by the archway that led back into the manse. As always, the man's hood obscured his face, but he could envision Fistandantilus's mocking look. He forced himself to smile.

"I've been expecting you, Dark One."

"I gathered as much." Wry amusement shaded Fistandantilus's voice. "Do you know, this is the first time I have ever received an imperial summons. It was . . . flattering."

Kurnos scowled, ignoring the sorcerer's derision. He had sent a messenger to the Tower of High Sorcery earlier that evening, bearing a sealed, nameless scroll, with instructions to leave his missive in a certain empty anteroom.

Fistandantilus stepped forward, toward Symeon's enchanted *khas* table. The game-pieces upon it stirred, looking up as he regarded them with unseen eyes. Kurnos didn't think the *khas* pieces could be afraid, but still, he couldn't shake the impression that they trembled.

"Fine workmanship," the sorcerer said, nodding. "Do you play, Holiness?"

Kurnos swallowed. It had been some time since his last good game of *khas*. He could find no opponent whose skills matched his own. The closest thing he had to a worthy rival was First Son Strinam, but the man was dull, unimaginative. He simply couldn't foresee the consequences of his moves, and defeating him proved too easy to hold interest. He'd trounced Strinam a dozen times in a row, playing in the evening's glow—using the white pieces now, as was his right. First Daughter Balthera hardly knew the rules. Quarath professed not to care for the game. Lord Holger—a fair player, who had beaten him in the past— was in the field, marching on Govinna even now. And so on.

"Yes," he said.

"Excellent," Fistandantilus declared, and sat at the table, before the dark pieces. "Let us play, then, while we talk."

The wizard made a gesture, and Kurnos felt a rushing, as if a gale had sprung up to blow expressly in his face. With a dizzying lurch, he was sitting at the table, before the white pieces. He shuddered, staring at the dark-robed form across from him. The mage had used sorcery on him! Fistandantilus met his shocked gaze, then shrugged, letting out a rasping laugh, and gestured at the table.

"The forces of light are yours, Holiness. Make your first move."

Kurnos gaped down at the pieces arrayed before him. All he knew of strategy, all the books he had read, fled from his mind. He forced himself to take a deep breath. With a glance up at Fistandantilus, he leaned forward and whispered to footsoldier. The tiny soldier bowed and strode forward, his mail rattling. His spear trembled in his hands as he eyed the dark form looming before him.

The dark mage snorted, his hand gesturing slightly, and one of his own pawns came to life and marched ahead to thwart Kurnos's.

The Kingpriest stared at the board. Fistandantilus's man had moved where he wanted it to go without the slightest word having been spoken. He knew the mage had done it to intimidate him, and it did. He steepled his fingers, trying to think of a gambit.

"You used the ring again," the sorcerer said, nodding at the emerald glittering on his finger.

Kurnos scowled, snatching his hands back. Rather than reply, he murmured to one of his champions, and the little Knight galloped diagonally across the board.

"I did," he admitted, when the piece came to a halt. "I sent the demon to slay my enemies, as you suggested. She failed."

He wasn't sure what response he expected Fistandantilus to make, but the wizard's shrug disappointed him all the same. "Did she?" he asked, advancing a second Footsoldier. "How?"

"That's why I asked you here," Kurnos replied. He spoke to one of his Wyrms, which then slithered through the ranks of his men, moving to threaten the wizard's ranks. "I commanded her to go to Govinna, to kill Lady Ilista and this Brother Beldyn. Last Moonsday, when I woke, she was back inside the gem."

Fistandantilus brought forward his Guardian. "I should think that is a good sign," he said.

"So did I," Kurnos snapped, glowering at the pieces. The dark mage's moves didn't seem to have any pattern or strategy, and that worried him. He was being toyed with. He advanced another Footsoldier to protect the Wyrm. "But I've heard rumors since that Beldyn is still alive, and . . . there's something wrong with Sathira."

That caught the wizard's attention. "Interesting," he said after a long moment, raising his gaze from the board. He retreated his Guardian two spaces—again, with no aim Kurnos could see—then clenched his age-spotted hand into a fist. "Let me see."

Kurnos felt a sudden chill on his hand. He looked to the ring, then caught his breath. It was gone from his finger. Glancing across the table, he saw Fistandantilus's fingers uncurl to reveal the emerald, glinting in his palm. The wizard raised the gem, peering into it, then waved his other hand over it, his fingertips weaving the air.

"*Apala ngartash,*" he murmured. "*Urshai maivak toboruk!*"

There was a sound like cloth tearing, and green light flared from the gem, billowing over the table like mist. The fog flowed around them, then, slowly, shapes appeared, pale and hazy, like ghosts. They stood in a well-appointed study, the details of which were vague. Kurnos recognized some of the figures—Durinen was sitting at a desk, and Lady Ilista was there as well—but the bearish warrior with them was unfamiliar, as was the fourth person. He knew, though, as soon as he saw the young man, with his white robes and long hair, that it was the Lightbringer.

He caught his breath. "What is this?"

"What Sathira saw, just before she attacked," Fistandantilus replied. "Now, watch."

The wizard made a flicking gesture with his fingertips, and the spectacle began. Kurnos watched, rapt, as the shadows took on the demon's familiar form, seizing Durinen and killing him, then two fighters running into the room, then the bearish warrior as well. In moments, all four were dead, and the demon was stalking the two priests.

He saw Ilista reach for her medallion, saw the resolve in her face, saw the demon lunge, its claws ripping into her, as she shielded herself with the medallion and gave a shout. A light flashed and the vision ended, the green glow vanishing like fog burned away by the sun. The ring went dark.

Kurnos sat back in his chair, speechless. So Ilista was dead. He would never forget the horrible sight, and he knew that, tomorrow night, Symeon would have company in his nightmares. Beldyn, who mattered most, was still alive. The Kingpriest wrung his hands, as Fistandantilus clenched his fingers about the emerald once more. With another twinge, the ring reappeared on his finger. Its grip felt even tighter than before.

"There is your answer," the wizard said. "The First Daughter hurt Sathira badly. She cannot leave the ring again until she recovers. A week, perhaps more. You may call upon her again then. I advise you do so, and do not hesitate this time." Pushing back, Fistandantilus rose from the table and began to turn away.

Ridiculously, after all the mage had told him, Kurnos's first thought was about their unfinished game. The archmage paused, glancing over his shoulder.

"Oh . . . yes," the sorcerer said. "It is my turn."

With that, he raised his finger, making a sharp gesture. As one, his pieces surged forward, swarming across the table and laying into the Kingpriest's men with sword and fang. Screams rang out across the balcony as the game pieces perished, cut to shreds by the sudden onslaught. In seconds, and against all the game's rules, his men had all perished.

"*Rigo iebid,*" Fistandantilus said as Kurnos gaped at the carnage.

The realm is fallen.

He was gone, melting into the shadows, leaving the sound of mocking laughter in his wake.

CHAPTER 23 ▼

It snowed the eve of Lady Ilista's funeral. It was the first of the season, blowing in on bitter winds off the Khalkists to the west. A light dusting that sparkled the air around the street lamps and filled the cracks between the cobblestones, it was the sort of snow that would be gone by midday, only a herald of the coming winter.

The snow kept folk inside, save for the watchmen on the city's high walls, who shivered as they huddled around smoldering braziers, and so the weather helped prevent the riots that might have transpired in the wake of the slaughter in the Patriarch's tower. There was worse on the way, fiercer storms that would howl down from the mountains and bury Taol's roads, as had happened last year. Some of the bandits' leaders looked on the coming snow as a boon. If the passes were clogged, after all, it would thwart the Kingpriest's troops. Tavarre, however—who had taken command of the city's defenders after Ossirian's death—scoffed at the notion, his scarred face sour.

"We didn't have enough food for *last* winter," he noted. "Another season like that, and half of Govinna will starve. When the spring comes, the *Scatas* will attack anyway, and by then we'll surely be too weak to hold against them."

He didn't mention what else troubled him. If the outriders' reports were correct, and two full *Dromas* were marching through Taol, it didn't matter when they came. Even with those who had pledged their swords to the Lightbringer since his arrival, the city's defenders were too few to stand against such a force. Govinna's gates might be impregnable, but that would make little difference when such a mighty foe started scaling her walls.

True to form, the snow turned to drizzle when dawn came, and fog settled in, filling the streets with gray murk. The city became a ghostly place, full of muffled sounds and eerie glows where lanterns burned. The mourning cloths outside the houses and shops hung limp, soaked through, and when the mourners made their way to the Pantheon, thousands strong, they seemed like phantoms in the gray. Unlike the wailing, pottery-smashing masses in the lowlands, the folk of the highlands were somber in the face of death, chanting in low voices, their hands ritually smeared with soot. Those who could afford to wore blue, but dyes were expensive in the highlands, so most came dressed in drab grays and browns, their faces daubed in crushed woad instead. The fog made them seem an army of drowned corpses, gathering in the courtyard in the foredawn cold.

The worship hall was dim, its vaulted ceiling lost in shadow without the daylight to illuminate it. What was strange, though, was the number of candles the clerics had set out. There were thousands of them, on shrines and in wall sconces, on silver candelabra standing throughout the room, and covering the dais where the god's altar stood. Of all the tapers, however, only one in ten were lit. The rest stood whole and dark, no flames dancing upon their wicks. Folk remarked at the strangeness of it, whispering and wondering. Somehow, it seemed wrong.

The bodies lay at the head of the hall, atop three wooden catafalques smothered in smoke from nearby censers. Clad in the chain hauberk he'd worn when he'd stormed the

Pantheon months ago was the hulking body of Lord Ossirian, his hands clutching his broadsword upon his breast. On another side, Durinen lay shrouded with a blue cloth to hide the ghastly wound that had killed him, but it was the figure in the middle, clad in full vestments, the sacred triangle painted upon her forehead, that drew the most looks. The former First Daughter had been in Govinna for the briefest time before her death, but the townsfolk grieved for her more than for the two men who flanked her. She had forsaken the church, the empire, and the Kingpriest to help the borderfolk and to bring them the Lightbringer's healing touch. She had given her life for him, it was said. Ilista had become a martyr, and they wept as they signed the triangle for her.

By the time the Pantheon's bells tolled the dawn watch, the worship hall was filled with people, pressed shoulder to shoulder on the pews and packing the aisles and apses as well. Still they came, spilling out into the vestibule and down the steps to the courtyard outside. Tavarre and the bandit chiefs stood near the front, their faces hidden by deep hoods, and the folk of Luciel held a place of honor nearest Ilista's bier. Wentha stood among them, and Fendrilla, and all the rest who had fled north to Govinna, brigand and villager alike. Only Cathan was absent, and a few folk glanced at one another, wondering where the young stalwart was—until a door opened at the room's far end and he entered, armored and hooded, his sword hanging by his side. He rested his hand on its pommel, looking over the crowd, searching for signs of danger. Finally he nodded, though his eyes remained narrow as he turned to speak a word to those in the anteroom behind him.

A gong sounded, and a hush fell over the crowd as the procession entered. It began with two young acolytes, dressed in gray and bearing lit torches. After them came an elderly cleric, one of the Little Emperor's men, swinging a golden thurible that trailed blue smoke in zigzagging arcs as he walked, into the room. Following him were four priestesses, singing a dirge, their voices echoing across the vast chamber. Then two more acolytes, and then the Lightbringer, and the mourners gasped as one.

The funerary rites in the Istaran church were clear and had been for centuries. They were specific about many details, among them the garb of the priest conducting the ceremony. He was to wear vestments of blue, unadorned and unhooded, and all the jewelry of his position. Beldyn, however, wore no rings or bracelets, no circlet on his brow. Only his holy medallion, glinting in the candlelight, hung openly around his neck. His robes were white, heretical at such a solemn occasion. It was neither of these facts, however, that made the folk of Govinna stare and murmur in shock.

It was the blood.

The stains were dried now, the color of rust. They covered the front of Beldyn's robes, stiffening the cloth, and smeared the cuffs of his sleeves. Bloodstains were even on his face still, a smudge on his chin and another on his temple. The clergy had taken pains to clean and prepare the bodies of the dead, but the Lightbringer had not washed since the attack. His long hair hung greasy down upon his shoulders, and the smell of the incense did not fully mask the whiff of uncleanness that rose from him. The silvery glow that shrouded him when he used his powers was a bare flicker now, yet his eyes blazed like blue stars as he took his place by the altar—Cathan by his side—and looked out upon the masses. Folk shifted beneath that terrible gaze, and many had to look away, bowing their heads. His were the eyes of a madman, flashing like lightning in a storm.

When the dirge ended, the stillness that fell over the worship hall was thicker than the fog outside. Beldyn held that silence for several minutes, raking the crowd with his eyes. Then he drew a breath, and his voice rang out like thunder across the hall.

"You have come," he said, "to hear a requiem, a memorial for the three who lie cold before you, cut down in the night.

You want assurances that they died fulfilling their purpose and therefore served the god's greater good. You want to know that, even in this dark hour, all will be well.

"You shall not have it. It is not true."

Again, gasps echoed around the hall. Some signed the triangle, murmuring warding prayers, but the Lightbringer silenced them with a glare.

"For centuries," he went on, "the church has told you such lies. The time has come for this to stop. I saw the thing that slew Lady Ilista and the others. It was a beast of purest evil, murderous and heartless. I will not simply accept her death was what Paladine intended.

"Some of you, no doubt, are thinking of the Doctrine of Balance that the church has held dear for millennia. We are told that without evil, good cannot exist. Even at midday, when the sun shines brightest, shadows remain. This has always been, the canon says. It always must be.

"Lies! In ages past, the Balance had its uses. It kept Paladine's power alive in the world, when the dark gods and their minions threatened to overwhelm all. Those days are past. The Queen of Darkness is gone from the world, her dragon hordes fled a thousand years since. We have hunted the servants of evil—the goblin, the ogre, the monster of nightmares—until they are all but destroyed in Istar. We have beaten back the cults that worship sin, yet Lady Ilista is still murdered by a thing of evil sent from the very Lordcity where the god's light shines brightest!

"Yes," he went on, as the folk of Govinna stared. "The author of this wickedness is the Kingpriest himself, Kurnos the Usurper. If you doubt it, ask yourself this: who else would send an assassin here? He fears me, fears the righteousness of my claim to the throne, so he does all he can to destroy me— even if it means truckling with darkest sorcery and demons from the Abyss itself!"

He opened his arms, displaying the bloodstains for all to see. "*Look!* See what the precious Balance has wrought! As long as we lack the will to destroy evil altogether, innocent blood will flow! The time for the old ways is over. We must kindle a *new* light, one that surrounds us, burning so brightly that the darkness and those who serve it flee forever!" He flung his hands up, reaching to the heavens. "*Sifat!*"

The light poured out of him then, spraying forth like the jets of some great fountain, arcing high into the air with a sound like the ringing of a great crystal bell. The glow hung in the air, bathing the mourners' open-mouthed faces, then it dropped again, raining down all over the room. Wherever it fell, it touched a candle, and that candle burst aflame . . . scores . . . hundreds . . . thousands of them, filling the room with their glow. As they did, the shadows they cast grew dim, until at last there was nothing *but* light, surrounding everyone, swallowing the gloom.

It began with just one man, surging to his feet halfway to the rear of the hall and thrusting his fist in the air. Then it spread, more and more folk jumping up to add their voices, until finally the whole Pantheon rang with the cry, and the city outside as well, a roar that cut through the morning air as the fog burned away in the sunlight.

"Death to the Usurper!" the folk of Govinna cried. "Life to the Lightbringer! An end to the Balance!"

Amid it all, his eyes twin suns, Beldinas smiled.

The catacombs held the smell of the old dead, a musty, spicy aroma that permeated the air and the stones alike. They were dark, close, and silent, older than the Pantheon, older than Govinna itself, a place harking back to the days when the Taoli were savages, scouring the wild hills with bow and spear and sacrificing their enemies to pagan gods. Missionaries from the church of Istar had dug them as a hiding place, where they could bury their fallen so the barbarians could not defile their bodies.

Times had changed. The church ruled now, and the barbarians had become civilized highlanders, but the dead remained, lying in niches mantled with dust and cobwebs. Each body was meticulously wrapped, from neck to feet, in strips of linen, but their heads remained uncovered, revealing bare skulls with scraps of colorless hair clinging to them. Their eyes stared sightlessly in the dark, teeth bared in rictus grins.

Cathan tried not to look at the bodies as he and Beldyn made their way through the cramped passages. The light of the torch he carried made the shadows leap in the corners of his vision, and that made his fevered brain—already edgy from the darkness deep beneath the earth in the cellars of the temple—see things that weren't there . . . or that he fervently *hoped* weren't there. Surely the corpses didn't stir as they passed, their skulls turning toward him, their bony fingers twitching. Surely he didn't *hear* the rustle of wrappings being shrugged off or the scrape of bone against stone. Even so, his heart leaped every time he brushed against a niche or stepped on a bone that had fallen from its resting place. He was terrified to think that if he looked back, he would see ghosts shambling after him, staring at him with dark holes whose eyes had long ago turned to dust.

"This door you're looking for," he whispered, his voice sounding horribly loud. "We're almost there, right?"

Beldyn peered through the gloom, then down at the scroll in his hands. He slowed down as he did so, which made Cathan even more afraid. If you stop, a childlike voice said in his brain, you'll give them a chance to catch up. They'll get you. . . .

"Yes," Beldyn said after a moment. "Pradian's writings say it's close."

"Good."

They went on, Cathan wishing someone else had come with them . . . like about one hundred armed men. Tavarre had offered them before they set out, though he couldn't afford to lose that many swords, but Beldyn refused. The scroll he held, the one Durinen had given him moments before the demon attacked, had something to say about the matter. The door would only open to Pradian's true heir and would let him and one other pass, so long as that other was faithful.

"I would have you, my friend," Beldyn had said that afternoon, after Ilista and the others were entombed. Cathan objected, saying there were better warriors among the bandits, but the Lightbringer shook his head. "You were the first to swear to me, and you have been true ever since."

Cathan sucked in a breath, caught a lungful of dust, and fell into a coughing fit.

The noise of his hacking and wheezing was still echoing back through the dark when the tunnel opened up before them into a burial chamber. It was not a large room, perhaps five paces on a side, but compared with the catacombs it felt as vast as the Pantheon's worship hall. A single pillar stood in its midst, carved with reliefs of twining dragons, and stone sarcophagi lined the walls, their lids sculpted to resemble long-bearded men in clerical garb. The high priests among the missionaries, Cathan guessed. The lid of one had crumbled, spilling out a tangle of bones and moldering robes. The skull that leered up at him from those leavings was still covered with leathery flesh. The image of Tancred, wasted and gaunt on his deathbed, flashed through his mind, and he had to shut his eyes to make the memory go away.

When he looked again, Beldyn had crossed to the chamber's far side. Cathan hurried after, torch held high, and when he came around the pillar he saw what caught Beldyn's attention. There, in the far wall, was the door.

It was hewn of stone, the same living rock as the walls, and intertwined roses snaked around it, carved into its frame. Perched high upon its lintel, looking down on them, was an alabaster falcon, wings half-spread, a triangle clutched in its talons.

They stared at the door in silence. Cathan felt no surprise when he saw it had no latch.

"What now?" he asked.

Beldyn studied the scroll a while longer, then nodded and tucked it into his belt. "Now we open it."

Cathan snorted a laugh, then stopped. As he watched, the monk pushed back his bloodstained sleeves—he still had not changed clothes—and studied the door.

"The *Miceram* lies in an ancient fane beyond this," he said. "Pradian put it there, then sealed the door shut. The geas he laid on it will be broken when one fit to wear the crown comes to claim it. So it is written. After that, we have only to face the guardian."

"Guardian?" Cathan asked, his voice rising. "What kind of guardian?"

Beldyn spread his hands. "The scroll does not say."

"Of course it doesn't," Cathan muttered. Gritting his teeth, he checked his sword to make sure it was loose in its scabbard, then, thinking better of it, drew the blade. "Well, we've come this far."

Smiling, Beldyn reached out and pressed his hands against the door. It was smooth, marred only by a small crack near its top. Licking his lips, he bowed his head and murmured a prayer.

"*Palado, ucdas pafiro,*" he intoned, "*tas igousid fo. Lob tis foro polam bidein unfifid, to Ceram ibin tarpid. So polo fat cifir. Bebam anlugud!*"

Paladine, father of dawn, I am thy chosen. Long has this door awaited the time foretold, when the Crown is needed again. That time is come. Let the way open!

He squared his feet on the floor, closed his eyes, and pushed.

Nothing happened.

Cathan watched, his heart falling, as Beldyn tried again and still a third time. He leaned into it with all his might. His face grew red, cords of muscle bulged in his neck, and sweat beaded on his brow, but still the door refused to budge.

"Damn it," Cathan muttered. "Don't tell me we've come this far, only to—"

"Cathan!" Beldyn hissed through clenched teeth. "Help me!"

Cathan stepped forward, eyeing the door suspiciously. "What—what do I say?"

"Nothing! Just *push*!"

Setting his sword down on the dusty floor, he stepped forward to take his place beside Beldyn, who was heaving with his shoulder now, grunting with the effort. Holding his breath, he set his hands on the door as well, and shoved as hard as he could.

All at once the air around them shivered, and sparks of red and gold poured out of the cracks where door met frame. With a deep growl the stone gave way, pivoting of its own accord and sending Cathan staggering to his knees. Beldyn stumbled too but stayed upright as, still streaming sorcerous cinders, the door rumbled open.

Snatching up his sword, Cathan sprang back to his feet. Images of dragons flashed through his mind, and the guardian became a black wyrm with fangs bared and flames leaping up its throat.

Several heartbeats later, after nothing had attacked them, he let the tip of his blade drop. There was no monster on the other side, only more cramped tunnel, winding out of sight. Seeing more niches carved into the walls, he sighed. At the very least, he'd hoped to get away from the dead.

Smiling, Beldyn stepped through the opening into the passage beyond. Cathan paused, took a deep breath, and followed.

CHAPTER 24 ▼

L ord Holger's breath smoked in the air as he stood outside his tent. He tried to hold still while his squire buckled on his shining, armor, but it was difficult. The lure of the fight sang in his blood, as it hadn't in years. He'd spent too long in Istar, serving at the Kingpriest's court, growing soft. That would soon change.

About time, he thought.

His squire, a gangly, dark-haired boy with a tuft of fuzz where a Knight's long moustache would one day grow, finished buckling Holger's greaves about his shins, then turned to strap spurs onto his master's metal-plated boots. However, when he reached for the old Knight's shield—an old battered thing engraved with the Solamnic kingfisher—Holger waved him off.

"No, lad. I won't be needing that yet."

The boy bobbed his head but kept the shield ready anyway, picking up his master's sword as well. Holger nodded with approval. They were not going into battle yet, but it was a squire's duty to be prepared, and the lad had learned his lessons well. He felt a certain sadness that the boy's tenure would end before long, but also a certain pride. When he returned to his family's castle in the spring, he would go with full commendations. Young Loren Soth would make a fine Knight one day.

It was after midnight, and the highland sky was clear, the stars glittering like chips of ice. That was better than the snow of the night before. There was nothing like a good snap of foul weather to muck up a battle. The camp stood in a rock-strewn valley east of the River Edessa, just off the main road to Govinna. The bulk of Holger's force had arrived earlier that day, tired from hard marching. Most of them slept now, the footmen in bedrolls and the officers in their own tents, but a few pockets of drunken *Scatas* remained awake, singing lewd songs around their fires. Holger would have preferred silence, but he'd long since learned soldiers weren't Knights. They needed their vices. Wine was the least of these and the one concession he made in the interest of morale. Better, he told himself, than the place swarming with camp followers.

He made his way across the camp, Loren dogging his heels. Several sentries raised their torches as he approached, then saluted when they recognized him. Finally, he reached the camp's northern end, where the ground rose to the valley's rim. He climbed the crumbling slope easily—city-softened or not, he still had a young man's vigor—and stopped at the crest, looking down into a bowl-shaped depression beyond. Below, barely visible among the ash trees and night's shadows, waited the army's advance riders.

They were only a small part of his forces, just a thousand strong, but they were enough for his purposes. Unlike the slumbering *Scatas* in the vale behind him, they were awake and armored, their horses ready to ride.

"All accounted for, milord," said a young Knight of the Crown, clambering up the hill to meet him. Sir Utgar, his name was, as fine a horseman as any in Holger's force. His blond moustache curled above a proud smile. "They await your orders."

Holger nodded. "Well, then," he replied, starting downhill.

The riders moved swiftly at his approach, scrambling to fall into order, their blue cloaks turning violet in Lunitari's ruddy light. A black-bearded, barrel-chested man, wearing a surcoat over matching scale armor—both gold in color, burnt copper in the moonglow—stood before them, waiting. He wore no robes, and a sword hung from his belt. Such was the field garb of the clergy of Kiri-Jolith. Unlike Paladine's priests, the Jolithan order had no compunctions against edged weapons. He raised his hands in greeting, curling his fingers to sign the battle god's horns.

Holger returned the gesture in kind, then looked to his men and cleared his throat. Amid the wind's muttering and the whickering of horses, the riders fell silent. Looking out at them—a sea of wind-weathered faces, watching him expectantly—he raised his voice to speak.

"You will ride north," he said. "At a fair pace, you'll reach Govinna by midmorning. When you do, you must assail it at once."

The riders shifted, nodding. A thousand was too few to capture a city, but they understood that wasn't the intent. Most had served a while in the imperial army, long enough to understand that first sorties were for scouting and testing the enemy's strengths . . . and weaknesses. The true fight would come later.

"Don't worry," he told them, eyes twinkling. "I don't expect you to take the battlements. If you do, though, don't worry about giving them back."

It was an old joke, but the men laughed anyway, and Holger chuckled along with them, then grew serious again, turning to the Jolithan priest.

"Father Arinus? Will you give us a prayer?"

The cleric had not laughed, hadn't even smiled at the joke. His face might have been hewn of stone as he stepped forward, the *Scatas* and Knights alike kneeling before him. Holger knelt too, as did Loren beside him. With deliberation Arinus pulled off his gauntlets and set them on the ground, then raised his bare hands over the soldiers. Brown leaves, stirred by the night wind, rattled on the limbs above him.

"*Jolitho Moubol,*" the war-priest prayed, "*Ricdas Follo, tas lonfam ciffud e nas punfasom fribas sparud. Couros icolamo du tam.*"

Mighty Kiri-Jolith, Sword of Justice, raise up thy shield and ward off our enemies' blows. We consecrate our blades to thee.

Steel rang as he drew his sword, a silver blade marked with gold filigree, then echoed as the riders followed suit. As one, they raised the weapons to their lips and kissed their quillons. Then they sheathed them again—all but Arinus, who instead set his against the palm of his left hand. Holger had seen this rite many times before, but he still bit down on one corner of his moustache as the Jolithan pressed the steel to bare flesh, then drew the blade across himself.

A few of the riders groaned as blood welled from the cut, but Arinus's expression still didn't change. Instead he clenched his fist, squeezing red droplets onto the rocky ground, then wiped his sword on his surcoat, leaving a crimson smear upon the gold. "*Sifat*," he declared, his voice betraying no pain.

"*Sifat*," echoed the riders. The blessing done, they rose and moved to their horses.

Holger stared after them as they rode away, a long dark line wending up the gully's far side. He wanted to follow, to feel the wind through the visor of his helm as they swept down on Govinna. He wanted to be there when the thrice-damned rebels saw for the first time what they had to face. Lightbringer or no Lightbringer, they would recognize their own doom. But he didn't follow. He still had work ahead, tactics to plan, before he assailed Govinna properly. His battle-yearning would have to wait a while longer.

Sighing, he turned and headed back toward the camp.

The tunnel changed as it delved ever deeper beneath the Pantheon. The dead and their niches continued, the ceiling low enough that Beldyn and Cathan had to stoop to keep from hitting their heads on it. Between the recesses, however, the stone walls gave way to plaster, smooth but crumbling, worn away in places. Where it held, it bore the colors of old frescoes, painted in archaic style and faded with age.

The pictures were hard to see in the wavering torchlight, and Cathan had to squint to make out what they showed. Here silver and bronze dragons soared high, locked in battle with wyrms of blue and green. There an army of warriors in antiquated bronze armor battled a foe whose image had long since vanished. In a third place, tattooed, naked savages thrust spears into men in white vestments, hung upside-down from oak trees.

"Martyrs to the god," murmured Beldyn, regarding the last. "You see now why the early clerics chose to build their fane down here."

Cathan shuddered, staring at the Taoli barbarians' hate-filled expressions. One wore a scar on his face, similar to Tavarre's. "They fought against the church and lost," Cathan said. "Now here we are, their heirs, doing the same."

"We will not lose," Beldyn declared, turning away. "They did not have the gods behind them."

He moved on, and so did Cathan, watching down the passage for signs of danger. None appeared. The silence of the crypt made a thunder of each echoing footfall. Finally, after what seemed like hours, the path ended at an archway, a triangle carved in its keystone. There were words, too, etched by the same hand, but age had worn them away until they were illegible. Dragons had still filled the skies when the arch was new.

Beyond, the passage gave way to steps, spiraling down even deeper into the rock. The stair was narrow, broad enough for only one man, the air above it alive with dust that glittered in the torchlight. Cathan swallowed, then pushed past Beldyn so he was in the lead as they descended. He tried not to look as frightened as he felt, but his sword still trembled in his hand, and sweat ran in runnels down his face as he craned, trying to see around the spiraling stair. Guarded. The crown was guarded. By what?

He decided he could gladly live to be a hundred without knowing the answer.

The steps wound a long way, farther even than the flight that first led them into the catacombs. By the time they reached the bottom, the tunnel's air had turned cold and stale, and dark, wet patches marred the walls. He didn't know how he knew, but Cathan felt sure the damp came from the River Edessa. They were below the river now, below everything. Halfway to the Abyss, it seemed—except for the bloody cold, of course.

At the foot of the stair, the catacombs resumed once more, niches and frescoes and all, older even than the ones above. Cathan shook his head, shivering and wondering. What must it have been like for the folk who dwelt here once? What kind of life was it, hiding in tunnels because existence on the surface was so dangerous?

"The light," Beldyn said as they looked down the hall.

Cathan glanced at him. "What?"

The monk's eyes gleamed, fever-bright. "Light," he repeated. "Put out your torch."

This far down? Cathan thought. *Are you insane?*

He did lower the brand, however, using his hand to shade it, and then he saw it too: A warm glow shone up the passage ahead, more golden than the ruddy torchlight. He quailed a little, then found his resolve and moved on down the hall. The light grew brighter as they walked, and when at last they reached a sharp bend in the passage, it was vivid enough to devour their torch light entirely. He stopped at the corner, his mouth going dry as he reached back to stay Beldyn. Sword tip quivering, he leaned forward and peered around the bend— and stopped, sucking in a sudden breath.

For their fane, the long-dead priests had chosen a vast, natural cave, hollowed out of the earth by countless years of dripping water. The cave was dry now, however. No pools filled the hollows of its uneven floor, and no moisture dripped from the stalactites that jabbed down from above, like the fangs of some immense stone dragon. Carvings of armored warriors and robed clerics marked the many stalagmites and the creamy flowstone that covered the cavern's walls. Above it all rose the god.

The image the priests had painted on the ceiling was of Paladine, but it was a different Paladine than Cathan had ever seen before. The church favored kindly images of the god: the Valiant Warrior, with his shining armor and noble face; the Dawn-Father, all long-bearded, white-robed gentleness; and the Platinum Dragon, coiled and soft-eyed. The image that glared down at the two of them, however, was stern and fierce, his curly hair and beard raven-black. This was the god's old face, the one whose followers had conquered half of Ansalon, tamed barbarians, subjugated kingdom and city-state alike to forge the empire. His ice-blue eyes reminded Cathan of the way Beldyn's had looked at Ilista's funeral, with just a glint of madness in them. He shuddered.

"What is it?"

Cathan jumped at the sound of Beldyn's voice. "We found it," he whispered over his shoulder.

They entered quietly, Beldyn staring at the god's image while Cathan looked about the cavern, searching for the guardian the scroll had spoken about. It had to be close by, lurking in the shadows, perhaps clinging to the wall, or even hanging from the ceiling. Wherever he shone his torch—barely useful now, in the golden glare—there was nothing to see. Hands sweating in his gloves, he led the way into the fane.

The glow's source lay ahead, but they couldn't make it out from the entrance. A row of six stalagmites, chiseled into statues of forgotten high priests, stood with their backs to them, blocking their view of the chamber's far side. Beldyn paused a few steps in, genuflecting to the glaring god above—those fearsome eyes which seemed to follow them—then signed the triangle and started forward again. Cathan stole ahead of him, sword ready, certain the mysterious protector was hiding behind the stalagmites.

It wasn't. On the other side of the statues stood several rows of pews, carved out of the same milky stone that made up most of the rest of the cave. Brass braziers, dark and pitted with age, loomed to either side, as did several silver censers, now tarnished black. Beyond, the floor rose toward the far wall, stopping at a ledge that served as a natural dais. The clerics had carved steps out of it, and upon it stood a triangular altar of white marble, veined with silvery blue.

Sitting atop the altar was the *Miceram*.

It was just as Beldyn had described it, reading from the scroll the night before. Hewn of bright gold and lined with red velvet, it bore ten points about its rim, each tipped with a sparkling, round ruby. An eleventh, the size of a hen's egg, glinted at the peak of its cap. The shimmering light spilled from it, washing across the fane. Like a star fallen from the sky, was Cathan's first thought.

"*Palado Calib*," Beldyn breathed. Tears glittered in his eyes. "It's even more beautiful than I imagined."

Cathan stared at the crown, afraid it would disappear if he moved abruptly, like a dream upon waking. After a moment, though, he blinked, shaking himself. Here was the *Miceram*, waiting as foretold, but what of the guardian?

Eyes narrowed, he grabbed hold of the nearest statue and leaned out, peering first past the altar, then to the left and right. Nothing—nothing to stop them from walking up and just taking the crown from the altar. He glanced again at the god's glowering, watchful face and frowned. Was this what Pradian's writings had meant? Was the scroll's warning of watchers merely intended to mean Paladine himself?

He'd nearly convinced himself of just that when a soft noise behind him raised the hairs on his neck. Stiffening, he glanced at Beldyn. The young monk had turned to look back toward the fane's entrance, and his face was the color of ashes, his blue eyes wide. Teeth clamped together, Cathan turned as well . . . and stared into the sightless eyes of the dead.

The corpses *had* risen, sliding out of their burial places to follow them down here. They had come in horrible silence, their only sound the scratch of bony feet against the stone floor. Flesh hung from their brown bones in gristly ropes. Dried entrails dangled from holes where their bellies had been. Tongues like strips of leather moved within their jaws, but to no effect. They had no breath to fuel their voices. There were already a score of them in the cavern, and many more were shambling behind, filling the passage where he and Beldyn had just been. It looked as if every corpse in the catacombs had awoken to confront them. To guard the *Miceram*.

"Oh, Abyss," he breathed.

The dead clerics shuffled forward, staggering like mummers' string puppets. Trying to swallow and realizing he lacked the spit, Cathan grabbed for Beldyn—who still stood rooted, paralyzed with horror—and shoved him back against the stalagmites. His sword came up as he moved to stand protectively before the monk—waiting for the gruesome revenants to attack.

Attack they did. He swung his sword as they drew near, striking the first at the base of its jawbone and shearing off its head. The skull flew, smashing to pieces on the floor. For a moment its body remained standing, long enough to make him wonder, but then the thing collapsed, clattering to the floor in a heap, and did not rise again.

He allowed himself a victorious grin, which vanished as two more lurched forward, bony fingers clutching, to take the fallen mummy's place. He lashed out again, cleaving through one corpse's collarbone and smashing it to the ground. The second reached out and seized his cloak, yanking him closer. Yelping, he brought his sword back up, slamming its hilt into the corpse's face. The creature's head snapped back, and he spun his blade around, cleaving through its wrist. The severed hand continued to cling to him even as he dropped the walking corpse with a swing that cut it in two beneath the ribs.

He laid low five more, piling the floor at his feet with bones, before they overwhelmed him. First, a corpse's bony claws got past his defenses, ripping through his leather cuirass. Blood beaded beneath his armor then began to seep. His skin burned as if Kautilyan fire had spilled on it, and he ground his teeth against the pain as he swept the dead priest's legs out from beneath, then drove the point of his blade into another mummy's skull. The strange wound already slowed him, however, and soon he had a second, a raking gash across his shoulder that numbed his entire sword arm.

Still he fought on, keeping himself between the corpses and Beldyn. The monk still hadn't moved. He simply stared at the dead priests in abject terror. Nothing stood between him and the *Miceram*, yet he didn't try to grab it or make a run for it.

"Move, damn it!" Cathan finally shouted, flailing against the growing forest of reaching, leathery arms. Still more entered the fane, two for every one he felled. "Get to the bloody crown! Get—"

He didn't have the chance to finish the sentence. A bony hand slammed into the side of his head, denting his helmet and sending him staggering. Black stars burst in his vision as another corpse grabbed his sword by the crossguard and yanked it from his grasp. A third caught him about the stomach, bowling him over backward. Its dead weight crashed down on top of him, blasting the air from his lungs. He whooped for breath, struggling to rise, but more dead priests set upon him now, seizing his arms and legs, holding him still. Snarling, he arched his back, twisting wildly, but there was nothing he could do. Darkness wavered at the corners of his vision, but he fought back valiantly, craning to look around, searching for a glimpse of Beldyn.

He gave a wretched moan. To his right, another knot of corpses had dragged the young monk down. Beldyn lay beneath their writhing forms, unmoving. "No," Cathan groaned.

A bony hand covered his nose and mouth, smothering him. Sobbing, he gave one last thrash of futile resistance, as the darkness bore him away.

CHAPTER 25 ▼

The men on Govinna's southern wall crouched low, peering through the crenellations that topped its battlements. They had arrows fitted on their bowstrings, quarrels notched on their crossbows, bullets ready in the leather pockets of their slings. Here and there, piles of stones waited to be thrown down to the ground below. Kettles of boiling water—oil was too precious, with trade cut off and winter coming—rested on hingeworks, steaming in the frigid air. Officers paced along the catwalk behind their men, and young boys dashed about, carrying orders and urgent messages.

Lord Tavarre took it all in with a glance as he elbowed his way toward the steps leading to the top of the city's formidable gatehouse. A crowd had gathered at the wall's base, jostling and shoving, shouting questions to the sentries above. To their credit, the watchers gave them no heed. Ossirian had taught his men well—this medley of bandits and town guards, with common folk thrown in.

Now, Tavarre thought, if they'll just follow me as well as they followed him, we might live to see the sunset.

He'd been in the Pantheon's cellar a quarter-hour ago, pacing before the great stone plug that led to the catacombs—had been there much of the day, in fact, staring down the dusty tunnel, but no matter how hard he'd squinted and scowled, Beldyn and Cathan hadn't emerged. He had heard from them, and had crossed from worry to fear. They had gone down into the crypt in the middle of the night. It was a bit past midday now, the sun hidden behind a pall of white clouds, and still they hadn't returned.

Then the runner had arrived, bearing a simple message that sent him running across the city, his heart in his throat. The *Scatas* had come.

He took the steps three at a time, his legs straining after the run from the temple. At the top a familiar figure awaited him: Vedro, his capable man from Luciel. He gripped a bow in his thick-fingered hands, his face grimmer than usual behind the cheek-guards of his helm.

"What do we have?" Tavarre asked.

Vedro spat on the flagstones, then waved out past the merlons. "See for yourself."

Tavarre pushed between a pair of archers to stare out at the hills. The high walls, perched at the summit of one of Taol's tallest hills, gave him a commanding view. He followed the road as it snaked off toward the southern fiefs, amidst leafless plane trees and moss-speckled boulders, sunlight glinting on the Edessa. He fixed his gaze on a dark mass, more than half a league off but coming closer.

He squinted, shading his eyes with his hand. "Horsemen only?"

"A thousand or about," Vedro said, spitting again. He'd been chewing some sort of bitter root, which left stains on his teeth.

"An advance force."

"Aye. Looks like the same lot what chased us, and we lost at the bridge," Vedro noted. "I sent runners to the other gates and the river too, to warn 'em. Wouldn't put it past the sneaky buggers to flank us while we concentrated on this lot."

"Mmm," Tavarre muttered, unconvinced. "More likely they're here to test us."

261

Another stream of brown juice shot from Vedro's lips. "Well, then. Best put on a good show, eh?"

Chuckling, Tavarre settled in to watch the riders approach. They took their time, and the sentries glanced at one another, muttering under their breaths. Many of Govinna's defenders were young and hadn't seen battle before. The older men were also edgy. The riders' deliberate, almost arrogant pace unsettled them all.

"Easy, lads," Tavare called. "We're behind walls, don't forget. We can handle a thousand." It's the ten thousand to come that will give us trouble, he thought, grimacing.

Someone—he didn't look to see who—handed him a cross-bow and a case of quarrels. He loaded the weapon and sighted down its length, then lowered it again. Behind him, the Pantheon's bells pealed, and the other churches joined in, ringing in harmony as they sounded the first bell of the after-noon. Down the wall, a jumpy archer loosed his shot. It flew high and long, but when it fell it was still far short of the riders. Vedro rounded on the bowman, thickening the air with curses, threatening to roast the man's balls over a brazier. After that, no one else dared let fly early.

Half a mile away, the *Scatas* began to pick up their pace. Fanning out at some unheard order, they reached to their saddles for bows. Tavarre hunkered lower, bringing up his crossbow as Vedro raised a hand, ready to order the first vol-ley. He stared, judging the distance—still too far, not quite yet. But nearly . . . nearly. . . .

"Loose!" Vedro roared.

A chorus of thrums sounded along the wall, then the receding buzz of arrows and quarrels as they streaked away from the city. Tavarre fired with the others, grabbing the string of his crossbow and pulling it back to reload as he tracked the missiles' flight. He lost sight of his own shot amid the volley, a deadly black cloud that dove at the approaching horsemen, falling all around them, and into their midst as well.

Men screamed and cursed. Most of the archers' shots missed, thudding into the ground and shattering against rocks and paving stones, but here and there a rider clutched himself and pitched forward against his horse's neck or toppled from the saddle with a crash of armor. Horses died too, shrieking as they threw their riders or fell on top of them—again, not many, but enough to raise a cheer from the bowmen along the wall. Fists jabbed the air in triumph.

"Quit yapping, you dolts!" Vedro barked. "There's plenty more where they came from. Loose again!"

The second volley was more ragged than the first, but no less deadly. Again the missiles rained down, and again men fell like scythed wheat, but they were using their oblong shields now, catching shots that might have killed them. One paused long enough to show his arrow-riddled shield—it had six shafts buried in its face—to the rider beside him. He paid for the mistake, a seventh shaft suddenly sprouting from his eye. Tavarre fancied it was his quarrel that knocked the man from his horse, but there was no way to be sure. A dozen other men could have made the shot. He didn't care. A fierce grin spreading across his face, he cocked to fire again.

Aided by their high vantage, many of the sentries loosed a third shot, and some a fourth, before the enemy was close enough to shoot back. After that, though, the defenders' victorious shouts turned to cries of alarm as the horsemen raised their bows, and guiding their steeds with their knees, sent their own swarm of arrows arcing upward. Most of those first shots hit the battlements, bursting into clouds of splinters to rain back onto the ground, but a few hit their mark. To Tavarre's left a man shrieked, his tunic soaking with blood as he grabbed at a shaft that had driven between his ribs. Another archer fell to his right, an arrow bristling in his throat. Still another shot came down a hand's breadth from the baron's left knee, burying itself an inch deep into the wooden catwalk. The closeness of it made him jerk away, throwing off his aim, and his next shot went out too far and long, past the rearmost riders.

After that the battle turned chaotic, men on either side shooting as quickly as they could, raining torrents of arrows and bolts down upon each other. Some on the wall started to pitch rocks, shouting with glee as the stones knocked men from their saddles. A few poured out the boiling cauldrons, raising howls from below. Meanwhile, the horsemen rode back and forth along the wall's length firing back. More than a hundred of them lay dead already, and more fell every minute, toppling from their saddles to lie still.

"For the Lightbringer!" Govinna's defenders cried, above the screams of the wounded and dying. Hearing the shout, Tavarre gave an involuntary shudder. Gareth had uttered those identical words on the Bridge of Myrmidons, just before he fell.

Today, though, it was the *Scatas'* turn to yield. After several more minutes of fierce battle, with a quarter of their number dead, the rest began to flee, galloping down the road and away.

"Ha!" Vedro declared, rising to fire at the few remaining attackers. "Looks like we gave 'em someth—

A sound, halfway between a crunch and a thud, stopped him in mid-sentence, and he sat down with a grunt on the catwalk. His bow clattered from his hands. Tavarre turned, and winced as he saw the arrow that had punched through Vedro's leather breastplate.

Vedro looked down at the shaft, a look of puzzlement on his face, as if he couldn't figure out how it had gotten there. Blood flecked his beard.

"Well," he said. "That's no good at all." He slumped sideways.

Tavarre was still staring at Vedro's unmoving form—he was still breathing, but raggedly, with blood foaming around the wound—as the city's defenders began to whoop and yell. Some shouted curses over the merlons, and others raised their weapons in the air. Shaking his head, Tavare looked up and saw the last of the horsemen galloping away, past the bodies of their comrades, past horses left riderless by the fighting, fleeing back down the road where they'd come. A scattering of arrows followed them, but the retreat was too fast, and the shots fell short.

Warily, he rose to watch the enemy go. He didn't join his men in their cheers, nor did the other nobles and seasoned warriors atop the wall. They knew, as he did, that this skirmish was only the beginning.

What was worse, the riders had hurt them badly. Looking along the wall, Tavarre saw men lying on the catwalk, some writhing and moaning, others ominously still. By his count, a hundred of his men had caught an arrow, and surely half of those were dead. His gaze settled once more on Vedro, sprawled at his feet, wheezing wetly. His men had killed more *Scatas* than they'd lost, but the Kingpriest's soldiers could afford to lose such numbers. The rebels didn't have them to spare. The next time the *Scatas* attacked, they would come in greater numbers. *Far* greater numbers.

Sighing, Tavare looked back across the city, toward the Pantheon. "Damn it, MarSevrin," he muttered. "Where are you?"

———◆◆◆———

I'm dead, Cathan thought.

He'd woken lying on bare stone, surrounded by silence, his nostrils thick with the spicy smell of the dead. After several faltering tries, he'd convinced his eyes to open . . . and looked into Paladine's black-bearded face, glowering down on him from above. Though he knew it was only a painting, he cringed, remembering how often—and how recently—he'd spoken hateful words about the god.

When he thought about it, though, he realized death shouldn't *hurt* so much. His flesh burned in a dozen different places where the corpses' claws had scratched him, and a dull throb filled his skull. He'd bitten his tongue, too, and a swollen knot formed there, aching terribly. There was a sharper pain, besides, a jabbing at the small of his back. He reached down underneath him to find out what it was and pulled out a shard of skull, scraps of hairy scalp still clinging to it. He shuddered, flinging it away.

He pushed himself up, but the pain in his head stabbed harder, making him slump down. Nausea whirled in his stomach, and the darkness closed in again, flickering in the corners of his eyes. For a moment, he thought he was going to pass out again, but he managed to stave off collapse, taking deep breaths of the musty air until the pain in his skull settled down to a dull roar. He sat up again, slower this time, and looked around, wondering how long he'd been unconscious. The way he felt, it had to be a good while.

He was still in the fane, lying in the same spot where the dead priests had dragged him down. Bits of the corpses he'd cut down lay strewn about him, and not far away—he had to look twice to believe it—was his sword. The torch he'd carried had long since guttered out, but the golden glow that suffused the room was plenty of light. He felt a thrill as he realized that the *Miceram* must still be there in the room with him.

But Beldyn wasn't.

He struggled to his knees and cast about. The young monk was nowhere to be seen—and the other mummies, the ones he hadn't destroyed with his blade, were gone as well. Reaching out, he snatched up his sword and heaved himself to his feet. There was no one down by the altar, though the crown still rested atop it, its rubies flashing crimson. He leaned against a statue, staring. There it was, the treasure he and Beldyn had come for—but what use was it, if he couldn't find the Lightbringer?

"Beautiful, isn't it?" asked a rough voice.

Cathan yelped, then whirled, his sword rising.

The man stood a few paces from him, clad in the flowing white robes of Paladine's clergy, and for a heartbeat he thought it was Beldyn. It wasn't. The priest was older, around forty summers of age, his skin was dusky, and his hair was cropped short, a black stubble instead of the Lightbringer's long, flowing locks. There was a hardness about his face, too, that was different from the otherworldly intensity of Beldyn's eyes. On his head rested a platinum diadem, studded with winking emeralds.

"Who—who—" Cathan stammered.

The swarthy man didn't look at him. His gaze was fixed on the *Miceram*.

"You see why I took it," he said softly. "I couldn't bear to see it on another man's brow."

Cathan blinked. There was something not right about the priest. The robes made it hard to tell, but he had the unsettling feeling the man's feet weren't touching the floor, and he was wavering a little, like smoke in a breeze. Looking closer, Cathan swore he could see *through* the cleric to the stone of the far wall. It came to him, with a feeling that was part excitement but mostly terror, that this was no living man, but a spectre of someone long dead.

Then he knew—the scroll. Beldyn had shown him the illumination.

"Pradian?" he asked in a quavering voice.

The first Little Emperor inclined his head toward Cathan. His eyes were pupilless, empty and white.

"Ah, good. You *do* know me. That will make this easier." He turned back to the *Miceram*. "I still remember bringing it here, you know. I was sure, then, that I would come back to claim it. So very certain. So very wrong."

Looking at the ghost, who was staring longingly at the Crown, Cathan felt a wave of sorrow wash over him. He knew of Pradian the Great—everyone in Taol had heard the tale of his rise and tragic doom. Cathan could see, beneath the ghost's arm, the dark stain where the arrow had slain him, as he rode back victorious from battle. How different things would have been, but for that one errant shot!

After a moment Cathan shook his head, raising his blade.

"Where's Beldyn? What have you done with him?"

Pradian stared. Either he didn't notice the sword pointed at him, or he didn't care. For a moment he said nothing, then waved a spectral hand. "Oh, him," he said. "The guardians have him . . . but he is of no concern. No, young Cathan— *you're* the one I've been waiting for."

"Me?" Cathan blurted. He stopped, frowning. "What do you mean?"

"I mean," the ghost replied, "that you are the one I foretold, so many years ago. Not your friend, the monk."

Cathan stiffened in shock. He followed the specter's gaze back to the *Miceram*, which glittered on the altar, its rubies dancing with light. He could feel something, an undeniable pull, like a lodestone tugging at him. He looked back at Pradian and swallowed. It felt as though the crown was trying to draw him toward it.

The urge to dash down to the altar flared, almost overwhelming him. He nearly gave in to the temptation, took one step forward, but in the end he staved it off, sweat beading on his upper lip as he stared at the crown. "But," he breathed, "that can't be. Beldyn's the one. Ilista saw him wearing it, and Durinen too. He opened the door."

"No," said Pradian. "It opened to *you*. As for the First Daughter and my successor . . . a trick, that. Easier for me to show the monk wearing the crown than to show you. They were more apt to follow that way. *You* were more apt to follow."

The pull strengthened. Cathan's whole body trembled, the hairs on his arms standing erect. It wasn't right, he knew that. It was some kind of trick. Beldyn was the rightful Kingpriest, wasn't he? And yet . . . if anyone knew who should claim the *Miceram*, wasn't it Pradian? He had put the crown here in the first place, after all.

All at once, Cathan was no longer standing by the row of statues, but rather right before the altar itself. The marble slab gleamed coolly in the *Miceram*'s light, free of the dust that mantled the rest of the catacombs. The crown glittered atop it, the rubies pulsing with their own inner vibrancy.

Cathan stared at it, his lips parted. He had never wanted something so much in his life.

"Take it," Pradian whispered gently. "Set it on your brow, and Istar is yours to rule, as it should have been mine. All who see you will bow before you—such is its power. Your enemies will surrender, your allies swear eternal fealty . . ."

His breath coming in quick gasps, Cathan laid down his sword, leaning it against the altar. He could see nothing now, nothing but the *Miceram*, and the power it could grant him. He imagined himself sitting on a golden throne as men and women from all over the empire knelt at his feet—priests, warriors, merchants and nobles all waiting to do his bidding. Everything he had ever dreamed of could be his: wealth and might. All he had to do was take the crown.

Smiling, he lifted the *Miceram* from the altar.

It was cool to the touch, heavier than he'd imagined—not gilded bronze, but solid gold. He weighed it in his hands a moment, then bent forward, pressing his lips to its central ruby—a gem so precious, it could buy a lifetime of comfort. *His* gem. Reverently, he lifted the *Miceram*, raising it toward his brow—

Suddenly, he stopped. His reflection, warped by the crown's curves, stared back at him from its golden surface. He saw his own eyes, wide and wild. There was madness in them, a crazed streak he hadn't seen since the dark days when he'd forsaken the god, before his world had changed. Before Beldyn.

Slowly, he lowered the crown again. "No."

He'd thought the ghost would say something, implore him to put it on. Instead, Pradian remained silent, watching him intensely. With an effort of will, Cathan tore his gaze from the crown and shook his head, stepping back.

"Beldyn asked me to come with him because he believed I was loyal," he said. "I won't betray him."

Pradian stared. "You would give up an empire?"

"The empire isn't mine to give," Cathan replied. "Beldyn

is the Lightbringer. The *Miceram* belongs to him. Now take me to him, and no more games."

The white light in the specter's eyes flared, and for a moment Cathan feared he'd chosen wrongly, that Pradian would attack him for his impudence. Instead, though, the ghost turned aside, and glided toward the wall behind the altar. Sighing, Cathan followed him.

"The true Kingpriest must have his subjects' love," the ghost said as they reached the wall. He turned, fixing Cathan with his colorless gaze. "Only a man who inspires such devotion is worthy of the Crown of Power. Remember this."

Pradian was gone, so suddenly his image remained burned on Cathan's eyelids. Before he could wonder about the apparition's disappearance, however, a soft click came from the wall before him. He looked and saw a crack had opened in the wall, glowing golden to match the crown. Now, as he watched, it widened and lengthened until it defined a doorway. It flared brightly, and the stone within it disappeared, revealing a shadowed passage beyond.

Holding his breath, Cathan stepped through the opening. On the other side was a small chamber, hewn from the living rock. On its far end was a simple shrine to Paladine, surmounted by the platinum triangle and dozens of white candles. Spectral, white flames flickered on each taper, without consuming them. Before the shrine, a body lay in repose: Beldyn, his robes dirt-smudged and flecked with blood. His face was white, his eyes shut, his chest rising and falling slowly.

Surrounding him were the legion of dead priests.

They filled the room, dozens of them, staring down at his motionless form. Then, sensing Cathan's presence, they turned, ancient sinews creaking. Their empty eye sockets seemed to stare right through him, utterly black. The stench of perfumed decay hung heavy in the room, half-choking him. He froze, his spine turning to ice, as he realized he'd left his sword leaning against the altar. All he had was the crown and his bare hands. If the corpses attacked him, they would rip him apart.

They did no such thing. Instead, seeing the crown in his hands, they bowed their heads and backed away, clearing a path to Beldyn.

Cathan stared at them, his nerves jangling. Cold sweat trickled down his back. Swallowing, he stepped forward, carrying the *Miceram* to the shrine where Beldyn lay.

CHAPTER 26 ▼

Tavarre huddled behind the battlements while an endless hail of arrows poured down. All around him, men screamed and fell as the shafts pierced their breasts, throats, skulls. Bodies littered the catwalk, some still moving, others not, and blood poured in runnels down the wall to the street below. Any moment, he knew, an arrow would find *him*— and, indeed, he was watching one shoot toward him out of the crimson sun when the nightmare tore apart and he woke, damp with sweat, to someone rapping at the door.

He sat up, reaching for the dirk he kept at his bedside. Kicking at the blankets that had tangled about his ankles, he got to his feet. The stone floor was freezing as he padded toward the door.

His first thought was the *Scatas* were attacking again. Whoever led the Kingpriest's forces would guess the city couldn't withstand a full assault. Tavarre was also well aware of that fact, as were a growing number of the men under his command—a potential morale problem there. More than just the dead and wounded had quit the wall after the battle. The desertions would only grow worse in the days to come.

When he flung the door open, he found himself looking at a young Mishakite priestess, a pretty thing of maybe eighteen summers, whose golden hair lay hidden beneath the hood of her blue robes. She gasped as he loomed before her, and he flushed as he realized he'd greeted her wearing nothing but a breechclout—to say nothing of the blade he was still flashing in his hand.

He lowered the dagger. "What is it? Have we lost more of the wounded?"

In the aftermath of the skirmish by the south gate, he'd ordered his men to bring the casualties back to the Pantheon. Now the church's worship hall stank of death and agony as the Mishakites tended the fallen, but there was little they could do for most but give them bloodblossom oil to soothe their pain as they died. Nearly half of the gravely wounded had perished since the battle—among them Vedro, who had hung on for hours, then expired an hour before sunset, brave fellow. More deaths would surely follow, though some would linger for days before succumbing to their wounds.

The Mishakite bowed her head. "Eight more, since even-song, my lord," she murmured, "but that isn't why I woke you." She lowered her eyes, signing the twin-teardrop sign of her goddess.

Tavarre frowned, then he knew, with a jolt. "It's the Light-bringer, isn't it?" he asked.

"Yes, lord," the priestess said, nodding. "He has returned. Only he . . ." She stopped, her sandaled feet shifting.

The hope that had kindled suddenly in his breast died just as quickly as he looked at her. She would not meet his gaze, so he reached out, cupping her chin and lifting it to make her look him in the eye. "What is it?" he demanded. "Is he . . . dead?"

"No, lord," she said. "Not dead. But . . ."

She trailed off, and he had to fight back the urge to grab her shoulders and shake her. "Tell me!" he demanded, his voice rising to a shout. "Tell me what's happened!"

Tears spilling from her brimming eyes, she told him.

The *Miceram* shimmered in the candlelight within Beldyn's chambers, its rubies glinting with crimson fire. It sat upon a cushion, which lay on top of a pedestal in the midst of the room. Neither Cathan nor Tavarre looked at the crown, however. Instead, their gaze was fixed upon the bed beside the pedestal, where the shell of the Lightbringer lay.

Beldyn's face was smooth, showing no signs of pain. Bruises darkened his flesh where the dead priests had seized him, and a few scratches on his arms had scabbed over, but he showed no other signs of injury, nothing that would threaten his life. The holy medallion on his breast rose and fell, rose and fell, his breathing was slow and deep, and his hands did not move. He might have been asleep, in the grasp of some pleasant dream—were it not for his eyes. They remained wide open, staring sightlessly at the ceiling. Though the room was dim, his pupils had shrunk to tiny points. Tears tracked down his temples, into his long, thick hair.

"I found him like this," Cathan murmured. "I tried to make him wake up . . . shook him, yelled at him . . . even slapped him. Nothing worked, so I carried him out of there, him and the crown, and brought them here. I did the best I could."

Tavarre stroked his beard. "You did well, lad," he murmured.

Cathan wanted to believe so, truly did, but still he felt sick. It wasn't supposed to be like this. Beldyn should be awake, not in this strange trance. The dying men in the worship hall needed him, and so did the living. He should have walked out of the catacombs with the *Miceram* shining on his brow, not come slung over Cathan's shoulder, arms and legs limp, head lolling like a dead man's. That wasn't part of the prophecy.

"What do we do?" he asked.

Tavarre didn't answer, the scars on his face deepening as

he thought. He pressed a hand against Beldyn's cheek, and Cathan knew what he would feel. The monk's skin was cold, clammy. Like a corpse, he thought miserably.

Sighing, Tavarre turned, gazing at the *Miceram*. He was silent for a long time. Then, brow furrowed, he took a step toward it.

"What are you doing?" Cathan asked, catching his arm.

Tavarre blinked, turning to look at him. "We need the crown, boy. Even without him, it may give us a chance."

He tried to pull loose, but Cathan didn't relax his grasp. "It isn't right," he said. "Everything that's happened has led up to Beldyn putting on the crown. Not you."

"That may be," Tavarre said, "but I doubt he'll miss it, in the state he's in. Let me go, boy."

"No."

They locked gazes, glaring at each other. Then, with a wrenching twist, Tavarre yanked himself from Cathan's grip. Doing so threw him off-balance, however, and he stumbled sideways. In that moment, Cathan stepped between him and the crown, reaching for the hilt of his sword.

Tavarre's gaze dropped to the blade. "You'd draw steel against me?" he asked, and laughed. "This is no time for games. I'd cut you to pieces."

"Maybe," Cathan replied and slid his sword from its scabbard.

He held it low, his gaze hard on Tavarre. They stared at each other. The baron's hand strayed across his body, fingertips brushing his own pommel.

"Damn it, boy," he growled. "Don't be an idiot."

Cathan's sword moved so swiftly that Tavarre had barely begun to draw his own before he felt it at his throat, the last four inches of its blade creasing his skin.

"I'm not an idiot," Cathan said, his voice like glass. "I swore to protect him, even if it costs me my life . . . or yours, lord."

Anger blazed in Tavarre's eyes—then faded. He slid his sword back home, a wry smile twisting his lips. "You have a lot of faith, Cathan," he said. "I think I liked you better when you had none."

Cathan shrugged, returning the grin as he lifted his sword away. "I don't blame you, but that door in the catacombs opened to *him*, my lord, not you. If you wore it, your men would fight to the death—but what good will that be, if they still lose?"

Tavarre opened his mouth to argue, then closed it again. It didn't matter how fanatical Govinna's defenders were. They were still outmatched, and he knew it. With a sigh, he turned back to the bed. Beldyn remained as before, silent, death-like, his eyes gazing at something neither man could see. The baron scratched his beard again.

"What *do* we do?" he asked.

Cathan blew a long breath out through his lips as he sheathed his blade. He walked to the bedside and laid his hand across Beldyn's lifeless fingers.

"Pray," he said.

———◆———

" . . . and so, Your Holiness, I implore you," droned the Seldjuki merchant, standing before the throne, "ease the restrictions your predecessor set on the sale of whale oil. My ships lie useless in the harbors of Lattakay. My men idle in taverns, drowning themselves in grog while their harpoons rust. If we can ply our trade freely again, I will send a tithe of my earnings to the church. The others in the whaling guild will do the same. . . ."

On and on he went, talking without pause. He was a ludicrous fellow, short and immensely fat, his bushy moustache making him look like one of the fabled walrus-men of Icereach. Extravagant jewels covered his clothes, and three peacock feathers jutted from his turban. The scent of ambergris clung to him like thick fog, and his nut-brown skin glistened rosily where he had applied too much rouge. Perhaps, in his youth, he had been a handsome dandy, but now he simply looked—and sounded—ridiculous. Still he prattled, oblivious to the scornful glances of the Kingpriest's courtiers all around him.

Kurnos, for his part, had stopped listening some minutes ago, settling back on his throne while the merchant yammered on. Ordinarily, he would have tried to show patience to the droning whaler, but today his thoughts left no room for the trivial business of the court. Rather, they were far away, roaming hungrily toward Taol. A courier had arrived at the Temple just last night, bearing news from Lord Holger. The army was in place, and the old Knight was certain that when he sent his men to battle, Govinna's impenetrable gates would fall. By Godsday, the highland rebellion would be crushed at last, its leaders dead, the borderfolk subjugated once more.

As for the upstart monk, the so-called Lightbringer . . .

The pain was so sharp, so sudden, that Kurnos had no time to brace himself. One moment, he was smiling lazily at his private thoughts. The next he bent forward with a grunt, grabbing at his left hand. It felt as though he'd dipped it in molten gold, and the pain got worse with every shuddering breath he drew. He bit down on his tongue, trying to swallow the agony, but could only stave it off for so long. Finally, he doubled over, clutching his fingers and letting out a ragged cry.

The fat whaler fell silent, his mouth hanging open as the crystal dome flared overhead, ringing with the echo of the Kingpriest's scream. The courtiers stared at Kurnos in shock. Strinam reacted first, the First Son stepping forward with concern in his eyes.

"Majesty?" he asked. "Are you all right?"

"I'm fine," Kurnos growled through clenched teeth. Stefara of Mishakal was hurrying toward the dais now. He waved her off, his face twisted into a snarl.

It was a lie. The agony was spreading, past his wrist and up his elbow. If someone had offered to cut off his arm with an axe just then, he would have given them the pleasure. He doubted even that would work. The ring would not release its grip so easily.

With an effort, he pushed himself to his feet and swept the hall with his gaze. It was hard to look imperious with tears streaming down his face, but he did his best.

"This court," he growled, his voice shaking, "is . . . adjourned. We will . . . resume . . . tomorrow."

The whaler made an indignant sound as Kurnos descended from the dais, making his way out of the Hall. The courtiers watched Kurnos go, whispering to one another as he shoved aside the curtains to enter his private antechamber. He wished them all dead. They would gossip about him, no doubt, while he was gone. There were already rumors spreading, he knew. The blighted rose garden, the dead hippogriff, Loralon's sudden dismissal from his position—and there were the darker tales of eldritch lights and strange sounds within the manse, late at night. It didn't matter how much the church strove to quell such idle talk. It still flourished in the wine shops and marketplaces. Now, after the scene in the Hall of Audience, there would be new gossip.

Kurnos didn't care. He only wanted to put a stop to the pain.

Bursting into his study, he slammed the door behind him, shot the bolt, and fell to his knees with a howl. He clutched his hand to his chest, its fingers curled like claws. From the way it felt, he expected to see his flesh charred black, falling off his bones, but it was still pink and unscarred, though slick with sweat—nothing passing strange . . . except the scorching sensation of the ring.

The emerald had flared to life, sickly green light dancing from facet to facet, Within, the shadows whirled, like moths trapped in a lantern glass. Amid the storm of darkness, the demon's eyes glared at him, hungry, eager, wild with blood-lust.

Say my name! she hissed in his head. *Say it and the pain ends. I must have vengeance! Say it!*

"No," he wept. "I don't need you. I won't do it. I—"

SAY MY NAME!

The ring flared, and the pain that came with it made Kurnos vomit—on his robes, on the floor. He fell on his hands and knees, sobbing. Flashes like Karthayan fireworks filled his vision as the pain spread through his chest, clawing closer and closer to his heart. He knew, when it got there, that he would die. The demon would rather kill him than be thwarted.

"Get out, then, you bitch!" he screamed, his throat burning. "Sathira!"

She burst from the emerald with such force that she knocked him back, sending him sliding across the marble floor. The shadows billowed like smoke from a holocaust, mushrooming up to the study's vaulted ceiling, spreading down the walls in rolling waves to pool across the floor. Candles blew apart, sending gobbets of hot wax flying through the air. The wine-colored lamp on Kurnos's desk burst into a storm of glass shards that tinkled onto the floor.

The Kingpriest lay still through it all, curled up in a ball, moaning as if someone had driven a spear through his stomach. He could only look up helplessly as the demon took on physical form—larger now than she had been, towering like an ogre, all sinuous, velvety blackness. Her baleful green eyes were as narrow as razor cuts as she glowered down at him, and for a moment he was sure she would seize him in her talons and tear him apart. She wanted to—he could sense it—but the magic that bound her held her back. For a long moment she seethed, the fires of the Abyss blazing in her eyes. Then, with such obvious loathing that Kurnos nearly laughed, she bowed to him.

"Master," she snarled. "I failed you. The monk lives. Say the word, and I will destroy him."

Unsteadily, Kurnos rose to his knees. The stink of bile was thick in his nostrils. He knew her words were a command, not an offer. If he denied her, she would return to the ring, and the pain would multiply until it killed him. There was only one way to end this. He had no choice. Did I *ever* have one? he wondered.

Wiping his mouth, he met the demon's malevolent gaze. "Very well," he said. "Go. Finish your task."

Sathira's eyes blazed with unholy joy. With a snarl, she streaked to the hearth set into the study's wall, then vanished up the chimney, leaving the chamber in ruins in her wake.

Alone, Kurnos slumped, his shoulders hunching in defeat. Weakly, he fumbled at his throat, pulling out his medallion. It felt deathly cold as he clutched it between his shaking hands.

"Help me, Paladine," he whispered. "I beg of you. . . ."

No reply came. In all of Kurnos's life, the god had never seemed farther away.

CHAPTER 27 ▼

Three days passed, and still Beldyn did not wake.

The rumors began to spread. Some said the Lightbringer was dead, others that he had fled Govinna after Lady Ilista's funeral. Tavarre tried his best to silence such gossip, but it would have been easier to dam the Edessa. Once the tales got out, they spread like the *Longosai* and just as dangerous, too. The sentries on the city's walls began to talk, casting anxious glances back at the Pantheon. Their morale was flagging, and Tavarre could only watch it happen. Even the rumors that cut closest to the truth—that the monk had withdrawn to commune with the god—drained the hope out of Govinna's defenders.

The desertions mounted.

Two young men posted by the city's western gate snuck away from their posts in the predawn gloom. Their replacements found that stretch of the wall unguarded when they arrived to relieve the pair, and after a furious search the two turned up in a tavern, half-drunk on raw wine. Tavarre punished them severely, stripping them naked and forcing them to prostrate themselves before each of the city gatehouses. As the day wore on, though, more and more sentries quit their posts—more than thirty desertions by sunset. Tavarre couldn't bring himself to blame his men. They were trapped, outmatched. They had lost Durinen and Ossirian both, and now, seemingly, the Lightbringer as well. It was a wonder *anyone* remained on the battlements by the following night's end. Still, many did, the light of belief shining in their eyes. Their watchword became *uso dolit*—*the god will provide*—and they spoke it over and over, awaiting Beldyn's return.

The rash of desertions continued through the third day, the ranks atop the wall dwindling every hour. That wasn't the worst of it, though, for that morning, an hour after dawn, a party of outriders came thundering out of the mists, galloping up to the southern gates and shouting to be let in. Riddled with arrows—two, without Beldyn's healing touch to aid them, died later that day from their wounds—they reported the news Tavarre dreaded hearing: the *Scatas* were breaking their camp and sharpening their blades, awaiting the command to march.

"It gets worse," said the lead scout, wincing against the pain of a shaft he'd taken through one wrist. "They've built a ram. Cut down a big ironwood, they did, an' put 'er on wheels, with a mantlet to cover. 'Twill sure move slow, but it looks strong enough."

Govinna's gates were mighty and had never fallen, not even in the worst of the *Trosedil*. But everything happened for the first time, sometime, Tavarre knew.

"Some of my officers are counseling surrender," he told Cathan that evening, as the sky outside Beldyn's bedchamber darkened to star-flecked black. It was a moonless night—Solinari would not rise for hours yet, and Lunitari had just set—and the fire that crackled in the room's great hearth couldn't fully stave off the chill. "Better to yield the city than see it burn, they say."

Cathan sat at Beldyn's bedside. He'd barely moved in days, sleeping in a chair in the room's corner, his sword across his knees. His eyes narrowed as he studied the baron's troubled face.

"You're not seriously considering it, though. Right?"

Frowning, Tavarre looked away. "A few of us must flee, if we want to live."

"Flee where?" Cathan pressed. "There's nowhere left to run—except the wilds, and winter's coming. One good blizzard, and the *Scatas* won't *have* to look for us. The storm will do their work for them."

Still, when Tavarre left again, returning to the wall with resignation-hardened eyes, Cathan found himself lingering over the idea of retreat. If the soldiers took the city—and they would—then he and the baron were both dead. If the *Scatas* didn't kill them where they stood, they would find their doom at the executioner's sword. He pictured his own head, dipped in tar and spiked above Govinna's gates, and felt sick. He was sure, too, that a worse fate awaited Beldyn.

Not that he'd notice, he thought bitterly, looking at the bed.

The trance had left a haunted mark on the Lightbringer. He had always been slender, but three days' starvation had left him gaunt, his cheekbones standing out sharply beneath his sunken eyes. Cathan hadn't been able to get him to take any food, though he *had* wet the monk's lips with a cloth soaked in watered wine. Still, despite his wasted state, he showed no sign of discomfort. His expression remained peaceful, as though he were enjoying some pleasant dream. At least he'll die happy, Cathan thought with a grimace.

His gaze drifted across the room, to the *Miceram* on its pedestal. It gleamed in the hearthglow, its rubies glinting with reflected starlight. He'd looked at it enough, these past three days, so it seemed an old friend. When he closed his eyes, he could picture every engraving, every scratch, every little dent. He had counted the gems' facets, noted their tiny flaws, learned which ones were wine-red and which leaned toward tawny. Looking at it, though, was all he ever did. Not once since he'd brought it here had he touched it.

Now he rose, knees popping, and walked to where it lay. Standing over it, he felt an ache inside him, like he hadn't felt since the fane, when he'd fought off the urge to put on the crown. He squeezed his eyes shut, trying to put the temptation out of his mind.

"You'll lose without it, you know," said a voice he recognized.

He gasped, opening his eyes as he whipped around. There, standing—or rather, floating—beside the hearth was Pradian. A knowing smile lit his face as he glided forward, the firelight, making him glow like a cloud at sunset. He made no shadow on the carpeted floor as he went to where the crown lay.

"You," Cathan said. "Damn it, what did you do to him?"

The ghost shook his head. "That makes no difference now. You need the *Miceram*'s power to win the coming battle. Without it, you will die—along with everyone else who still stands against the *Scatas*. You don't have the strength to hold the defense, and you know it."

Cathan didn't answer; he only stared at the crown, aglisten in the firelight. He reached out, brushing its surface with his fingertips. It was cold to the touch, but there was something else, too: a strange new sensation, like the crackling air before a summer storm. It made him jerk his hand away, and he stepped back from the pedestal.

"It's all right, lad," Pradian said, leaning forward. "It feels strange, I know, but you'll get used to it. You'll have to, if you're going to stop the *Scatas*."

"Me, stop the *Scatas*?" Cathan repeated, then looked at the ghost. "How?"

The spectre only smiled. "I can't tell you. Only the crown can do that."

Cathan swallowed, feeling the truth of the specter's words. He reached out again, and this time nothing stopped him. The crown lifted off the pedestal easily and quickly warmed in his grasp. Cathan turned, raising it high.

"Go on," Pradian urged, his blank eyes shining. "All you have to do is put it on."

Cathan held still, the *Miceram* poised above his own head.

He took a deep breath. Then, with a slow smile, he brought it down. . . .

. . . and set it on the bed beside Beldyn.

Pradian's swarthy face had been exultant. Now it changed: "Fool!" he thundered. "The *Scatas* will take it back to the Lordcity and give it to the false Kingpriest who sits the throne there! Do you want that?"

"No." Cathan smiled slyly. "Neither do you. It will be the end of your claim to the throne. You'll have lost your war at last . . . unless you wake Beldyn."

The ghost scowled. For a long moment, neither of them moved . . . then, slowly, Pradian nodded. "Very well," he said, "but remember what you're giving up, boy."

"It was never mine in the first place."

With one last glare, the ghost turned away, gliding to Beldyn's bedside. His eyes lingered hungrily on the *Miceram*, then he bent low, his mouth seeking the Lightbringer's. Their lips met, and light blazed, the crown's gold and Beldyn's silver aflame together. Cathan fell back as the light stung his eyes, throwing up his arm to block it out—and it was gone, and Pradian with it, the ghost vanished into the air.

Beldyn's eyes flickered open.

Uttering a wordless cry, Cathan ran over and seized the monk's wasted hand. He pressed it to his cheek, laughing and weeping at the same time. "*Palado Calib*," he said, and could say nothing more.

Weakly, the Lightbringer smiled. His eyes went to the crown, lying beside him. His free hand reached out, shaking, to brush its central ruby. "*Site ceram biriat, abat*," he whispered, then turned to look at Cathan. "Thank you, my friend. I've been through a lot, but now I know how I can stop the *Scatas*. Help me up. Let me show you."

Beaming, Cathan helped lift him from the bed. Beldyn was weak still, his legs trembling as he got to his feet, but he refused any help. Instead, he nodded to the *Miceram*, his eyes gleaming in its golden light.

285

"Bring that," he said.

Cathan laughed, reaching for the crown—then stopped as a sound broke through the air, jarring him: a clarion warhorn. He listened to it, not believing, then bowed his head with a moan. He knew the call.

They were too late. The battle was beginning.

———◆•◆•◆———

Sathira swept across the highlands, skimming over the rocky ground. It was easy to keep hidden in the night's shadows, so she could move swiftly across the land, unimpeded by broken ground, tangled bracken or the white-frothed streams that tumbled through cuts on their way to the thundering Edessa. She flowed over them all, hissing with anticipation. She could smell the monk's reek on the wind.

At last, she reached the crest of a tor crowned by a tall, mossy boulder. She perched atop the stone, her green eyes flaring as she beheld Govinna. There it was, sprawled on its twin precipices, sparkling with lamplight. In its midst, high-towered and copper-roofed, loomed the Pantheon. Loathing swelled within her at the sight of it. She had failed here, thwarted by the thrice-damned priestess. The pain of her banishment flashed hot in her memory.

The priestess was dead now, though. She could protect Brother Beldyn no more.

Sathira became aware, suddenly, of a commotion to the south. Born of shadows, she could see in darkness as well as day and now beheld a great dust cloud, rising beyond the city. The Kingpriest's army, she realized, letting out a harsh, hissing laugh. The siege was about to begin. The notion that those on both sides of the coming battle were servants of Paladine—or believed themselves to be—amused her greatly. The dark gods would be pleased indeed.

She crossed the remaining miles to the city in minutes. As she expected, most of Govinna's sentries had left its north gates, to face the approaching *Scatas*, but a few still remained. She killed three of them as she streaked over the wall, barely slowing as she ripped them open with her wicked talons. Hot blood dripped from the battlements as she dove into the narrow streets, leaving the other guards to stare in horror at the tattered remains of their fellows.

Getting into the Pantheon was even easier. Searching, she found an open window and glided through it into the dark halls. Bloodlust surged within her as she slid through the church. The Lightbringer's stench was everywhere, making it hard to tell which way to go. It was strongest in the cloisters, though, so she headed that way, her claws opening and closing eagerly.

Finally, she came to a closed door, where the stink was stronger than anywhere else. The stench came from within. These were Beldyn's quarters. She snarled a laugh, then her eyes flashed bright green, and the door blew off its hinges. Splinters rained onto the floor as slipped into the study. Glancing around to make sure the room was empty, she swept through to the bedchamber, where the reek was strongest. She stopped, letting out a furious growl.

The monk was gone.

Frustration boiled within her as she glared around the room. The Lightbringer's odor lingered over the bed, but no one was in the room. Furious, she streaked about, shredding tapestries and smashing the shrine to Paladine in its corner, then turned and shot back out into the study . . . and stopped.

She was no longer alone. A young acolyte stood in the doorway, staring at the smoldering ruins of the door. Now his gaze lifted, and the color drained from his face. He froze, his eyes wild with terror.

In an eyeblink she had him, seizing him with claws locked around his neck, pricking his flesh. She shuddered with pleasure. He twitched in her grasp, choking.

"Where is he?" she barked. "The Lightbringer! Where has he gone?"

The boy didn't answer. She saw, in his wide, frightened eyes that he really didn't know. She tightened her grip, her talons digging deeper, and he struggled a moment longer then fell limp, blood pouring from the savaged ruins of his throat. He crumpled to the floor when she let him go and lay twitching and bleeding in the dark.

Then she was out the door again, streaking down the hall, her eyes ablaze with emerald fire. Beldyn was out there somewhere. She *would* find him.

Tavarre's horn carried beyond Govinna as well as within. Its blare echoed among the hills, where the second and fourth *Dromas* of the imperial army waited. They had halted a mile south of the city, standing ready, weapons and shields in hand. Torches flickered among their ranks, but for the most part they carried no lights. They needed none to see their goal. Even in the dark night, there was no mistaking Govinna's towering walls.

The *Scatas* had little in the way of siege equipment, but what they had was menacing. Dozens of scaling ladders lay on the ground, and at the rear was their great battering ram, a tree trunk three times as wide as a man was tall, hewn from a great ironwood tree. A massive, bronze head in the shape of a clenched fist covered its end, gleaming in the stars' glow.

Standing near the ram with his officers, Lord Holger glanced up at the trumpet's blare. His face tightened into a scowl. He'd just been considering sending a man forward to request a parley before the battle was joined. The borderfolk didn't seem keen on giving him that chance, though. Already he could see swarms of them, lit by blazing braziers, thick atop the curtain wall.

"I don't believe it," said Sir Utgar, standing near Holger's right hand. "They think they can fight us? Are they fools?"

Several other men chuckled, but Holger shook his head. "Worse," he said. "They have nothing to lose. Loren, my shield."

The knights exchanged looks as his squire hurried forward. Holger Windsound never wore his shield unless a fight was imminent. He held still as Loren buckled the massive, circular targe to his arm, then reached across his body to rattle his sword in its scabbard.

"What are your orders, milord?" Utgar asked.

Holger drew a deep breath. The freezing air stung his nostrils but kept him alert. He signed the triangle and Kiri-Jolith's horns, then drew his blade, holding it high.

"Full attack," he said. "Let's end this quickly."

Runners dashed off down the ranks, shouting the order. In reply, the army's falcon and triangle banners lifted high, and the war drums roared, booming for all to hear. Bellowing in reply, the *Scatas* raised their swords and spears and began to march, their blue cloaks like pools of ink in the night. Among them, the white and gold robes of clerics flashed, mimicking the stars above.

Holger watched them go while his officers dispersed. Loren brought him his percheron, which blew out its lips at the prospect of battle. Taking the reins, the old Knight swung up into the saddle, spurred his steed, and led his men to war.

Tavarre stood among Govinna's remaining defenders, glowering as the *Scatas* started forward. Down the wall, a few more men threw down their weapons and ran—but only a few. The rest stared as the soldiers advanced, as inexorable as a flood. There seemed to be no end of them.

Grimacing, Tavarre sounded the horn again. It was done. The soldiers would take the wall, break the gates. He would die here with his men, and all he had wrought, everything he'd done since his beloved Ailinn died, would come to nothing. He laughed softly to himself—he'd been foolish to think he could defy the Kingpriest.

Bloody well better take a few with me then, he thought. He brought his horn to his lips, letting fly a third ringing blast. The men and women atop the wall echoed it, their weapons punching the air.

"For the Lightbringer!" they cried.

The *Scatas* moved too quickly and too slowly all at once. Marching at such a deliberate pace, they seemed to take forever to cross the last mile to the city, but at the same time Tavarre could scarcely believe it when his archers began to loose their arrows, which flew and fell among the advancing soldiers.

The footmen lost many to that first volley, more than the horsemen had in the first sortie. Packed in close formation, the *Scatas* had little room to evade the barrage, and the first ranks dropped in waves, leaving those behind to stumble over their bodies. A few raised their shields in time, drawing curses from the men on the wall. Tavarre got one of them with a shot from his crossbow, piercing him through the knee with a steel quarrel. The man staggered and fell. Tavarre let out a whoop, pulling back his string to reload.

Once again, the tenor of the battle changed as the *Scatas* returned fire. White-fletched arrows peppered the battlements, and Govinna's defenders began to fall. Beside Tavarre, a woman screamed and sprawled across a merlon as an arrow sliced open her neck. Her blood spattered the baron, but he didn't even bother to wipe it from his face as he aimed and fired again and again. Another man, just down the wall, spun in place, then fell from the battlements, two shafts lodged in his breast.

So it went, for what seemed like hours, men and women falling on either side, some dead as soon as they hit the ground, others thrashing for a time before falling still or trying to drag themselves away. Tavarre emptied a case of quarrels and yelled for more. Elsewhere along the wall, the archers grabbed enemy arrows and fired them back. It made no difference, however, how many the borderfolk slew. For every soldier who fell, a dozen or more marched behind. They pushed forward relentlessly, stepping over their dead, weathering stones and boiling water as well as the constant rain of arrows.

Now the ladders came, as Tavarre knew they would, pushing forward through the masses of imperial soldiers, their bearers seeking patches of wall to assail. A deep rumble shook the earth, and the enormous ram followed, pushed by fifty men as it made its slow, creaking way toward city's proud gates.

"Aim for them!" Tavarre barked, waving at the *Scatas* driving the ram. "The ones with the ladders too! Slow them down!"

The battle's noise was so fierce that only a handful of borderfolk heard him, but his orders spread nonetheless, from one man to his neighbor, on down the line. The ram quickly shuddered to a halt as half the men pushing it fell, pierced by bowshot and crushed by thrown stones. The same happened to most of the ladder-bearers, but not all—here and there, along the wall's length, ladders swung upward to thump against the battlements. Soldiers scrambled up, two or three rungs at a time.

Govinna's defenders acted quickly, grabbing up long-handled military forks and hurrying across the battlements. Thrusting hard, they shoved the ladders back, sending them toppling over. The climbing men screamed as they plummeted, then fell sharply silent as they crashed into the ground.

Victory cries rang out across the wall, but Tavarre didn't join in. Already, more *Scatas* were picking up the ladders, and the ram lurched forward again. More arrows and quarrels poured down, and for a second time the attack stopped. The ladders rose and fell again, a second time, a third, but the soldiers kept coming, picking them up and planting them anew in the blood-soaked ground.

Out of bolts again, Tavarre threw away his crossbow and grabbed up a fork. Below, the ram was moving yet again, on toward the city. This time, though, it refused to stop, and the city's defenders gritted their teeth as it rumbled up to the gatehouse. The gleaming, fist-shaped head smashed into the gates.

Tavarre winced, feeling the crunch of the impact beneath his feet, and watched as the *Scatas* backed the ram away again, ducking beneath the continuing deluge of arrows, then surged forward another time, smashing the great tree into the city's doors. Tavarre shut his eyes, a cold feeling running through him as he wondered if he'd just heard splintering. Another few blows like that, and legendary or not, the gates would come down. After that . . .

He glanced at the Pantheon, his mouth twisting. If only he'd taken the *Miceram*, rather than leaving it for Beldyn. He wasn't sure what difference the crown would have made, but still, anything would be better than standing here, waiting for death.

Uso dolit, his men had said, when their fellows deserted. *The god will provide.* Tavarre laughed bitterly at their blind faith, gripping his sword as the ladders rose again. "Well," he muttered, "the god had better damn well hurry up."

CHAPTER 28 ▼

The crash of the *Scatas'* ram against Govinna's gates boomed across the city, shaking the steps under Cathan's feet as he wound his way up the Patriarch's Tower. Lurching sideways, he threw out his sword arm to anchor himself against the wall. When he had his balance back, he muttered a curse. Beldyn continued to climb before him, untroubled by the trembling ground. He was already disappearing around the stair's next bend. Grunting, Cathan dashed after him. They were nearly at the top now.

Beldyn paused when they reached the landing leading to the Little Emperor's chambers, his gaze fixed on the door. The bodies were long gone from the study beyond, as was the blood that had spattered the floor, but the smell of death still lingered, like the after-scent of smoke in a burnt-out ruin. Beldyn put a hand to his brow, then ran it down his face with a shuddering sigh. Cathan said nothing, his own thoughts dark. He looked down at the *Miceram*, cradled in the crook of his left arm. He'd tried to get Beldyn to put it on, but the monk had declined.

"Not here," he'd said.

"Where, then?" Cathan had asked.

Beldyn had smiled. "Follow," was his only reply. And so here they were, leaving the study behind and moving ever

293

upward, toward the tower's crenellated roof.

The boom of the ram shook the city again as they emerged into open air once more. Cathan stumbled to one knee, nearly dropping the crown as he saved himself from sprawling into the balustrade, then rose beside the monk. The night wind whirled about them, whipping at Beldyn's robes and making his long hair whirl as he looked south across the city. In the *Miceram*'s metallic glow, his face seemed made of burnished gold, and his eyes flashed as he beheld the battlefield below.

Cathan had seen the Kingpriest's army before, on the high-road south of Luciel, but the sea of torch flames and star-flashing armor beyond Govinna's walls awed him. The enemy seemed to go on forever, particularly compared with the thin line of defenders atop the wall. The siege ladders rose and fell, and the ram rumbled back from the gates. The huge fist on its end shone with fireglow as it pulled away, paused, then rushed forward again, its impact loud enough to rattle windows and send shingles sliding off of roofs all over Govinna. Still the gates did not give, and the ram hauled back yet again.

Swallowing, he turned to Beldyn, raising the crown. "Will you *please* put this on now?"

The monk met his gaze, smiling. His eyes were stranger than usual, silver sparks dancing across their surfaces like bugs on water. "Not yet," he said, shaking his head. "There is still something I must do."

Bowing his head, he clasped his sacred medallion, squeezing it until his fingers turned white. His lips moved silently, forming words Cathan didn't recognize. When he opened his eyes again, the air around him had already begun to sparkle with silver light. His mouth a hard line, he flung his free hand outward, toward the walls.

Cathan gasped. He knew the gesture. He'd seen it before. In his mind, he was at the Bridge of Myrmidons, watching as the *Scatas* slew Sir Gareth and his men. Beldyn had performed the same ritual then. Now the air about him sang with phantom chimes.

"No," Cathan breathed, his eyes wide. "Are you going to—"

He never finished the question. At that moment, Beldyn's eyes flared with holy light, and his voice rang out, pure and musical, as he focused his will upon Govinna's fabled, unconquered gates.

"*Pridud!*" he bellowed.

Break!

———◆———

Tavarre leaned on his fork, added his weight to that of the three other men who strove to push the ladder down from the wall. Despite their efforts, though, the ladder refused to budge. The Kingpriest's soldiers had managed to plant it firmly in the body-strewn earth below, and it simply would not move. It shook slightly as the *Scatas* started up it.

Glancing to either side, Tavarre saw a half-dozen other ladders standing firm against the best efforts of Govinna's defenders. He spat a vile oath. After six failed assaults, the *Scatas* would hold back no longer. His forces were crumbling around him, dashing what last, frail hopes he held.

Disgusted, he gave the fork one last, useless shove, then fell back. When the first soldier appeared at the top of the ladder, he lunged, thrusting the weapon home. The *Scata* let out a ghastly shriek as the fork punched through his plumed helm, then toppled backward. Blood sprayed in an arc from his face as he tumbled out of sight. He took the fork with him, wrenching it from the baron's hands and bearing it with him to his doom.

Furious, Tavarre stumbled back, yanking his sword from its scabbard with a noisy ring. The red rage of battle flashed before his eyes.

The second soldier up the ladder died as well, and the third, each impaled on the weapons of Tavarre's men. The fourth was ready, however, and managed to duck a clumsy thrust, grabbing his attacker's fork and yanking it forward, dragging its wielder with it. The man, a youth in the colors of

Govinna's guardsmen, stumbled forward and caught the soldier's sword through his stomach. Glaring from behind his helm, the *Scata* climbed up onto the battlements, swinging his bloody blade to clear a space for his fellows.

Moments later, that fourth soldier was writhing on the catwalk, laid open from breast to groin by Tavarre's own blade, but the damage was done: dozens of the *Scatas* were up, clambering over the merlons to take his place. Swords dancing, they pushed outward, cutting down the city's defenders with deadly precision. The borderfolk fought valiantly, but the trained soldiers outmatched them in blade-on-blade battle. Quickly, they gave ground.

Tavarre roared, laying about with his sword. He shouted curses as he rained down blow after blow, driving the blade through one soldier's chest, then turning to hack into another man's knee. The soldier cried out, stumbling, and the baron's blade opened his throat. Blood splashed the stones.

Another *Scata* pushed forward, lashing out and getting past Tavarre's hurried parry. He flinched away, but a hot pain shot across his cheek. Another scar, to join those he'd already earned. Laughing carelessly, he slapped the soldier's sword away with his own, then grabbed the collar of the man's cloak and spun, hurling the man off the wall. The *Scata* screamed all the way down to the cobbled street below.

Rage wasn't enough, though. Even as Tavarre fought, his men died around him, the one to his left clutching at sickly bulges trying to escape his slashed stomach, the one to his right with his hands covering a face soaked in blood. So it went: Govinna's defenders melted away, while more and more *Scatas* gained the top of the wall.

Tavarre roared with incoherent fury. It was over. He'd lost.

"*Palado,*" he prayed, splitting a *Scata's* helm, "*mas pirhtas calsud. Adolas brigim paripud . . .*"

Paladine, welcome my soul. Forgive the evils I have wrought . . .

Before he could finish the prayer, however, the wall suddenly lurched beneath his feet, leaping so violently that he stumbled against the merlons, nearly tumbling over. Elsewhere on the wall, bandits and soldiers alike staggered, some falling to their knees as the ground leaped beneath them. Others weren't so lucky, and pitched over the side.

At first, Tavarre thought it was the battering ram, finally bashing down the gates. Looking down, however, he saw that wasn't so. The ram was away from the wall, its pushers staring in shock toward the city. He frowned. If the *Scatas* hadn't shaken the wall, what had?

Then a borderman beside him cried out, jabbing his finger back toward the Pantheon. "Look! The tower!"

A *Scata* came at him just then, but Tavarre stopped him, hammering him in the face with the pommel of his sword. As the man crumpled, senseless, the baron glanced back, to where the borderman had pointed. He sucked in a cold breath, a weight settling inside him. There, atop the Pantheon's tallest spire, stood Beldyn.

Tavarre shuddered, understanding even as the Lightbringer turned his hand palm-up, shouting a second time. *"Pridud!"*

The gates shivered, deep cracks rippling through them. The wall bucked again, bordermen and *Scatas* alike crying out as they stumbled against one another. A few continued to pursue the fight, but now most of them halted, all eyes turning to stare up at Beldyn. Those nearest the gates began to edge back. Below, the attackers did the same, some shying away warily while others—including most of the ram-pushers—simply wheeled and fled.

Tavarre gaped at the white-gleaming figure on the tower's top. High above, Beldyn's fingers curled into a fist. "No!" the baron cried. "You're going to—"

"PRIDUD!"

For the third time, the wall shuddered even harder. The gates twisted, bulging outward for a sickening instant. A cyclone of white light swirled around them. Then, with a blinding glare and a roar, they exploded. They were gates no longer, a mass of torn wood and metal, splinters raining down on either side of the wall. Bits of wreckage flew outward, pelting the road and smashing the cobbles. A piece of rubble slammed into the mighty, fist-headed ram, cracking it in half and sending it tumbling end over end. The debris kept falling, for minutes.

Tavarre stared numbly. Around him, a few of the *Scatas* moved in, their blades leveled at his chest and throat. He hardly noticed, even when they grabbed his own sword by the quillons and yanked it from his grasp. Below, other *Scatas* shouted victory cries as they poured through the hole where Govinna's mighty gates had been.

"Gods' blood," Tavarre murmured, staring up at the Patriarch's Tower, where Beldyn still shone like a silvery beacon. Tears sheeted his eyes, turning the Lightbringer into a blur as the *Scatas* knocked him to his knees. "*Pilofiro*, what have you done?"

———◆◆◆———

Within the Pantheon's dim halls, Sathira shrieked with pain as the wave of holy power struck her. It tore at her shadowy form, and for a moment she feared it would rip her apart, send her howling back to the shelter of the emerald, as had happened when the First Daughter had defeated her. It didn't, though: the pain was excruciating, but it passed. The spell's focus was elsewhere, far from the temple, so the torment abated, leaving her reeling and shivering in its wake.

Hissing hatefully, the demon shut her eyes, seeking the source of the godly force. It took her a while—the echoes of the agonizing blast still lingered—but after a moment she found what she was looking for. The pain still burned, like a smoldering cinder in her mind. She growled, focusing. Where was it? *Where?*

Her eyes slitted open, looking up. A cackling laugh erupted from her, a sound that had nothing to do with mirth. The Lightbringer was *above* her.

With an eager snarl, she swept on through the church, bound for the tower.

———◆◆◆———

Cathan watched everything, appalled, as the last of Govinna's defenders either fell or surrendered. Most gave up their swords as the Kingpriest's army enveloped them. A few held out, however, fighting on, despite the fact that they had already lost. One by one, their flashing blades fell still, swallowed by the press of soldiers on all sides. Sickened, Cathan wondered how many of those last brave few were men he knew. Were any of them from Luciel? Was Lord Tavarre one of them?

The *Scatas* were pouring into the city now, surging through its winding, narrow streets, the light of their torches spilling down the lanes. More and more they came, no end to them, thousands strong. He could hear their shouts of triumph, the conquering hymns of the priests who walked among them. Closer and closer they came, bearing down on the Pantheon. They would tear the place apart if they had to, he knew. Before much longer had passed—and before they could flee to a safe place—the soldiers would be surging up the tower. He eyed the stairs. They were tight, and their curve might make it easy for him to fight, but even so, he couldn't hold out forever. They'd kill him, take Beldyn, and that would be it. Everything they'd fought for would end.

He turned to the monk, stricken. Beldyn leaned on the balustrade, shoulders bowed, gazing down at the advancing soldiers. White light sparkled around him, but within the aura he was clearly exhausted. He looked haggard, many times his years, and he slumped further, nearly toppling over the rail. The inexplicable magic he'd worked had spent him, as it had at the bridge. He had no strength left.

"What have you done?" Cathan breathed.

Beldyn turned, shuddering with fatigue. His eyes were

blue suns, terrible to behold. "What I had to," he said, his voice breaking. "I saw my fate, while I lay in that trance. The enemy must come to me. It is what the god intends."

Cathan stared, aghast. "What are you talking about?" he demanded. "You mean Paladine meant for us to *lose*?"

"No, my friend." Beldyn said with his smile returning, "but the battle cannot be won with swords. The answer is in your hands."

Frowning, Cathan looked down. He still held the *Miceram* in his grasp.

"*Site ceram biriat, abat,*" Beldyn said. "It's time for you to crown me."

Cathan swallowed, turning the crown in his hands. Its rubies shimmered from within. A giddy laugh burst from his lips.

"I've never done a coronation before," he said. "I don't know how."

"There's nothing *to* know," Beldyn replied, easing himself onto one knee. "Put it on my head and name me Kingpriest. The rest is just ritual claptrap, anyway."

Again, Cathan hesitated. Then, taking a deep breath, he stepped forward and raised the *Miceram*. He held it above Beldyn's head, heavy in his hands, and shivered. The wind had turned frigid, all of a sudden.

"Beldyn," he spoke, then stopped, shaking his head. "*Beldinas*. In Paladine's name, and with this crown, I hereby—"

Then, suddenly, his voice died in his throat. Two green eyes had appeared, burning slits just behind Beldyn's back. He stared, horror swelling in his breast as his gaze locked with Sathira's. The demon laughed, a low, growling sound that cut through Cathan's spine.

"Too late," she snarled, and lunged.

Cathan was quicker, though. Dropping the crown with a clatter, he shoved Beldyn aside. The monk grunted as he sprawled across the tower's roof, but he was out of the way. Raising his sword, Cathan stepped in front of the demon.

She slowed, glaring, then laughed again and lashed out, swiping at the blade with her talons. With a horrible rending sound the weapon burst apart, scattering tangled fragments everywhere. As Cathan stared at the useless hilt in his hand, she brought her sinuous, shadowy arm down on him.

White stars burst in his head, and fire blossomed as her claws furrowed his chest, ripping through his armor like wet parchment. It wasn't a death blow, although he cried out, tumbling in a heap, the wind exploding from his lungs. Sathira glided after him, cackling, talons outstretched—

And flinched, letting out a hiss of pain.

Cathan stared from where he lay, his eyes wide. She glared at him from a few feet away, her eyes aglow with loathing, but though she clearly wanted to kill him, something stopped her. He furrowed his brow, then looked down and saw what it was.

Whether her claws had done it or whether it was from the force of hitting the ground, the little leather pouch he used to hold slingstones had burst open, spilling out the pieces of the holy sign he'd smashed after Tancred died. He stared at the bits of white porcelain, fanned out upon the rooftop, then glanced up at the demon. She stared back, her green eyes blazing with hate, then turned with a hiss and swept toward Beldyn.

"No, you don't," Cathan said, and threw one of the pieces at her.

It struck her in the back, bouncing off as if she were solid flesh, rather than shadowstuff. Sathira gave a terrible scream, writhing in agony, and he wasted no time, pelting her with more bits of the holy sign until she fell back, crumpled in on herself, and shrank into little more than a ragged cloud of blackness with two motes of green fire suspended in its midst. All the time she shrieked curses upon him, upon Beldyn, upon Paladine himself. Cathan didn't let up until he'd run out of pieces, and they lay scattered about her shapeless, howling form.

On the far side of the roof, Beldyn rose to his feet. He regarded Sathira for a long moment, helpless and seething, then went and picked up the *Miceram*. Cathan watched, holding his breath, as Beldyn turned back to the demon.

"*Scugam oporud*," he spoke softly.

Demon begone.

With that, he set the Crown of Power on his head.

Sathira froze, her eyes flaring wide. A terrible shriek, the worst yet, like metal tearing a hole in the sky, erupted from her shadow mouth. Beldyn cried out too, howling in pain and ecstasy. He flung his arms out, the *Miceram* blazing with the fires of dawn.

And the world filled with light.

CHAPTER 29 ▼

In the years to come, poets wrote that the light that ended the Battle of Govinna came from the heavens, a bright, shining beam streaking down from the firmament. The poets weren't there, though. To the bordermen and *Scatas* who were, the light came from atop the patriarch's spire, rising *up* into the night-black sky.

Those closest saw it best, and none was closer than Cathan. He saw the *Miceram* flare brightly, its glow shifting from red-gold to Beldyn's brilliant white. Then the light burst forth, engulfing monk and demon alike. Sathira let out a final tormented howl that choked off into silence, and she was gone, destroyed by the crown's holy power, sobbing back to the deepest pits of the Abyss in burning agony.

The light did not disappear with her death, however. It burned brighter still, a lance of silver that shot up into the heavens, so high goatherds looked upon it twenty leagues away and wondered what it was. It stayed that way a long time, drawing awestruck stares from soldier and bandit alike as flares of holy power pulsed along its length. Finally, with a watery pealing sound, it burst open, spilling light across the city.

Cathan flinched as the glow swept over him, expecting it to burn the flesh from his bones, but this radiance was cool, smelling of rain and rose petals. As it bathed him, he felt it ease his mind, driving out despair, fear, rage. His pain—strong where Sathira's claws had torn into him—faded away. Joy welled up within him, deeper than any he'd felt in his life, even at Wentha's healing. He wanted to laugh, sing, fling up his arms and shout with bliss.

The holy power passed, spreading outward through the Pantheon and into Govinna beyond. It overtook the Kingpriest's forces, stopping them in their tracks, stunned. It flowed from street to street, courtyard to marketplace, through windows and around statues. It leaped across the gap that split the city's east half from its west and scoured the green roofs of Govinna's temples, leaving shining copper in its wake. On the curtain wall and beyond, men gaped as it rushed toward them, then flung up their arms when it struck, passing by in a rush, washing over both armies like an eldritch wind.

It healed as it went, leaving the wounded stirring in its wake, exclaiming in wonder. Men who had lain dying on the ground moments before, their life-blood seeping from ghastly wounds, drew breaths suddenly devoid of pain and rose, their fevered minds calm once more. Flesh mended, bones set straight and true, severed hands and arms appeared anew where bloody stumps had dangled moments before. Even those who had been on death's hard edge smiled as they rose to their feet, their injuries gone as if they had never existed. When it was over, only the dead remained, scattered on the stony ground, but even they seemed different. Their faces had smoothed, even those who had perished in agony, now at peace with the god.

The chanting began on the walls, among the borderfolk who had fought in Beldyn's name, but it spread quickly, clamoring across the city and echoing from the hills. Both sides lent their voices now, joining in a chorus of joy. Never before, in all of Istar's history, had such a cry arisen, weapons and fists punching the sky as both sides bellowed together: "*Cilenfo! Pilofiro! Babo Sod!*"

The Healer! The Lightbringer! The True Kingpriest!

The next day, as the turquoise sky dimmed in the east, the plaza outside the Pantheon filled once more. This time, however, it wasn't only the folk of Govinna who crowded there. Alongside them, blue cloaks flapping in the evening breeze, stood the *Scatas* of the imperial army. Men who had sought to kill one another only scant hours before now jostled for a better view, looking toward the temple's broad steps.

Lord Holger stood at the rear of the crowd, Loren at his side. He glanced back at his officers, arrayed behind him, and his moustache twitched with sorrow. There were breaks in their ranks, for not everyone had lived to see the holy light. Sir Utgar and other friends of Holger's were dead. It would be hard explaining things to the dead men's families. Holger wasn't even sure he understood it himself yet.

Coughing into his gauntleted hand, he stood erect and started across the plaza, the other Knights marching behind. The crowd parted before him, *Scatas* saluting and bordermen staring as he and the others strode toward the Pantheon. Holger had expected, when he'd ordered the attack yesterday, that he would soon make this very march. At that time, he'd thought it would be to accept the rebels' surrender. Now, however, he went for a wholly different reason. He went to make peace.

As the Knights approached the church, a second party emerged from the portico. At its head stood Tavarre of Luciel, his scarred face grave, his mail shirt tattered from the fighting. With him were the other bandit chiefs, men Holger had sworn to hunt down and destroy. Instead, the old Knight stopped on the temple's steps, bowing deeply to his former enemy. His officers followed suit, then the bordermen repeated the gesture

Gravely, Tavarre stepped forward, drawing his dagger from his belt. Holger held his breath, his old campaigner's instincts sending his hand to his sword, but he held back.

This was a highland ritual, one the Taoli had performed since their barbarian days. Tavarre tugged off his left glove, set the blade to the palm so bared, and drew it swiftly across his flesh. The baron's face twitched as blood welled out, bright red, dripping upon the steps. He sheathed the dirk again, extending his injured hand toward Holger.

"*Bas cor purdamo*," he spoke in the church tongue.

Old woes forgotten.

Holger paused, and all over the plaza breaths stilled as his hand shifted to his own dagger and drew it out. His gauntlet clattered to the ground as he cut himself in turn.

"*E parpamo*," said the old Knight, uncustomarily smiling.

And forgiven.

They clasped hands then, their blood mingling, then leaned forward to kiss each other formally on the cheek. So the imperial army and the bandits of the Taol made their peace, and a great cheer arose from the crowd, voices rising in jubilation.

The cry only lasted a moment, however. Stillness descended again as a pair of figures appeared in the temple's doorway.

The first was a young warrior, clad in a snow-white tabard. His eyes swept over the mob, looking for signs of trouble. He then stepped aside, letting the second man come forward.

Tears stung Holger's eyes as he beheld Beldinas Light-bringer up close for the first time. Though he was weary and pale, the young man made a surprisingly regal figure, mantled in shining light and embroidered robes. His hair tumbled in rich waves over his shoulders, and his eyes burned with zeal. On his brow, gold and rubies and all, was the Crown of Power, the *Miceram* worn by the Kingpriests of old.

Site ceram biriat, abat, Holger thought, staring at the crown and the onetime monk who wore it.

Slowly, the old Knight doffed his helm and fell to his knees. Behind him, his officers did the same. They all drew their swords, kissed their quillons, and laid them upon the steps. They bowed their heads as Beldinas strode up to them, signing the triangle. When Holger looked up again, brushing white hair from his eyes, his cheeks were damp and glistening.

"Holiness," he said, "I cry your pardon. I have defied you, in my blindness."

Beldinas shook his head. "The fault is not yours, Lord Knight. You have been tricked by the servant of darkness who sits the throne. I ask you to help me set this aright. Will you follow me?"

Holger drew a long, slow breath. In the silence a hawk skirled, riding the winds above the city. Exhaling, he leaned forward, touching his forehead to the floor. "We shall, my lord," he said.

A murmur ran through the crowd, then fell silent as Beldinas raised his hands in blessing.

"Let it be so, then," he said. "We shall remain in this place three days longer to tend our dead. When that is done, let us go forth to the Lordcity, and none of us rest until we have thrown Kurnos the Usurper down from his ill-gotten throne!"

The people's shouts ran long and loud across Govinna.

Of late, the messengers within the Great Temple had come to view the imperial manse with dread. Indeed, most within the church grew nervous when they looked upon the Kingpriest's palace, but it was the messengers who feared it most, for they had to go inside there.

They had been going back and forth for days now, bearing missives from the imperial courtiers. None knew the contents of the scrolls, but there was no question the news was bad. Any good messenger gained a sense, when he delivered a message, of whether the tidings he bore were good or ill, and it would have taken a blind gully dwarf not to guess rightly in Kurnos's case. Each time, his mood grew fouler, until the Temple's messengers took to quarrelling over who would deliver the next one—or rather, who would not.

Handril, a skinny, straw-haired acolyte who'd lost the latest argument, swallowed as he approached the manse's great platinum doors. The Knights who stood watch outside kept still as he raised his hand and rapped. After a time, the doors cracked open, and Brother Purvis emerged. The old chamberlain looked older and frailer than Handril had ever seen him, his back stooped and weary, his brow an anxious wrinkle. He said nothing as he turned and led Handril in. They walked through the rich entry hall and on down sunlit passages. Finally, at the top of a long, curving stair, they came to a halt before the golden doors of the Kingpriest's private audience hall.

Purvis gave the boy a sympathetic look. "He awaits within, lad. Give him the message, and do not linger." Pushing the doors open, he gestured Handril through.

It was dark within, the curtains drawn, a few candles flickering. It took Handril's eyes a moment to adjust to the gloom, so the first thing he noticed was the stench. It was a stale smell and sour, the reek of dried sweat and grime. He wrinkled his nose, wondering how long it had been since Paladine's Voice on Krynn had bathed. Biting his lip, he stepped inside.

"H-Holiness?" he asked.

Nothing.

There was no one on the throne or anywhere else he could see. Scalp prickling, Handril looked about, but there was no sign of the Kingpriest. Slowly, he crept toward the dais, an ivory scroll-tube in his hands. His sandals clapped against the marble floor as he went, then halted. There was something there—many somethings, in fact, scattered upon the dais and down its steps to the floor. Handril peered at them, then started forward again.

He was nearly to the dais when he saw what the things were, and a frown creased his face. Why had the Kingpriest strewn *khas* pieces about the floor? Stopping again when he reached them, he bent down and picked one up, his breath catching when the dim light touched it. Handril knew little of *khas*, but he knew enough to understand that the white champion in his hand should not be slumped against his horse's neck, his back raked with tiny sword wounds. He rose again, shivering, turning to look around—

The hand that seized his throat was like a band of iron, squeezing off all but a thin trickle of air as it jerked him forward. Handril wanted to shout, but all he could manage was a squeak as Kurnos loomed out of the shadows.

The Kingpriest was a terrible sight, a pale, drawn apparition whose beard stuck out in red tangles. His robes were dirty and disheveled, and the sapphire tiara on his head sat askew amid tufts of silver-frosted hair. The worst, though, were his eyes. They were wide and red-rimmed, and a wild sheen lit them. They were filled with anger, fear, and madness.

"What do you want?" Kurnos hissed.

It took Handril several wheezing breaths to find his voice. "A—a dispatch, sire," he gasped, raising the scroll-tube. "From the—First—Daughter."

The Kingpriest's eyes narrowed to twitching slits. His grip tightened, and black spots whirled before Handril's eyes. With a growl, he snatched the tube from the messenger's hand and shoved the boy back, letting him go.

"Out," he snapped.

Clutching his bruised throat, Handril all but sprinted from the room.

Kurnos stood silently for a time, staring at the scroll-tube, then, scowling, he opened it and slid out the roll of vellum. Violet wax sealed the message, bearing the seal of the Revered Daughters of Paladine. He tore this away, then unfurled the message and read it.

A moment later he flung it away.

Word of the Battle of Govinna had reached the Great Temple six days ago. A courier, caked with road dust, had arrived from the borderlands, bearing word from Lord Holger. Kurnos's heart had leaped as he unfurled *that* scroll—and died, just as suddenly, as he read the old Knight's account of what had happened. The traitorous bastard had changed sides, gone over to the damned Lightbringer! Even now, the wretched pretender was marching toward Istar itself, with both the bandits and the imperial army at his back.

Kurnos had quit the basilica at once, hiding in the manse to keep the news from his court. It didn't work. Holger had sent other missives to Istar, and soon the Temple's halls echoed with whispers about the Crown of Power and silvery, healing light.

The writs of *Nio Celbit*—withdrawal of support from the reigning Kingpriest—had started arriving the next morning. Nubrinda of Habbakuk was first, declaring her intention to side with Beldinas when he arrived. It made sense, of course—how could she not, when he wore the *Miceram* and had thousands of *Scatas* at his command? Kurnos cursed her anyway, declaring her *Foripon* along with Holger and every soldier who marched with him.

He'd hoped the denunciation would give the other hierarchs pause. He was wrong. Soon after, Stefara of Mishakal had dispatched a writ of her own, then Peliador of Kiri-Jolith. Marwort, the court wizard, revoked the support of the Orders of High Sorcery, and Quarath of Silvanesti had done likewise for the Chosen of E'li—the first of Paladine's clergy to forsake Kurnos's reign. Even the high priests of Branchala and Majere, whom Kurnos had appointed after his coronation, denounced their patron. When he'd woken this morning, only the First Son and First Daughter had remained loyal . . . and now he'd lost Balthera. Kurnos felt his reign crumbling like rotten mortar.

Snarling a vile oath, he raised the scroll-tube high, then smashed it down on the floor at his feet. Splinters of ivory skittered across the floor.

A cold laugh rasped behind him. "Really, Holiness," mocked Fistandantilus's voice. "That's hardly decorum befitting an emperor."

Kurnos whirled, hands clenching into fists as he faced the Dark One, barely visible in the room's smothering shadows.

"You!" he growled, stabbing a finger. "You foul, lying bastard!"

The sorcerer inclined his head.

"You said you'd help me," Kurnos snapped. "You said you wanted me on the throne!"

"So I did," the dark wizard replied. "Apparently I underestimated the forces arrayed against you."

Kurnos reached to his left hand, where the emerald ring sparkled, the darkness that had haunted it gone. It had refused to let go of his finger before. Now he could pull it off easily. "*Underestimated?*" he shrieked and flung it at Fistandantilus.

The sorcerer caught the ring easily, eyed it, then closed his hand around it. "Even I can be mistaken, Holiness. I did not think the young man would find the *Miceram*. Now the Lightbringer comes to Istar. You cannot stop him."

"*You* could."

Fistandantilus shrugged. "To what end? You have lost the throne anyway."

The room fell silent. Kurnos trembled with fury. He'd lost the army, the church, Sathira . . . and the people of the Lordcity would soon follow, once word of the miracle of Govinna got out.

"Is there nothing I can do?" he asked.

Chuckling, Fistandantilus raised the ring. He peered through the emerald a moment, then passed his fingers above it, leaving trails of green sparks in the air as he muttered an incantation. The air around the gem shivered, and a faint rumble sounded from it, like the roll of distant thunder. With a viridian flash, it vanished.

Kurnos felt a sudden pressure on his finger, and a groan burst from his lips. The ring was back.

"Now," the dark figure hissed, staring at him from the depths of his hood, "listen carefully, Holiness. When the Lightbringer comes, he will confront you. His men will search you for blades, but they will not have cause to notice the ring, and that will be his undoing. The enchantment I have laid upon it is a killing spell, released when you speak the word *Ashakai*. Get close to the boy, point the ring at him, then . . ." His voice trailed into silence.

Kurnos stared at the emerald. Within it, where Sathira's shadows had lurked, a tiny stormcloud billowed and flashed, spitting forked lightning.

"What about me?" he asked with a shudder, looking back up. "What will happen—"

Fistandantilus was gone.

Spitting an oath, Kurnos looked back at the ring again. For a moment, he considered turning it on himself. The sorcerer had told him how to use it. All he had to do was point it, speak the word . . . then one last flare of pain . . . he wouldn't have to endure the shame of being cast down from the throne . . . the sapphire tiara lifted from his brow . . .

"No," he whispered, the word no more than a breath.

Kurnos had nothing left. All he'd striven for, all he'd been, was ashes now. He'd betrayed his god, and Paladine had turned his face away. There was one last thing he could claim, before the game was over, one sweetness to temper the bitter thing his life had become. He laughed, the mad glint in his eyes becoming a flame.

He would have revenge.

CHAPTER 30 ▼

I s that it?" asked Wentha. "Is that Istar?"

Cathan held his sister steady as she leaned forward, afraid she might fall from his saddle. She had ridden with him the whole distance from Govinna, her eyes wide with wonder at the sight of the lowlands, the aqueducts towering over the rolling fields, the towns with their whitewashed villas and domed cathedrals, the sapphire waters of Lake Istar, where the floating boat-city of Calah stood, all towering masts and gliding outriggers.

All of it was as strange to her as it was new to him, which was part of the reason Cathan had taken her along, when most of the common folk—from Luciel and Govinna both—stayed behind. Mostly, though, she'd come because he couldn't bring himself to leave her behind again, as he'd done that summer. No one had argued with his choice, though Tavarre and Holger—both commanders of Beldinas's legions now—frowned on the notion of bringing a young girl when there might still be battles ahead. In the end, Cathan was the Lightbringer's favorite, and the Lightbringer had said yes.

Now, looking ahead along the marble-paved High Road, Cathan smiled, a shiver of awe running through him. "Yes, Blossom," he said. "That's it."

The army had been marching steadily for more than a month, coming down from the highlands with the winter's first blizzards at its back, then crossing the grasslands of the empire's heart. Lowlanders had gathered to watch in amazement as they passed, murmuring at the strange sight: *Scatas* and Taoli marching together, priests and soldiers alike singing hymns to Paladine . . . and at the force's heart, the shining figure of Beldinas, bestride a mighty chariot and wreathed in light, the *Miceram* glittering on his brow. Seeing him, the lowlanders bowed their heads, signing the triangle in reverence. A century past, the *Trosedil* had raged across their fields, and all still knew the legend of the Crown of Power. Truly, whoever the strange man in the chariot was, he was the Paladine's chosen.

Now the army stood halted on a cliff along the shore of Lake Istar. It was a misty morning, fog filling the hollows and eddying across the water. Just ahead, a huge arch straddled the road, twined with bas-reliefs of roses and dragons, divine triangles and falcons' wings. Atop it blazed three great fire urns, their flames leaping high, and a huge, plaque of gold shimmered at its apex, etched with letters ten feet high:

> *Calsa, A gomo duruc, du nosom forbo ciforud.*
> *Calsa du forbo sebais mif usas.*
> *Calsa, bosodo arburteis, du Istar.*

> *Welcome, O noble visitor, to our beautiful city.*
> *Welcome to the city beloved of the gods.*
> *Welcome, honored guest, to Istar.*

Two miles down the road, the Lordcity shone like a jewel at daybreak. Its domes and minarets, gold, alabaster and lapis, strove skyward from within its mighty walls, topped by the bloody finger of the Tower of High Sorcery. Keen eyes could spot the fabled Arena, the Kingfisher Keep, the silken canopies of its market stalls. Trees—cedar, almond, orange, and others—showed green in its gardens, and statues and fountains dotted its plazas. Sails of countless colors flew in its harbor, and spread out across the waters beyond. Amid it all, like a silver promise, shone the Great Temple.

Looking upon Istar for the first time, Cathan felt a rush of tears. He thought back to the springtime, and the man he had been: a godless outlaw squatting in a ditch, waiting for a priest to rob. What would he have said then if someone had told him that he would one day follow a savior to the empire's heart? He shook his head. Paladine's games were strange indeed.

"It's even more beautiful than I imagined."

He recognized the musical voice at once and lowered his eyes as Beldyn came up alongside him. The Lightbringer had descended from his chariot and stood on foot now, his strange eyes fixed on the sprawling city. His was a conqueror's face, hungry and fierce, eclipsed by the *Miceram*'s light.

"Lady Ilista would have been proud to see you here today, sire," Cathan said softly.

Beldyn nodded, then glanced up at the brightening sky. "I know. She is."

A shout rose from the lookouts. At once, everyone was on their feet, muttering and staring about. Tavarre had sent a handful of outriders ahead to the city to make sure the road was clear. There was no sign of any more *Scatas* or other threats, but both the baron and Lord Holger wanted to be sure before they approached the Lordcity. Thinking the scouts had spotted the riders, Cathan stared down the High Road toward Istar's gilded gates.

"What is it?" he wondered. "I don't see anything."

Wentha sighed, as if he were a simpleton. "Not *there*. In the sky!"

Cathan blinked, confused—then he saw something too. There, silhouetted against the cloudrack, was a large, dark shape, part eagle, part lion. There had been wild griffins in Taol once, and the borderfolk still told tales of them, but Cathan had never seen one before. Now his mouth opened as he watched it glide toward them, riding the high winds above the cliffs. As it drew nearer, he saw the creature wasn't alone: a rider sat upon its back, white-robed, a long shock of golden hair trailing behind.

His horse whinnied, shying as it scented the flying beast. Cathan patted its neck to soothe it, but the animal remained skittish, as did the other soldiers' mounts. Horses were griffins' natural prey, which was why the highlanders had hunted them out, long ago. The beast's rider knew this too, it seemed, for he didn't try to land near the army. Instead, the griffin lit upon a neighboring hillock, and its rider climbed down. Cathan watched the tall figure speak in his mount's ear, then turn and head toward them, across the stony ground.

"An envoy," Beldyn said, nodding toward the rider. "I must parley with him."

"Not without me, you're not," Cathan muttered, swinging down from his horse.

Leaving Wentha in his saddle, he went after Beldyn, his hand on his sword. Several others—Tavarre and Holger, as well as other Knights and bandits—hurried to join them. The white-robed figure raised a delicate hand, and Cathan felt a fresh pang of wonder. He had never seen an elf before either.

"*Sa, Pilofiro,*" the elf said, his face cool and haughty as he signed the triangle. *Hail, Lightbringer.*

"I am Quarath, Emissary of Silvanesti. I speak on the church's behalf."

Beldyn nodded, interlacing his fingers in the elven holy sign. "*Sa,* Quarath. I have come to enter your city. May I?"

The elf nodded, then frowned, glancing up toward the mass of the army. "You may, but they must remain outside the gates."

"What?" Tavarre barked, his scarred face darkening. "Leave them here?"

Quarath glanced at him, lips pursed. "It is custom. No force so large has marched into Istar since the Three Thrones' War. However," he went on, raising a finger to forestall Tavarre's and Holger's objections, "you may bring a smaller detachment—say, a hundred men. In return, we shall yield a hundred priests as hostages, including the First Son and First Daughter of Paladine." He raised an eyebrow. "Does this suit you?"

Tavarre's furrowed brow said it didn't, and Holger looked displeased as well, but Beldyn inclined his head, smiling. "Very well. Continue, Emissary."

"The hierarchs will meet you at the gates," Quarath went on. "From there, we shall lead you to the Great Temple. Lord Kurnos"—his upper lip curled as he spoke the Kingpriest's name—"has quit his manse and awaits you in the basilica. He has offered to surrender the throne—but only to the Lightbringer himself."

Cathan joined Holger and Tavarre in surprise at this, followed by suspicious scowls. Beldyn's eyes narrowed—but only for a moment. "If that is how the Usurper chooses," he said. "Return to the city, Emissary, and tell them I come."

Bowing, the elf turned and strode back toward his waiting griffin.

"Sire," Holger murmured as they walked back toward the army. Behind them, the griffin vaulted into the air, carrying Quarath back to Istar. "I must object."

Beldyn smiled. "I know. The man has tried twice to kill me, but his demon is no more, and Kurnos stands alone. And," he added, glancing at Cathan, "I will be protected. I would see the Usurper's face as I dethrone him. Will any of you challenge that?"

If he hoped anyone would defy him, they disappointed him. Even Tavarre shook his head, looking at his feet.

"Good," Beldyn declared. "Bring my chariot, and choose your men. We march to the Lordcity at midday."

Cathan's throat tightened as the city gates drew near. The huge, gold-chased doors stood shut, and scores of archers looked down from above, arrows notched on their bows. Swallowing, he touched his battered sword and watched the bowmen, waiting for them to make a move.

Thus far, the hierarchs had proven true to Quarath's word. The hostages had already come out of the city and waited with the Lightbringer's army—along with Wentha, who stayed behind at Cathan's insistence. That did little to assuage Cathan's fears, however. Beldyn had spoken often, during the long march, of Kurnos's evil and treachery. What, to a man like that, were the lives of a hundred of his own clergy? The hierarchs didn't need to be complicit. Like with Pradian, all it would take was one archer, one well-aimed arrow . . .

No one fired. Instead, the gates shuddered and rumbled open, their great falcon and triangle crest splitting to reveal the city beyond. As they did, a great din rose from within, thousands of voices rising in joyous shouting and song.

Looking upon the folk of the Lordcity, Cathan thought back to the day Beldyn had first come to Govinna. That was nothing beside this. It seemed everyone in Istar had turned out to welcome the Lightbringer. There were more of them than Cathan, living his life in a highland village, had ever thought to see in one place. They packed the streets, crowded on rooftops, leaned over balconies—even perched in the trees. They raised their arms and cheered, throwing white rose-petals in the street, so many the cobblestones looked mantled in snow. Hands lifted children high, and drums and shawms and chimes made a racket even louder than the mob's roar. Merchants and scholars, nobles and commoners, priests of every god of good— all had come, hoping to glimpse the Lightbringer and the Crown of Power. All chanted the same two words over and over: *"Babo Sod! Babo Sod!"*

The True Kingpriest!

Smiling, Beldyn raised his hands in greeting, and his chariot rumbled forward. His escort went with him, Cathan riding beside, watching the crowd with gritted teeth. Kurnos didn't need a crack archer to do his work. One person hidden amidst the adoring throngs would do the trick. Any one of them might be carrying a crossbow beneath his cloak or a dagger up his sleeve. Any one of them might be waiting for the chance to strike. Cathan's stomach clenched at the thought.

When they emerged from the gatehouse's shadow, a party of august men and women, clad in all colors of robes, came forward to stand before them. Quarath stood among them, smiling. Beldyn's chariot halted, and he looked down at the elf regally. The *Miceram* sparkled and shone in the noon daylight. A hush rippled through the crowd as the Emissary bowed.

"Welcome, Holiness," Quarath said and gestured at the robed figures behind him. "These are the hierarchs of a holy church. We have done wrong, following the wrong leader, who has reigned here until now. We cry your forgiveness."

The mob murmured at this, and beside Cathan, Tavarre chuckled.

"Clever," the baron muttered, "asking mercy in front of so many people."

Cathan nodded, scouring the crowd with his gaze as Beldyn raised his hands, signing the triangle over the clerics. The crown flared with ruby light.

"*Tam paripo*," Beldyn pronounced.

I forgive thee.

There were more introductions, each of the high priests kneeling in turn to receive the Lightbringer's blessing, then Quarath bowed again and gestured for Beldyn to follow. The throng parted as the hierarchs led the way down the broad street, past shrines and colonnades, obelisks and lush gardens. The masses stayed thick all the way, so their progress was slow, and by the time the party reached the arched entrance to the broad expanse of the *Barigon*, Cathan, nervous about possible treachery, was shaking in his saddle, his hand white-knuckled about his sword's hilt.

The great plaza was empty, Solamnic Knights standing guard at its various entrances, and desolate-looking after the mad press of the streets. The Great Temple seemed incomparably beautiful to Cathan, all marble and crystal, swaying trees and explosions of bright-colored birds above its fabled gardens. Its gold spires glistened against the cloudless sky, and the basilica dome sparkled like a diamond. Cathan momentarily forgot his fears, and stared in mute amazement. Beside him, Beldyn smiled, his eyes aglow.

"*Efisa*," the Lightbringer whispered, in a voice so quiet only Cathan could hear. "I'm home, at last."

He climbed down from his chariot, and the rest of the party dismounted as well, handing their reins to a cluster of waiting acolytes. Cathan eyed each young priest carefully, studying their faces, looking for strange shapes beneath their cassocks, but there was nothing. Still gripping his sword, he fell in at the Lightbringer's side.

Onward Quarath led them, across the plaza to the church's long, wide steps. Beldyn climbed without pause—and so Cathan and the others—then stopped before its high, platinum doors, waiting as they swung silently open. Then, genuflecting and signing the triangle, he entered the Temple.

They passed quickly through a vast, airy atrium—so quickly, in fact, that Cathan was only vaguely aware of a succession of silken arrases, intricate mosaics, and pools filled with glittering, jewel-hued fish. Busts of long-dead Kingpriests, carved of serpentine and turquoise, looked down from pedestals, each glaring or smiling in his own manner. The air danced with butterflies and dulcimer music.

At the hall's end stood another pair of doors, bearing the falcon and triangle. They remained closed as the party drew near, and Quarath stepped forward to open them. Before he could, however, both Tavarre and Holger moved to interpose.

"Sire," the baron said to Beldyn, "I think it wise if my men go in first."

Beldyn waved his hand. "Very well, but draw no weapon unless you must. No man has ever killed another in the basilica. I would not have you be the first."

Nodding, Tavarre gestured to a handful of men, bandits and Knights alike. Cathan remained by Beldyn's side as the others moved forward, touching their blades but not unsheathing them. His scarred face resolute, the baron cracked the doors open and led them through.

The wait seemed to last forever. Cathan's eyes darted this way and that, returning again and again to the hierarchs. They were a strange lot, powdered and perfumed, jewels sparkling on their fingers, wrists, throats, and brows. He felt a stir of loathing at the sight of the clerics. These were the same who had allowed the plague to ravage his home and his family. At the same time, though, he thought of Ilista, and a strange sympathy swelled in him for those who dwelt within the Temple's walls. Surrounded by such beauty, was it any wonder so few of them could conceive of how his people had suffered?

No longer, he told himself. Symeon had been complacent; Kurnos was corrupt. Things would be different when Beldinas reigned.

Finally, the doors opened again, and Tavarre emerged, his gaze stern.

"The way is clear, Holiness," he said, bowing to Beldyn. "My men have searched the hall, and it is empty—save for the wretch himself."

Beldyn's mouth became a hard line. "Come, then. Let us end this."

They entered the cavernous Hall of Audience, the bordermen staring in wonder at the blue-tiled floor, the rose-petal walls, the crystal dome gleaming overhead. The sound of their footsteps, of rattling armor, echoed through the great chamber as they strode toward the dais at the far end. Cathan's eyes narrowed upon the golden, rose-wreathed throne and the man who sat upon it.

Kurnos glowered at them, resplendent in silver robes, jeweled breastplate, and sapphire tiara. He swept his gaze over the approaching party, and his face reddened to match his beard when he saw the hierarchs and Lord Holger. Finally, as the group halted before the dais, his eyes settled on Beldyn. Cathan shivered. He had never seen hate so intense, so unreasoning.

"So," the Kingpriest sneered, "you're the whelp who plots to steal my throne."

The Knights and bandits muttered at this, but Beldyn held up a hand, stilling their noise. On his brow the *Miceram* blazed a bright light. Next to it, Kurnos's tiara seemed but a trinket. When he smiled, it was as though his blazing eyes could cut steel.

"I am the Lightbringer," he said, the crystal dome ringing with his voice. "I wear the Crown of Power, lost long ago. The god has chosen me to rule."

Kurnos frowned, then barked a derisive laugh. "Idiot boy. *I* am Paladine's voice upon Krynn."

"Blasphemer!" Beldyn snapped, his face suddenly becoming a terrible mask of rage. "You say such a thing, *you* who used dark magic to murder Lady Ilista and tried to kill me as well?"

The hierarchs started, glancing at one another in shock. The Kingpriest stiffened, the color draining from his face.

"I did it for the good of the empire," Kurnos muttered.

"No. You did it for yourself."

For more than a minute, silence reigned within the hall. Cathan held his breath, waiting—for what, he didn't know. Finally, Beldyn spoke again in granite tones.

"Uncrown, Usurper. Leave my throne, or I will drag you from it."

Kurnos sat still. Muscles jumped in his face, and the fingers of his right hand worked restlessly, toying with a ring on his left mounted with a huge emerald. Finally, with a shuddering sigh, the Kingpriest rose to his feet. Bowing his head, he stepped away from the throne, lifted the sapphire tiara from his head, and set it on a golden armrest. His eyes glistening, Kurnos stepped off the dais's highest stair.

"Very well," he said. "The empire is yours, Lightbringer. I would ask one thing of you, though, before your men take me."

Beldyn nodded. "Speak."

"I ask for mercy," the Kingpriest said. "I have sinned. Absolve me, Beldinas."

Gasps echoed through the hall as all eyes turned toward Beldyn. For a moment his brows knitted as though he might refuse, but then the Lightbringer spread his hands.

"So be it," he said. "*Bridud.*"

Approach.

Smiling, Kurnos started down the stairs. At Beldyn's gesture, Cathan moved to meet him and searched him for weapons. He was loath to touch the false Kingpriest, but he did so and not gently, grabbing Kurnos's arms and legs, then stripping off his jeweled breastplate and checking beneath. He was sure he would find a dagger somewhere among the man's vestments, but even though he searched a second time, he found nothing.

"Well?" Beldyn asked.

Cathan hesitated, uncertain, every instinct telling him something was wrong. There was something in Kurnos's eyes that troubled him—a hidden smile, lurking deep beneath the mad sheen. Finally, though, he stepped back.

"He is unarmed, Holiness."

Smiling, Beldyn beckoned Kurnos to him.

Mistrust simmered in Cathan's breast as the Kingpriest stepped forward and knelt before the Lightbringer. Slowly, Kurnos bowed his head. He twisted the ring on his finger again, Cathan noticed, moving the emerald around and around in curious fashion.

"*Usas farno,*" Beldyn intoned, his eyes shining as he signed the triangle, "*tas adolam aftongas?*"

Child of the god, dost thou forswear thine evil?

Kurnos took a deep breath, let it out. "*Aftongo,*" he murmured.

Around and around the emerald went. Around and around . . .

"*Tas scolfas firougos, tenfin ourfas?*"

Wilt thou repent thy misdeeds, as long as thou livest?

"*Firougo.*"

Cathan's eyes locked on the emerald. There was something wrong about it, a strange flashing in its depths. Like lightning, he thought, his heart lurching within his breast as Beldyn reached out and laid his hand on the Kingpriest's head, speaking the rite of absolution.

Kurnos brought up his hand, pointing the ring at the Lightbringer's heart. "*Ashakai,*" he said.

Cathan surged forward with a shout.

Beldyn's eyes widened.

Lightning, green and blinding bright, flared from the emerald. Thunder roared, filling the hall.

The next thing Cathan knew he was lying on the ground, with Kurnos beneath him. The tiles were smeared red where the Kingpriest's head lay crooked—unconscious, but not yet dead. The stink of ozone filled the air, and with it the sickly smell of charred flesh. Terror seizing him, Cathan rolled off Kurnos and looked up, expecting the worst.

The Lightbringer was unhurt.

The pain hit, hot and sharp. Cathan looked down and saw the wound, his leather breastplate and the padding beneath that had burnt away, the flesh beneath it seething red and black, smoke curling from his side.

It seemed everyone started shouting at once. Men ran forward, seizing Kurnos and hauling him away. He heard Holger barking orders, saw Tavarre dashing toward him, his scarred face twisting as he fell to his knees to try to help. He ignored them all, staring at Beldyn. The Lightbringer looked back, his face white, horror staining his diamond-bright gaze. Suddenly the regal figure was gone, and he was a young monk once more.

"Holiness," Cathan said thickly. There was a warm, iron-tasting wetness in his mouth. Blood, some distant part of his mind said. "Are you all right?"

Stunned, the Lightbringer didn't answer.

"Beldyn!" Tavarre shouted, cradling Cathan's head in his hands. "Get over here and heal him, damn it!"

Cathan smiled. "It's all right," he whispered. "Actually, I feel fine."

Letting out his breath, he died.

CHAPTER 31 ▼

A thousand blasphemies whirled through Tavarre's mind as he stared at Cathan's lifeless face. The lad's breast had stilled, his gaze fixed, staring blindly at the crystal dome above. Cathan was gone.

Stung with tears, the baron closed those sightless eyes, then laid Cathan on the floor, smoke still curling from where the magical lightning had struck him. The wound was ghastly. Tavarre took the time to cover it with Cathan's hands, folding them on top of the horrible sight. Drawing a shuddering breath, he looked up at the others.

Everyone else—the hierarchs, his men, even Lord Holger— was too aghast to move or speak. Their eyes showed white, their mouths hung open. Among them, the Lightbringer too was aghast. His glow seemed to dim as he realized what had happened.

"He saved me," Beldyn said, his brow furrowing as if he didn't understand. "He saved my life. . . ."

You let him die! Tavarre wanted to scream. You had the power to heal him and you did nothing! He wanted to smash the basilica's dome, tear down the Temple stone by stone. He wanted to pull Paladine down from the heavens and beat him blue.

Tavarre rose, twisted, and stalked to where Kurnos lay. The Kingpriest was stirring now, moaning in pain. The blow against the floor had rattled his wits, but it hadn't killed him. Another injustice, there. Snarling, Tavarre yanked his sword from its scabbard. The hall rang with the scrape of steel as he raised it above the groaning figure.

"Now you die," he spat.

"Wait!"

Tavarre's sword was heavy. It took effort to divert the blow. He did so anyway, striking the mosaic floor a hand's breadth from Kurnos's neck. Tiles cracked beneath the blade. He stumbled, thrown off-balance, then turned to look toward the Lightbringer.

"Wait?" the baron demanded. "Holiness—"

"I will not have people say I took the throne by assassination," Beldyn said. His eyes blazed with fury. "Take off his ring, the emerald one. I would see it."

Tavarre didn't move. He stared at the Lightbringer, his anger turning to disgust. Kurnos was a murderer, a coward, a fool. He deserved to die, not just to be stripped of his precious jewelry. The Abyss awaited him, and Tavarre saw no need to keep it waiting long.

It was Quarath who obeyed, stepping forward and bending down to prize the green gem from Kurnos's finger. The Kingpriest writhed as it came free, groaning again but still not waking. The elf took the ring to Beldyn, who turned it slowly between his fingers, studying it in the dome's cool light. Color played across its facets. Finally, he clasped the magic ring in his fist and looked up.

"Bring him to me," he said determinedly.

Tavarre had never felt the same devotion toward the Lightbringer that Cathan had, but now, looking into his fierce, wrathful gaze, he couldn't help but obey. The desire to kill left him—for now, at least—and sheathing his sword, he bent down to bear Kurnos up.

The Kingpriest's head lolled as the baron lifted him, and one of Holger's Knights stepped forward to help while

Kurnos blinked and tried to regain his senses. His mouth a lipless line, Tavarre half-dragged the fallen priest to Beldyn, then shoved him to his knees and stepped back, ready to draw steel once more if he must.

"Awake, wretch!" Beldyn growled, hurling the ring.

It struck Kurnos in the face, and he jerked as it clattered to the floor, his eyes flaring open. He stared blindly for a moment, his hand rising to touch the place where his hair had turned sticky with blood, then he started as he remembered everything, trying to draw back from the accusing circle of faces. Tavarre grabbed his shoulder, holding the false Kingpriest still. In time, he stopped struggling, and slumped.

"I could have you killed," Beldyn declared, golden light swelling from the *Miceram*. "One word, and any man here would cut your throat for me—or bring me the blade to do it myself. You have spilled blood in the church's most sacred heart. It would only be fitting to spill yours in return."

Kurnos glared at him hatefully. "Do it, then," he snarled.

Within the holy light, blue eyes flashed with rage, and Beldyn raised his hand, opened his mouth to give the order they all expected—then he stopped himself, sighing.

"No, you aren't worth the trouble," he said, "and death is too sweet a reward. No, Kurnos—your punishment will not be so easy. You will live, imprisoned in the High Clerist's Tower in Solamnia. You will have the rest of your days to think on what you've done. Perhaps, in time, you will earn the god's forgiveness—but you shall never have mine.

"Look, all of you!" he shouted, turning to the men and women gathered about him. He gestured at Kurnos. "*This* is what comes of the Balance. By allowing evil to remain in the world, we invite it into our own hearts. As long as we tolerate sin, we leave the door open for it to corrupt us.

"No more of this. It is time to cast off the old ways. As long as I rule this empire, I will not rest until wickedness and witchcraft are driven from the realm. The time of darkness is ended—and so begins a new age, of light everlasting."

As he spoke, the *Miceram*'s glare grew bright around him, so bright the hierarchs and soldiers had to squint against the radiance. Cloaked in light, Beldyn walked to where Cathan lay. Tavarre stared as he passed, and a murmur ran among the hierarchs as they realized what he meant to do.

Quarath came forward as Beldyn stood beside the body, reaching out to touch the young monk's arm. "Sire, do not attempt this. Not even the Kingpriests of old claimed such power."

Beldyn said nothing, only turned to stare at the elf. Quarath stiffened, paling, then stepped back. The audience hall was silent as Beldyn knelt, the white light shimmering around him. He laid his hand upon the scorched patch on the young man's wounded side and shut his eyes. His lips working soundlessly, he reached to his breast, pulling out his medallion to clasp it in his hand. Then, gently, he bent low and pressed his lips to Cathan MarSevrin's forehead.

"*Palado,*" he prayed, "*ucdas pafiro, tas pelo laigam fat, mifiso soram flonat. Tis biram cailud, e tas oram nomass lud bipum. Sifat.*"

A moment passed. Then another. Nothing happened.

Tavarre stepped forward. "Holiness," he said gently. "He's dead. There's nothing you can—"

"*No!*" Beldyn shouted, stopping him with a wild look. He looked every bit as mad as Kurnos, and Tavarre fell back.

"Enough!" the Lightbringer shouted, the crystal dome ringing with his words. "Hear me, Paladine! All my life I've served thee. With all my heart, I have worked thy will. *NOW WORK MINE!*"

Suddenly, it happened. The white glow surrounding him flared like an exploding star and flowed down his arm, washing over Cathan's body. Beldyn's back arched as divine power surged through him, so intense the other men cried out in pain as they beheld it. His face shifted from agony to rapture and back again, and tears of blood trickled down his cheeks. The air shivered, and the ground shook. Above, the basilica's dome rang with a terrible clamor, blaring to match the Lightbringer's blazing glow. . . .

At last it faded, the crown's light dimming once more.

Beldyn slumped back with a groan, his face bathed with sweat. He would have fallen had Quarath not rushed forward to catch him. His body, his face, were lost in a silvery cloud. Tavarre only gave him a quick glance, however. His eyes, and everyone else's, were elsewhere.

Cathan stirred and took a breath.

No one made a sound as his breast rose, then fell, then rose again. His eyelids flickered open, and a puzzled frown creased his face. Then he turned his head, and a gasp ran through the room as the onlookers beheld his eyes.

Before, they had been dark, like stormclouds ready to break. The god's power had changed them, though, drawing the darkness away. Now they were dead white, with neither pupil nor iris. It was like looking into the milky gaze of a blind man, and Tavarre found himself glancing away, so he wouldn't have to meet their blank stare. But Cathan was not blind: his god-touched eyes turned toward Beldinas, slumped in Quarath's arms. Slowly, he smiled.

"Thank you," he murmured.

The monk shook his head. "It's only right. You gave your life for me. I have only given it back."

Cathan nodded, understanding. His eyes closed again, and he slept.

Everyone watched as Quarath helped Beldyn stand. He was weak, shaking and pale, but still he pushed the elf's hands away. Tavarre tensed, sure he would fall, but though he swayed on his feet, he remained upright. Beside him, Quarath dropped to his knees, his golden hair spilling over his face as he bowed his head.

"*Sa, usas gosudo*," the elf murmured.

Hail, chosen of the gods.

As one, everyone in the room—from low-born bordermen to the hierarchs of the holy church—knelt as well, repeating Quarath's words. Beldinas Lightbringer regarded them all with a smile, then turned toward the dais and climbed the steps to his throne.

The Great Temple of Istar held many secrets, places only a handful of high clerics had ever seen. The *Fibuliam* within the sacred chancery was only one. There were also reliquaries filled with holy artifacts, treasuries brimming with gold and jewels, hidden sanctuaries where the church's leaders could gather in times of trouble. Of all the church's secrets, however, none was guarded more closely than its dungeon.

The prison was small, less than a dozen cells and a room where the clergy could conduct the rites of inquisition. It was not a place for common criminals—the Lordcity had a vast jail for such miscreants—but rather for those the hierarchs felt were dire threats to church and empire. Black traitors, high priests of the dark gods, and those declared *Foripon* had all languished within its walls. The only way in or out was a long, narrow stairway that cut deep into the earth, guarded not only by a squad of handpicked Solamnic Knights, but also by glyphs graven into the walls that would burn anyone trying to escape to ashes. No one in the empire's history had ever broken out of the dungeon, and Kurnos knew he wouldn't be the first.

His cell was small, bare stone with a straw pallet, a clay pot for night soil, and nothing else. It had no windows—there was nothing to look out on anyway—and its thick, ironwood door blocked out all sound and light. The air was frigid, damp, and musty, and a strange, sharp smell hung in the air. The scent maddened him for hours as he tried to figure out what it was— then he recognized it, wishing at once that he hadn't.

It was his own fear.

Kurnos had no idea how long he lay there, curled in a ball and staring at nothing. With nothing to see or hear, time became ambiguous. Hours might have passed, or days. In the gloom, his mind drifted back to the last time he'd ventured so far beneath the Temple. It had been the night after his coronation, when he'd come down to the *Selo* and gazed into the empty crypt. He'd worried, then, that he might soon lie within it. Now he wept—how naïve he had been! He would never lie beside the other Kingpriests now—no, his grave would be plain, nameless, unconsecrated.

He sobbed for a long time, unable to stop himself. When the fit finally ended, his breath hitched in a throat that felt like he'd swallowed razors. "Oh, Paladine," he sobbed. "How I've failed thee. . . ."

"Your god cannot hear you, Kurnos."

He cried out at the cold voice, close in the darkness. The chill in the cell suddenly grew biting, painful. Robes whispered in the shadows, and he shrank away, whimpering.

"Go away," he moaned.

"Not yet," Fistandantilus hissed, so near that Kurnos could feel the wizard's breath on his ear. "I have something to say to you first. After that, we are finished."

Kurnos trembled uncontrollably. He didn't know where to look. The sorcerer's voice seemed to be everywhere, a part of the blackness. It took him nearly a minute to find his voice.

"Speak, then."

Fistandantilus smiled. It was too dark to see, and his hood would have hidden his face even if the cell were in full daylight, but Kurnos sensed the cruel grin anyway.

"Very well," the wizard said. "I want to thank you."

"What?" Kurnos blurted. "*Thank* me? Beldyn's alive. I failed!"

"Yes. I know you did."

Kurnos stared blindly at nothing, his mouth working silently.

"I *wanted* Beldyn to live," the dark wizard hissed, his voice barely more than a breath. He chuckled. "If I truly desired his death, I would have killed him myself."

"I don't—I don't understand." The world swayed like the deck of a storm-tossed galley.

"Of course you don't," Fistandantilus sneered. "You're a fool, Kurnos, a Footsoldier upon my own private *khas* board. You dreamed of ruling this empire, but my designs are greater.

To achieve them, I need a true holy man on the throne. Now, with your help, I have him.

"I saw Brother Beldyn first, you see—years before Lady Ilista, in fact. I searched Ansalon for the man I wanted . . . and found a boy. I thought to wait until he came into adulthood, but the god called Symeon earlier than I'd hoped, so I had to act.

"I knew there would be discord within the clergy if he simply came here, you see," the dark wizard went on. "Many would have been reluctant to follow him—he's young, after all, and from a heretical order. The hierarchy would have factionalized, and another war could have begun. I needed the church united . . . so I turned to you."

Kurnos moaned, shrinking beneath the weight of the wizard's words. Tears streaked his face. "Me?" he breathed.

"You. I fed your yearning for power, gave you the tools to craft your own downfall. If you succumbed to evil in your desire to keep the throne—used demoniac magic—the hierarchs would have to look favorably upon Beldyn. It took more trouble than I expected, perhaps, but in the end you did as I knew you would.

"The empire will follow him now," Fistandantilus finished, pitiless. "Those who matter have beheld his power and the depths of your depravity. I am done with you."

Kurnos wanted to scream, to curse, to grab the sorcerer in the darkness, smash his skull against the wall . . . but he found suddenly that he couldn't move. His body might have been made of lead, rather than flesh.

"You bastard," he sobbed. "I'll kill you . . . I'll kill—"

"No, Holiness," Fistandantilus whispered. "You won't, but you'll tell them about me now, won't you? They probably won't believe you, but then again, they might. I'm afraid I can't take that chance. *Sathira*."

There was no light in the cell, but after Fistandantilus spoke the name, the shadows grew deeper still, thickening until they were almost solid. A loud rush of unholy wind, more wintry than the chilliest Icereach gale, filled the room. Kurnos felt the last fragile threads of his sanity fray as the demon's familiar presence took form. He mewled in terror . . . then his mind finally gave way, and he began to laugh and laugh, an uncontrollable glee that turned to screams as two slits of green appeared in front of his face.

"My old friend," Sathira growled. "I have longed for this."

Her talons found him, tearing through skin, flesh, bone. Kurnos shrieked with delight and knew no more.

"Enough," Fistandantilus said after a while.

Sathira did not heed, continuing to rip ragged strips from the twitching thing on the floor. Blood sprayed the walls. She hissed with delight, devouring Kurnos, digging deep to claw out the choicest bits. Fistandantilus felt neither joy nor disgust at the sight—only annoyance that she did not readily obey him. He raised a hand, snapping his fingers.

"I said *enough!*"

The demon flinched as a spark of white light struck her, then cowered away from the fleshy ruin, snarling. She watched the wizard with menace in her green eyes. He paid her no mind. He knew spells that could tear her to pieces if he chose, and she knew it.

She had served him well. Twice she could have destroyed the young monk, if she'd chosen, and twice she had let herself appear to be defeated. That had been her end of the bargain they had struck.

"Go now," he said, making a gesture. "Back to the Abyss and your queen."

Her eyes flashed, a flare that lit the room for an eyeblink, displaying the scattered bits of wet bone and gristle that covered the floor. With an inward swirl of wind and a sound like distant thunder, Sathira was gone.

Fistandantilus stood alone in the cell, looking down at what had once been the Kingpriest of Istar. He could see very well, despite the lack of light, and he knew he could not leave things like this. If the guards found this dripping mess, there would be questions. Worse, the Lightbringer might come up with answers. That would not do.

Shrugging, he raised his hands, weaving his fingers through the air. Spidery words slipped from his tongue, and the sharp, darkly euphoric rush of magic filled him, an old friend. His *only* friend. Focusing his will, Fistandantilus spun the power into a spell.

The air in the cell shivered, growing warm. When it stilled, the gory mess the demon had made was gone, and Kurnos lay whole once more, his body unharmed, his eyes closed in peace. Seeing him as he was now, the guards would think he had simply died in his sleep. Not even the new Kingpriest, with all his divine might, would guess the horrible truth.

Fistandantilus nodded, smiling within his hood. "Farewell, Holiness," he said. In a flickering, he vanished from the cell.

EPILOGUE ▼

TWELFTHMONTH, 923 I.A.

Cathan couldn't feel his legs.

He'd been kneeling all night upon the stony path in the Garden of Martyrs, surrounded by the grandeur of the Great Temple—basilica, manse, cloisters, and riots of fruited trees and night-blooming flowers. Birds sang above, and nocturnal lizards, bred to resemble tiny silver and gold dragons, shuffled through the undergrowth. Behind him, the Kingpriest's private rose garden—blighted and brown when he'd first beheld it, more than a fortnight ago—had turned a brilliant green, and though it was the wrong time of year, huge, fragrant blooms covered the trellises with crimson and gold.

He paid no attention to any of it. His eyes were fixed on the cenotaph.

It was a tall, oblong slab, hewn of moonstone, that glistened blue in Solinari's light. Many such monuments loomed among the garden's almond trees, graven with hundreds upon hundreds of names: the honored dead, who had given their lives for the holy church. The earliest were older than the Temple itself, from the days of the first Kingpriest's rise, and they went on from there, down through the empire's history. Here were the missionaries who had perished in the crusades to civilize the borderlands. Over there were the casualties of the Annexation Wars, which had made provinces of the once-proud kingdoms of Seldjuk, Falthana, and Dravinaar. Three separate stones, set far apart from the others, bore the names of the victims of the Three Thrones' War. A great many people had died in the god's name over the centuries.

The cenotaph where Cathan knelt, however, was mostly blank. The sculptor Nevorian of Calah had chiseled the first names into its smooth surface over the past few days. Cathan stared at them, a hardness in his throat.

Gareth Paliost, Knight of the Sword.
Durinen, Patriarch of Taol.
Ossirian, Lord of Abreri.
Ilista, First Daughter of Paladine.

There were others, too: Gareth's Knights, Tavarre's man Vedro, and those who had fallen—on either side—in the Great Battle of Govinna. What held Cathan's notice, more than any of them, was the long, blank expanse beneath. It gave him a strange feeling, and not just because one day—perhaps soon—the space would be filled. What troubled him most was that his name had nearly been there.

Some had argued, in fact, that his name still belonged on the cenotaph. He *had* died, after all—was he any less a martyr, because the Lightbringer had restored his life? The scholars would, no doubt, keep debating the matter for months, but he knew he would have plenty of chances, in the coming years, to earn an unchallenged place on the monument.

For this day, Cathan MarSevrin would become a Knight.

That hadn't been an easy thing, either. Lord Holger had been hard against knighthood for him and still was. The Solamnic orders, he contended, required years of training in arts both martial and courtly. Knighthood wasn't something awarded lightly—and only seldom to a commoner or to one so young.

Beldinas had listened to the old Knight's arguments, his face blank behind the *Miceram*'s glow. Then, leaning forward on his throne, he had made his reply.

"*Est Sularus Oth Mithas*," he'd said. "The Solamnic oath—
My Honor is My Life. Who better to swear it than one who has
already *given* his life?"

In the end, Holger had relented, consenting to Cathan's
admission to the Knights of the Crown, the lowest of the
orders. By the time Cathan himself learned of their decision,
it was far too late for him to object. Now he kept silent vigil,
the dawn still hours away, unable after all this kneeling to
sense anything from the knees down—not even prickling.

How long, he wondered, could a man's feet feel asleep
before they turned black and fell off? What would happen if
he couldn't walk properly when the time came? Had Huma
Dragonbane limped to *his* dubbing?

"He used a cushion, you know."

Cathan stiffened, his heart lurching at the sound of the pleasant, jocular voice. He turned, looking over his shoulder, and saw
the man who had spoken. It was a short, corpulent monk in a
white pavilion of a habit. He leaned against another cenotaph,
hands folded across his vast belly, a little smile twitching the corners of his mouth. Cathan blinked, confused. He hadn't been in
Istar long, but he was certain he would remember such an odd
fellow. Yet he was sure he'd never seen the man before.

"What?" he exclaimed.

The monk smiled. "You were wondering how Huma got
through his vigil. He knelt on a pillow. The Knights didn't
start this bare-ground nonsense until a few hundred years
later. Idiotic, if you ask me."

"What?" Cathan managed to repeat. "Who *are* you?"

"Always the same question," the monk replied, his enormous belly jiggling as he waddled closer. He looked up at the
moonstone slab, sorrowful. "Lady Ilista asked the same thing.
She knew me as Brother Jendle, but that's not important—*you're*
the one who matters. If you'd kindly remove your tunic. . . ."

A pudgy hand reached out, plucking at the plain gray shift
Cathan had donned for the vigil. Cathan flinched away. "What?"
he asked again.

"Don't you know any other words?" Jendle asked, his brow creasing. "Your *tunic*. I need to make sure you're who I think you are. I have a message, and I'd hate to give it to the wrong man. On your left side, please—there should be a scar."

When he met Brother Jendle's eyes, he froze. They were an odd color, a golden brown dancing with silver light. There was something about them that reminded him of Beldyn, and as he looked into them his doubts faded. Swallowing, he reached up and unlaced the neck of his shirt, then pulled it up, over his head. Beneath, towards his left side, was a large patch of puckered flesh, hairless and shiny, the kind of mark burns left. It was the only sign that remained of the lightning blast that had killed him.

Jendle bent forward, squinting and grunting as he examined it, then straightened with a satisfied nod. His eyes lingered on the scar.

"How did it feel?" he asked. "To die, I mean?"

Cathan sighed. Everyone—even Beldyn—asked him that question. "Everything went dark," he said. "Then there was a bright light, and I opened my eyes. Nothing else."

The monk nodded, chins bunching. "Probably best, that. Now hold still. This won't hurt a bit."

"Wh—" Cathan started to say again. Before he could say anything more, though, the monk reached out, extending a bulbous finger to touch his scar.

The world wrenched about him. Suddenly, he was no longer in the garden, but floating *above* it, staring down at the trees and stones below. There, in its midst, were Brother Jendle . . . and *him*. His own body knelt before the monument, where he'd been a heartbeat ago. He tried to cry out at the sight, but no sound came from his lips.

You have no lips, he thought, staring at the fleshly form he'd left behind.

He began to rise. Soon he was gazing down at the whole Great Temple—vast and magnificent, the basilica glittering at its heart—then the entire Lordcity, its lights aglow along Lake

Istar's shore. Higher still, he floated over the other cities of the heartland: island-bound Calah, crowded Odacera across the water, Kautilya's glowing bronze foundries. The other provinces came into view next, from the jungles of the north to Dravinaar's southern desert. Shifting, he looked west . . . yes, there was Govinna, nestled among the hills, and beyond it the western realms, Solamnia, Kharolis, and Ergoth. He beheld the elven forests, the mountains that hid the fabled kingdom of the dwarves, the frozen isles of Icereach. All of Ansalon lay beneath him, surrounded by shining sea.

He felt himself shifting away toward the sky. There were the moons, red and silver, and the constellations his father had taught him: the Book of Gilean, the Fivefold Serpent, the Platinum Dragon that was Paladine's emblem, all laid out in their patterns across the velvety night. And there, among them, was something unusual. Something *moving*, streaking swiftly among the stars, flames raging around it. He squinted—or would have, if he'd had eyelids—and tried to look closer, make out its shape.

A hammer?

Yes, that was it. A great, burning hammer, flashing toward him, toward the blue ball of Krynn. It loomed larger every moment, throwing off fiery red tongues as it spun, startling him with its hugeness. The thing seemed miles across, as vast as the whole Lordcity, and he cringed as it neared, terrified that it would slam into him. When the moment came, however, the huge burning hammer missed him by an arm's length, shooting by with an incredible roar.

Then it was past, plummeting now, wreathed in fire as it dove toward Ansalon. Toward Istar.

Cathan shut his eyes, crying out, as it struck. . . .

He snorted, his head snapping up, thunder echoing in his ears.

Cathan glanced around. He was back in the garden, before the cenotaph, but of Brother Jendle there was no sign. Above, the sky was the color of plums, heralding the sunrise—hours had passed, the silver moon set, the night gone by. A dream, he told himself. You fell asleep—on your vigil!—and dreamed of fat monks and burning hammers.

Then, why wasn't he wearing his tunic?

Looking down, he saw it there, wadded on the ground before him. He gaped a moment, then snatched it up and dragged it over his head again.

He was still wondering when he'd taken it off when a soft cough sounded behind him. Starting, he turned to see a dark-haired youth standing down the path. Lord Holger's squire. He looked sullen, but Cathan expected that. Loren Soth had trained since childhood for the honor he was about to earn. Half a year ago, Cathan had been a god-hating outlaw, and today he would be made a Knight.

"It's time, sir," the squire said.

He did not look at Cathan's eyes; the scar was not the only mark death had left behind. In the days since, Cathan had found that few people could meet his blank gaze for long. Even Wentha couldn't keep from glancing away. Cathan knew it would be that way for the rest of his days, and it hurt to think of it—but it was better, he told himself, than the alternative.

He bowed his head, signing the triangle, then rose and started forward. Three steps later he stopped, staring at his feet. He could feel them fine! No pain, no numbness . . . not even prickling. He lifted one, shaking so it rattled in his boot.

"Sir?" Loren ventured again. "Are you well?"

Cathan flushed, lowering his foot again. "Yes. I'm fine."

Perplexed, he followed the squire away from the cenotaph, toward the gleaming basilica. The ceremony would soon begin.

First, though, he had to speak with someone.

Solamnic dubbings didn't often draw crowds. They were usually private ceremonies, held in the Kingfisher Keep and attended only by the Knights themselves. On this cool winter's day, however, matters were different. After all, not every Knight had returned from the dead.

The tale of Cathan's resurrection had spread far. Throughout the Lordcity and in the empire beyond, folk spoke in hushed tones of the Lightbringer's greatest miracle. It rapidly eclipsed all the other stories of Beldinas's ascension, overshadowing, even, the mysterious news of the death of Kurnos the Deceiver. So when the time came, thousands of Istarans turned out in the *Barigon*, to watch Cathan's knighting.

The Knights arrived in a mass early that morning. They followed Lord Holger into the square, their armor shining in dawn's light, and the burgeoning crowds parted as they strode across the plaza and up the stairs to the church's looming portico.

Soon after the hierarchs emerged from the Temple, bejeweled and kohl-eyed, wearing their grandest robes. Most were the familiar faces that had greeted the Lightbringer by the western gate two weeks before, but not all. A new First Son stood in place of Strinam, who had been Kurnos's favorite, and the high priests of Habbakuk and Majere were new as well. Such was always the way when a new Kingpriest claimed the throne.

Quarath stood among the high priests, his thin lips curled into a polite smile. He had sent a griffin-riding messenger to Silvanesti, bearing word of the Lightbringer's triumph to Loralon and inviting his former *shalafi* to return and take his place again in the imperial court. Yesterday the reply had come. The old elf had chosen to stay in his wooded homeland, but had sent his blessing to Beldinas.

Watch this new Kingpriest, Loralon's message had bidden. *Help him rule.*

Quarath's smile widened. He would do just that.

Finally, as the sun hung crimson above the Lordcity's eastern wall, a row of trumpeters, standing on a balcony overlooking the *Barigon*, raised platinum horns to their lips and blew a thunderous fanfare. An excited murmur rippled through the crowd, quickly building into cheers. Holger and his senior Knights scowled. The dubbing ritual was supposed to be a solemn occasion, not a jubilant one. There was no containing the crowd's elation, however, as the Great Temple's doors opened and the Knight Aspirant emerged.

Cathan hesitated, flushing when he saw the clamoring throngs, and for a moment he looked as if he might turn and flee back inside. In the end, though, he swallowed and strode forward. Clad in shining plate and long, white tabard, he walked to the front of the gathering atop the stairs, then lowered himself to one knee. Behind him, following the ritual, came his Guard of Honor. These elicited more murmurs from the crowd. While most such escorts consisted of three elder Knights, Cathan's were more unusual.

The first was Tavarre of Luciel, the scarred bandit lord wearing a red, fur-lined cloak over a chain hauberk washed with gold. In his hands he carried a gleaming shield, one of the three gifts every aspirant received for his dubbing. Behind Tavarre, bearing the second gift—a pair of silver spurs on a blue satin pillow—came a honey-haired girl, at thirteen summers just on the edge of marrying age. Suitors had already begun to line up for Wentha MarSevrin's hand. She blushed at the sight of the shouting mob then took her place behind her brother.

It was the third member of the honor guard, however, who drew the most gasps. The crowd turned wild as he emerged, breaking into a frenzy of shouting and song, and this time the Knights didn't object. It was, after all, the first time a reigning Kingpriest had ever carried an aspirant's sword.

Beldinas Lightbringer smiled as he strode out of the Temple, wreathed in holy light. In place of the white robes he had worn when he entered the city, his vestments were the crimson of dawn, a symbol of his new order. In his hands, point upward, he carried Cathan's blade—not the battered *Scata*'s weapon he had worn for much of the past year, but a fine, newly forged weapon, long of blade and keen of edge. Set into its golden hilt were several chunks of what appeared to be white stone—they appeared jade, perhaps, or onyx—but which were actually ceramic, pieces of the holy symbol that had helped defeat the shadow demon atop the Pantheon.

The crowd fell silent as the Kingpriest came forward. He looked out upon them, the *Miceram* flashing on his brow, then gazed down at Cathan. His eyes shone like sunlight on water as he opened his mouth.

"Cathan MarSevrin," he intoned. "The imperial court and the Knights' Council have heard of your deeds of bravery, courage, and sacrifice." He paused, his face turning grave as the last word echoed across the plaza. "In recognition, we intended to declare you a Knight of Solamnia. However, we have chosen not to do so."

A chorus of shock erupted from the crowd. Atop the steps, the confusion was no less. Everyone glanced around in confusion. Only Beldinas and Cathan showed no surprise.

The Lightbringer raised his hands for silence. The crowd obeyed, but there were frowns of perplexity among the onlookers now.

"I understand your disappointment," he told them. "You came here to see a dubbing. You shall have it, but not the kind you expected.

"Just now, as I was preparing for this ritual, young Cathan came to me and told me of a vision he had, while he kept his vigil. In it, Paladine spoke to him, in the same guise he took when he sent Lady Ilista on her quest to find me. The god showed him a burning hammer falling upon the empire."

At this, the onlookers muttered, signing the triangle and touching their foreheads to ward off evil. Even some of this hierarchs shifted, their eyes flicking skyward, as if the hammer might be poised over their heads even now.

Beldinas only smiled. "*Lisso, usas farnas,*" he declared.

Peace, children of the god.

"These are glad tidings, not an omen of disaster! Paladine sent this vision to show that we are right in rejecting the Balance that has corrupted this empire for so long. *We* are that burning hammer—all of us—and it is our god-granted duty to strike wherever we can and purge the evil that remains among us.

"There shall, then, be a *new* Knighthood," he concluded, the crown blazing, "an Istaran Knighthood, that shall be the vanguard in this holy war. It shall be open to all who would see the end of wickedness, and Cathan MarSevrin shall be the first of its number."

As citizen, Knight, and cleric alike looked on in amazement, Beldinas raised the sword high, lowering it to touch Cathan's shoulders with the flat of the blade—left, then right, then left again.

"*Fe Paladas cado, bid Istaras apalo, tam Gidam codo,*" he declared.

In Paladine's name, with Istar's might, I dub thee Knight.

"Rise, Sir Cathan, of the Order of the Divine Hammer."

Cathan got to his feet, his eyes brimming with tears. The Kingpriest handed him his sword and the people of Istar cheered anew, their shouts rising into the brightening sky.

Collections of the best of the DRAGONLANCE® saga

From *New York Times* best-selling authors Margaret Weis & Tracy Hickman.

THE ANNOTATED LEGENDS

**A striking new three-in-one hardcover collection
that complements *The Annotated Chronicles*.
Includes *Time of the Twins*, *War of the Twins*,
and *Test of the Twins*.**

For the first time, DRAGONLANCE saga co-creators Weis & Hickman
share their insights, inspirations, and memories of the writing of this
epic trilogy. Follow their thoughts as they craft a story of ambition,
pride, and sacrifice, told through the annals of time and
beyond the edge of the world.

September 2003

THE WAR OF SOULS Boxed Set

**Copies of the *New York Times* best-selling War of Souls
trilogy paperbacks in a beautiful slipcover case.
Includes *Dragons of a Fallen Sun*, *Dragons of a Lost Star*,
and *Dragons of a Vanished Moon*.**

The gods have abandoned Krynn. An army of the dead marches
under the leadership of a strange and mystical warrior. A kender holds
the key to the vanishing of time. Through it all, an epic struggle
for the past and future unfolds.

September 2003

Tales of
Ansalon's ancient past

WINTERHEIM
The Icewall Trilogy, Volume Three
Douglas Niles

Inside the forbidding confines of Winterheim, a royal captive is
scheduled for execution. A do-or-die assault on the ogre fortress comes
from without, but rebellion is spurred from within.

A WARRIOR'S JOURNEY
The Ergoth Trilogy, Volume One
Paul B. Thompson & Tonya C. Cook

The mighty Ergothian empire is gripped by civil war. Centuries before the
first Cataclysm sunders Ansalon, two imperial dynasts struggle for supreme
power. Amid this chaos and upheaval, a brave young peasant shakes the
towers of the mighty as his fate and the destiny of Krynn collide.

SACRED FIRE
The Kingpriest Trilogy, Volume Three
Chris Pierson

At long last, the Kingpriest has overstepped his power. His chief
opponent is the warrior who was once his most faithful disciple,
but even that does not sway the visions of a fanatic.
Because of his blindness, all Istar will suffer.

October 2003